CAUGHT UP
in the Tribulation

J.B. MᶜKISSACK

A NOTE FROM THE AUTHOR

Biblical prophecy is complex and open to multiple interpretations, with no single, definitive understanding of how end-time events will unfold. After decades of studying these prophecies, the author believes the timeline presented in this novel aligns with Scripture, while acknowledging that other interpretations are also possible—though some clearly are not. The author encourages readers to approach prophecy with humility, exploring these themes while avoiding rigid perspectives.

The story delves into speculative interpretations of prophecy, spiritual warfare, and the struggle between good and evil. It is not meant to assert definitive truth about future events, but rather to provoke thought and inspire reflection that may lead to deeper faith.

The name of the Antichrist character has been intentionally chosen so that it does not numerically add up to 666 in real life, ensuring no accidental association with real individuals who might share the same or a similar name.

Please remember that this is a work of fiction. Names, characters, businesses, places, events, and incidents are products of the author's imagination or are used fictitiously. Any resemblance to actual persons, living or dead, or real events is purely coincidental.

Ultimately, this book aims to entertain, challenge perspectives, and explore the possibilities within prophecy. By engaging with this story, readers are encouraged to reflect on their faith while recognizing it as fictional storytelling—an imaginative journey rather than doctrinal teaching.

And yes, this is indeed a disclaimer.
For more information visit: www.jbmckissack.com

DEDICATION

To God, the source of all grace, truth, and light. This book is offered in gratitude for Your unending mercy and love, and for the transformative work You have done in my life.

To my beloved wife, Tammy, my companion in life and ministry. Your unwavering love, patience, and support have been the foundation that has carried me through this journey. Thank you for walking beside me, believing in me, and for your steadfast encouragement, even when the road was uncertain.

To my daughters, whose love and laughter have filled my life with joy and meaning. You are constant reminders of God's goodness, and I thank Him every day for blessing me with such incredible gifts.

Finally, I dedicate this book to all who long for Christ's return and seek His will in their lives. May this story ignite your imagination and draw you into a deeper understanding and relationship with God. In a world filled with shadows, may you walk in faith, pursue truth, and cling to the light of Jesus. Be encouraged to hold fast to His promises and stand firm in your journey of faith.

CONTENTS

ACKNOWLEDGMENTS

First and foremost, I give thanks to God for His boundless grace, for reaching out to me, transforming my life, and faithfully guiding, correcting, and helping me through every step of this journey.

To my beloved wife, my partner on this incredible journey of life and ministry—you have been my rock, a source of love and strength. Thank you for reading this novel with me every step of the way, and for your unwavering love and support.

I extend my deepest gratitude to my dear friend, Mark Morgan, for the countless hours of conversation and our deep dives into God's Word. Your unwavering support for the pre-wrath interpretation of scripture has been invaluable. For over twenty years, you have listened, shared insights, and encouraged me as this novel took shape.

Finally, a special thanks to my friend, Robin Rutherford, for meticulously reading through multiple versions of this manuscript and tirelessly marking it with red ink. Your patience, attention to detail, and dedication to helping me refine this story have been invaluable. I am deeply grateful for your support in shaping this final work.

CAUGHT UP
in the TRIBULATION

1

SILENT DESCENT

"The Dark to Come"

The air inside the camp was heavy, almost smothering, thick with the stench of despair and the agony of broken spirits. Rebecca sat alone in her cell, the rough stone walls pressing in on her like the weight of her suffering. Her body trembled with exhaustion, her once-strong frame now frail from weeks of malnutrition and abuse. Her knees were drawn to her chest as she huddled in the farthest corner, her body instinctively trying to make itself as small as possible, as if disappearing could somehow offer relief.

Her hands, raw and calloused, gripped the thin, filthy blanket that had done little to keep her warm during the freezing nights. Her lips moved soundlessly, her throat too dry and her spirit too shattered to form the words she longed to speak. It had been days—no, weeks—since she had last felt God's presence, since she had last prayed and truly believed He was listening.

The silence was overwhelming, pressing in on her like the weight of the stone walls. With no sounds of machinery or voices, it was as if the entire camp had been abandoned, as if she were the last soul left, but she knew better. She knew they were still out there, watching, waiting.

Her head dropped to her knees as she began to shake, the tremor starting deep within her bones and spreading outward. She couldn't hold on much longer. The silence, the stillness, it felt like it was closing in on her. She longed to cry out, but her voice had abandoned her days ago, just like her hope.

Tears welled in her eyes, hot and thick, as she stared blankly at the barred door, invisible in the surrounding blackness. Yet somehow, she could still feel it, the iron bars, not just trapping her body, but imprisoning her soul. The darkness around her seemed to echo her despair, wrapping itself around her like an oppressive shroud.

"I can't... I can't do this anymore." The words slipped through her cracked lips, barely more than a whisper in the oppressive darkness, so faint that even she wasn't sure if she had spoken them aloud.

Rebecca leaned her head back against the cold stone, her heart pounding with fear and hopelessness. "Where are You, God?" she whispered, her voice cracking with desperation. "Have You abandoned me? Have You forgotten Your promise? I can't... I can't feel You anymore."

The tears came harder now, uncontrollable, her body shaking with sobs. She had tried, tried so hard to be strong, to endure, to hold onto her faith. But the days had stretched on endlessly, each one darker than the last, filled with the torment of isolation and the relentless cruelty of her captors. The beatings, the interrogations, the constant threats against her life, they had worn her down to the point where she no longer recognized herself.

Her lips moved again, forming a prayer that felt weak, almost futile. "Jesus, please..." she breathed, the words barely more than a sob. "Please, help me. I don't have any strength left. I can't do this anymore. I can't keep holding on. If You don't save me, I'm going to break. I'm going to fall apart, and I don't know how to get back up."

Her body slumped forward, her forehead pressing into her knees as she wept, her sobs echoing in the empty cell. "Please, God, don't leave me here. I don't know how much longer I can survive this..." Her voice faded into broken whispers as her prayer became a raw, aching plea. "I need You. I need You to save me. Please... please..."

For a moment, there was nothing but silence, her tears soaking the rough fabric of her prisoner's clothes. The darkness around her seemed to close in, smothering any remaining sliver of hope. And then, just as she felt she might drown in her despair, a voice, soft and urgent, cut through the stillness.

Rebecca's eyes were pressed into her knees, her body shaking with silent sobs, when something in the air shifted. Slowly, almost unwillingly, she lifted her head. A sharp, blinding light pierced the darkness, so intense that it seemed to carve through the void itself. She recoiled, the sudden brightness gripping her with a fear so raw it felt like a physical force wrapping around her chest. The light wasn't a beacon of hope, it was oppressive, cold, and unnatural, casting twisted shadows against the stone walls of her cell.

For a heartbeat, she froze, terror seizing her, her breath faltered. Her mind raced, unable to understand if this was another cruel trick or something more sinister.

Then, through the stillness, a voice broke the silence, barely more than a whisper.

"Rebecca..."

She froze. Who—or what—was calling her name?

"Before the Darkness"

Rebecca was unaware of the suffering that awaited her, the weight of a darkness yet to descend. Still, in the quiet corners of her soul, a faint tremor stirred, as if the air itself whispered of trials to come, a shadow she could neither name nor escape. A chill crept through her as her eyes drifted to the skyline, where dark clouds gathered, obscuring the setting sun. For a brief moment, she could almost feel the weight of the cross she no longer wore, the emblem that had once given her strength, now hidden away, out of sight, out of fear.

The sky was an eerie shade of gray, a dull haze rising from the streets below. She stood on the balcony of her small apartment, staring out at the towering buildings that loomed like monuments to a world she no longer recognized.

The air was thick with dread, as if the world were holding its breath. Something was coming—something none of them could clearly define, but it was coming.

Her phone buzzed in her pocket, pulling her from her thoughts. She glanced down at the screen: "Global Unrest Escalates: Martial Law Declared in Three Major Cities," "New Ethics Code Mandates Compliance," "Religious Institutions Under Investigation."

Rebecca's heart pounded. It was happening faster than she had imagined. The quiet erosion of everything she believed in was no longer silent—it was a full-scale assault. She swiped the screen away, feeling the weight of it pressing down on her.

Behind her, the apartment felt cold, despite the warmth of the sun slipping behind the clouds. James sat at the small kitchen table, his brow furrowed as he watched the news on the television—a steady stream of chaos unfolding, dark prophecies coming true.

"Have you seen this?" he asked, his voice low and tight with worry. "The protests are getting worse. People are being detained for... anything. Anyone who's even slightly out of line."

Rebecca nodded, but said nothing.

A sudden crack of thunder split the air, and she flinched, the tension in her body snapping like a taut wire. This wasn't just a storm brewing in the sky. It was the world itself groaning.

James stood and crossed the room, placing a hand on her shoulder. "We need to be careful," he said, though his voice lacked conviction. "We just have to keep our heads down, stay together."

Rebecca nodded, but deep down, she knew it wasn't that simple anymore. Without the cross she once wore, she felt exposed, her strength fading with the world around her. The world was changing—had changed—and they stood at the edge of something far more terrifying than they could fathom.

The storm was coming.

She couldn't stay cooped up in the apartment any longer. The tension was unbearable. She needed to be around people who shared her concerns, people who understood what was at stake.

The next morning, she and James met up with her friend Sarah at their usual spot, a small café tucked away from the city's relentless bustle.

The city hummed with the relentless energy of progress. Glass-and-steel towers pierced the sky, their mirrored surfaces reflecting a world in constant motion. On the streets below, people moved with purpose, eyes fixed on the screens in their hands, oblivious to the changing landscape around them. Billboards loomed over the crowds, flashing slogans that echoed the new mantra of society: "Embrace the Future," "Liberation Through Unity," "One World, One People."

At the corner of 5th and Main, a once-vibrant church stood in stark contrast to the bustling city. Its doors were chained shut, a faded sign hanging from the rusted gate: Sold—Future Site of the Liberty Tower. The stained-glass windows, which had once depicted scenes of hope and redemption, were now cracked and grimy, their colors dulled by neglect. The cross that had crowned the steeple lay in pieces on the ground, trampled and forgotten.

Phones, tablets, and TV screens streamed a relentless flow of news about these distressing times: Nation's Last Prayer Breakfast Canceled Amid Protests, New Education Reform: Religion Removed from History Curriculum, Faith-Based Organizations Lose Tax-Exempt Status. The headlines scrolled endlessly, a litany of the world's drift into secularism.

Inside a nearby café, the air was thick with the smell of coffee and the murmur of conversation. At a corner table, a small group of friends gathered, their faces tense with concern. Rebecca Marshall, a schoolteacher in her early thirties, glanced up at the television mounted on the wall. A news anchor was discussing the latest government initiative—mandatory ethics classes in schools, designed to replace outdated religious teachings with a new, inclusive moral code.

"They're not even trying to hide it anymore," Rebecca muttered, her fingers tightening around her coffee cup.

Next to her, Sarah Rivers—a petite woman with a quiet strength in her eyes—nodded grimly. "It's happening faster than I thought it would. First, they took prayer out of schools, then they started rewriting the textbooks. Now this. They're systematically erasing everything we believe in." There was an edge to her voice, a quiet defiance, born from the same tenacity that had driven her to reclaim her maiden name. It was more than a name to her—it was a hard-won symbol of escape, a reminder of why she could not afford to lose any more freedoms.

Across the table, James, Rebecca's husband, let out a frustrated sigh. "And what can we do? If we speak out, we're labeled as intolerant or backward. The last time I brought up my faith at work, my boss gave me a warning about creating a hostile environment."

The group fell into a heavy silence, the weight of the world's indifference pressing down on them. Outside, the city buzzed on, oblivious to the small group huddled in the corner, clinging to their faith in a world that seemed determined to shake it free.

Rebecca broke the silence, her voice barely above a whisper. "We have to stay strong. I know it's hard, but we can't let them take this from us. Not our faith. Not our hope."

James reached across the table, taking her hand in his. "But what happens when they come for more? When it's not just our jobs on the line, but our freedom—our lives? How do we fight against something this big?"

Sarah's gaze drifted to the window, where the church across the street stood as a grim reminder of the world they were living in. "I don't know," she admitted. "But I do know that we can't do it alone. We have to stick together, support each other. That's the only way we'll make it through this."

The conversation was interrupted by the sound of the café door opening. A man in a dark suit entered, his presence commanding immediate attention. He glanced around the room before settling his gaze on the group in the corner. Rebecca felt a chill run down her spine as their eyes met. There was something unsettling about him—something that made her instinctively wary.

The man approached the counter, his movements smooth and deliberate. As he placed his order, his voice carried across the room, calm and authoritative. "I'll take a black coffee, no sugar. And make it quick. I have a meeting at the Department of Education in fifteen minutes."

James leaned in closer to the group, his voice low. "Do you think he's...?"

"One of them?" Sarah finished the question. "Maybe. He certainly fits the profile. But it doesn't matter. We can't let fear control us. We have to keep calm and keep a low profile."

The man took his coffee and left as quickly as he had arrived, leaving an uneasy tension in his wake. The group watched him go, their conversation taking on a new urgency. A new alert appeared on Sarah's phone: 'A New Dawn is Coming, Be Part of the Change'. These news alerts had been included in the latest phone software update, and there was no way to turn them off.

As they finished their drinks and prepared to leave, Rebecca paused to look at the church one last time. She could still remember the sound of the choir singing on Sunday mornings, the feeling of peace that had filled the sanctuary. Now, it was all gone, just another casualty of a world adrift in its pursuit of progress.

But deep down, she knew that the battle was coming. There was still hope, still a chance to stand firm in the face of the storm. And as long as there was faith, there would be something worth fighting for.

She just prayed that it would be enough.

"Tension"

The fluorescent lights in the staff room hummed softly, casting a sterile, indifferent glow across the space that felt as unforgiving as the day's discussions. Rebecca sat at the far end of the room, her posture straight, shoulders tense. The red pen in her hand felt heavy, as if burdened by more than just its ink, as she marked a student's essay with what focus she could muster. Each stroke of the pen seemed louder than it should, the room amplifying her every small movement against the backdrop of voices that drifted from a few tables away.

At one of the central tables sat Miss Keller, a sharp-eyed, middle-aged woman known for her no-nonsense approach and firmly held views. Her short, efficient gestures and crisp voice were unmistakable markers of her presence. Leaning forward, she directed her question at the younger teacher across from her, breaking the soft hum of the room with words that sliced through the quiet.

"Did you hear about the recent policy update?" Keller's tone held an edge of satisfaction, as if the news was overdue justice.

Mr. Thompson, the young teacher who had joined just last year, nodded, his brow creasing as he considered her question. He was thoughtful, cautious even, choosing his words with care. "Yeah, I did. It's pretty clear the administration wants to make sure this school is no place for certain... outdated influences," he said, his voice trailing off as if he regretted the implication.

A thin, satisfied smile pulled at Keller's lips. "It's about time. We can't have students being influenced by those who cling to beliefs that should have been retired decades ago. School is for facts and forward-thinking, not for old notions dressed up as guidance," she said, the finality in her tone leaving little room for disagreement.

Rebecca's chest tightened. She felt the weight of their words pressing into her, the room suddenly heavy and more oppressive. The discussion had been a familiar one over the past months, creeping from meeting agendas to hallway conversations and now more boldly and direct.

Keller leaned back, her eyes sliding over to Rebecca, a gleam of something more personal sparking in their depths. "Remember when that incident happened last year?" she said, feigning a casual tone that fooled no one. "A teacher who decided to pray with a student—what was her name? Oh, right, Rebecca."

The pen paused mid-stroke in Rebecca's hand, suspended over the paper as if time itself had stopped. The room seemed to shrink, the walls pressing inward. She glanced up, locking eyes with Keller, whose expression was a blend of knowing and provocation.

"Yes, Rebecca," Keller continued, her voice adopting a tone of practiced neutrality, though her gaze was unyielding. "A... memorable moment. You were put on temporary suspension for that, weren't you?"

Rebecca took a slow, deliberate breath. The sting of that period hadn't faded, even after months. "I was. The student asked for help, and I couldn't turn her away," she replied, her voice steady but heavy, as if each word was a stone placed carefully to maintain balance.

Thompson shifted uncomfortably, his brows drawing together as he glanced at Rebecca with a mixture of sympathy and curiosity. It wasn't judgment; it was an attempt to understand the reasoning that had driven her decision. "Why risk so much, Rebecca?" he asked gently, as if trying to bridge the chasm that was forming in the room.

"Because it mattered to her," Rebecca said, keeping her gaze steady. The memory of that moment came back in a rush—the look in the student's eyes, the silent plea for comfort. "It wasn't about pushing an agenda. It was about offering support when it was needed most." Her confession hung in the air, fragile but resolute.

A short, humorless laugh broke from Keller as she crossed her arms over her chest. "Well, you certainly learned your lesson, didn't you, Rebecca?" she said, her eyes narrowing. The words were sharp, each one edged with a challenge that dared Rebecca to respond.

Rebecca's jaw tightened, but she refused to flinch. "I learned a lesson, alright," she said, her voice low but unwavering. "The lesson that standing by your beliefs comes with consequences." The tremor in her hand stilled, replaced by a resolve that had always been there, just beneath the surface.

Keller's smile was thin and unyielding. "Consequences that should teach you when to adapt," she said, her voice softening into a tone that bordered on condescension. "Stubbornness has no place in a school that's moving forward."

The frustration that simmered within Rebecca finally surfaced. "Is that what you call it, adapting?" she shot back, her voice tight but controlled. "Ignoring what students truly need just to meet policy standards? I helped that student because she reached out. Isn't that what we're supposed to do—support them, guide them?"

Keller's expression hardened, the brief warmth in her voice extinguished. "Support them, yes, but not by holding onto beliefs that could make others feel uncomfortable. We're here to ensure a safe environment, Rebecca. That doesn't happen by placing personal beliefs above the well-being of everyone."

The tension in the room vibrated, each word pulling it tighter, as if the cords of an invisible net had wrapped around them all. Rebecca's pulse quickened, each beat pounding in her ears, a reminder that she was teetering on the edge of something that could not be undone. The silence that followed was heavy, broken only by the distant sound of footsteps in the hallway and the soft, persistent hum of the lights.

Thompson cleared his throat, his eyes darting between the two women. He looked as if he were weighing whether to intervene, the strain of the conversation now visible in the furrow of his brow. "Alright, let's take it down a notch," he said, his voice carefully measured, attempting to coax the moment into something less volatile. "We're all here for the students, every single one of them, and we're on the same team."

The silence stretched on but lost some of its sharpness. Rebecca's eyes met Thompson's, and she allowed herself a small, grateful nod. The tension hadn't lifted, not entirely, but it had retreated just enough for them to take a collective breath.

Keller turned back to her laptop, the click of keys resuming with an insistence that felt almost defiant. The room, though less strained, still carried the memory of the exchange. Rebecca looked down at her stack of papers, the neat margins now smudged as her vision blurred momentarily. She blinked hard, clearing her eyes and focusing.

The conversation wasn't over. Not here, not in the walls of the school, not in her own mind. As the faint hum of the lights and the rhythmic clatter of typing filled the silence, Rebecca wondered how long she could hold onto what defined her before the cost grew too great.

"A New Doctrine"

The city's central plaza was packed with people, a sea of faces all turned toward the towering stage that had been erected overnight. The air buzzed with a mixture of excitement and apprehension as citizens gathered for the much-anticipated government announcement. A large banner hung above the stage, emblazoned with the words, "Unity Through Progress—A New Era of Social Harmony."

Rebecca and Sarah stood near the back of the crowd, trying to blend in as best they could. James had decided to stay home, wary of what the day might bring, but Rebecca had insisted on coming. She needed to see it for herself, to witness the direction the world was taking, even if it filled her with dread.

The stage was flanked by large screens displaying the government's seal—a stylized globe encircled by olive branches, symbolizing peace and unity. A row of officials in sharp suits stood on the platform, their expressions solemn as they prepared to deliver the news. At the center stood the Director General, a commanding figure known for his persuasive oratory and his vision of a unified nation. His real name, Nabal Malakar, carried a foreboding resonance, as if crafted to evoke both strength and dread. But he insisted, with absolute authority, that he be addressed solely as "Director General," a title that reinforced his persona as the unchallenged authority for the position given to him as part of the New World Order.

As the clock struck noon, the Director General stepped forward, his presence commanding immediate attention. The crowd fell silent, the hum of anticipation tangible. He began speaking, his voice amplified by the speakers positioned around the plaza.

"Fellow citizens," he began, his tone measured and reassured, "we stand on the brink of a new era. An era where tolerance and harmony are not just ideals, but realities. Where every person, regardless of their background, belief, or identity, can live free from fear and discrimination."

A ripple of applause spread through the crowd, but Rebecca remained still, her heart sinking with each word. She knew where this was leading. They had heard the rumors for weeks now—whispers of new policies, of changes that would alter the very fabric of society.

The Director General continued, his gaze sweeping over the crowd. "For too long, outdated and divisive doctrines have held us back, creating barriers between us. It is time for us to move forward, to embrace a new doctrine—one that promotes unity above all else. Therefore, I am pleased to announce the implementation of the Social Harmony Act."

The applause grew louder, but Rebecca could only hear the rushing of blood in her ears. The Social Harmony Act—she had feared this day would come. The act was more than just a policy; it was a mandate that would force everyone to conform to the new world order, stripping away the freedoms that had once been taken for granted.

The Director General's voice took on a firmer tone. "Under this act, all forms of religious expression that could be deemed exclusive or intolerant will be restricted. Places of worship must align with the principles of inclusivity, and any teachings that contradict the values of our united society will no longer be permitted. We must ensure that no one is made to feel inferior or excluded because of outdated beliefs."

The crowd erupted in cheers, but there were pockets of silence—groups of people exchanging uneasy glances, realizing the implications of what had just been announced. Rebecca felt Sarah's hand grip her arm tightly, and she turned to see the fear in her friend's eyes.

"This is it," Sarah whispered, her voice trembling. "They're going to shut us down."

Rebecca nodded, her throat tight. The announcement had confirmed their worst fears. The Social Harmony Act was a direct attack on their faith, on everything they believed in. The government had made it clear: there was no room for dissent in this new world. Conformity was not just encouraged—it was required. This event and the announcements were mirrored all over the world, signaling a global shift toward a new order where deviation from the prescribed norms would not be tolerated.

As the Director General continued to outline the specifics of the act, a debate began to stir in the crowd. Some people shouted their approval, hailing the act as a step toward a more inclusive society. Others, however, voiced their concerns, their words drowned out by the cheers and the blaring speakers.

One man near the front raised his voice in protest, his tone desperate. "What about freedom of religion? What about our right to believe what we choose? You can't just take that away!"

The Director General's response was swift and cold. "Freedom of religion is not freedom to discriminate. We cannot allow beliefs that harm the fabric of our society to persist. This act is about ensuring that everyone, regardless of who they are, feels valued and accepted. We must all be willing to make sacrifices for the greater good."

The crowd roared in approval, and the man was quickly drowned out. Rebecca's heart ached for him—for all of them. They were being silenced, one by one, in the name of progress and unity. And with each cheer, with each shout of approval, the divide between those who conformed and those who resisted grew wider.

The Director General concluded his speech with a rallying cry. "Together, we will build a world where harmony reigns, where love and acceptance are the foundation of our society. This is our destiny, and it is within our grasp. Let us embrace this new doctrine and move forward into a brighter future."

The applause was deafening, but Rebecca could only feel a deep sense of loss. As the crowd began to disperse, she turned to Sarah, her voice barely audible over the noise. "What are we going to do?"

Sarah shook her head, tears welling in her eyes. "I don't know. But we can't stay here. I don't feel safe."

They hurried away from the plaza, weaving through the throngs of people who were still celebrating the announcement. The city, once a place of refuge and hope, now felt hostile, foreign. Every step they took was heavy with the realization that their world had changed irrevocably.

As they reached the edge of the plaza, Rebecca glanced back at the stage, where the officials were shaking hands and congratulating each other. The banner overhead fluttered in the breeze, its message stark against the clear blue sky: "Unity Through Progress."

But Rebecca knew that this unity came at a price. A price she wasn't sure they could afford. As they walked away, she felt a growing sense of isolation, as if the ground beneath her feet was crumbling, leaving her with nothing to stand on.

The future of their faith in this new world was uncertain, but one thing was clear: the battle was just beginning, and it was a battle they couldn't afford to lose.

"Family Divided"

The house was quiet, save for the soft hum of the refrigerator in the kitchen and the distant murmur of a television in the living room. Rebecca sat at the dining table, her hands wrapped around a mug of tea that had long since gone cold. She stared at the patterns on the wood grain, her mind replaying the events of the day over and over again—the announcement, the cheers, the feeling of being surrounded by a world that was slipping further and further away from her.

The front door creaked open, and James walked in, his shoulders slumped with the weight of a long day. He glanced at Rebecca, his expression weary. "How was it?" he asked, his voice betraying a mix of curiosity and dread.

Rebecca sighed, not looking up. "Exactly what we feared. They've made it official—any religious beliefs that don't align with their new doctrine are considered harmful. The Social Harmony Act... it's going to change everything."

James hung his coat on the back of a chair and joined her at the table. For a moment, they sat in silence, the tension between them thick and unspoken. Finally, James broke the silence. "I'm not surprised, honestly. We've seen this coming for a while now. But... I think we need to talk about what this means for us. For our family."

Rebecca finally looked up, her eyes tired but resolute. "What do you mean?"

James hesitated, choosing his words carefully. "Rebecca, you know I've been thinking a lot about everything lately. About what's happening in the world and how we're going to get through it. I don't want to see our family torn apart by this. I don't want to lose you... or our daughter... because of something we can't control."

Rebecca's heart tightened. "What are you saying, James? That we should just give in? Abandon our faith?"

He shook his head, frustration flickering in his eyes. "No, I'm not saying that. But we have to be realistic. We have to adapt if we're going to survive this. I'm worried about what will happen if we push back. What if they come for us? What if we're arrested, or worse? We have to think about our daughter."

Rebecca bit her lip, the weight of his words pressing down on her. "So, what do you want us to do? Pretend we believe in their new doctrine? Go along with everything, just to keep the peace?"

James leaned forward, his voice low and urgent. "I'm saying we need to be smart. Maybe we don't have to be so open about our beliefs. We can still keep our faith, but do it quietly. We don't have to make ourselves targets."

Rebecca shook her head, her hands trembling. "James, we can't just hide who we are. What kind of example would that set for Emily? For ourselves? We've always taught her to stand up for what's right, no matter the cost. Are we just going to throw that away now?"

James ran a hand through his hair, his frustration growing. "I'm trying to protect our family, Rebecca. This isn't just about us anymore. We have to think about the future, about what kind of world our daughter is going to grow up in. Do you really want her to suffer because we refused to bend just a little?"

Before Rebecca could respond, their teenage daughter, Emily, walked into the room, her ear buds dangling from her neck. She had clearly overheard their conversation, her expression a mix of confusion and concern. "What's going on?" she asked, her voice cautious.

James and Rebecca exchanged a glance, neither sure how to explain the situation. Finally, Rebecca spoke, her tone gentle. "We were just talking about... everything that's happening. The new laws, the changes. It's going to be tough for people like us—Christians."

Emily frowned, her brow furrowing in thought. "But isn't it just about being more accepting? I mean, that's what they keep saying at school. That everyone should be free to believe what they want, as long as it doesn't hurt anyone else. What's so bad about that?"

Rebecca felt a pang of sorrow as she realized how deeply the new teachings had already influenced her daughter. "It's not just about accepting others, Emily. It's about being forced to deny what we believe in, to go along with things we know aren't right. They're taking away our freedom to live out our faith. They don't want us to live by the Bible."

Emily shrugged, her tone uncertain. "But maybe Dad's right. Maybe we don't have to make a big deal out of it. We can still believe what we want, just... you know, keep it to ourselves. Isn't that enough?"

Rebecca stared at her daughter, struggling to find the right words. "Emily, faith isn't something you can just keep to yourself. That kind of faith is dead faith! Our faith is part of who we are. It's not just about what we believe—it's about how we live, how we treat others, how we follow God's teachings. If we start hiding that, if we start pretending, we're not just lying to the world—we're lying to ourselves."

Emily looked down, clearly torn. "I just don't want us to get in trouble. I don't want anything bad to happen to us."

James reached out, placing a hand on Emily's shoulder. "We don't want that either, honey. But we also don't want to lose ourselves in all of this. We're just trying to figure out the best way to handle it."

The room fell into a heavy silence, each of them lost in their own thoughts. The family that had once been so united in their faith was now grappling with a division that had never existed before—a division born out of fear, uncertainty, and the relentless pressure of a world that demanded conformity.

Rebecca felt a tear slip down her cheek as she realized a divide had crept into her family. She wanted to protect them, to keep them safe from the dangers that seemed to be closing in. But she also knew that compromising their faith, even in small ways, would only lead to a greater loss.

She reached for James's hand, squeezing it tightly. "We'll figure this out," she said softly, though she wasn't sure if she was reassuring him or herself. "We'll find a way to stay true to our faith, to protect our family... somehow."

James nodded, but the doubt in his eyes was unmistakable. "I hope so," he murmured. "I really hope so."

Emily quietly left the room, retreating to her own thoughts as the weight of the conversation settled over the family. Rebecca watched her go, her heart aching with the realization that the world they had once known was slipping away, and with it, the certainty that had once guided their lives.

As the night wore on, the house remained silent, the tension thick in the air. Each of them was left to grapple with the choices they would soon have to make—choices that would define not just their faith, but their very identities in a world that no longer welcomed them.

And in that silence, Rebecca knew that their journey was only just beginning—a journey that would test not just their beliefs, but the very bonds that held their family together.

"The First Wave"

The small church hall was filled with the soft murmur of voices as the congregation gathered for their midweek prayer meeting. The room was dimly lit, the only illumination coming from a few scattered lamps and the flickering candles on the altar. The atmosphere was heavy, not with the usual warmth of fellowship, but with a quiet, almost tangible tension.

Rebecca, James, and Emily sat in the back row, close to the exit—a habit they had developed in recent weeks, ever since the new laws had been announced. Sarah had slipped into the pew next to Rebecca's at the last minute. The meetings had grown smaller, with many members of the congregation too afraid to attend, fearing the repercussions of being associated with a faith that was now considered dangerous.

Pastor Daniels, a man in his late fifties with a kind but weary face, stood at the front, flipping through his Bible with deliberate care. He looked up at the congregation, his eyes filled with both determination and sorrow.

"Brothers and sisters," Pastor Daniels began, his voice steady but confident, "we are indeed living in troubling times—times that shake us and challenge our faith. But let me assure you, this is not the Great Tribulation that the Bible warns us about. I know many of you are worried, asking, 'Could this be the start of the end?' But Scripture gives us clarity.

15

"You see, the Word is clear: Jesus will return for His church before the Tribulation begins. He will come back in a way that is unseen by the world, and in that moment, we who believe will be caught up, taken out of harm's way before the terrible events described in Revelation unfold. This rapture, as the Apostle Paul described in 1 Thessalonians 4:16-17, will be a sudden disappearance, a 'snatching away' of all true believers. One moment we'll be here, and the next, we'll be in His presence.

"Yes, things may get worse before that moment. The Bible tells us we'll face 'wars and rumors of wars,' and we may feel pressure as believers. But rest assured, God has not appointed us to endure the Tribulation. The trials we experience now are simply tests of our faith, not punishments. The Great Tribulation will be a time of consequences for a world that has turned away from God—not for His faithful church.

"Now, I know some of you are concerned about the Mark of the Beast. Let me be clear: we won't be here when that mark is introduced. Revelation 13 describes the mark as a symbol of allegiance during the Tribulation—a time when the Antichrist will reign openly. The mark itself may well be a microchip implanted under the skin, a device to track and control those left behind. But you don't need to worry about that, because God will take His people out before that time arrives. He will not allow us to face that kind of tribulation.

"This is a promise we can hold onto. We are His bride, and He will rescue us before the darkest days. While we may face challenges or persecution, these are not the same as the events described in Revelation. God's love is greater than any trial we face, and His promise to take us home stands firm before the Great Tribulation begins."

As Pastor Daniels paused, a soft murmur of relief rippled through the congregation. Heads nodded, and a few "Amens" echoed from the pews.

"Do not lose hope, my friends," he continued with renewed fervor. "We are safe in His hands, and the blessed hope of His soon return is our comfort. Stand strong, and keep looking up—for our redemption draws near. It can happen at any moment."

Rebecca glanced around the room, noting the worried expressions on the faces of the people she had worshipped with for years, but the pastor's words gave them hope. These were people she had shared joys and sorrows with, people who had become like family. But now, many were afraid to even attend church.

Just as Pastor Daniels was about to continue, the doors at the back of the hall burst open, and a young man stumbled in, out of breath and wide-eyed with fear. His clothes were disheveled, and his face was pale as he made his way to the front of the room.

"Pastor!" he gasped, his voice trembling. "They—they've started arresting people. In the city square, just now. They took them away in vans—Christians who were praying, refusing to leave when the police told them to stop. They—" He paused, struggling to catch his breath. "They said it was for inciting public discord. For spreading intolerance."

A ripple of shock and fear spread through the room, the murmur of voices growing louder. Pastor Daniels raised his hands, calling for silence, though his own face was stricken with the news.

"Calm yourselves, please," he urged, though his voice betrayed his own alarm. "We knew this day might come, but we must not let fear take hold. This is most likely the beginning, the first wave, and there will likely be more. But we must remember why we are here. We are here to stand firm in our faith, to support one another, and to trust in God's plan, even when we do not understand it."

Sarah clutched Rebecca's hand tightly, her knuckles white with tension. "This is it," she whispered, her voice barely audible over the anxious murmurs of the congregation. "It's starting."

Beside Rebecca sat her daughter, Emily, her young face a mixture of confusion and fear. Emily's eyes flickered between the pulpit and the congregation, trying to grasp the gravity of what was happening. Rebecca gently squeezed Sarah's hand, a familiar gesture of comfort she had offered many times since stepping into Sarah's life when she needed it most. It had taken Sarah years to overcome her past, and reclaiming her maiden name, Rivers, had been more than a legal victory—it felt like the grace that had found her, flowing back into her life.

Emily leaned closer to her mother, her voice soft but urgent. "Mom, what's happening? Is it turning bad now?"

Rebecca kept her gaze forward, her voice steady but low. "Just whisper a prayer, sweetheart. We'll be okay."

Rebecca looked at Sarah, her heart pounding in her chest. The reality of the situation was sinking in—this wasn't just a theoretical threat anymore. It was real, and it was happening now. People were being arrested, taken away simply for praying in public. The thought of what might happen to them—what might happen to her, to her family—was terrifying.

James leaned in close, his voice low and urgent. "We need to be careful, Rebecca. This could get worse, fast. We have to think about what we're going to do if they come for us."

Rebecca looked at him, her mind racing. The fear was there, gnawing at the edges of her resolve, but so was something else—a quiet, stubborn determination. She had always known that following Christ could come at a cost, but she had never imagined it would be this. Yet, deep down, she knew that she couldn't turn away now. Not when her faith was being tested like this.

Pastor Daniels cleared his throat, drawing the congregation's attention back to him. "I know that what we face is daunting," he said, his voice filled with a quiet strength. "But let us not forget that we follow a Savior who faced the ultimate persecution, who suffered and died for our sins. He did not shy away from the cross, and neither can we shy away from the trials before us. We must stand together, support one another, and above all, trust in God's providence."

He paused, looking out at the sea of anxious faces. "If any of you feel that you must leave, I understand. But know this: whether we are here together or apart, we are united in Christ. And that unity cannot be broken by any law, by any government, or by any persecution."

A few people shifted in their seats, clearly torn between their fear and their faith. But no one moved to leave. The silence in the room was thick with the weight of their collective decision.

Rebecca felt a surge of emotion well up inside her—fear, yes, but also a deep sense of resolve. She looked at James, then at Sarah, and saw the same determination reflected in their eyes. Emily, however, showed a clear sense of fear and a need for protection. Yet, they would not abandon their faith, not even in the face of what was to come. It was a decision made in that moment, wordlessly, as the reality of their situation settled in.

Pastor Daniels raised his hands in prayer, and the congregation followed suit, bowing their heads together. The prayer was simple, a plea for strength and protection, for wisdom and courage in the days ahead. But as they prayed, there was a sense of solidarity in the room, a powerful bond formed by their shared faith and their shared resolve to stand firm, no matter the cost.

When the prayer ended, the congregation remained seated, unwilling to break the fragile moment of unity that had formed. Rebecca felt the tears welling in her eyes as she realized just how much this community, these people, meant to her. They were her brothers and sisters in Christ, and together, they would face whatever came their way.

As they slowly began to file out of the hall, Rebecca caught Pastor Daniels' eye. He gave her a small, weary smile, nodding in understanding. They both knew that this was just the beginning, that the road ahead would be difficult and fraught with danger. But they also knew that they would not walk it alone.

Outside, the night air was cool and crisp, a stark contrast to the warmth and tension that had filled the church. Rebecca, James, and Sarah stood together for a moment, taking in the quiet of the evening, the calm before the storm. Emily clung to her mother, yearning only to be home.

"We'll get through this," Rebecca said softly, though she wasn't sure if she was speaking to them or herself. "We have to."

James placed a hand on her shoulder, his expression serious. "I had my doubts, but whatever happens, we stick together. We keep our faith. No matter what."

Sarah nodded, her eyes still wide with fear, but James's words gave her a newfound resolve. "We can't let them take this from us. We just can't."

As they walked home in the darkness, Rebecca couldn't shake the feeling that their world was changing in ways they couldn't fully comprehend. The first wave of persecution had arrived, and with it, a new reality—one where their faith would be tested in ways they had never imagined.

But as they walked, hand in hand, Rebecca knew that they would face it together. And that, perhaps, was the greatest strength they had.

Caught Up in the Tribulation

2

UNSEEN DOMINION

"The Rider Revealed"

Rebecca stood at the kitchen sink, staring out the window into the darkened street. The faint glow of the streetlamp illuminated little more than the foggy night, its weak light barely piercing the stillness outside. She held the edge of the counter, her knuckles white as she tried to steady herself. The unease she'd felt earlier had only grown, an invisible weight pressing against her chest.

Behind her, James was flipping through channels on the muted television, his movements impatient, agitated. He finally settled on the news, where a serious-faced anchor spoke over a scroll of headlines that seemed to blur together: "Religious Restrictions Expand Nationwide," "Prayer Gatherings Disbanded for Public Safety," "Unity Act Gains Unanimous Approval in Congress."

James exhaled sharply and sank into the worn couch. "They're dismantling everything," he muttered, rubbing his hands over his face. "Bit by bit, they're tearing it all down."

Rebecca turned away from the window, her arms crossed over her chest. "It's what we've been expecting, isn't it?" she said softly, though the words felt hollow. "We knew it would come to this."

"Knowing doesn't make it easier," James replied. "It doesn't make it less terrifying."

She nodded but said nothing. Instead, she moved to the table, picking up her Bible. Its pages were worn from years of study, the edges smudged with fingerprints. She opened it, trying to focus on the familiar words, but the sense of foreboding only deepened.

And then it hit.

Rebecca clutched her chest, her breath catching as a wave of dread surged through her. Her Bible slipped from her hands, falling to the floor with a dull thud. The sensation was sharp, overwhelming, unlike anything she had felt before. This wasn't fear in its usual form—it was primal, ancient, and vast. It wrapped around her like chains, pulling her into a suffocating grip.

"Rebecca?" James's voice was sharp with concern. He was on his feet in an instant, his hands steadying her as she swayed. "What is it? What's wrong?"

She couldn't answer. Her chest heaved, her breaths shallow, as if the air had grown too thick to inhale. Her vision blurred, and she squeezed her eyes shut, her trembling hands pressing harder against her chest.

The world fell away.

Rebecca opened her eyes to find herself in a place that defied description. She stood in the presence of a great multitude, a vast expanse of angelic beings stretching into infinity. The air shimmered with a brilliance that was both awe-inspiring and terrifying, charged with a tension that made her heart pound.

In the center of it all was the Throne, radiant with a light so pure it seemed to pulse through the very fabric of existence. Rebecca's gaze was drawn to the scroll held in the hand of the One who sat upon the Throne. It was sealed with seven seals, its surface emanating a power that resonated through the gathering.

A voice rang out, clear and resonant, carrying an unshakable authority. "Who is worthy to open the scroll and break its seals?"

The question hung in the air, followed by a silence so profound it seemed to stretch into eternity. Even the mightiest angels lowered their heads, their radiance dimming under the weight of the moment. Rebecca could feel it too, the crushing sense of unworthiness pressing against her soul.

Tears pricked her eyes as the silence grew heavier, the tension unbearable. She wanted to cry out, to plead for someone to step forward, but no sound came.

And then, He appeared.

Jesus stepped forward, His presence a perfect blend of majesty and humility. The crowd parted as He approached the Throne, their reverence palpable. His radiance was not blinding like the Throne's light—it was warm, steady, and deeply comforting. Yet, His expression was solemn, His steps purposeful.

"You are worthy," the voice declared, and the words shattered the tension like a flood breaking through a dam. Relief rippled through the assembly as Jesus took the scroll. The heavenly host erupted in praise, their voices lifting in a symphony so beautiful it brought tears to Rebecca's eyes.

But as He broke the first seal, a new tension filled the air. The sound of the seal breaking was sharp and violent, a crack that echoed through the expanse. From the scroll emerged a rider on a white horse, majestic and imposing. The rider held a bow and wore a crown, his presence exuding conquest and authority. Yet Rebecca sensed the deception beneath his radiant exterior.

This was not of God.

The rider raised his bow, his intent clear—a false peace masking his true purpose. Rebecca's chest tightened as she watched, unable to look away. Jesus's gaze remained steady, though sorrow shadowed His eyes.

Rebecca's vision blurred as light and shadow spun around her once more. When she opened her eyes, she was back in the living room, her breath ragged, her hands clutching James's arms.

"Rebecca!" James's voice was sharp, his face pale. "What happened? Are you okay?"

She struggled to catch her breath, her words barely above a whisper. "The first seal... it's broken."

James's eyes widened, his brow furrowing as he tried to make sense of Rebecca's words. "The first seal is broken?" he repeated, his voice edged with concern and confusion. "Rebecca, what does that even mean? What seal? What are you talking about?"

Rebecca sat on the edge of the couch, her hands trembling as they clutched at her knees. Her breathing was shallow, her face pale. "It's... the scroll," she murmured, her voice barely audible. "The seal... I saw it. It broke. I—" Her words faltered, her gaze darting around the room as if searching for something unseen. "It's happening, James. It's all happening."

He crouched in front of her, his hands gripping her shoulders gently but firmly. "Rebecca, slow down. I don't understand. What did you see? What's happening?" His voice softened, but the worry in his eyes deepened as he searched her face for answers.

Her eyes met his, glassy and filled with a mix of fear and disbelief. "I... I was there," she whispered. "I saw Him. The scroll, the seals... the rider. James, the rider—he was so... wrong, and yet everyone thought he was good."

James tightened his grip slightly, his heart pounding. "You saw a rider? Rebecca, listen to me. You're scaring me. What are you talking about? Where were you?" His tone was gentle, but there was an urgency behind it, an unspoken plea for her to make sense of the words spilling from her lips.

"I don't know!" she cried, her voice cracking as tears welled in her eyes. "I don't know how to explain it. I was here, but I wasn't. I felt it, James. It was real. Too real. The first seal... it's broken. The end... it's starting."

James exhaled slowly, trying to steady himself as he saw the raw panic etched across her face. He reached up, brushing a strand of hair from her damp forehead. "Rebecca, you've been under so much stress lately. Maybe you just—" He stopped himself. He didn't want to dismiss her, not when she was this shaken, but he didn't understand. And it scared him.

"Come on," he said softly, his voice steadying as he made a decision. "You're exhausted. Let me help you to bed. We can talk more about this in the morning, okay?"

Rebecca blinked at him, the fight draining out of her as her body sagged under the weight of what she'd experienced. "I... I don't know if I can sleep," she whispered, her voice trembling. "What if I—"

"You need to rest," James interrupted gently, standing and pulling her up with him. She didn't resist as he wrapped an arm around her shoulders, guiding her toward the bedroom. "You've been through something overwhelming. Whatever it was, we'll figure it out. I'm here, Rebecca. You're not alone."

She leaned into him, her steps unsteady, her mind still swirling with fragments of the vision she couldn't fully explain. As James helped her into bed, he knelt beside her, smoothing the blanket over her trembling form. "I'm here," he said again, his voice firm but filled with tenderness. "Just rest. We'll figure this out together."

Rebecca turned her head, her eyes meeting his once more. The tears spilled over now, unchecked, and her voice was barely a whisper. "I'm scared, James."

His heart broke at the vulnerability in her words. He took her hand in his, squeezing it gently. "I know," he said softly. "But I've got you. I'll stay right here. We'll get through this."

As her eyes fluttered shut, James sat back, watching her as her breathing began to even out. He didn't move , afraid to leave her alone in this fragile state. His mind raced with questions, none of them with clear answers. What had she seen? What could have shaken her so deeply? And what did she mean about seals and riders?

He reached out, brushing her hair back from her face as she shifted slightly, a faint murmur escaping her lips. "I'll figure this out," he whispered, though he wasn't sure if he was promising her or himself.

The room was silent now, save for the faint sound of her breathing. But James's heart remained heavy. Something had happened— something he couldn't understand, something that had shaken Rebecca to her core. And as he sat there, keeping watch over her sleeping form, he couldn't shake the creeping unease that whatever it was, it wasn't over.

Not even close.

James lingered for a moment longer, his heart heavy as he watched Rebecca's face finally relax into something like sleep. She had been so shaken, her words scattered, her hands trembling in his. He wanted to understand, to help, but the only thing he could do now was let her rest. With a quiet sigh, he slipped out of the room and into the living room. As he sank onto the couch, his mind raced with worry, even as his own exhaustion pulled at him.

Manipulating"

As Rebecca slipped into a restless sleep, her body betrayed the turmoil of her mind. Her breaths quickened, her hands gripped the sheets, and her legs twitched against the mattress. Within minutes, she was tossing and turning, her face etched with unease. Outside the dream, the bedroom was silent, but inside, Rebecca's soul was being dragged into a terrifying vision.

The air around her was suffocating, clinging to her skin like a wet shroud. Every breath felt like a struggle, the atmosphere charged with an unnatural energy that vibrated through her body. Darkness surrounded her, not an ordinary darkness, but something alive, pulsating, shifting as though it were watching her. The ground beneath her feet wasn't solid; it rippled like liquid shadow, unstable and unnerving.

Rebecca spun in place, her arms wrapping around herself as panic rose in her chest. "Where am I?" she whispered, but her voice was swallowed by the oppressive silence. The void pressed closer, thick and choking, as though it were daring her to move.

Without warning, a force yanked her forward. She stumbled but didn't fall, her body obeying the unseen pull as the world around her changed in an instant. She found herself standing in a grand hall, its walls gleaming with gold and mirrors. The reflections within the mirrors twisted and warped, the faces staring back at her stretched into grotesque smiles that didn't belong.

Before her was a long table, surrounded by men and women dressed in sharp suits. They sat stiffly, their expressions serene but their eyes hollow and lifeless. Low whispers filled the room, voices that slithered through the air like serpents. Rebecca's gaze was drawn to the shadows stretching unnaturally from each figure. They moved independently, tendrils coiling around the politicians' necks and wrists, their darkness deeper than the void that had brought her here.

A particular shadow leaned forward, its form indistinct except for two burning red eyes that pierced the gloom. Its rasping voice cut through the whispers, sharp and venomous. "Sign it," it commanded, and the man at the head of the table nodded, his pen trembling as he scratched his signature onto a thick document.

Rebecca moved closer, though she didn't remember taking a step. She looked over his shoulder at the paper, but the words blurred as though they were alive, writhing to escape her understanding. Still, their intent was clear—laws designed for control, restrictions wrapped in the guise of unity. The weight of their implications pressed against her chest like a stone.

"They'll believe it's their idea," the shadow hissed, its voice thick with triumph. The man nodded again, his hand steady now as though the dark force had claimed full control.

Rebecca opened her mouth to scream, to warn him, but no sound came. The air grew heavier, and her vision blurred. The room dissolved like smoke, and she was flung into another scene.

The bright lights of a newsroom blinded her for a moment. She blinked, adjusting to the new surroundings. A well-dressed anchor sat behind a desk, her polished smile gleaming as she spoke into the camera. Rebecca watched in horror as a shadow loomed over the woman, its clawed hands resting on her shoulders. It leaned close, whispering into her ear. The anchor's lips moved in perfect sync with the words fed to her.

Behind her, screens flickered with images of protests, violence, and crumbling cities. "Unity," the anchor said, her voice calm and hypnotic. "Harmony through compliance." The camera panned to an audience behind the scenes. Their faces were slack, their eyes glazed with a hollow acceptance that sent chills down Rebecca's spine.

"Stop it!" Rebecca tried to shout, but the words were strangled in her throat. She reached forward, desperate to shake the woman free from the shadow's grasp, but the room shattered before she could take another step.

Now she stood in a gallery, the walls jagged and unnatural. Paintings hung crookedly, their vibrant colors replaced with smears of blood-red and inky black. Sculptures writhed as if alive, their shapes monstrous and wrong. Artists worked feverishly nearby, their faces pale and gaunt, their hands trembling under the weight of the shadows that hovered over them.

"It's bold," a voice murmured behind her, smooth and approving.

"No," Rebecca whispered, her stomach churning. "It's wrong. It's so wrong."

A shadow turned sharply, its blazing red eyes locking onto hers. Rebecca froze as it surged toward her, its tendrils reaching out to ensnare her. She stumbled backward, her heart pounding in her chest as terror gripped her. It was aware of her. It saw her.

"You don't belong here," the shadow hissed, its voice a venomous growl. The tendrils lashed out, and Rebecca raised her arms instinctively to shield herself. Before they could reach her, the scene dissolved into nothingness.

She was thrust into the final vision with no warning. Before her stretched a vast sea of people, their numbers so great they disappeared into the horizon. They marched in eerie unison, their heads bowed, chains clinking with every step. The air was thick with their murmurs, prayers not to God, but to something else, something dark and consuming.

Rebecca's gaze was drawn upward, and her breath froze. A towering figure loomed over the crowd, its form cloaked in impenetrable darkness. Two eyes burned like fire, their malevolence penetrating. The figure raised its arms, and its voice thundered through the void.

"You are mine," it declared, its tone dripping with authority. "You serve me."

The crowd didn't resist. They dropped to their knees, their chains tightening as they murmured pledges of allegiance. The weight of their submission pressed against Rebecca's chest, making it hard to breathe.

"No!" she screamed, her voice finally breaking free. "They don't belong to you!"

The figure's burning eyes snapped toward her, and its gaze was like a physical blow. Rebecca fell to her knees, her body trembling under the weight of its attention.

"You cannot stop this," it said, its voice echoing with a dreadful finality. "The world is already mine."

Rebecca tried to push herself up, to resist the crushing force, but the ground trembled violently beneath her. Shadows surged forward, consuming the crowd, the world, and finally her.

Rebecca jolted awake, gasping for air. Her body was drenched in sweat, her hands gripping the sheets as though they were the only thing keeping her tethered to reality. Tears streamed down her face as she whispered, "God, help us. Please, help us."

The room was silent, but the whispers from her dream echoed in her ears, and the darkness outside the window felt far too close.

"A Pastor's Lament"

The church was empty now, save for the solitary figure of Pastor Daniels, seated in the front pew. The evening sun cast long shadows through the stained-glass windows, filling the sanctuary with a melancholy light that mirrored the heaviness in his heart. He was the same man who had once welcomed Rebecca and James when they first arrived, his sermons a source of comfort and conviction during their journey of faith. But now, the once-vibrant church, filled with the voices of a joyful congregation, was a hollow echo of what it had been. The pews, which had once held families like theirs, were mostly vacant—a testament to a world that had lost its way.

The pastor, whose shoulders now bore the weight of sorrow and loss, stared at the altar with tear-filled eyes. His thoughts drifted to his late wife, who had been the love of his life and his unwavering support in ministry. She had passed away two years earlier, her body slowly ravaged by cancer. The illness had taken its toll, draining the life from her day by day, but through it all, she had never lost her faith. She had faced her suffering with grace, her belief in God's goodness never wavering, even as her physical strength ebbed away.

He remembered the days when the church had been full—when Sunday was a sacred day, a time for worship and rest. Families dressed in their Sunday best, children laughing as they ran up the steps, eager to join their friends in Sunday school. The church had been a beacon of hope, a place where the community gathered to seek solace, strength, and purpose.

But those days seemed like a distant memory now. The world outside had changed. The rise of secularism, the push for personal pleasure above all else, and the relentless attacks on the church had taken their toll. Scandals, both real and exaggerated, had been eagerly seized upon by the press, magnified and broadcast to the masses. Every failing of the church was used to further weaken its influence, to convince the world that it was an outdated institution, no longer relevant in modern society.

Sunday had once been a day of rest, a day to reconnect with God and family. But now, it was just another day—a day to recover from Saturday night's indulgences, or to prepare for the workweek ahead. The shops were open, the streets were busy, and the world seemed to have forgotten the meaning of the Sabbath. The pastor's heart ached as he thought about how easily society had dismissed the importance of this day, replacing it with trivial pursuits and self-serving agendas.

The pastor sighed, his thoughts returning to his wife. How he wished she were here with him now, to comfort him, to offer her wisdom and strength. She had always been his anchor, the one who had kept his faith grounded even in the face of adversity. Without her, he felt adrift, struggling to keep his faith alive in a world that seemed determined to snuff it out.

He bowed his head, hands clasped together, and prayed for guidance, for strength, for the wisdom to lead his dwindling flock through these dark times. He prayed for the courage to continue preaching the truth, even when the world around him no longer wanted to hear it.

But as he prayed, he couldn't shake the feeling of despair that clung to him like a shroud. He had seen the enemy's work firsthand—how Satan and his minions had infiltrated every aspect of society, how they had turned people away from the truth and toward a path of destruction. The church, once a bastion of hope and righteousness, was now seen as an obstacle to progress, a relic of the past that needed to be dismantled.

The pastor's thoughts were interrupted by the sound of the church doors creaking open. He lifted his head and saw a familiar face—Sarah, one of the few remaining faithful members of his congregation. A longtime friend of Rebecca and James, she had been a steadfast presence in the church, known for her unwavering support and quiet strength. She walked in, offering him a small, sad smile as she approached, sensing the weight of his burdens.

"Pastor," she said softly, sitting down beside him, "I wanted to check on you. It's been a hard day for all of us, but I know it's been especially hard for you."

The pastor nodded, grateful for her presence. "Thank you, Sarah. It has been difficult, but your faith and support mean more to me than you'll ever know."

Sarah hesitated for a moment before speaking again, her voice tinged with concern. "I've been thinking about everything that's been happening—the world, the church, and all the changes we're seeing. It's hard not to feel like we're losing the battle."

The pastor sighed deeply. "I know what you mean. The church is under attack from all sides—spiritually, morally, even legally. And the worst part is, many people don't even realize it. They're blind to the enemy's influence, to the lies that are being fed to them every day."

Sarah nodded, her eyes downcast. "It feels like everything we've worked for, everything we believe in, is being torn apart."

The pastor placed a reassuring hand on her shoulder. As his fingers gently rested on her, a spark seemed to ignite within Sarah. It was a simple touch, yet it stirred something deep inside her—a longing, a need for connection that she had kept buried for so long. The warmth of his hand, the strength it conveyed, made her heart race in a way she hadn't felt in years. She found herself leaning into the touch, craving the comfort and reassurance that his presence provided. It was more than just the words he spoke; it was the unspoken bond that passed between them in that moment, a connection that went beyond the surface.

"You're right, Sarah. The world is changing, and not for the better. But we must remember that the battle is not ours alone. God is with us, even in the darkest times. We may feel small and powerless, but our strength comes from Him. And as long as we keep our faith, as long as we continue to stand firm in the truth, we are not defeated," Pastor Daniels said the words to her as if they were memorized, his voice steady but lacking its usual conviction.

For a moment, as the words left his lips, a shadow of doubt crossed his mind. He glanced down at his hand, which had begun to tremble slightly, and clenched it into a fist as if trying to grasp the certainty that seemed to be slipping through his fingers. "Do I even believe what I said?" The thought echoed in his mind, lingering like an unwanted guest.

Seeing the momentary uncertainty in his eyes, Sarah felt an even stronger pull toward him. She needed more than just spiritual guidance; she needed someone who understood her fears, who could share in her burdens. In that brief touch, she felt as if she had found that person. The longing in her heart, which had been dormant for so long, suddenly felt alive, pulsing with a desperate need for connection, for something— or someone—to hold on to.

She looked into his eyes, searching for something deeper. "Thank you, Pastor," she whispered, her voice trembling slightly. "I needed to hear that."

Pastor Daniels noticed the tremor in her voice, the vulnerability in her gaze. A sudden warmth spread through him, a realization that he, too, was in need of something more—something beyond the role of a shepherd. He forced a smile, then hesitated before speaking again, as if wrestling with his own thoughts. Finally, he said softly, "Sarah, you can just call me Tim."

The simplicity of the gesture caught Sarah off guard, and she felt her heart skip a beat. It was as if, in that moment, he had reached out across the distance between them, inviting her into a more personal space, a connection that went beyond the formalities of their relationship. She nodded, her emotions swirling as she whispered, "Thank you... Tim."

Pastor Daniels—Tim—felt a strange sense of relief at hearing his name on her lips, as if something that had been tightly wound inside him had begun to loosen. He wasn't sure what it meant, but he knew that the bond between them had shifted, deepened in a way that was both comforting and unsettling.

"A Glimmer of Hope"

Sarah excused herself and left, her footsteps echoing softly through the quiet sanctuary. She paused at the door, glancing back at Tim, who remained seated in silent contemplation. Her heart ached with a mix of gratitude and sorrow—gratitude for the words of comfort he had offered, but sorrow for the uncertainty she sensed in him, mirroring her own. With a heavy sigh, she stepped out into the fading light of day, leaving him alone in the vast, empty church.

As she walked away from the church, Sarah's thoughts were consumed by the pastor's touch, the warmth of his hand on her shoulder. It had been such a simple gesture, yet it had unlocked a flood of emotions she hadn't allowed herself to feel in years. She realized that she longed for more than just spiritual leadership; she needed someone to walk this dark path with her, someone who could offer more than just words of comfort. She needed a companion, someone who could fill the void that had grown in her heart over the years of struggle and loss.

Tim, meanwhile, was closing up the church. He lingered in the sanctuary, his thoughts heavy with the day's burdens. As he extinguished the candles and locked the doors, his mind kept returning to the brief moment with Sarah—the way she had looked at him, the way her body had responded to his touch. He couldn't deny the spark of connection he had felt, and it unsettled him. He had been a man of God for so long, had dedicated his life to his ministry, but in that moment, he realized that he, too, was in need of something more—someone to share the weight of his burdens.

As he walked out into the night, locking the church doors behind him, Tim found himself praying not just for strength, but for clarity. He asked God to guide him, to help him understand what was happening in his heart. Was this connection with Sarah a sign of something deeper, something ordained by God? Or was it a distraction, a temptation that could lead them both astray?

Sarah walked home, her heart heavy with the weight of the day's revelations. She tried to focus on her prayers, on the words Tim had spoken, but her mind kept drifting back to that moment in the sanctuary. The longing she felt was undeniable, and she wondered if it was a sign from God or a temptation she needed to resist. All she knew was that something had shifted in her heart, and she couldn't ignore it.

Tim, too, found himself struggling with his thoughts as he walked away from the church. The sanctuary, which had always been his place of solace, now felt empty without Sarah's presence. He realized that he had come to rely on her more than he had admitted, not just as a member of his congregation but as a friend, a confidante—perhaps even something more.

As the night closed in around them, both Sarah and Tim were left to grapple with their emotions, each wondering if the connection they felt was a gift from God or a test of their faith. Whatever it was, they knew that their lives were about to change in ways they had never anticipated. In the quiet of their separate homes, they each sent up a prayer, asking for guidance, for strength, and for the wisdom to navigate the uncertain path ahead.

"The War on Salvation"

Rebecca lay in bed, her eyes fixed on the faint patterns of moonlight that stretched across the ceiling. Sleep felt impossible. The previous night's dream clung to her like a shroud, the burning eyes of the shadow figures etched in her memory. The way they had looked at her, as though they could see into her very soul, had left her shaken to her core. The pressure of their gaze, the weight of their malice—it had been unbearable.

She had felt their intent. It wasn't just a dream; it was something more. All day, the oppressive sensation lingered like a storm cloud hanging over her. She had been distant, barely able to meet James's concerned gaze as he repeatedly asked if she was all right. She couldn't find the words to explain, even if she wanted to. How could she describe the evil she felt stirring in the world around her, or the way it seemed to press against her, suffocating and relentless?

James lay beside her now, his breaths slow and even. She envied his peace, even as she feared disturbing it. She was exhausted, yet the thought of closing her eyes terrified her. What if the dream returned? What if the shadows were waiting for her again?

Turning carefully so as not to wake him, Rebecca reached for her phone on the nightstand. Lowering the brightness to a soft glow, she opened her Bible app, praying for comfort. The screen illuminated the darkness as she scrolled aimlessly, hoping for a passage that would soothe her frayed nerves.

Her finger paused on the "open at random" option, and she hesitated, then tapped it. The screen loaded, and there it was: Revelation. The words struck her like a physical blow. Of all the books, why this one?

She considered closing the app, but something compelled her to read on.

The hours passed as she read. Her heart pounded with every verse—visions of destruction, beasts, plagues, and the sealing of the faithful. The descriptions mirrored too much of what she had felt in her dream, stirring her unease further. Her hands trembled as she read of the war waged by Satan and his angels, the final conflict for the souls of men. It felt too real, too familiar.

Finally, exhaustion claimed her. Her grip on the phone loosened, and it slipped from her hand onto the blanket as her eyes fluttered shut. She drifted off, her last thought a silent plea for peace.

Rebecca was there again.

The darkness was suffocating, denser and colder than before, as though it had been waiting for her return. This time, she was drawn into a massive chamber—a place that felt alive with malice. The walls seemed to breathe, their surface consuming all light, leaving the air oppressive and heavy. The faint flicker of red runes etched into an enormous obsidian table was the only source of illumination, their glow writhing like serpents.

Figures loomed around the table, shifting shapes cloaked in shadow. Their forms were terrifyingly abstract, as if their very presence defied human understanding. Some had burning eyes that glared with a hatred so intense, Rebecca felt her knees weaken beneath her. Others were faceless voids, emanating cold, bone-deep dread.

At the head of the table sat Satan himself, his form both beautiful and horrifying. His radiance was a sickening mockery of light, and his throne twisted upward like jagged claws reaching to claim the heavens. His eyes burned with pride and hatred, and his voice, smooth yet venomous, filled the chamber.

"This is no longer a war of flesh and blood," he said, his tone resonating with a dark authority. "This is a war for their souls."

Rebecca's heart raced as his words echoed in her mind. She wanted to run, to hide, but her body refused to obey. She was frozen, an unwilling witness to the council of darkness.

Satan's gaze swept across the table, and every figure straightened, their anticipation visible. "Strike the shepherds," he commanded. "Turn the leaders of their churches into instruments of confusion. Let them doubt, let them fall. Without their shepherds, the flock will scatter. Strike the shepherd and the flock will scatter."

One of the shadowed figures leaned forward, its voice grinding like stones. "And their message?" it rasped. "How shall we twist their words?"

A cruel smile curved Satan's lips. "We will corrupt it," he said, his tone dripping with malice. "Turn their gospel into one of self-indulgence and prosperity. Let them forget the sacrifice, the cross. Let them worship themselves and their good deeds in the name of their God."

The council roared its approval, a sound that reverberated through Rebecca's very bones. The shadows shifted and writhed, their excitement filling the chamber as they fed on the despair their plans would unleash.

Satan's voice rose above the cacophony. "Let the world be so mired in confusion that they cannot see the light. Bring war to their minds, their homes, their churches. Persecute them until they curse the name they once held dear. Break them, body and soul, until they bow before me."

Rebecca's heart shattered at the weight of his words. She wanted to scream, to stop them, to plead for mercy, but she could do nothing but watch as the council plotted the destruction of all she held sacred.

Suddenly, the chamber shifted. The table, the shadows, even Satan's form blurred and dissolved, leaving Rebecca alone in the vast, oppressive void. Her chest heaved as she gasped for air, her spirit crushed under the weight of what she had witnessed.

And then, as if in defiance of the darkness, a faint light brightened her soul, a flicker, small but unwavering. It called to her, a whisper of hope in the suffocating blackness.

Before she could embrace it, the darkness surged, swallowing her whole.

Rebecca jolted awake with a cry, her body trembling and drenched in sweat. The phone lay beside her, its screen dark. James stirred but didn't wake, his steady breathing a sharp contrast to the chaos in her mind.

She sat up, clutching the blanket as tears streamed down her face. The whispers from the council still echoed in her ears, the weight of their plans crushing her spirit. She whispered a desperate prayer, her voice shaking. "God, help us. Please, help us."

The room was quiet, but she could feel the battle consuming the world and closing in on her.

"A World Ensnared"

The world seemed to unravel with every passing moment, its foundations cracking under the relentless weight of corruption, greed, and despair. Rebecca could feel it even in her waking hours, a suffocating pressure that clung to her spirit. But now, in the aftermath of her second dream, the truths she had glimpsed in the unseen realm played vividly in her mind. They were more than visions; they were reflections of a reality taking shape around her.

The earth, once a masterpiece of divine intention, its foundation layered with hope and virtue, was crumbling. Societies that had stood as beacons of justice and truth dimmed like dying embers. Their light, snuffed out by the weight of compromise and corruption, gave way to shadows stretching ever deeper.

Across the globe, the spiritual war raging in the unseen realm broke through with terrifying clarity. Governments, originally designed to protect and serve, became dens of avarice and tyranny. Laws no longer upheld justice; they were twisted tools wielded by leaders whose hearts had been warped by the whispered lies of demons. Rebecca saw them, faces familiar from news screens and headlines, signing decrees with trembling hands, their decisions shrouded in invisible chains.

"The people will follow," one shadow had hissed in her dream. "They'll accept the leash as long as you promise them bread and circuses."

The leaders nodded, their hollow eyes gazing at the documents before them, oblivious to the darkness curling around their shoulders.

The media, once heralded as the cornerstone of free thought, was no better. Rebecca's vision blurred and shifted to crowded studios where smiling anchors delivered poisoned truths. Their words dripped with manipulation, glorifying the self and scorning the notion of absolute morality. The airwaves buzzed with messages that lauded indulgence and belittled sacrifice, their venomous reach extending into homes and hearts. Deception reigned, the masses consuming the lies with eager devotion.

Rebecca saw a child sitting before a flickering screen, their wide eyes drinking in every fabricated word. The voice of the shadow behind the anchor whispered, "Truth is irrelevant. What matters is belief, and belief, we can shape."

Her heart ached at the sight. The children. The youngest, the most vulnerable, were being led astray before they could even grasp the depth of what was being stolen from them.

Homes, the bedrock of human flourishing, were splintering under the weight of materialism and immorality. The dream took her into countless living rooms, each one cold despite the glow of modern comforts. Parents and children sat in separate rooms, their faces illuminated by the blue light of devices, the silence between them a chasm too wide to cross. Arguments broke out over fleeting desires, love was traded for convenience, and truth for what felt good in the moment.

Rebecca tried to cry out, tried to warn them, but her voice was lost in the sea of selfish pursuits.

Her surroundings shifted again, this time to church sanctuaries. She had hoped to find refuge there, a flicker of light amidst the darkness. But the pulpits were not safe. False prophets, their smiles radiant and their words sweet, stood before eager congregations. Their messages promised prosperity, indulgence, and happiness, carefully avoiding the cross. The call to sacrifice, to repent, to carry the burdens of faith was drowned out by sermons designed to tickle ears and stroke egos.

Rebecca stood among the crowd, unnoticed but horrified. She wanted to scream, to plead with them to open their eyes. But as she reached out, she saw the shadow lurking just behind the preacher, feeding him words that danced on his lips like honey laced with poison.

"Give them what they want," the shadow whispered. "If they feel good, they won't notice the chains tightening."

Even the faithful remnant, small and scattered, struggled under the weight of these lies. Their voices, once bold, now wavered, as the world pressed harder against them. The truth they clung to felt like a fragile ember, barely holding against the winds of deception.

Rebecca's heart broke as the earth itself groaned under the burden of its decay. Forests withered, rivers ran dark, and the skies carried an oppressive weight. The air buzzed with the laughter of the unseen, the forces of darkness reveling in their apparent victory.

And then she saw him.

The rider on the white horse.

His figure loomed in the distance, silhouetted against the smoldering horizon. He smiled, his face alight with a beauty that chilled her to the bone. It was a beauty that masked rot, a smile that promised salvation while hiding conquest. He carried a bow, but no arrows, yet his influence spread effortlessly across the earth. His voice echoed in her ears, smooth and commanding.

"They have chosen me," he said, his words a mockery of triumph. "I will give them what they ask for."

The world beneath his steed seemed to bow in submission, bending to his will. Nations crumbled, their people willingly enslaved. The shadows around him surged forward, spreading across the land with devastating speed.

The vision shifted once more. She stood on the edge of the abyss, staring down into its endless depths. The council of darkness convened below, their whispers rising like smoke. Satan sat at its center, radiant yet corrupt, his eyes blazing with hatred. His generals leaned close, their plans spreading like wildfire.

"We've only begun," one shadow rasped.

Rebecca's spirit trembled under the weight of the evil that surrounded her. The earth was unraveling, the forces of darkness growing bolder. She knew the worst was yet to come.

But then, faint and flickering, the light appeared in her inner being, deep inside. It was small, almost imperceptible, yet it pierced the oppressive blackness surrounding her. Though fragile in appearance, the light was steady. It didn't grow brighter, but it endured, unyielding against the tide of shadow.

The light didn't shout or rage. It simply existed, a quiet defiance in the face of overwhelming darkness. And that was enough.

The light caught Satan's attention. His head jerked up, his fiery gaze locking onto her with a sudden and searing intensity. The movement was sharp, almost violent, and every shadowy figure in the abyss followed his gaze. A deadly silence fell over the council of darkness. The pause lasted only a heartbeat before Satan moved.

In one swift, predatory motion, he lunged upward, his form stretching unnaturally as his hand shot toward her heart. His clawed fingers burned with malevolent energy, and the air around him crackled with fury. Shadows swarmed behind him, writhing like a living tide, their twisted forms racing to support his assault.

Rebecca awoke with a start.

She sat bolt upright in bed, gasping for air. Her chest heaved as though she had been underwater, her lungs desperate to fill themselves. Her heart pounded a relentless rhythm, each beat driving the terror deeper into her veins. Tears streamed down her face, hot and unbidden. Her hands clutched the blanket in a death grip, trembling as the vision clung to her like a second skin. She pressed her hand against her chest, as if to make certain her heart was still there. She could feel it pounding, a fierce and frantic reminder that she was still alive.

Beside her, James stirred. His soft murmur reached her ears, but he didn't wake. His peaceful breathing was a stark contrast to the chaos she had just escaped. She glanced at him, her heart aching. He had asked her so many times if she was all right, but how could she explain this? How could she describe the evil she had faced, the shadows that sought to crush her very soul?

Rebecca leaned back, pressing her trembling body against the headboard. The weight of her exhaustion was overwhelming, but the thought of closing her eyes again filled her with dread. Sleep had become her enemy, and she hated it.

The darkness of the room seemed to press against her, but somewhere deep within, the faint flicker of the light still remained. She couldn't feel it as strongly now, but she knew it was there.

Her voice broke as she whispered into the void, "God, help us. Help me. I don't know how to fight this."

The room was silent, but she clung to the memory of that light. It had endured, even in the heart of pure blackness. Though the terror still gripped her, though the tears continued to fall, the light gave her a fragile, reassuring hope.

3

PERSECUTION BEGINS

"Seal of Deceit"

Over the last two centuries, the world had steadily unraveled, drawn into Satan's web of deceit and domination. The rider on the white horse galloped forth, his conquest hidden beneath false peace. Nations welcomed his arrival, blind to the darkness taking root. Governments, corrupted by whispered lies, abandoned justice for tyranny. Truth became a casualty, crushed beneath greed and oppression.

Satan's influence reached into every sphere of life. The media, once a tool for enlightenment, became a weapon of manipulation, spreading half-truths and glorifying self-indulgence. Families splintered under the weight of materialism and immorality. Even the Church faltered. False teachers rose, distorting the gospel into empty promises of prosperity while silencing the call to repentance.

The enemy's plans grew bolder. Persecution began with subtlety but escalated as laws turned against believers. Rebecca saw it all—families torn apart, churches emptied, and the faithful crushed under the weight of fear. Yet their light, though flickering, endured.

At the center of it all, Rebecca's vision revealed Satan, triumphant in his throne of shadows, directing his forces with precision. "Strike the shepherds," he commanded, his voice a venomous whisper. "Let the flock scatter. Twist the truth until they can no longer see the light."

The storm had been building for generations, and now the world teetered on the edge of its darkest hour. Yet even amidst the growing despair, the faint light of Christ's victory endured—a defiance against the shadows. The forces of darkness celebrated their power, but the faithful prepared to stand firm, knowing the story was not yet over.

"The First Decree"

The midday sun blazed down on the steps of the Capitol, its heat radiating off the marble columns that loomed over the crowd gathered below. Cameras clicked and whirred, capturing every angle of the historic moment. Reporters jostled for position, their microphones extended toward the stage where the nation's leaders were preparing to address the public. A large banner draped over the front of the podium bore the words: "Unity for All—A New Era of Peace."

Rebecca sat at home, the television screen flickering with the live broadcast of the event. James was next to her, his face set in a grim line, and Sarah had joined them, her hands clasped tightly in her lap. As soon as the situation felt tense, Emily retreated to her room. The air in the room was thick with anticipation, a sense of dread that had been building for weeks, ever since the first rumors of the new legislation had begun to circulate.

The camera panned over the crowd before settling on the podium, where the President stood flanked by advisors and high-ranking officials. His expression was stern, resolute, as if he was about to deliver news that would change the course of history. And, in a way, he was.

"Ladies and gentlemen," the President began, his voice carrying through the speakers with practiced authority, "we stand at a crossroads in our nation's history. For too long, we have allowed divisions to fester, driven by outdated beliefs and practices that have no place in a modern, united society. Today, we take the first step toward a future where harmony and peace are not just aspirations, but realities."

Rebecca felt her heart begin to race, her breath catching in her throat. She knew what was coming, but that didn't make it any easier to hear. She glanced at James, whose jaw was clenched tightly, his eyes fixed on the screen.

"In recent years," the President continued, "we have seen the damaging effects of intolerance and exclusion, often rooted in religious doctrines that seek to divide rather than unite. While freedom of belief is a cornerstone of our nation, we must also recognize that certain practices and teachings are incompatible with the goals of a just and equal society."

The words hit Rebecca like a physical blow. Incompatible. Just a few months ago, the idea that her faith could be deemed incompatible with society would have seemed absurd. But now, as she watched the President deliver his decree, it was all too real.

"Therefore," the President said, his voice firm, "it is with a heavy heart, but with unwavering conviction, that I announce the signing of the National Unity Act. This legislation will prohibit any public expression of beliefs that are deemed harmful or discriminatory. Places of worship must adhere to guidelines that promote inclusivity and social harmony. Any teachings that conflict with these principles will be subject to regulation and, if necessary, prohibition."

Rebecca's hands trembled as she gripped the edge of the couch. The National Unity Act—it was the end of everything she had known, everything she had taken for granted. The government was not just targeting extremists or fringe groups; they were coming for her, for every Christian who refused to conform to the new norms.

James clenched his fists, his knuckles turning white as he swore under his breath, his voice trembling with barely suppressed rage. "This is it. They're going to make it illegal to be a Christian in this country!" His words cut through the tension in the room like a blade, his anger fueled by a deep sense of betrayal and fear for what lay ahead.

The outburst hung in the air, heavy and charged. Sarah flinched at the sharpness in James's voice, her eyes widening in alarm. She instinctively shrank back, her mind flashing to memories she had worked hard to bury, where anger had always meant danger.

Rebecca noticed the sudden change in Sarah's demeanor. Gently, she placed a hand on James's arm, her touch firm but calming, as if trying to absorb some of his fury before it could do more harm. "James, please," she said softly, her voice steady, though her own fear simmered just beneath the surface. She didn't want to add to the tension, but she couldn't ignore the way Sarah had recoiled. "We need to stay strong, for each other."

James exhaled sharply, his anger still simmering but now tempered by the awareness of the impact his words had on the others. He glanced at Sarah, who had drawn into herself, her eyes avoiding his. Rebecca's touch grounded him, reminding him of the delicate balance they were all trying to maintain. He softened, trying to let go of the anger, at least for now.

Sarah forced a small smile, a shaky attempt to reassure them. "I'm fine," she murmured, though the words felt heavy on her tongue. She wasn't sure who she was trying to convince—James, Rebecca, or herself—but she knew she couldn't let them see how much the anger had rattled her. Not after everything she had been through. She had to be strong, for them, for herself.

As they focused on the scene unfolding on the screen, Sarah's eyes filled with tears as she shook her head in disbelief. "How can they do this? How can they just... take away our rights like this?"

The words trembled on her lips, and as she spoke, memories she had long tried to bury began to resurface. The images were vivid, each one sharper than the last—images of a man whose face was contorted with rage, whose words cut deeper than any physical blow ever could. He wasn't her husband, though he had taken every liberty as if he were. Sarah had never known the safety of a loving relationship, had never been raised in the church or taught the comfort that faith could bring. Christianity, to her, had always been something distant—something that other people seemed to understand, but that had no place in her chaotic life.

She remembered the way he had torn her down, piece by piece, until there was nothing left but a hollow shell of the person she had once been. His words, his fists, had shattered her self-esteem, leaving her feeling worthless and unlovable. There were nights when she had come close to ending it all, convinced that the world would be better off without her in it. The darkness had been so thick, so suffocating, that she had almost succumbed to it entirely.

It was during one of those dark days that she had met Rebecca. It seemed like a chance encounter at the time, but looking back, Sarah knew it had been divinely orchestrated. Rebecca had seen something in her that day—a flicker of the person she could become, hidden deep beneath the layers of pain and despair. She had reached out to Sarah with a kindness that was foreign to her, and for reasons Sarah couldn't explain, she had accepted it.

Rebecca had slowly, patiently shared her faith with Sarah. She talked about her beliefs, about the freedom that could be found in Jesus, about a love that was unconditional and unwavering. Sarah had scoffed at first, convinced that it was all a fairy tale, something too good to be real. As the days turned into weeks, and the weeks into months, she found herself drawn to the hope that Rebecca spoke of, a hope that she had never known. Then, one day, almost without realizing it, she believed.

The change in Sarah was almost immediate. She found a strength she hadn't known she possessed, a sense of worth that had been buried under years of abuse. The man she had been with couldn't stand the new Sarah. He tried to break her again, to tear her down as he had done before, but this time, something was different. The prayers of Rebecca, James, and Pastor Daniels had taken root, and in a moment that could only be described as divine intervention, circumstances shifted. The man was suddenly out of her life, removed in a way that was almost miraculous. It was as if God had heard their prayers and acted in a way that left no doubt that He was in control.

As these memories flooded her mind, Sarah found herself back in the living room, the warmth of the past moments still clinging to her, but mixed with the cold reality of the world they now faced. The fear of losing everything she had fought so hard to gain—the peace, the faith, the freedom—threatened to overwhelm her.

Rebecca noticed the tear slipping down Sarah's cheek and gently reached out, placing a comforting hand on her knee. "We've been through so much already, Sarah," she whispered, her voice filled with the strength of someone who had seen the darkness and found the light. "We won't let them take this from us. We're stronger now, because we have each other and because we have Him."

Sarah nodded, wiping away the tear. She forced a small smile, though her heart still trembled with the fear of what was to come. "I'm fine," she said softly, though the words carried the weight of her past and the uncertainty of her future.

Rebecca squeezed her hand reassuringly. "We'll get through this," she said, her voice firm. "Together."

With that, the three of them turned their attention back to the screen, steeling themselves for the battle that lay ahead, knowing that whatever came next, they would face it together, with their faith as their anchor.

As the scene in the living room faded into the background, the story of their struggle was only beginning to unfold. The fight for their faith, for their rights, and for their very souls was far from over. They would need every ounce of strength, every bit of the faith they had come to cherish, for the trials that lay ahead in the chapters yet to come.

On the screen, the President continued to speak, and they once again focused on the broadcast. "These measures are not taken lightly," he was saying. "But they are necessary if we are to build a society where all individuals are valued and respected, regardless of their background or beliefs. We must be willing to make sacrifices for the greater good, and that includes rethinking the ways in which we express our faith."

The crowd outside the Capitol erupted in applause, a wave of approval that seemed to drown out the dissenting voices. The camera zoomed in on the President's face, capturing the resolve in his eyes. To him, this was not just a political maneuver—it was a moral crusade, a righteous cause in the name of unity.

Rebecca felt a cold chill settle over her. This was the moment she had feared, the moment when her faith became a liability, a mark against her in the eyes of the state. She had always known that being a Christian meant standing apart from the world, but she had never imagined that it would mean standing in opposition to her own government.

As the press conference continued, the President outlined the specific measures that would be implemented under the National Unity Act. Churches would be required to submit their sermons for review, ensuring that no message of exclusion or intolerance was preached. Religious symbols would be banned from public spaces, and any violation of these new laws would result in severe penalties—fines, imprisonment, or worse.

Rebecca's mind raced, the implications of the decree hitting her all at once. This wasn't just about public expression—it was about control, about forcing believers to choose between their faith and their freedom. For many, it would be a choice they couldn't make.

James turned to Rebecca, his voice low and urgent. "What are we going to do? If they start enforcing this... we could lose everything. Our church, our community... even our daughter."

Rebecca swallowed hard, the weight of the decision pressing down on her. She had always been a woman of faith, a woman who believed in the power of prayer and the strength of conviction. But now, faced with the reality of what was to come, she wasn't sure if she was strong enough to endure it.

But as she looked into James's eyes, she knew that they had no choice. This was their cross to bear, their trial in the face of a world that had turned its back on the very principles they held dear.

"We stand firm," she said finally, her voice steady despite the fear that gnawed at her insides. "We don't give in. We don't back down. No matter what."

Sarah nodded, wiping away the tears that had spilled down her cheeks. As she did, her mind raced with thoughts she hadn't dared to voice. She couldn't go back to the way she was before—before her faith had freed her, before it had given her life and hope when she had thought all was lost. The darkness she had escaped from was too real, too close, and the fear of losing what she had found in her faith was almost paralyzing. The thought of having it taken away, of slipping back into that void, was more terrifying than anything the world outside could throw at her.

Sarah knew she couldn't let that fear control her. The faith that had brought her out of the shadows was the only thing that could sustain her now. She turned to Rebecca and James, her voice steady despite the turmoil inside her. "We have to trust that God will see us through this," she said, her words laced with a quiet determination. "It won't be easy, but we have to keep our faith. It's all we have left."

The weight of her words hung in the air, a reminder to all of them that no matter what came next, they had to hold on to the faith that had carried them this far.

The press conference ended with a final, resounding statement from the President: "Let this be a new beginning for our nation—a beginning where all people, regardless of creed or color, can live together in peace and harmony. We are stronger together, united in our common purpose."

The screen transitioned into the commentators as the broadcast ended. James turned it off, leaving the room in silence, except for the ticking of the clock on the wall, each second a reminder of the world that had just shifted beneath their feet.

"We'll need to be careful," James said quietly, his voice heavy with resignation. "They'll be watching us now, looking for any excuse to make an example of us."

Rebecca nodded, knowing he was right. The government had made its stance clear—there was no room for dissent, no tolerance for those who refused to conform. The days ahead would be dark, filled with uncertainty and fear. But they had made their choice, and they would face whatever came with their heads held high.

As the three of them sat together in the dim light of the living room, Rebecca felt a sense of calm settle over her. It wasn't the calm of certainty or peace, but the calm of resolve. They were entering a new chapter of their lives, one that would test their faith in ways they had never imagined, but they would face it together, with the strength that came from knowing they were on the side of truth.

No matter what happened, they would not be shaken.

"Mandatory Compliance"

The fluorescent lights in the government building flickered slightly, casting a harsh, sterile glow over the sparse interior. The walls were painted an unremarkable shade of gray, and the air was thick with the scent of industrial cleaner, a sharp reminder of the cold, impersonal nature of the place. Rows of chairs were lined up in front of a large screen at the front of the room, where the words, "Sensitivity Training: Building a Unified Society," were emblazoned in bold, blocky letters.

Rebecca sat in the middle row, her heart pounding as she took in her surroundings. She had received the summons a few days ago—a formal letter from the Department of Social Harmony, informing her that she was required to attend a mandatory sensitivity training session. Failure to comply, the letter warned, would result in immediate legal action and possible transfer to a reprogramming facility. The letter had left no room for doubt: this was not a request—it was an order.

James sat beside her, his jaw set in a hard line, his eyes fixed on the screen. He had received the same letter, and they had both known there was no avoiding it. They had to go, had to sit through whatever this was, if only to buy themselves a little more time to figure out their next move.

Rebecca's daughter, Emily, had been called in for a different session earlier that week, one specifically designed for the youth. The government had been strategic, targeting the younger generation first, knowing that if they could sway the children, they could undermine the parents. The sessions were framed as educational and necessary for social harmony, but everyone knew the truth—they were grooming the youth to become informants, encouraging them to report on their parents if they held Christian beliefs.

But Emily, sharp and aware of what was happening, had seen through their lies. She didn't tell them anything, protecting her family as best she could. Yet, despite her silence, Rebecca and James had been flagged. The authorities were monitoring them now, and they even knew that Sarah might be a friend and fellow Christian. The net was closing in on all of them.

When Emily returned home, her face pale and eyes wide with what she had witnessed, she had warned her mother in a hushed voice. "It's not just training," she had whispered to her mother, her voice trembling. "It's brainwashing. They'll say it's about tolerance and unity, but it's really about breaking you down, making you doubt everything you believe in. They're trying to get us to turn on each other."

Rebecca had steeled herself for what was to come, but now that she was here, in this cold, impersonal room, the reality of it was almost too much to bear. The room was filling up with other attendees—people she recognized from her community, from church, even from her children's school. They all wore the same tense expressions, the same look of quiet fear.

As the room grew more crowded, the door creaked open again, and Sarah walked in, her steps tentative and hesitant. She paused near the side of the room, her eyes darting around, taking in the nearly full seats, the cold stares of strangers, and the oppressive atmosphere that seemed to weigh on her chest. She felt exposed, vulnerable, like a deer caught in the headlights, unsure where to go or what to do.

A security agent standing near the door, armed to a nearly ridiculous level with gear and weapons, barked at her with a voice that cut through the room like a knife. "Take a seat now! Time to begin!" He jabbed a finger toward an empty chair right in the middle of the front row—the last place she wanted to sit, or anyone for that matter.

Sarah froze, the command echoing in her ears, but she couldn't bring herself to move. She glanced around desperately for an alternative, hoping to find a less conspicuous spot, but there was nowhere else to go. The agent's eyes narrowed as he took a step closer, his voice dropping to a low, menacing growl. "I said, take a seat. Now. Or there will be consequences."

Her heart pounded in her chest as the threat hung in the air, heavy and suffocating. Rebecca and James, seated a few rows back, watched in helpless silence, their hearts aching for her. They could see the fear in her eyes, the way her hands trembled as she forced herself to comply. Sarah moved to the front row, each step feeling like it might be her last, and sat down in the chair the agent had pointed out, her body tense and rigid, as if bracing for an impact.

The room seemed to close in around her, the weight of the situation pressing down on her shoulders, but she knew she had no choice. She had to do what they said, had to survive this somehow. Rebecca and James exchanged a glance, their hearts heavy with worry and sorrow for their friend. They knew what sitting in that seat, under those harsh lights, would do to Sarah—how it would make her feel exposed and powerless, a painful reminder of the vulnerability she had fought so hard to overcome.

The door at the front of the room opened, and a woman in a crisp, navy suit entered. She was tall, with perfectly styled hair and a practiced smile that didn't reach her eyes. She moved to the front of the room, her heels clicking sharply on the tile floor, and took her place behind a sleek, metal podium.

"Good afternoon, everyone," she began, her voice smooth and professional. "My name is Ms. Aldridge, and I'll be leading today's sensitivity training session. The purpose of this training is to help you better understand the values of our new society and to ensure that all citizens are equipped to contribute positively to our nation's unity and harmony."

Rebecca clenched her fists in her lap, resisting the urge to roll her eyes. She could already see where this was going—Ms. Aldridge was going to lecture them about tolerance and inclusivity, all while subtly undermining their beliefs and pushing them toward conformity.

Ms. Aldridge continued, her voice taking on a more serious tone. "In recent years, we've seen how divisive and harmful certain beliefs can be, particularly those that promote exclusion or intolerance. Our goal here today is to address these harmful beliefs and to help you realign your thinking so that it is more in line with the values of our society."

She clicked a button on a remote, and the screen behind her flickered to life, displaying a series of images: protesters holding signs with hateful messages, news clips of violent clashes between different religious groups, statistics on the rise of hate crimes.

"As you can see," Ms. Aldridge said, gesturing to the screen, "these are the consequences of intolerance and division. These are the kinds of behaviors and beliefs that we must work together to eliminate. And it starts with each of you, here in this room."

Rebecca felt a knot form in her stomach. This was worse than she had expected. Ms. Aldridge wasn't just trying to convince them to be more tolerant—she was framing their faith as a threat to society, something that needed to be eradicated.

The presentation continued, with Ms. Aldridge outlining the "new moral framework" that citizens were expected to adopt. It was a carefully crafted doctrine of inclusivity, one that left no room for the absolute truths of Christianity. Every belief, every value, was presented as relative, subject to change in the name of progress.

Rebecca could feel the pressure mounting with each passing minute. She glanced at James, who was sitting rigidly in his seat, his expression unreadable. She knew he was struggling, just as she was. How could they sit here and listen to this? How could they be expected to renounce everything they believed in, everything that had guided their lives?

As the session wore on, Ms. Aldridge moved on to the "interactive" portion of the training. The attendees were divided into small groups and given scenarios to discuss—situations where they would need to choose between their personal beliefs and the new societal norms.

Rebecca's eyes locked onto Sarah, seated among a sea of tense faces. As she moved closer, her heart sank. Sarah sat with her head bowed low, shoulders hunched, as if trying to disappear into herself. She wasn't looking up, avoiding any interaction with those around her. The anxiety and fear seemed to radiate from her in waves, almost tangible in the oppressive atmosphere of the room.

Sarah's thoughts were spiraling out of control. Her heart pounded so hard it felt like it might burst out of her chest. The walls of the room seemed to close in, and the voices around her became a disorienting blur. She felt a wave of nausea rise up, and her hands began to tremble uncontrollably. It was as if the air had thickened, making it impossible to breathe. All she wanted was to disappear, to be anywhere but here, trapped in a room full of people who had no idea of the terror clawing at her insides.

Rebecca, seeing Sarah's distress, quickly made up her mind. She had to get to her, to comfort her, to somehow shield her from the nightmare she was obviously living. As the attendees started to move into groups, Rebecca tried to maneuver her way over to Sarah, hoping they could at least stay together.

Just as she was about to reach Sarah, a security agent stepped in front of her, blocking her path. "Step back," he ordered, his voice cold and authoritative. "You're not assigned to this group."

"But she's—" Rebecca began, her concern overriding her caution.

"Step back," the agent repeated, more forcefully this time. His eyes narrowed, and his hand hovered near the weapon strapped to his side. "Now."

Rebecca hesitated, glancing at Sarah, who was now being forcibly guided by another agent into a different group. Sarah's eyes were wide with fear, her body stiff as she tried to resist, but she was no match for the agent's grip. Her anxiety spiked, sending her mind reeling into a dark abyss of panic. The room felt like it was spinning, and she was being pulled deeper into a nightmare from which there was no escape.

The agent barked at Sarah, "Comply, or there will be consequences." His voice was a harsh slap to her already fragile state, and she found herself moving despite every fiber of her being screaming to run, to hide.

Rebecca was forced to watch from a distance, helpless as Sarah was pushed into a group where she didn't belong, where she would have to face her fears alone. Rebecca's heart ached as she was ordered away, the reality of their situation sinking in even deeper. This was no mere training; it was a test of endurance, of breaking them down piece by piece.

Sarah, feeling utterly defeated, let herself be placed in the group, her mind racing with thoughts of how she couldn't go back to the way she was before her faith had freed her. The life, the hope she had found in Christ—she was terrified it could all be taken away in a place like this. She had no choice but to comply, to survive this ordeal, praying desperately for the strength to make it through without losing herself in the process.

Rebecca couldn't see Sarah from where she was seated, and her husband, James, had been placed in another group. They were presented with a scenario where a teacher, much like herself, had to decide whether to remove religious content from her curriculum to comply with the new guidelines. The discussion quickly grew tense, with some members of the group expressing a willingness to conform, while others, like Rebecca, grappled with how to remain true to their faith.

"I just don't see how we can do this," Rebecca said quietly, her voice trembling with emotion. "How can we be expected to deny our beliefs, to pretend they don't matter? Isn't there some way to find a middle ground? They're asking us to condemn what we hold sacred, to say our beliefs are bad and harmful."

One of the other attendees, a man named Mr. Hayes, shook his head. "There is no middle ground," he said flatly. "They've made that clear. Either we comply, or we face the consequences. It's that simple."

Ms. Aldridge walked by their group, listening in on the conversation. She smiled politely, but there was a steely glint in her eyes. "Remember," she said, her tone deceptively kind, "this isn't about denying your beliefs. It's about adapting them to fit the needs of a modern, inclusive society. You can still have your faith, but it must be practiced in a way that doesn't harm others."

Rebecca's hands tightened into fists. "But what if our faith teaches us things that are considered... harmful by your standards? What if we believe in absolute truths that don't change with the times?"

Ms. Aldridge's smile didn't falter, but her eyes grew colder. "Then you'll need to make a choice, Mrs. Marshall. Adapt, or face the consequences."

The words hung in the air, heavy with the threat that lay beneath them. Rebecca felt a surge of anger and fear rise up in her chest. This was exactly what she had feared—being forced to choose between her faith and her freedom. She refused to deny Christ.

James heard Rebecca's voice and turned to see her, his eyes pleading with her to stay calm, but Rebecca could see the same conflict etched in his gaze—the same struggle to reconcile what was being demanded of them with the truths they held dear. The tension between them was intense, both grappling with the impossible choice before them, torn between compliance and conviction.

The session dragged on, each moment more agonizing than the last. Rebecca forced herself to participate, to keep her head down and avoid drawing any further attention, but every fiber of her being screamed in silent protest. This wasn't just sensitivity training—it was indoctrination, plain and simple. Every word, every exercise was designed to erode their beliefs, to force them into compliance with a worldview that felt so fundamentally wrong.

As the session neared its end, Ms. Aldridge announced that each attendee would be required to sign a statement of compliance before leaving. The statement declared that they agreed with the principles outlined in the training and would adhere to the new guidelines in all aspects of their public and private lives. As Rebecca scanned the document, her eyes caught a troubling clause buried within the dense text: a commitment that, at a future date, attendees "will" be asked to make further sacrifices to renounce old, ancient Christian beliefs. By signing, they were agreeing in advance to comply with whatever was demanded of them in the future, all for the sake of societal unity.

Rebecca stared at the paper in front of her, her hand frozen above the pen. How could she sign this? How could she, in good conscience, agree to something that went against everything she believed in? It was a trap—a carefully worded agreement that would bind her to deny her faith in Jesus, not just now, but at some unknown time in the future, when the demands would become even more unbearable.

She looked at James, who had already signed his form, his face pale and strained. He met her gaze, his expression pleading. "Rebecca, please," he mouthed. "Just sign it. We'll figure out what to do later, but we can't afford to fight this right now."

But Rebecca couldn't bring herself to do it. Her hand shook as she gripped the pen, her mind racing. She knew what this meant—if she refused to sign, she would be marked as non-compliant. She would be a target.

Ms. Aldridge noticed Rebecca's hesitation and approached her with that same cold, polite smile. "Is there a problem, Mrs. Marshall?"

Rebecca looked up at her, the conflict raging within her. Every instinct told her to sign, to get out of this room and keep herself safe. But something deeper, something stronger, held her back.

"I can't sign this," Rebecca said, her voice trembling but firm. "I can't agree to something that goes against my faith."

The room went silent, all eyes turning to Rebecca. Ms. Aldridge's smile faded, replaced by a look of thinly veiled irritation. "Mrs. Marshall, I strongly advise you to reconsider. Non-compliance will have serious consequences."

Rebecca swallowed hard, her heart pounding in her chest. But she knew she couldn't back down now. "I won't sign it," she said again, her voice stronger this time. "I can't."

Ms. Aldridge's expression hardened. She motioned to one of the security guards stationed at the door, who immediately stepped forward. "Very well, Mrs. Marshall. You leave us no choice."

The guard took Rebecca by the arm, his grip firm but not rough. James stood up, his face a mask of fear and helplessness. "Wait, please— don't take her. She just needs more time."

Ms. Aldridge shook her head. "The time for hesitation is over. We must ensure that all citizens are aligned with the values of our society. If Mrs. Marshall cannot comply, she will be transferred to a reprogramming facility for further assistance."

Rebecca felt her heart sink as the reality of her situation hit her. She was being taken away—not just from this room, but from everything she knew. She would be sent to a place where they would try to break her, to force her to conform.

As the guard led her toward the door, she felt a strange sense of peace wash over her. She had made her choice—a choice to stand firm in her faith, no matter the cost. Though she didn't know what awaited her, she knew that she was not alone. She would not be shaken.

As she was escorted out of the room, James's voice echoed after her, filled with desperation. "Rebecca, I'm sorry—I'm so sorry..."

But Rebecca didn't look back. She kept her eyes forward, her heart steady, as she was led to the door in silence. Suddenly, the quiet was shattered.

"Stop! Please, stop!" Sarah's voice rang out, trembling with panic. Rebecca's heart lurched as she heard the desperate cries of her friend, and she turned just in time to see Sarah break from her seat, her face contorted with fear.

"Don't take her! You can't take her!" Sarah screamed, rushing forward, her hands outstretched as if she could physically prevent the guards from leading Rebecca away. Her voice was raw, filled with a terror that seemed to echo through the room. "Please, don't take her from me! She's all I have—she knows me, she knows where I've come from!"

Rebecca's blood ran cold as she watched the scene unfold. Sarah, usually so composed, had lost all self-control, her fear and desperation overtaking her completely. She tried to reach out to Rebecca, but a guard stepped in front of her, blocking her path. "Get back!" the guard barked, but Sarah didn't stop. She pleaded, her voice cracking with emotion, "You can't take her! Please, don't do this! She's my sister in Christ— she's all I have left!"

The guard's face hardened, and as Sarah tried to push past him, another guard swiftly moved behind her. Without warning, the guard raised a Taser and fired. The electric shock hit Sarah like a lightning bolt, and she crumpled to the floor, her body convulsing as the current surged through her. A collective gasp filled the room as Sarah lay motionless, her face twisted in pain and shock.

Rebecca's heart shattered as she watched Sarah being lifted under each arm by the guards, her limp body dragged across the floor, her feet trailing behind her. One of her shoes slipped off in the process, left behind like a silent witness to the violence that had just occurred. Tears streamed down Rebecca's face as she called out, "Sarah! Oh God, Sarah!" But there was nothing she could do—nothing but watch in horror as her friend was carried out, her body lifeless and discarded.

Rebecca was led out of the room behind Sarah, her legs trembling with every step. Her mind raced with guilt and fear, a constant loop of "Should I have signed the statement?" running through her thoughts. The weight of it all pressed down on her chest, suffocating her, as she realized the true cost of their faith in this dark and twisted world.

4

CAMP

"Gray Despair"

The air was thick with the smell of damp concrete and disinfectant as Rebecca stepped out of the transport van and into the cold, gray courtyard of the reprogramming camp. The high, featureless walls loomed around her, topped with razor wire that glinted menacingly in the dim light. Armed guards patrolled the perimeter, their faces expressionless, eyes hidden behind dark sunglasses. The entire facility exuded the feeling of a place where hope came to die.

Rebecca's wrists ached from the cuffs that had bound her during the journey, and her legs trembled as she was led through the heavy iron gates that clanged shut behind her with a finality that sent a shiver down her spine. She tried to steady herself, drawing on the deep well of faith that had carried her this far, but the oppressive atmosphere of the camp seemed to sap her strength with every step.

The guards ushered her into a stark, windowless building where she was processed with clinical efficiency: fingerprinted, photographed, and stripped of her personal belongings. Her wedding ring—a symbol of her love and commitment to James—was pried from her finger with cold detachment, leaving her feeling even more vulnerable, more exposed.

They handed her a plain gray uniform, identical to those worn by the other detainees she had glimpsed in the courtyard. The fabric was rough and ill-fitting, but it was the least of her worries. She knew the real trials were yet to come.

After processing, Rebecca was led down a narrow corridor lined with metal doors, each one bearing only a number, with no name to mark its occupant. The sound of her footsteps echoed off the walls, mingling with the distant hum of machinery and the occasional muffled cry. Finally, they stopped in front of one of the numbered doors. The guard opened it, revealing a small, bare cell furnished with only a metal cot, a toilet, and a sink.

"This is where you'll stay," the guard said flatly. "You'll be brought to the reprogramming sessions according to your schedule. Cooperate, and things will be easier for you."

Rebecca nodded numbly, stepping into the cell as the door clanged shut behind her. She stood there for a moment, staring at the blank walls, trying to process the reality of her situation. She had known that refusing to sign the compliance form would lead to consequences, but she hadn't fully grasped what that meant until now.

Taking a deep breath, Rebecca sat down on the cold metal cot, the thin mattress offering little comfort. She closed her eyes, attempting to center herself, to pray, but the words seemed to elude her. All she could think about was Sarah.

She hadn't seen Sarah since they had been separated. The last she saw of her, Sarah had been unconscious, and Rebecca's heart twisted with worry. She had asked repeatedly about her friend's condition, her whereabouts, and what was being done to her, but each question was met with silence. The guards ignored her pleas, offering only threats to gag her if she didn't remain quiet.

A deep ache settled in Rebecca's chest, a longing to be held by James, to feel the comfort of his arms around her. She couldn't shake the image of his face as she was led away—helpless, stricken with worry. What must he be going through now? Did he even know where she was? Was he out there, desperately trying to find a way to help her?

The questions swirled in her mind, adding to the oppressive weight of her situation. She felt so isolated, cut off from everyone she loved, everyone who understood the depth of her faith and the strength it took to defy a world that sought to strip it away.

But she knew she couldn't allow herself to give in to despair. She had to find a way to endure, to survive whatever came next. For herself, for Sarah, for James. They were counting on her to stay strong, and she couldn't let them down.

She opened her eyes and stared at the blank ceiling above her. In the silence of her cell, Rebecca whispered a prayer, her voice trembling but resolute. "Lord, give me strength. Help me to endure. Guide me through this darkness and keep my heart steadfast in faith. I trust in You, no matter what comes."

With that, Rebecca lay down on the cot, curling up into a tight ball, and allowed herself to rest, if only for a moment. She knew that the days ahead would be long and filled with trials, but she also knew that her faith was the one thing they couldn't take from her—no matter how hard they tried.

Even as these gray walls threatened to overwhelm her, Rebecca felt a flicker of resolve ignite within her. She had come this far because of her faith, because she believed in something greater than herself, greater than the forces trying to break her. She had to hold on to that belief; it was now all she had.

The first reprogramming session was even worse than Rebecca had feared. She was led into a sterile room and strapped into a chair, facing a large screen. As the guard left, the sound of the heavy metal door locking behind her echoed unnervingly loud in the otherwise silent space. The room was dimly lit, with the only light coming from the screen, which cast a harsh, flickering glow across her face, amplifying the sense of isolation and dread.

A voice crackled through an overhead speaker, cold and detached. "Welcome, Mrs. Marshall. You are here because you have refused to align your beliefs with the principles of society. This session is designed to help you understand the importance of social harmony and the dangers of holding onto outdated, harmful doctrines."

The screen flickered to life, bombarding Rebecca with a rapid montage of images: scenes of violence and unrest, interspersed with slogans about unity and tolerance. The relentless onslaught was accompanied by a low, droning sound that seemed to vibrate deep within her skull, overwhelming her senses. The noise was so intense, so penetrating, that it became impossible to think clearly, as if it was designed to drown out any thought or resistance, seeping into her consciousness with an almost unbearable force.

The voice continued, relentless. "Your beliefs are a threat to the peace and unity of our society. By holding onto them, you are endangering not only yourself but those around you. You must let go of these harmful ideas and embrace the values of inclusion and progress."

Rebecca clenched her fists, her nails digging into her palms as she tried to block out the voice, the images, and the overwhelming pressure to conform. But the onslaught was unrelenting, the message drilled into her mind with every passing second. It felt as though the room itself was closing in on her, suffocating her with its insistence.

She wanted to cry out, to tell them they were wrong, that her faith was not a threat, but the words remained trapped in her throat, strangled by the oppressive atmosphere of the room. Each minute of the session stretched into an eternity as the images continued to assault her senses, eroding her resolve bit by bit. The relentless droning sound made it nearly impossible to think clearly, clouding her mind and seeping into her consciousness. The constant barrage of images, each one blaming her faith for the world's violence, felt like a direct attack on her soul, forcing its twisted message into the deepest corners of her thoughts.

When it finally ended, Rebecca was unstrapped from the chair and led back to her cell, her legs barely able to support her weight. She collapsed onto the cot, her body trembling with exhaustion, her mind numb from the relentless barrage of lies and propaganda.

Yet even in her weakened state, a small, stubborn voice within her refused to be silenced. It whispered to her, reminding her of who she was, of the faith that had sustained her through every trial, every hardship. She clung to that voice, to that small ember of hope, as though her very soul depended on it.

The days that followed were a blur of reprogramming sessions, each one more grueling than the last. The methods varied—sometimes it was the screen, other times it was a series of questions designed to confuse and disorient her, to make her doubt her own beliefs. They showed her testimonials from people who had "seen the light," who had renounced their faith and embraced the new order, their faces serene and content.

Rebecca knew that it was all a lie. These people had been broken; their spirits crushed under the weight of the pressure to conform. She knew that if she wasn't careful, the same thing could happen to her.

She wasn't the only one in the camp, of course. During mealtimes and in the brief moments of respite between sessions, she caught glimpses of the others—men and women, young and old, all clad in the same drab gray uniforms, their faces marked by the same haunted expressions. Some met her gaze with a flicker of recognition, a silent acknowledgment of their shared struggle, but most kept their heads down, their spirits already broken by the relentless indoctrination. Rebecca found herself constantly scanning the faces, desperately searching for any sign of Sarah, but there was none. The absence gnawed at her, adding another layer of fear to the already suffocating atmosphere of the camp.

One day, as Rebecca was being led back to her cell, she heard a commotion from one of the other corridors. The harsh voices of guards shouting orders echoed through the sterile halls, followed by a loud crash and the unmistakable sounds of a struggle. Rebecca's heart leaped into her throat as she craned her neck, desperate to see what was happening. Just as the guards tried to hurry her along, she caught a fleeting glimpse of the scene.

It was Sarah!

Rebecca's breath froze as she saw her friend being forced to her knees, surrounded by guards. Sarah's face was a mask of pain and exhaustion, her eyes blackened with bruises, and her once neat hair hung in tangled, matted strands around her battered face. The sight of her, so broken and bruised, sent a wave of despair crashing over Rebecca.

Before she could react, before she could even call out to her friend, the guards pushed Rebecca forward, forcing her down the corridor and away from the scene. The last image of Sarah, on her knees with her spirit crushed, burned itself into Rebecca's mind, haunting her with every step she took back to her cell.

Later, Rebecca heard whispers from some of the other detainees, passing through the camp like a chilling wind. The rumors spoke of a man who had refused to comply during his reprogramming session—had refused to utter the words they demanded, had refused to renounce his faith. He had been taken to a different part of the camp, a place whispered about with fear, where the pressure was more intense, and the methods more brutal. The thought of what he might be enduring sent shivers down Rebecca's spine, but no one spoke of a woman. Rebecca clung to the hope of hearing something, anything, about Sarah, but the silence was deafening.

The image of Sarah, battered and broken, haunted her. It was a burden she couldn't shake, one that weighed heavily on her heart. Though her body was exhausted, drained by the relentless reprogramming sessions, she spent every moment she could on her knees on the cold concrete floor of her cell, praying fervently. She begged God to help Sarah, to be with her, to give her strength in whatever hell she was enduring.

Tears streamed down Rebecca's face as she cried out to God, not for herself, but for Sarah. The depth of her anguish was poured out in those prayers, her soul aching with the fear of what might have become of her friend. The cold, hard floor beneath her knees was nothing compared to the pain in her heart, and the silence of the camp was broken only by the sound of her quiet sobs, as she prayed and cried for Sarah, pleading with God to intervene.

That night, as Rebecca lay on her cold, hard cot, the thin blanket offering little warmth against the chill that seemed to seep into her very bones, her thoughts were consumed by Sarah and the man she had heard about—the one who had refused to break, who had stood firm in his faith despite the unimaginable pressure. She didn't know his name, had never seen his face, but in her heart, she felt a deep connection to him, as if their shared struggle had bound them together in a way that transcended the walls of the camp.

Her mind drifted to Sarah, the image of her bruised and battered face flashing before her eyes. She wondered what horrors her friend was enduring, and the thought twisted like a knife in her chest. Rebecca's heart ached with the weight of not knowing, of fearing the worst, and she fought to keep her own resolve from crumbling under the relentless assault of doubt and fear.

As Rebecca lay there in the darkness, she found strength in the thought of the man who had refused to comply. If he could stand firm, if he could hold on to his faith even when the forces against him seemed insurmountable, then so could she. She prayed with all her might that Sarah could too—that somewhere, somehow, her friend was finding the strength to endure, to resist, to hold on to the faith that had brought them both so far.

Rebecca closed her eyes, whispering a prayer into the silence of the night. "Lord, give us the strength to stand firm, to hold on to You, no matter what they do to us. Be with Sarah, wherever she is, and help her to feel Your presence, to know that she's not alone, and be with that man, whoever he is—give him the courage to keep fighting, and help us all to remember that we're not just enduring this for ourselves, but for each other, and for You."

As the prayer left her lips, Rebecca felt a flicker of hope ignite within her—a small, fragile flame that she clung to in the darkness, a reminder that even in the depths of despair, they were not alone.

The days dragged on, and the sessions continued, chipping away at her defenses, wearing her down little by little. There were moments when she felt herself wavering, moments when the pressure to conform became almost unbearable. But in those moments, she would close her eyes and pray, drawing strength from the God she knew was with her, even in this dark place.

Finally, after what felt like an eternity, the door to her cell opened, and a guard stepped inside. "You're being moved," he said curtly.

Rebecca's heart skipped a beat. "Moved? Where?"

The guard didn't answer. He simply motioned for her to follow, and Rebecca had no choice but to obey. She was led through a maze of corridors, deeper into the heart of the camp, until they reached a door marked "Special Containment."

Inside, the room was stark and empty, save for a single chair in the center. The guard gestured for Rebecca to sit, and she did so, her heart pounding in her chest.

A moment later, the door opened again, and a man in a lab coat entered, his expression cold and clinical. He carried a clipboard, which he glanced at before speaking. "Mrs. Marshall, you've been identified as a high-risk detainee—someone who poses a significant threat to the social harmony we're trying to achieve. Your refusal to comply with our methods has been noted, and we will be implementing more... intensive measures."

Rebecca felt a surge of fear, but she forced herself to remain calm. "I'm not a threat," she said quietly. "I'm just trying to stay true to my faith."

The man raised an eyebrow, as if amused by her defiance. "Your faith is precisely the problem, Mrs. Marshall. It's what's keeping you from embracing the new order, from becoming a productive member of society. But don't worry—we have ways of helping you see the light."

He gestured to the guard, who stepped forward and strapped Rebecca into the chair, securing her wrists and ankles tightly. The cold metal bit into her skin, and she could feel her heart racing, but she refused to let the fear show on her face. She knew that they would use any sign of weakness against her, and she was determined not to give them the satisfaction.

The man in the lab coat walked over to a control panel on the wall, his movements precise and methodical. "This process is designed to help you understand the futility of resistance," he said, his tone detached. "You will be shown the truth, and in time, you will come to accept it."

Rebecca's heart skipped a beat as the room darkened, leaving only a harsh, white light focused on her. The silence was suffocating, broken only by the faint hum of the machinery around her. She closed her eyes, trying to block out the fear, trying to pray, but the words seemed to slip away from her grasp.

The screen in front of her flickered to life, displaying a series of images and messages, each one more disorienting than the last. They were designed to confuse, to break down her sense of reality, to make her question everything she had ever believed. The droning voice returned, echoing in her mind, repeating the same phrases over and over, demanding her submission, her compliance.

"Your faith is a lie. Your beliefs are dangerous. You must renounce them for the greater good."

The voice was relentless, a cold, mechanical monotone that hammered away at her will, trying to break her down, to make her surrender. The pressure was immense, like a vice tightening around her mind, squeezing the life out of her resistance. Rebecca could feel her resolve slipping, the constant assault on her senses wearing her down. But even as the voice droned on, even as the images blurred together into a nightmarish whirl, she clung to the one thing they could never take from her—her faith.

But then, the screen in front of her changed. The images shifted from the abstract scenes of violence and chaos to something far more personal. The first image was of James, her husband, but not as she remembered him. His face was twisted in agony, his body contorted as if he were being tortured. His eyes, filled with unspeakable pain, locked onto hers through the screen, and his lips moved silently, forming the words "Please, Rebecca, make it stop."

Rebecca's heart lurched, her breath catching in her throat. She knew it wasn't real—knew it had to be some sick trick, a manipulation designed to break her—but the sight of James suffering, even in this fabricated nightmare, was almost more than she could bear.

Before she could recover, the image shifted again. This time it was Emily, their daughter. She was bound to a chair, her face streaked with tears, her voice trembling as she begged, "Mom, please... just do what they say. I can't take this anymore. Please, I need you. I need you to stop this."

Tears welled up in Rebecca's eyes, and she shook her head, trying to dispel the horrific images, but they kept coming. The screen flickered once more, and now it was her mother—her mother who had passed away years ago—appearing before her, looking as real and solid as if she were actually there. "Rebecca," her mother said, her voice gentle yet laced with sorrow, "you have to let go of these foolish beliefs. Think of your family. Think of what you're putting them through. Do you really want to be responsible for their pain?"

Rebecca's hands trembled violently as she gripped the arms of the chair, her knuckles white with the effort. The images of her family, of her friends—each one more agonizing than the last—continued to flash before her eyes, each of them begging her, pleading with her to comply, to stop their suffering. It was an all-out assault on her heart, her mind, her soul.

The voice returned, colder and more menacing than before. "You see what you're doing to them, Rebecca? Your stubbornness, your refusal to comply—it's causing them unimaginable pain. This is your fault. You could stop all of this. You could save them. All you have to do is let go of this foolish faith, and it will all be over."

Rebecca's entire body shook with the effort of holding on, of resisting the overwhelming urge to give in. The images, the voices—they were so real, so vivid, it was like her worst nightmares had been brought to life. Even as the pressure mounted, even as her resolve began to crack under the weight of the horror being shown to her, she fought to hold on to the truth.

"They're lies," she whispered to herself, though the words were barely audible over the droning voice and the terrifying images. "They're just lies. God, help me, they're lies."

Still the images persisted, and with each passing second, the line between reality and the fabricated horrors on the screen blurred further. She could feel her grip on her sanity slipping, her mind teetering on the edge of despair.

Then, in a moment of clarity, she realized what they were trying to do—how they were using the images of her loved ones, the people she cared about most in the world, to twist her emotions, to manipulate her into breaking. They were attacking the very core of who she was, trying to make her believe that by holding on to her faith, she was causing unspeakable harm to those she loved.

"No," she choked out, her voice hoarse and raw. "No, I won't... I can't."

The stream of images wouldn't stop. James, Emily, her mother—they continued to plead with her, their voices growing more desperate, more heart-wrenching with every passing moment. The pain in their eyes was unbearable, and Rebecca felt as though her heart was being torn apart, her soul crushed under the weight of their suffering.

Finally, when she thought she could take no more, when the pressure was so intense that she feared she might lose herself completely, she did the only thing she could think of. She prayed. Not for herself, but for them—for James, for Emily, and for Sarah, wherever she was. She prayed for their safety, for their strength, and for God to protect them from whatever horrors might come.

Then as she prayed, the images began to blur, to distort, as if her words were somehow pushing them back, reclaiming her mind from the darkness that sought to consume her.

"I won't give in," she whispered, the words a vow as much as a prayer. "I won't give up my faith. No matter what you do, I will not abandon Him."

The images on the screen flickered, then vanished, leaving only the droning voice and the oppressive darkness of the room. But Rebecca knew, deep in her heart, that she had won this battle. The war was far from over, and she knew they would try again, that they would use every trick, every manipulation, to break her, but she also knew that no matter how dark the path ahead, she would not walk it alone.

The man in the lab coat approached her, his expression unreadable. "You are stronger than most," he said, his voice carrying a note of begrudging respect. "But everyone breaks eventually. You will too, in time."

Rebecca met his gaze, her eyes weary but defiant. "You're wrong," she said, her voice hoarse but steady. "My strength doesn't come from me. It comes from God."

The man studied her for a moment, then turned away, signaling to the guard. "Take her back to her cell," he ordered. "We'll continue tomorrow. Bring in the next one."

As Rebecca was unstrapped from the chair and led back to her cell, an overwhelming exhaustion settled over her. Her body was weak, her mind battered, but her spirit remained unbroken. She had faced the darkness, and though it had nearly consumed her, she had held on to the light.

Back in her cell, she collapsed onto the cot, her body trembling with fatigue. But as she lay there, she whispered a prayer of gratitude, thanking God for giving her the strength to endure. She knew that the battle was far from over, that the days ahead would be even more difficult, but she also knew that she was not alone.

Rebecca closed her eyes, letting the darkness of sleep take her. Tomorrow would bring new challenges, new trials, but she would face them with the same unyielding faith that had carried her through this day. No matter what they did, no matter how much they tried to break her, she would not surrender. Her faith was her shield, her strength, and it would carry her through the storm—she hoped.

"The Underground Church"

The narrow, unmarked alley was shrouded in darkness, the only light coming from a distant streetlamp that flickered weakly, casting long, distorted shadows against the crumbling brick walls. James pulled his coat tighter around him as he made his way through the alley, his heart pounding in his chest. Every sound—a distant car, a sudden rustle in the garbage bins, the faint hum of the city—felt like a potential threat, a reminder of the ever-present danger that hung over him and those like him.

He had received the location just that morning, a cryptic message slipped into his pocket by a stranger on the street. It had been scrawled on a small piece of paper, simple but clear: "11 PM. The old mill. Basement. Knock three times, pause, then once more. *Sanctuary.*" No signature, no indication of who had sent it, but the code word— *Sanctuary*—told James all he needed to know. It was the signal Pastor Daniels had said they should use if secrecy was vital, an assurance that this was genuine. James knew immediately what it meant. It was an invitation to the underground church, a place where believers could gather in secret, away from the prying eyes of the government.

As he reached the end of the alley, James spotted the old mill—a dilapidated building that had once been a thriving center of industry but it had long since fallen into disrepair. The windows were boarded up, and the doors hung crooked on their hinges, as if the building itself had been abandoned by time. But James knew better. This place, though crumbling and forgotten, had become a sanctuary for those who refused to let go of their faith.

He approached the rusted metal door at the side of the building, his hand trembling as he raised it to knock. One, two, three... one. The sound echoed in the stillness of the night, and for a moment, James feared that no one would answer, that he had been led into a trap. Then he heard a faint shuffling on the other side of the door, followed by the soft click of a lock being turned.

The door creaked open, revealing a tall man with a rough, weathered face and kind eyes. He gave James a brief nod, stepping aside to let him in. "Welcome," the man said in a low voice. "You're safe here. For now."

James stepped inside, his eyes adjusting to the dim light of the small, narrow hallway. The man quickly shut the door behind him, bolting it securely before leading James down a flight of creaky wooden stairs. The air grew cooler as they descended into the basement, the faint sound of voices growing louder with each step.

At the bottom of the stairs, they reached a heavy wooden door, behind which the voices grew clearer—soft, murmured prayers and the quiet rustle of pages turning. The man knocked softly, and the door was opened by a woman with a warm, welcoming smile. "Come in," she said gently, her voice soothing. "We've been hoping you would come."

James entered the room, immediately struck by the contrast between the harsh, cold world outside and the warmth and light that filled this hidden space. The basement was small, with low ceilings and exposed pipes, but it had been transformed into a place of worship. A simple wooden cross hung on one wall, surrounded by candles that flickered softly, casting a warm, golden glow. A few rows of mismatched chairs had been arranged in front of the cross, and about a dozen people were seated, their heads bowed in prayer.

As James moved closer, he recognized some of the faces—members of his community, people who had once attended his church, before it had been shut down. They looked up as he approached, their expressions a mixture of relief, determination, and sadness. Here, in this hidden room, they could be themselves, free from the oppressive scrutiny of the world above. Here, in this room, the power of prayer was multiplied by the faith of each person in the room.

The man who had let James in gestured for him to take a seat, and he did so, sinking into one of the chairs with a heavy sigh. The woman who had greeted him closed the door quietly and took her place at the front of the room, standing beside the cross.

"Thank you all for coming tonight," she began, her voice steady and calm. "I know it's not easy, and I know the risks we take by being here, but we are here because we believe—because we know that our faith is worth fighting for, even in the face of persecution."

The others murmured their agreement, and James felt a sense of solidarity wash over him. He had been so alone these past few weeks, so overwhelmed by fear and doubt, but now, surrounded by his fellow believers, he felt a renewed sense of strength. They were not just fighting for themselves—they were fighting for each other, for their community, for the God who had never abandoned them.

The woman led them in prayer, her voice soft but filled with conviction. "Lord, we come to You in this dark time, seeking Your guidance and protection. We ask for the strength to remain steadfast in our faith, even as the world turns against us. We know that You are with us, even here in the shadows, and we trust in Your promise that You will never leave us nor forsake us."

The room fell silent as they prayed together, each person offering their own quiet plea to God. James closed his eyes, his heart swelling with emotion as he felt the presence of the Holy Spirit wash over him. It was a feeling he hadn't experienced in days, not since Rebecca and Sarah had been taken away, and it brought him a sense of peace that he hadn't realized he was missing.

When the prayer ended, the woman began to speak again, addressing the group with a quiet urgency. "We've received word from other underground churches across the city," she said. "The persecution is spreading, and the authorities are cracking down harder than ever. They're raiding homes, monitoring communications—doing everything they can to root us out. We need to be vigilant. We need to stay connected, but we also need to be careful."

A man in the back of the room raised his hand, his voice filled with concern. "What about the others? The ones who've been taken to the camps? Have we heard anything?"

The woman nodded solemnly. "We've had some reports. It's bad—worse than we imagined. They're trying to break them, to force them to renounce their faith. Some have... given in. Others are holding strong, but the pressure is immense. We need to keep them in our prayers, and if there's anything we can do to help them, we must do it."

James's heart ached at the mention of the camps, his thoughts immediately turning to Rebecca. He hadn't heard anything since she was taken away, and the uncertainty gnawed at him constantly. But hearing the others speak of their loved ones, their friends who were also enduring the horrors of reprogramming, gave him a small measure of comfort. He wasn't alone in his pain, and neither was Rebecca.

The woman continued, her voice firm. "We may be small in number, but our faith is strong. We are the body of Christ, and no matter what they do to us, they cannot take that away. We must stand together, support one another, and continue to worship in secret. This is our refuge, and we must protect it."

She motioned for everyone to stand, and they did so, joining hands as they began to sing a hymn—softly, so as not to attract attention, but with a deep, unshakable faith. The words of the hymn filled the room, a gentle but powerful declaration of their belief in God's enduring love and mercy.

James felt tears welling in his eyes as he sang, the emotion of the moment overwhelming him. He thought of Rebecca, of her courage, of the strength she must be drawing on even now. He knew that wherever she was, she was holding on to the same faith, the same hope that had brought him here tonight.

The hymn ended, and the room fell into a peaceful silence. The woman smiled, her eyes shining with tears of her own. "Thank you," she said softly. "Thank you for being here, for standing with us. We will continue to meet, to worship, to pray. And we will continue to fight for our faith, no matter what."

The group began to disperse, some staying behind to speak quietly with one another, others slipping out into the night, careful to avoid drawing attention. James lingered for a moment, taking in the warmth and light of the room one last time before he, too, prepared to leave.

As he turned to go, the door at the back of the room creaked open, and a familiar figure stepped inside. James's chest tightened as he recognized Pastor Daniels, the man who had once led their church before it was shut down. His face was gaunt, and his clothes hung loosely on his frame, but there was a fire in his eyes that hadn't dimmed despite the trials he had endured.

"Pastor Daniels," James whispered, his voice filled with a mixture of relief and shock. "I... I thought they had taken you."

Daniels shook his head, a small, tired smile playing at the corners of his lips. "They tried," he said, his voice low and gravelly from disuse. "But by the grace of God, I've managed to stay one step ahead of them."

He approached James, placing a hand on his shoulder. "I made sure the message reached you, James. It's not safe to stay in one place for too long, but I had to see you, to know that you were still holding on."

James nodded, swallowing the lump in his throat. "Rebecca... she's been taken, and Sarah, too. I don't know where they are or what's happening to them."

Pastor Daniels' expression grew somber, and he nodded slowly. "I've heard about the camps. The things they're doing there... it's worse than anything we imagined. They're trying to break the faithful, to force them to accept a twisted version of the gospel—a gospel stripped of truth, of the atoning sacrifice of Jesus. It's Satan's plan to lead God's people away, to lure them into a false sense of security with a message that sounds good on the surface but is filled with half-truths and lies."

James clenched his fists, anger and sorrow swirling within him. "How do we fight that? How do we protect them when they're in there, being fed those lies?"

"We fight with the truth, James," Daniels replied, his voice steady and resolute. "We pray, we support each other, and we hold on to the true gospel—the one that proclaims Jesus as the only way to salvation, that reminds us of His sacrifice on the cross. We cannot let them twist the

Word of God to suit their agenda. We must be vigilant, we must be strong, and we must trust that God is with us, even in the darkest places."

James felt a surge of determination as he listened to the pastor's words. He had come to this underground church seeking solace, seeking a reminder that he was not alone in his fight. Now, as he stood beside Pastor Daniels, he realized that he was part of something much greater—a spiritual battle that had been waged since the beginning of time, a battle between truth and deception, light and darkness.

Pastor Daniels looked around the room, his eyes meeting those of each person who remained. "We are the remnant," he said quietly. "The ones who will stand firm, no matter what. They can take our churches, our homes, even our lives, but they cannot take our faith. We must hold fast to the truth and be ready to stand against the lies, no matter the cost."

The group nodded in agreement, the weight of the pastor's words settling over them like a heavy blanket. They knew the road ahead would be hard, filled with trials and persecution, but they also knew that they were not alone.

As James prepared to leave, Pastor Daniels pulled him aside, his voice dropping to a whisper. The others filed out of the room, leaving the two men alone in the dimly lit basement, the flickering candlelight casting long shadows on the walls.

"James," Daniels began, his voice heavy with the weight of what he was about to say, "There's something you need to know—something I've heard about Rebecca and Sarah."

James's heart tightened in his chest, a mixture of hope and dread swirling within him. He looked into the pastor's eyes, searching for any sign of what was to come.

"Rebecca... she's holding strong, James," Daniels said, his voice softening as he spoke. "She's refusing to comply with their demands, refusing to renounce her faith. From what I've heard, she's enduring the reprogramming with a steadfastness that's nothing short of miraculous. They're trying to break her, but she's clinging to her faith with everything she has. You should be proud of her."

James felt a wave of relief wash over him, his heart swelling with pride and gratitude. He had known Rebecca was strong, but hearing that she was standing firm in the face of such overwhelming pressure brought him a sense of peace he hadn't felt in days. "Thank God," he whispered, his voice thick with emotion. "Thank God she's holding on."

Pastor Daniels nodded, his expression somber. "But there's more, James. I've heard some troubling news about Sarah."

A shiver ran down James's spine, the sense of dread returning with full force. "What is it?" he asked, his voice trembling.

Daniels hesitated, his eyes flickering with a mix of anger and sorrow. "They've been... brutal with her, James. More brutal than we imagined. She's been proclaiming her faith, telling anyone who will listen about what Jesus has done for her, about how they can have the same freedom she's found in Him. They hate her for it. They've been mocking her, taunting her, telling her that she's not free, that she's nothing but a prisoner."

James clenched his fists, his knuckles white with the effort of holding back the anger that surged within him. He could picture Sarah, her defiant spirit refusing to be crushed, even as they tried to tear her down. "What else?" he asked, his voice tight.

"They're beating her, James," Daniels continued, his voice trembling with barely contained emotion. "They're trying to silence her, to make her give up, but she won't. She's been saying things like, 'You can kill this body—I hate it anyway—but you cannot kill the woman God has made me into.' They can't stand it, and it's driving them mad. But Sarah... she remains steadfast."

Tears welled up in James's eyes as he listened to the pastor's words, his heart breaking for the woman who had endured so much already. "How... how can she keep going?" he whispered, his voice barely audible.

"It's because of her faith, James," Daniels said, his voice filled with admiration. "She's found a strength in Christ that they can't touch, no matter how hard they try. She's made peace with her past, and now, no matter what they do to her, she's free in a way they'll never understand."

James nodded, swallowing hard as he tried to process what he had just heard. He could picture Sarah's defiance, her unwavering faith in the face of unimaginable suffering. It was both inspiring and devastating, a reminder of the power of faith but also of the cost that often came with it.

Pastor Daniels hesitated, his gaze drifting away as if struggling with something deep within him. "James," he began, his voice faltering, "there's something else I need to confess. Something that's been weighing on me..."

James noticed the way Daniels' voice trailed off, the unspoken words hanging heavy in the air. He caught the flicker of emotion in the pastor's eyes, a shadow of something that he hadn't seen before—something that made his heart sink.

"Pastor..." James prompted gently, though his voice held a note of concern.

Daniels' eyes met his, and for a moment, James saw a vulnerability in the older man that he had never seen before. "James, I... I care about Sarah. I care about her deeply. But lately, I've been struggling with feelings that I know are." The pastor stopped short and did not finish his confession.

James felt a pang of understanding and sadness as he watched the pastor grapple with his emotions. He had always respected Daniels for his unwavering commitment to the gospel, to doing what was right and maintaining a good image to protect his ministry, but just for a moment, he saw the man's humanity, the struggle that came with being in a position of spiritual leadership.

Before Daniels could say anything more, James bowed his head and whispered a silent prayer. "Lord, give him strength. Protect him from the enemy's lies and give him the wisdom to navigate this trial. Help him to remain strong in his calling, and to find peace in Your truth."

When James looked up, he saw that Daniels had composed himself, though the struggle was still evident in his eyes. "Thank you, James," the pastor said quietly, his voice now steadier. "I needed to..." but once again, he couldn't finish his sentence.

James nodded, his respect for the pastor deepening. "It's late," he said softly, then headed to the door and quietly left.

As he made his way home, James whispered a prayer under his breath, a prayer of thanks for the underground church, for the strength of his fellow believers, and for the hope that still burned within him, even in the darkness of this time.

"Help from the Shadows"

Back in the old mill, Pastor Daniels remained seated long after James had left, the soft glow of the candlelight flickering across his troubled face. His heart was a storm of emotions, a mixture of guilt, fear, and something he was afraid to name, a feeling he feared might be a kind of love for Sarah, a love he knew was forbidden as a pastor. He had always been steadfast, unwavering in his commitment to God's calling, but now the lines had blurred, and the struggle within him was tearing him apart.

He looked around the basement, the makeshift sanctuary that had become a refuge for the few remaining believers who dared to defy the oppressive regime. The old, cracked walls seemed to close in on him, a stark reminder of the dangers they all faced. But it wasn't the fear of being caught that weighed on him tonight; it was the battle raging in his soul, a battle he was terrified of losing.

Daniels rose from his seat, the wooden chair creaking as he pushed it back, and walked slowly toward an old blanket hung up as a makeshift door. He hesitated for a moment before pushing it aside, revealing a small room beyond. The space was sparse, with only a twin-sized bed pushed against the wall and a pile of blankets on the floor. This was where he slept now, where he hid from the world outside.

The room had been shown to him by a community of homeless people he had once ministered to, a group that had come to his aid when he had nowhere else to turn. He remembered how he used to visit them with members of his church, bringing food and the Word of God to those who had nothing. He had been humbled by their faith, a faith that, in many cases, seemed stronger than his own. They had so little, yet their trust in God was unshakable, their belief in His provision absolute.

When the government had sent armed teams to his church, intent on arresting him for refusing to water down the gospel he preached, he had narrowly escaped. He could still see the flashing lights, hear the pounding on the doors, the shouts as they ransacked his house looking for him, but he had fled before they could catch him. He ran through the darkened streets, heart pounding, until he found himself in the one place he knew they wouldn't look—among the homeless.

The people there had sheltered him without question, taking him in and hiding him from the authorities. It was their network, their eyes and ears on the streets that had kept him informed about what was happening in the camps, about the fate of his church members, and most recently, about Sarah. They were his lifeline, his connection to the world he had been forced to leave behind.

Daniels sat on the edge of the bed, the old springs creaking beneath his weight. He stared at the pile of blankets on the floor, his mind heavy with thoughts of Sarah. The news he had shared with James weighed on him—the knowledge of the beatings she had endured, of her steadfastness in the face of such cruelty. Her words echoed in his mind: "You can kill this body; I hate it anyway, but you cannot kill the woman God has made me into." Her courage both inspired him and tore at his heart, deepening the feelings he knew he couldn't afford to have.

He bowed his head, resting it in his hands, the flickering candlelight casting long shadows on the walls. "Lord," he whispered, his voice thick with emotion, "give me the strength to overcome this. Help me to remain true to You, to the calling You have placed on my life. Don't let me fall into temptation; don't let me betray the trust You've placed in me."

Tears filled his eyes as he prayed, the weight of his responsibilities as a pastor pressing down on him like never before. He knew that the battle wasn't just against the forces outside, but also against the desires within him, desires that threatened to lead him down a path he knew he couldn't take.

When he finally lifted his head, he wiped his eyes and blew out the candle, plunging the small room into darkness. He lay down on the bed, pulling the blankets up around him, trying to find some comfort in the familiar, but the turmoil within him made it impossible to rest. His thoughts drifted back to Sarah, to her courage, to the love he couldn't allow himself to feel, and to the mission he couldn't abandon, no matter how much it tore at his soul.

As sleep finally began to take him, Pastor Daniels whispered one final prayer, a prayer for strength, for guidance, and for the wisdom to navigate the dark and dangerous path ahead. "Lord, help me to stand firm, to lead Your people in truth, and to resist the temptations that seek to destroy me. Be with Sarah; do not let them darken her light. In Your name, I pray."

With that, he closed his eyes, surrendering to the exhaustion that had been building within him for days.

"Breaking the Chains"

Under the dim, flickering light of his cell, the man whom Rebecca had been fervently praying for sat in silence, his body a map of bruises and cuts that would slowly transform into scars, each one a testament to the brutality he had endured. His once-powerful frame, honed by years of rigorous discipline, now bore the marks of relentless beatings, his muscles marred and his spirit tested. The guards had tried everything—mockery, violence, starvation—yet nothing could force him to denounce his newfound faith. To them, it was inconceivable that a man like him, a former guard who had once enforced the ironclad rules of this hellish camp, would abandon it all for a belief that seemed so utterly irrational and useless. Everything had changed the day Sarah was brought into the camp.

He remembered that day with painful clarity. Sarah had been dragged through steel doors, her body already battered from the abuse she had suffered in the outer camp. Yet, despite the bruises and the obvious physical pain, there was something about her—something unbroken, something that refused to yield. He had been assigned to guard the section where her cell was located, just another routine duty in the monotonous life of watching over the "detainees" and leading them to their reprogramming sessions. From the moment she arrived, Sarah was different. There was a light in her that drew him, a light he couldn't understand.

One night, as he stood watch outside her cell, he found himself pausing, his attention caught by the sound of her voice. She was praying, her words a soft, steady stream of conviction that sent a shiver down his spine. She prayed not just for herself but for the other prisoners, for the guards—she prayed for him. Her words were filled with grace, with forgiveness, and with a faith so deep it was unmistakable, reaching out to touch even the darkest corners of his soul.

He couldn't stay away. Night after night, he found himself lingering near her cell, listening to the words she spoke in the quiet hours when most had lost hope. Finally, one night, unable to contain the storm of emotions within him, he stepped closer to the bars and spoke, his voice gruff but underlined with an emotion he had long forgotten—something akin to desperation.

"Why do you do it?" he asked, his voice low and strained. "Why do you hold on to this... faith, even when it's costing you everything?"

Sarah looked up at him, her eyes glowing with a light he had never seen before—a light that seemed to pierce through the darkness within him. "Because it's not just faith," she said, her voice calm and unwavering. "It's real. I was lost in a living hell, desperate for something I didn't even know I needed. But then Jesus saved me, and no matter what they do to me, they can't take away the peace I now have. You can find that peace too. He's waiting for you, even now."

The words, though they sounded cliché, hit him like a thunderbolt. For years, he had lived a life of rigid discipline, dedicating himself to martial arts and the structured existence of the camp, believing that control and strength were the solutions to everything. But in that moment, something deep within him cracked—not his will, but his heart. He realized how empty his life had been, how all the discipline and control in the world couldn't fill the void inside him.

He found himself opening up to her, confessing the doubts and fears that had haunted him for so long—the fear that everything he had believed in was a lie, and the fear that there was nothing beyond the cold, harsh reality he had known. His dedication to perfecting his mind and body through Jeet Kune Do, which he had mastered, suddenly seemed hollow. Sarah, with her kindness and compassionate spirit, that felt like a balm to his wounded soul, shared the gospel with him—the truth about Jesus. As she spoke, he felt a sense of peace washing over him, a hope that had been absent from his life for as long as he could remember. It was as though something heavy and dark had lifted from his shoulders, a weight that seemed to have been placed upon him from ancient times, replaced by a lightness he couldn't explain. He didn't fully understand what was happening, but he knew one thing: he believed her, and in that belief, he was changed.

In a hushed voice, he asked, "What is your first name?" Her last name had been the only one given to the guards, a tactic designed to strip the prisoners of their humanity, reducing them to mere numbers in the system. "Sarah," she replied softly, her eyes searching his, filled with compassion.

"And yours?" she asked, sensing the connection forming between them.

"Bruce," he answered, a name that once carried the weight of a different life, now whispered in the dim light of a cell that had become a place of transformation.

But that peace was short-lived. Another guard had overheard their conversation and reported him. He was dragged from his post, beaten mercilessly, and thrown into a cell, the same cold, dark place where he had once watched over others. Now, he was one of them—a prisoner for his newfound faith.

Through the beatings, the torture, and the taunts, he held onto what Sarah had given him. He had found a faith that no amount of brutality could take away. Now, as he lay in his cell, he knew he had to act. The guards had taunted him relentlessly, telling him how they planned to beat Sarah to death for what she had done to him. They said they were going to savor each moment of her suffering.

He couldn't let that happen to her. She was an angel in his mind. He wouldn't let them kill her. The memory of the guards' taunts echoed in his mind—how they had gloated about their plans to break her, to make an example of her by slowly beating her to death. It was during one of these brutal punishments that Rebecca had caught a glimpse of Sarah, forced to her knees, her face bloodied and bruised as the guards took pleasure in her suffering. The image of Sarah haunted Rebecca ever since.

Eventually, Rebecca managed to pass by Sarah's cell. She stumbled on purpose, falling with her face against the bars. Sarah, startled, looked up just as Rebecca whispered, "I love you, sister. I'm in cell 17B." The guard quickly intervened, yelling at Rebecca to "Move on!" but the message had been delivered.

Bruce began working on a plan, his mind methodically piecing together every detail he had observed during his time as a guard. His intimate knowledge of the camp's layout, the routines of the guards, and the blind spots in their security gave him an edge that few could match. Still it wasn't just his experience that fueled his determination; it was the discipline and mental fortitude he had cultivated over years of mastering Jeet Kune Do—a path he had been drawn to since childhood, largely because of his shared name with the legendary Bruce Lee.

As a boy, Bruce had felt a strange kinship with the martial arts icon, not just because of their shared name but because of the philosophy behind Jeet Kune Do. It wasn't merely about fighting—it was a means to transcend the physical and cultivate deeper mental and spiritual discipline. While religion often offered structured paths to spiritual connection and a set of beliefs to follow, Bruce found that Jeet Kune Do presented a different kind of spirituality, one rooted in self-mastery and adaptability.

Bruce Lee's teachings about water—how it could be both gentle and powerful, shapeless and yet able to overcome obstacles—resonated deeply with him. Unlike religion, which often required adherence to a set doctrine, Jeet Kune Do was fluid, evolving with the practitioner's understanding and experience. This fluidity reflected a broader philosophy: to adapt to life's challenges, respond with awareness, and maintain balance amid uncertainty.

For Bruce, Jeet Kune Do became more than a fighting style; it became a way of life. The principles of fluidity, economy of motion, and mental clarity allowed him to act without hesitation. These teachings shaped him, turning him into a man of precision and control—one who could anticipate an opponent's move before it was even made. It was not just a method of combat but a philosophy of existence, a path that paralleled the spiritual quests of traditional religions, yet allowed for personal interpretation and growth.

Now, in this hellish camp, the freedom he now felt in his newfound faith had seamlessly blended with his self-discipline. Those principles were more crucial than ever. The liberation of his spirit gave him strength, while his unwavering discipline kept him focused. Every step of his plan needed to be flawless, every action calculated with precision. He couldn't afford a single mistake—not with Sarah's life hanging in the balance.

With the routines of the guards imprinted in his mind and his understanding of the camp's vulnerabilities, Bruce began to formulate his escape plan. It wasn't just about physical strength or combat skills; it was about using his mind, his training, and his faith—newly ignited by Sarah—to outmaneuver those who sought to destroy them. The stakes were higher than they had ever been, but Bruce knew he had to succeed. The woman who had directed him to a source of light that had freed his soul, who had given him something to believe in beyond his own strength, needed him, and he would not let her down.

Bruce knew that escaping the camp alone would be impossible. The walls that held him were not just made of concrete and steel; they were fortified by fear, oppression, and the ever-watchful eyes of those who had long since abandoned compassion. He needed someone on the inside—someone he could trust with his life and with Sarah's. The thought of her suffering was like a knife twisting in his soul, driving him to a place he hadn't been in a long time: desperation, and in that desperation, he did something he had never done before: he reached out to God.

"Please, God... let me talk to Lance. I need his help." The words were simple, almost hesitant, as if he wasn't sure God would listen to someone like him. But faith, even the size of a mustard seed, has the power to move mountains. Bruce, though unaccustomed to prayer, was beginning to understand that God hears every word His children speak to Him—no matter how small, no matter how uncertain.

It wasn't long after this quiet plea that Lance, a guard who had always seemed somewhat out of place among the others, suddenly felt an inexplicable urge to be transferred to Bruce's section. The desire was strong, almost as if something deep within him was guiding his actions, though he couldn't explain why. Lance had no idea which section Bruce was in—cell assignments were kept secret, especially in Bruce's case. The authorities were intent on keeping everything about Bruce under wraps, not wanting the truth of what had happened to get out. Asking directly would have raised suspicion, so Lance kept his curiosity to himself, trusting that this strange compulsion would lead him where he needed to be.

To Lance's surprise, a sudden schedule change resulted in his transfer to Bruce's section without him ever having to request it. The timing was so precise, so unexpected, that it felt like more than just a coincidence.

Lance was different from the other guards. While they had been hardened by the cruelty and brutality of the camp, Lance retained a softness, a humanity that had not yet been extinguished. He was a short man, compact in build, but with a sharp mind and an intensity that drew Bruce's attention from the start. There was something about Lance that resonated with Bruce, something that made him believe that maybe—just maybe—we are alike in the world.

Unbeknownst to Lance, the timing of his transfer and the connection that had formed between him and Bruce was not a coincidence. It was an answer to Bruce's prayer, a divine orchestration that neither of them fully understood but would soon realize was part of a greater plan—one that could mean the difference between life and death, freedom and captivity. God heard his prayer months before he even whispered it and God drew them together.

Bruce took it upon himself to help and mentor Lance, to share his knowledge of Jeet Kune Do. It wasn't just about teaching Lance the physical aspects of the martial art; Bruce shared with him the deeper philosophy, the mental discipline, and the balance between strength and gentleness that Jeet Kune Do embodied. Lance had absorbed these teachings eagerly, finding in them a sense of purpose that had been missing from his life. As they trained together in the shadows of the camp, a bond of trust grew between them—a bond that Bruce knew he could rely on now.

Since his arrest, Bruce had been confined to his cell, kept under close watch by the guards. It was a punishment for his defiance, a way to break him by isolating him from the others. Yet even in his confinement, Bruce continually prayed that Lance would come.

One night, as the camp settled into its uneasy quiet, Bruce heard the familiar sound of footsteps approaching his cell. The rhythmic sound of boots on concrete echoed down the corridor, a constant reminder of the oppressive watchfulness that defined every moment of life in this place. Moving closer to the bars, Bruce peered into the dimly lit corridor, his eyes narrowing as they adjusted to the shadows.

"Bruce," a voice whispered, barely audible over the distant hum of the camp's machinery.

Lance stood before his cell, his face half-hidden in the darkness, but the determination in his eyes was unmistakable. Bruce glanced upward, a quiet prayer of gratitude escaping his lips. "Thank you," his heart swelling with the realization that his desperate plea had been answered. Lance knew the story—he knew it was the prisoner, Rivers, who had gotten Bruce into this mess. What puzzled Lance was how a man like Bruce, disciplined and unyielding, could be so profoundly influenced by her. He couldn't fathom how, even under the crushing brutality of this camp, Bruce remained unbroken, seemingly changed in ways Lance couldn't yet understand.

Glancing around to ensure they were alone, Lance leaned in closer, his voice low and urgent. "I've been thinking... We need to get you and Rivers out of here. They're going to kill her, Bruce. You know that, right?"

Bruce nodded, his heart heavy with the truth in Lance's words. "I know," he murmured, the weight of the situation pressing down on him like a vice. Lance leaned closer to the bars, his voice urgent but steady. "We have to act fast. We don't have much time."

Lance's voice dropped to barely a whisper. "I've been studying the shifts, the routines. There's a window—during the guard change, it's the only time when security is weak enough to get through."

Bruce listened intently, his mind racing through the possibilities, calculating the risks. "I can do this, Lance, but it will take a miracle— and guess what? Miracles happen. You need to tell Sarah—I mean, Rivers."

Lance hesitated, glancing around to make sure they weren't overheard. His hand moved to his pocket, and for a brief moment, he pulled out a master key. He held it between his fingers, the cold metal glinting faintly in the dim light. Bruce's eyes widened, hope igniting within him. Then, Lance pulled it back, his face set with grim determination.

"I can't give it to you now, Bruce," Lance said, voice low but firm. "It's too risky. If they find it on you before we're ready, it's over—for both of us." He took a step back, slipping the key into his pocket. "I'll get it to you right before the escape, I promise. Just be ready."

Bruce nodded, his resolve unwavering despite the disappointment. "I understand," he said, voice steady. The plan was still in motion, and he was fortified by the belief that this, too, was part of a greater divine plan for their liberation.

Lance's gaze flickered with the gravity of what they were planning. "I can't tell Rivers; it's too risky. You know this is all or nothing, right? If we're caught...

Bruce met his gaze through the bars, his expression unyielding. "We won't get caught. It's not just about strength or skill; I feel as if I am on a much greater mission. We're not just fighting to survive—we're fighting for something much bigger."

Lance's grip tightened on the bars, a silent affirmation of what they were about to attempt. "I'm with you, Bruce. Whatever it takes."

They spent the next few minutes finalizing the details, their voices low but their resolve unshakable. Lance would discreetly pass by and look in on Sarah for Bruce. She was being broken and battered more with each day. Every second counted.

As Lance prepared to leave, Bruce whispered one final instruction, his voice filled with the weight of what was to come. "Be careful, Lance. We only get one shot at this."

With that, Lance slipped away into the shadows, leaving Bruce alone once more in his cell. But now, there was a plan—a sliver of hope in the darkness. As Bruce settled back onto the cold, hard floor, he closed his eyes and whispered a prayer for strength, for wisdom, and for the courage to do what had to be done. He could talk to God. Wow!

5

SECOND SEAL

"The Fiery Red Horse"

Rebecca lay on the thin cot, her body aching from the brutal conditions of the camp. Every muscle screamed for rest, her mind teetering on the edge of exhaustion. The days of persecution had ground her spirit down, and though her faith held firm, her nights were her only reprieve. The visions that once haunted her sleep had been mercifully absent, granting her the solace of dreamless, deep slumber.

But tonight was different.

As her body sank into the depths of sleep, the vision took hold.

A fragile stillness blanketed the earth, a deceptive peace masking the storm about to break. The first seal's revelation lingered like a shadow, its impact hidden from humanity, blind to the spiritual war raging just beyond their sight.

In the heavenly realm, the Lamb again approached the scroll, His presence radiant and resolute. The angelic host stood silent, their eyes fixed on Him as He reached out and broke the second seal. The crack reverberated through the cosmos, a sound that tore through time and space, announcing the horror to come. Rebecca's body shuddered as the sound of the seal breaking passed through her like a wave.

From the scroll emerged a fiery red horse, its color burning like fresh blood. Its rider, cloaked in shadows, held a massive, blood-stained sword. His presence radiated menace, a harbinger of violence and conflict. Rebecca's soul quaked as she understood his power to take peace from the earth, to ignite hatred, division, and war.

The vision shifted—homes shattered by discord, streets stained with blood, nations turning on one another with savage ferocity. The fiery red horse galloped relentlessly, leaving chaos and despair in its wake. The cries of the innocent rose, a terrible symphony that echoed in her ears.

The angelic host watched, their faces etched with sorrow, as the evil of the rider descended. His sword gleamed with dark purpose as the earth trembled beneath his charge. Peace was ripped away, and hatred spread like a plague, consuming everything in its path.

Rebecca felt the tension, the horror, as if it were all around her, suffocating and inescapable. The fiery red horse had been unleashing its fury for two thousand years since the birth of the Church. ·

Rebecca awoke with a gasp, her chest heaving as she clawed her way back to reality. Her body trembled, her sweat-soaked hair clinging to her face as her heart thundered against her ribs. She pressed a hand to her chest, feeling its erratic rhythm as though to confirm it was still there.

The vision lingered, vivid and unrelenting. She couldn't shake the sight of the fiery red horse, the gleaming sword, or the screams of those caught in the rider's wake. She knew her torment was tied to the horsemen. Tears welled in her eyes as she curled up on the cot, her whispered prayer trembling in the stillness.

"God, help us. Help me. I don't know how to endure this."

The darkness of the camp was quiet, but in her spirit, the echoes of the vision roared. The fiery red horse was loose, and the world was about to be consumed.

"Make it Stop"

Rebecca's exhaustion overtook her, and despite her resistance, sleep claimed her. But it was not the restful oblivion she longed for. Her spirit was dragged into a dark, ethereal realm, a place far removed from the light of Heaven. The air was thick with malevolence, alive with an ancient energy that pulsed like a living heartbeat. Shadows moved with sinister intent, and a suffocating sense of dread wrapped around her like a shroud.

At the center of the unholy gathering stood Satan himself, commanding and dreadful. His dark robes absorbed what little light existed, and his eyes burned with a sinister intelligence. Hovering before him was a massive, glowing map of the world, alive and shifting, its pulsing surface illuminating the twisted forms of his demonic generals. These beings, grotesque and cruel, radiated power and malice, their anticipation fueled by a dark energy as they waited for their orders.

Satan raised his hand, silencing the murmurs of his gathered host. His voice, deep and resonant, filled the air with both authority and menace. "The time has come," he intoned, "to shatter the illusion of peace.

Humanity clings to safety like fools. We will rip it from their grasp and drown them in chaos."

Rebecca watched, frozen, as Satan gestured to the map. On its surface, nations and leaders shifted like pieces on a game board. "Exploit their greed," he continued, his voice dripping with venom. "Feed their lust for power. Let them tear each other apart. We will make them thirst for conquest and bloodshed."

The map pulsed as Satan, the rider of the white horse, a specter of deception, stood over it. He smiled coldly. "My work is done. The groundwork is laid. Now, the fiery red horse will ride, and humanity will ignite its own destruction."

A tall, imposing demon stepped forward, his burning eyes reflecting the cruel joy of his master's command. "It shall be as you will, my lord," he hissed. "The nations will rise against each other. Their leaders will become pawns, their armies, instruments of our chaos."

The demon generals erupted in jeers and laughter, staking claims on the earth with vicious delight. "The East is mine," snarled one, his form slithering with malice. "Discontent already thrives there."

"The North shall fall under my command," another declared. "I will turn brother against brother before the year's end."

Rebecca's heart pounded as their taunts and schemes filled the air. The generals relished their task, reveling in the chance to manipulate humanity into destruction. For them, this was not merely a war—it was a game, and the souls of men were their pieces to be played and discarded.

Satan leaned closer to the map, his predatory grin widening. "Do not forget the righteous," he said, his tone venomous. "Twist their understanding of scripture. Make them believe their wars are holy, that their violence is justified by the will of God. Let them stain their hands with blood in my name, while they think they serve the light."

The demon commander bowed low. "They will beg for mercy," he said with cruel satisfaction, "but none will come."

The chamber erupted with laughter, a sound so vile it seemed to pierce Rebecca's very soul, vibrating through her body with an intensity that made her knees buckle. The demons reveled in their cruelty, their voices a cacophony of mockery and malice, feeding the oppressive atmosphere with their dark joy.

Rebecca, trembling at the edge of the shadows, gasped before she could stop herself. The sound was small, but it echoed in the eerie silence that followed the demonic chorus. Satan's gaze snapped toward her, his burning eyes locking onto hers with a force that rooted her in place.

His smile widened, cold and predatory, as he took a deliberate step toward her. "Ah," he said, his voice low and venomous, each word curling through the air like smoke. "So fragile. So weak. I will break you." His grin twisted into something even darker, his words laced with triumph. "You will be my puppet, your strings pulled at my whim. Your every thought, every breath will serve me."

Rebecca's mind screamed for release, her chest tightening as the oppressive air closed in around her. The vision blurred, but the images seared themselves into her consciousness, the pulsing map, the gloating demons, and above all, Satan's triumphant gaze as he prepared to unleash war and chaos upon the earth.

Even as she was wrenched from the vision, the weight of his words clung to her like chains, her soul trembling under the memory of his cruel promise.

Rebecca awoke with a jolt, her chest gasping as though she had been suffocating. Her sweat-soaked body trembled, and tears streamed down her face. She clutched the thin blanket, her heart racing as the echoes of the vision roared in her mind.

"God," she whispered, her voice breaking, "make this stop."

The darkness of her room was silent, but the terror lingered, sharp and suffocating, and the world stood on the brink of devastation.

"The Unseen Hand of War"

In the dark realm, this was no vision, one of the demon generals, Maldris, wasted no time; he ascended from the ethereal realm, his presence a dark, invisible shadow that slithered across the globe. Moving with purpose, his influence spread like a contagion as he deployed his demons to infiltrate governments and the corridors of power, unseen by mortal eyes but felt in the cold, calculated decisions that would soon plunge the world into chaos.

In the opulent chambers of a government office, a powerful leader sat behind a grand desk, his brow furrowed as he weighed the consequences of his next move. Unbeknownst to him, Maldris stood by his side, a spectral figure that whispered dark thoughts into his ear, fueling his paranoia and ambition. The leader hesitated, feeling a strange compulsion gnawing at the edges of his consciousness, as if his decisions were being guided by something beyond his understanding. It was a fleeting moment of clarity, a brief acknowledgment of the unnatural influence over him, before the haze of ambition clouded his mind once more. With a single command, the wheels of war were set in motion, his actions now fully under the shadow of the demonic influence.

"Your enemies plot against you," the demon's voice was a soft, insidious hiss, curling into the leader's mind like smoke. "They seek to undermine your authority, to strip you of power. You must strike first, show them your strength, or be crushed beneath their heel."

The leader's hand trembled as he reached for the red phone on his desk, the one that connected him directly to his military commanders. His hesitation wavered under the weight of the demon's influence. The leader's thoughts, once clear, became muddled with fear and suspicion. He saw threats in every shadow, betrayal in every ally.

"Do it," Maldris urged, his voice now a commanding presence. "Order the strike. Let them know that you will not be trifled with. War is the only path to secure your legacy."

In a distant military command center, the same unseen force manipulated the minds of generals and strategists. The demon moved among them like a phantom, invisible yet pervasive, twisting their perceptions and clouding their judgments. Maps of contested territories lay spread before them, lines drawn in blood as they plotted their next moves.

"Launch the offensive," the demon whispered into the ear of a decorated general, who stood rigid before a digital map of the world. "Show no mercy. Your enemies are weak, ripe for the taking. Their defeat will ensure your nation's dominance for generations to come."

The general, once a man of honor and restraint, felt a dark satisfaction seep into his soul. In his hand, he held a phone, programmed with military encryption, ready to send thousands of troops into battle. The demon's words echoed in his mind like a sinister mantra. With a single command, the wheels of war were set in motion.

In the shadowy corners of the world, the demon's influence reached even further. Extremists gathered in secret, their hearts already poisoned by hatred and zealotry. The demon fed their rage, whispering promises of glory and martyrdom, igniting the flames of violence in their souls.

"Take up arms," the demon urged, his voice like fire in their veins. "Purge the earth of those who oppose you. Your cause is just; your enemies are unworthy of mercy. Rise, and bring about the cleansing that the world so desperately needs."

As the extremists armed themselves, preparing for acts of terror and violence, the demon's laughter echoed in the dark recesses of their minds, a sound that only they could hear—a sound that drove them to the brink of madness.

Throughout the world, the effects of the demon's influence began to manifest. Nations that had once enjoyed uneasy peace now teetered on the brink of war. Assassinations were plotted in secret, leaders overthrown, and civil unrest spread like wildfire. In cities and villages, neighbors turned against one another, suspicion and fear replacing trust and camaraderie.

In a bustling marketplace, once filled with the sounds of commerce and laughter, a mob gathered, their faces twisted with anger. A single spark, a whispered lie, was all it took to ignite their fury. The demons watched with satisfaction as the mob turned on an innocent family, their cries for mercy drowned out by the roar of hatred. Blood was spilled in the streets, and the demons reveled in the chaos they had wrought.

The world was now a tinderbox, with the demon generals holding the match. Their unseen hand guided events from the shadows, their influence pervasive and inescapable. The fires of war had been lit, and they would soon consume all in their path.

The second seal had been broken, and the rider on the fiery red horse had been unleashed upon the earth. Peace was shattered, and the world would soon be bathed in blood. The stage was set for the great and terrible events that were to follow, as the forces of darkness moved ever closer to their ultimate goal: the complete subjugation of humanity and the thwarting of God's plan for salvation.

"The Earth Ablaze"

The earth, once a vibrant symphony of diverse cultures and life, now lay under the oppressive shadow of impending doom. Globally, the seeds of discord planted by the demon generals and their hordes had sprouted into a raging inferno of conflict. The world was ablaze, both literally and figuratively, as wars erupted across every continent, each more brutal and senseless than the last.

From the deserts of the Middle East to the jungles of Africa, the air was thick with the acrid stench of burning cities and the cries of the wounded and dying. Smoke billowed into the sky, blotting out the sun, as once-thriving metropolises were reduced to rubble. In Europe, ancient capitals that had stood for centuries were now war zones, their streets littered with the debris of civilization and the bodies of those caught in the crossfire.

In one city, a skyscraper toppled, its steel frame twisted by the heat of a thousand fires. The building crumbled like a house of cards, sending plumes of dust and ash into the sky as it collapsed onto the streets below. Panic-stricken civilians ran in all directions, their faces masks of terror as they fled from the advancing flames. The roar of the inferno was deafening, drowning out the desperate pleas for help and the screams of those who could not escape.

Elsewhere, in a once-peaceful village, the night sky was ablaze with the glow of burning homes. Families huddled together, seeking refuge in the shadows as armed militants stormed through the streets, their weapons flashing in the darkness. The demon lieutenant's influence gripped the scene, his malice evident in the ruthless brutality of the attackers, who showed no mercy to those they encountered. The village, once a place of warmth and community, had become a battlefield where the innocent were slaughtered without hesitation.

In the midst of this global upheaval, the demon commander moved unseen, his presence felt in every corner of the earth. He whispered words of hatred and vengeance into the ears of generals and soldiers, fueling the fires of war with lies and deceit. His influence spread like a plague, infecting the minds of men and women who had once known peace, turning them into instruments of destruction.

Bombs fell from the sky, their explosions shaking the very ground as entire neighborhoods were obliterated in an instant. In the aftermath, the survivors stumbled through the wreckage, their eyes hollow with shock and despair. The world they had known was gone, replaced by a landscape of devastation where the strong preyed on the weak, and hope was a distant memory.

The demon's hand was evident in the brutality of the conflicts, the sheer scale of the destruction. Borders that had once separated nations were now meaningless, as the violence spread like wildfire, consuming everything in its path. The earth was a battlefield, and no place was safe from the chaos that reigned.

"A Fragile Routine"

In the aftermath of the devastation that gripped the world, James and Emily tried to hold onto the fragments of a life that once felt secure. The days were long and heavy, the weight of fear hanging over them like a storm cloud that refused to pass. The once-bustling city had grown eerily quiet, its streets now patrolled by armed enforcers under the guise of maintaining order. James, a man who had once thrived in his work, now found himself caught in a system that valued conformity over contribution.

The alarm blared in the dim light of their apartment, signaling the start of yet another grueling day. Emily stirred in her bed, her eyes dull with the fatigue that had become her constant companion. School was no longer a place of learning but a mandatory indoctrination center where the children were taught to serve the "greater good"—a phrase that now tasted bitter on everyone's tongue. She dreaded going, but there was no choice. The rules were strict; the consequences for disobedience severe.

James, already dressed, leaned over the kitchen counter, staring at his phone. The screen flashed with the latest news: more cities in flames, more lives lost. The world was crumbling, and yet, he was expected to report to work as if nothing had changed. Even sickness was no excuse—there was no room for weakness in this new world order. The message was clear: work was not just a duty; it was a requirement for survival.

"Emily, it's time," James called, his voice heavy with the resignation that had settled into their lives.

Emily shuffled into the kitchen, her school uniform neat but devoid of any pride. "Dad, why do we have to keep doing this?" she asked, her voice barely above a whisper. "Why do we have to pretend that everything is okay when it's not?"

James sighed, setting his phone down. He walked over to her, placing a hand on her shoulder. "Because if we don't, they'll come for us. And if they come for us, we won't be able to help your mom or anyone else. We have to survive, Emily. We have to keep going, no matter how hard it gets."

"But what if the war reaches us?" Emily's eyes, once filled with innocence, now reflected the harsh reality of the world outside. "What will we do then?"

James looked away, his heart heavy with the burden of the truth he could no longer shield her from. "We'll have to leave," he said finally. "When—not if—but when the war reaches us, we'll have to go somewhere safe. We'll have to find a way out, find a place where we can survive."

Emily nodded, her fear mirrored in her father's eyes. The news app on James's phone suddenly came to life again, an emergency alert flashing across the screen. Another city had fallen. Another wave of destruction was on its way.

"We can't stay here forever, Dad," Emily whispered, her voice trembling with the realization of what that meant. "We'll have to leave soon, won't we?"

"Yes, Emily," James replied, his voice barely audible. "We will. But for now, we have to keep going. We have to keep trying to live, even if it's just pretending."

James hesitated, the weight of the truth pressing down on him. He knew they couldn't ignore the unspoken fear that had haunted them since the day Rebecca was taken. He looked into Emily's eyes, seeing the same worry that gnawed at his own heart. "Emily," he began, his voice trembling slightly, "I know you're worried about Mom. So am I. Pastor Daniels told me... he told me she's been transferred to the inner courts of the camp."

Emily's eyes widened, fear flashing across her face. "The inner courts?" she whispered, her voice barely audible. "Dad... some of the kids at school said that people don't come back from there."

James nodded, swallowing the lump in his throat. "I know," he said, his voice thick with emotion. "They say... they say that's where they use the extreme measures, where they break people. And many... many never make it out. That is why we need to pray without ceasing for your mom."

Tears welled up in Emily's eyes, and she looked away, biting her lip to keep from crying. "Do you think she's...?" Her voice broke, unable to finish the thought.

James reached out, gently turning her face back toward him. "We can't lose hope, Emily," he said, his voice firm despite the despair he felt inside. "Your mom is strong. She's survived this long, and I believe she's still fighting. But we have to be ready, Emily. We have to be strong for her, for each other."

Emily nodded, wiping away her tears. "I miss her so much, Dad. It's been so long..."

"I know, sweetheart. I miss her too," James whispered, pulling her into a tight embrace. "But we have to keep going, for her. We have to believe that we'll be together again someday, no matter what happens."

Emily clung to her father, the weight of their shared burden heavy on her small shoulders. "We will see her again," she murmured, as much to reassure herself as to convince her father.

"Yes, we will," her dad replied, holding her close, trying to shield her from the harsh reality of their world. But even as he spoke, the doubt gnawed at him, and the question lingered in his mind—how long could they hold on before the storm finally consumed them?

The phone continued to flash with the horrors of the world outside, a constant reminder that their fragile routine was just that—fragile. The storm was coming, and they both knew it. It was only a matter of time before the war that raged across the globe found its way to their doorstep.

As Emily and James made their way to the door, a heavy silence hung between them. The weight of the morning's conversation pressed down on both of them, unspoken fears threading through their thoughts like a dark undercurrent. Emily reached for the door handle but hesitated, her hand hovering just above the cold metal. Her mind raced with the possibilities her father had laid out—leaving, running, trying to find safety in a world that seemed to have none left.

James, lost in his thoughts, nearly walked into her, stopping just short of bumping into her back. He placed a gentle hand on her shoulder, his concern momentarily breaking through the fog of his own dread.

Emily turned to face him, her eyes wide with the question that had been gnawing at her since their conversation began. "Dad... if we leave, how will Mom find us?"

The question hung in the air, heavy and heartbreaking. James felt a pang of sorrow deep in his chest, a sharp reminder of how much they had already lost—and how much they still stood to lose. He searched for the right words, something to give his daughter a semblance of comfort, but all that came was a sigh, filled with a mixture of helplessness and resolve.

"We'll find a way, Emily," he finally managed, his voice barely above a whisper. "No matter what happens, we'll make sure she knows where to find us. I promise."

But even as he said it, the doubt gnawed at him. How could he promise something so uncertain, so fragile in a world where everything was being torn apart? Emily, sensing his unease, offered a small nod, accepting his words even if they didn't fully comfort her. She didn't ask for more, knowing that there were no easy answers left for them.

She finally grasped the door handle, her small fingers gripping it tightly as if it was the last piece of stability in a world spiraling out of control. With one last look at her father, she pushed the door handle in, then turned, a trick required to open the failing handle and pulled the door open, stepping out into a world that had become increasingly hostile and unpredictable.

She finally grasped the door handle, her small fingers gripping it tightly as if it were the last piece of stability in a world spiraling out of control. With one last look at her father, she pressed the handle inward, then turned it—a trick needed to open the faulty latch, then pulled the door open, stepping out into a world that had become increasingly hostile and unpredictable.

James followed, the door closing behind them with a soft click that echoed in the quiet hallway. They walked side by side, their footsteps synchronized, each step forward a small act of defiance against the chaos that sought to consume them.

In their shared silence, there was a determination to keep moving forward, to survive not just for themselves but for each other—and for Rebecca, wherever she might be.

"The Earth Below Engulfed"

In the spiritual realm, the vision of the unfolding apocalypse was unbearable to the righteous. The devastation was staggering, the scale of human suffering beyond comprehension. The hand of the demon commanders and their legions wrought destruction in every act of violence, every senseless death. This was the fulfillment of prophecy. The opening of the second seal was fueled by the evil nature of carnal man, but was orchestrated by unseen spiritual forces, ominously clear to those in the heavenly realm.

The rider on the fiery red horse swung his massive sword in a single, devastating arc. Dripping with the blood of nations, the blade symbolized the division and strife unleashed upon the world. It was not merely a weapon of war but an instrument of spiritual conquest, designed to pit brother against brother, nation against nation, and soul against soul.

The earth was a patchwork of conflicts. Cities lay in smoldering ruins, their streets choked with the dead and dying. The cries of the innocent rose like a haunting symphony, their suffering reverberating across the surface of the earth. In the camp where Rebecca and Sarah endured the weight of persecution, the echoes of these horrors were inescapable. The daily cruelty, the erosion of hope, was a microcosm of the broader chaos. Rebecca prayed fervently for strength, while Sarah, frail but unwavering, fought against the lies that threatened their spirits.

The Church, splintered and battered, faced its darkest hour. Under the fiery red rider's attacks, its leaders were hunted, its congregations scattered. What had once been a stronghold of truth now struggled to survive, with faithful remnants clinging desperately to the promises of God. Sarah fought oppression with quiet resolve, while Rebecca, haunted by her visions, bore the crushing burden of the unfolding tribulation.

Heaven was overwhelmed with sorrow for the people of the earth, trapped in a nightmare from which there was no escape. The forces at work were far beyond human control. This was not merely human folly but the deliberate machination of darkness, intent on the utter undoing of God's creation. The demon commander's laughter echoed in the unseen realms as Satan's schemes bore fruit in the pain and despair of the faithful.

A deep sense of dread settled over creation. This was only the beginning. The chaos and destruction would worsen as the remaining seals were broken. The fires of war, ignited by the rider's sword, would burn until nothing was left but ash. For Sarah and Rebecca, every day became a battle to cling to their faith as the world outside their camp descended further into madness.

Yet even as the second seal brought horror upon the earth, a glimmer of hope remained. All of creation understood that the rider's power, and indeed all the forces of darkness, was limited. A limit to this torment would be reached. The judgment to come was inescapable, and the suffering of the present age, terrible as it was, would one day give way to a new dawn—a dawn where peace and justice would reign forever.

But for now, the nightmare raged on.

6

GLOBAL SYSTEM

"The Unifier Emerges"

The world held its collective breath as screens flickered to life, broadcasting an event that had captured the globe's attention. Every news channel, every social media platform, and every public square buzzed with the same image—a grand stage set before the United Nations headquarters, draped in flags from every nation. The very air seemed charged with anticipation, as though the earth itself sensed that a monumental shift was about to unfold.

James, Emily, Pastor Daniels, and four others huddled together in the dimly lit basement of their makeshift church, their faces illuminated by the glow of the television. The underground church had scattered after the raid, with survivors retreating into deeper hiding, seeking shelter in safe houses known only to a trusted few. Now, they gathered in tense silence, their hearts heavy with foreboding as the world's most powerful leaders prepared for what had been billed as the "Summit for Global Unity."

At the center of the stage stood a man who had risen to prominence in what seemed like the blink of an eye. He towered above the gathered leaders, his figure commanding attention, yet his demeanor disarmingly warm. Dressed impeccably, his sharp features softened by a charismatic smile, he radiated an aura that had captivated billions. His eyes, however—piercing, intelligent, and cold—revealed the calculating mind behind the charm. This was the man the world had come to know as the Unifier, Ben Reshan, a leader who had emerged from the chaos of global turmoil, offering a vision of peace and prosperity that had United Nations under his banner.

The camera zoomed in on Reshan's face as he approached the podium. His voice, smooth and resonant, carried the authority of a man who had already achieved great things, yet hinted at even greater ambitions.

"People of the world," he began, his tone confident and measured, as the chaos of war continued to consume the globe. The fires of conflict had spread unchecked, leaving cities in ruins and nations shattered. The airwaves were abuzz with news of battles raging on every continent, each report grimmer than the last. "We are in a world engulfed by flames," he continued, his voice rising above the desperation that gripped so many. "But we now stand at the precipice of a new era. An era where the divisions of the past will be no more, where the barriers that have separated us are dissolving, and where we, as a global community, will finally achieve the peace and prosperity that has long eluded us."

His words carried a promise that felt like a lifeline to a world drowning in violence. He projected the assurance of a savior, the one who would rise from the ashes of war to forge a new order. But beneath the surface, his eyes gleamed with a different kind of resolve, one that hinted at a vision far beyond mere peace.

Applause erupted from the crowd, a sound that seemed to echo across every corner of the globe, amplified by screens in homes, public spaces, and devices everywhere. But in the quiet basement where James and Emily sat, the reaction was much different—a heavy silence, a noticeable tension, as the words echoed in the hearts of those who knew what was truly unfolding.

Reshan's voice rose with fervor, drawing the masses deeper into his vision. "For too long, we have allowed our differences to divide us—differences in race, culture, and religion. But today, we cast aside those divisions. Today, we declare a new identity, one that transcends the past and unites us as one people under a single global system."

James felt a shiver run down his spine. He had always known this day would come—the day when the world would bow to a single leader in the name of peace. But hearing it declared so plainly, so seductively, filled him with dread.

On the screen, Reshan gestured toward the sea of flags behind him, symbols of a world now united under his influence. "This is our moment," he proclaimed. "A moment to set aside the conflicts of the past and embrace a future where we work together as one global community, not as separate nations."

Again, the applause thundered, and the camera panned to the faces of the world's leaders—some beaming with awe, others cloaked in reverence, their devotion unmistakable. As the camera moved, it briefly captured faces marked with doubt and fear—those few who sensed that something far more sinister was at work. The shot lingered only for a fleeting moment before shifting away, as if to downplay their presence. But behind the scenes, anonymous monitors identified these possible dissenters, taking down their names swiftly and silently.

Emily leaned closer to her father, her voice barely above a whisper. "He's dangerous, Dad. I can feel it."

James nodded, his gaze fixed on the screen. "I know. But look at them—most people don't see it. They're ready to follow him, wherever he leads. It's as if the wars were started just so he could swoop in."

Pastor Daniels sat quietly, the weight of the world pressing heavily on his chest, as though the very air he breathed had thickened with despair. Since the scattering of his church, an unsettling stillness had settled deep within him—a silence that seemed to carry more questions than answers. Was this quiet the voice of God calling him to wait, to trust in His timing, or was it the subtle, creeping seduction of his own flesh, pulling him into resignation? The doubt gnawed at him.

The sadness, deep and unshakable, washed over him as he watched the people on the screen—oblivious, blinded by the charisma of the Unifier, their hearts seduced by the very darkness he had long preached against. Where were they now? Those who had once filled the pews, eager to worship, to learn? Scattered, lost to the deceit of a world that had turned its back on truth.

What haunted him most wasn't their blindness. It was his own silence. Had God called him to this quiet place, to observe, to wait for the right moment? Or was his silence a sin of complacency, a retreat into himself? The questions gnawed at his soul.

Reshan's voice softened, taking on an almost paternal tone, as though guiding a wayward child back onto the right path. "To achieve this vision, certain sacrifices must be made. We must be willing to set aside the beliefs that divide us and embrace a new global doctrine—one that promotes unity, tolerance, and understanding."

James clenched his fists. He knew what was coming—the subtle twisting of truth that would ensnare the souls of millions.

"And so," Reshan continued, his voice laced with quiet authority, "I am pleased to announce the formation of the Global Faith Initiative, a unified belief system that will bring all religions together under a single, inclusive doctrine. The Council of Unity, composed of spiritual leaders from around the world, will guide us on this path of enlightenment."

In the basement, the air grew thick with horror as the announcement settled over the group. The faces of religious leaders flashed across the screen, each one pledging their support, their expressions serene as though they had found the ultimate truth. But to James, Emily, and the others, it was nothing less than a declaration of war on faith itself.

"He's consolidating power over all nations and religions," James whispered, his voice tight with anger. "He's twisting every belief system to suit his agenda."

Emily's eyes widened in fear. "What are we going to do? If he succeeds, there won't be any place left for us... for anyone who believes in the truth."

Reshan's voice broke through their thoughts once more, this time carrying an even greater weight. "This is our destiny. A world united, a world at peace, a world where all are free to live and believe as they choose under the protection of the Global Faith Initiative. Together, we will create a future that is bright, just... and inevitable."

The applause grew deafening, the camera zooming out to reveal the sea of faces, all swept up in the fervor of the Unifier's vision. Ben Reshan's image, now larger than life, filled every screen, every device, a symbol of a world ready to bow before him.

In the dimly lit room where the underground church gathered, there was no applause—only the heavy silence of those who knew the world had crossed a line from which there was no return.

"We need to warn the others," Pastor Daniels said, his voice trembling with urgency. "This is it. If we don't stand now, it'll be too late."

James nodded, his face set in grim determination. "We'll keep the faith alive. No matter what he does, we won't stop."

As the broadcast ended, Reshan's final words lingered in the air like a dark omen. "All religions are tied to our home, this celestial ball traveling gracefully through the cosmos—the earth, our mother, Gaia. We are the protectors of this living, breathing organism, and if we do not act, she will shake us off as if we are mere fleas. But I promise you, change is coming."

The crowd roared, swept away by his vision. The world was being drawn into a lie, one that would soon demand their souls. And in that basement, James and his small band of believers knew that their fight was only just beginning.

Tim Daniels, the pastor without a church, sat in silence, his mind drifting to Sarah, the once-fiery soul who had been the heart of their small congregation. She had burned with a passion for the Gospel, a flame so bright it seemed unquenchable, even in the face of persecution. But now, as the world darkened and the weight of torment pressed down upon her, he feared that her fire might be extinguished, snuffed out as though a torrent of despair was pouring over her. He prayed for her, though his own prayers felt like faint whispers lost in the storm, growing weaker by the day. The oppressive weight of a world spiraling into chaos seemed to be smothering his spirit too, yet he clung to hope—fragile as it was—pleading with God to rekindle the flame, not only in Sarah but in himself as well.

He sat there, lost in the quiet turmoil of his thoughts, unresponsive to those around him. One by one, they left him to his silence, slipping away until he was alone once more—alone with the weight of a world crumbling and the echoes of his unanswered prayers.

"Escape Day"

Bruce sat on the edge of his cot, the dull hum of the facility's machinery the only sound breaking the oppressive silence of his cell. His eyes, heavy with sleeplessness, traced the cracks in the concrete floor, his mind a storm of thoughts. He heard the familiar sounds of Lance's footsteps just before the door to his cell slid open.

Lance's face was tense but determined, his eyes flickering with the same intensity that Bruce had come to both admire and trust. "Everything's set," Lance whispered, crouching low as if the walls themselves might listen. "I cut the barbed wire on the back fence. It's held together with a thin wire, so they won't detect it unless they're really looking. You'll be out before the guards make their rounds."

Bruce's heart raced, but his face remained a mask of calm. He had been waiting for this moment, hadn't he? For hours, days, weeks—he had dreamed of freedom, of escape from this suffocating place. Yet now, as Lance laid out the final piece of the plan, doubt gnawed at him, an insidious whisper threading its way through his mind.

"I'll give you the key tomorrow," Lance continued, his voice barely above a breath. "After that, it's up to you. Make your move... or don't."

Bruce swallowed hard, his throat dry. He nodded, though his body felt frozen in place. Lance gave him a hard look, as though trying to read the thoughts flickering behind his eyes. Satisfied, Lance slipped away, leaving Bruce alone once more in the dim light of his cell.

As his footsteps faded, the flood of doubts washed over him with brutal force. He could picture it—slipping through the wire, darting into the shadows, disappearing into the night. But just as easily, he could see the guards catching him, dragging him back, beaten and worse off than before. But a way out was whispered into his fear; he saw an image of himself standing before the tribunal, accepting their terms, surrendering to the system.

Maybe, just maybe, they would release him. No job, no future, but at least he would be free. He could leave all of this behind. He could blend back into the world, the way it was before. He could survive.

"Go back," a voice hissed in his mind. "You've seen what they can do. You don't stand a chance. Think of yourself for once. You can once again focus on building yourself up, making yourself better, stronger."

Bruce clenched his fists. The voice was so clear, so reasonable. He could almost feel the weight lifting from his shoulders at the thought of surrendering. He wouldn't have to run. He wouldn't have to risk his life. He could escape in a different way—by letting go.

He closed his eyes, his breathing ragged as the tension tightened its grip on him. And then, as if from nowhere, a presence filled the room. It wasn't a voice this time—but a force. Strong. Unyielding. It seized his spirit with such intensity that it nearly stole his breath. For a moment, Bruce wondered if his mind was playing tricks on him, but the presence was undeniable—more real than the concrete walls around him. There was no sound, yet it felt as if something were swirling within the confines of his cell, like a whirlwind—but not of the physical world. It was something deeper, something spiritual, a force that defied explanation.

With it came a flood of compassion—unexpected, overwhelming. His thoughts turned to Sarah, her face flickering in his mind like a distant, fading memory. Her passion for the Gospel, her courage in the face of darkness, her unwavering faith even when everything else crumbled. How could he leave her behind? How could he turn his back now? If he backed out, would he be guilty of her death?

As if the presence had physically gripped him by the shoulders, Bruce felt his spirit lift, courage filling him like a rush of wind in his lungs. It was as if the very walls of the cell had brightened, though the light remained dim and unchanged. He stood, his heart beating with newfound resolve. The doubts, the fear—they still lingered, but now, they were mere shadows compared to the strength rising within him.

He wouldn't turn back. He couldn't. This wasn't just about him. It was about Sarah. It was about standing for something greater, something more than survival. And in that moment, Bruce knew—he would take the key. He would make the move.

There was no going back now.

"Unbroken Silence"

Sarah braced herself as the heavy steel door clanged open. The dim, cold light from the hallway spilled into her cell, casting long, jagged shadows on the walls. She barely had time to stand before the guard stormed in, his boots thudding against the concrete floor.

"Well, well," the guard sneered, his voice dripping with contempt. "The saint still holding on, are we?" He paced the small space like a predator, his eyes scanning her with cold amusement. "What's it going to take to break you?"

Sarah's fists clenched, her body rigid as she locked eyes with him, refusing to flinch. "You'll never break me."

The guard chuckled darkly, a cruel smile tugging at his lips. "We'll see about that. They all break eventually."

He stepped closer, his presence suffocating as he loomed over her. She could smell the staleness of his breath, feel the weight of his malice bearing down. "Why don't you just make it easy on yourself, huh? Surrender, give up this nonsense. We all know you don't really believe all that God nonsense. You're scared. I can see it."

Sarah's heart pounded in her chest, but she didn't back down. "You don't know anything about me."

"Oh, but I do," the guard mocked, circling her. "I know people like you. Tough on the outside, fragile on the inside. You'll beg before the end, you'll see."

He stepped in closer, grabbing her arm with a force that made her gasp, pain shooting through her shoulder. She wrenched it free, her body instinctively fighting back. But the guard was quicker, his hand flying up to strike her across the face. The blow was brutal, knocking her back against the cold wall, her head swimming with pain.

Still, Sarah didn't yield. She wiped the blood from her lip with the back of her hand and glared at him through the haze of pain. "You'll have to do better than that."

Rage flashed in the guard's eyes, his smile twisting into a snarl. He lunged at her, pinning her against the wall, his face inches from hers. "You think you're tough, huh?" he growled. "Let's see how tough you are. Why can't that God of yours save you? Is it because he is powerless?"

The struggle was fierce. Sarah kicked and clawed, her body reacting on pure survival instinct. Every muscle in her body screamed with pain, but she fought, her mind refusing to surrender even as her body weakened.

The guard's strength was overwhelming, and with a final shove, he sent her crashing to the floor. She hit hard, the impact knocking the breath from her lungs. For a moment, she lay still, her vision blurred, the room spinning.

The guard stood over her, breathing heavily, his face flushed with anger and satisfaction. "Not so tough now, are you?"

Sarah's body was crumpled on the floor, her chest rising and falling with shallow, labored breaths. Blood trickled from her mouth, pooling on the cold concrete beneath her. She looked broken, fragile—a shadow of the defiant woman who had stood just moments before.

The guard kicked her with the full weight of his body and spat at her, his voice low and menacing. "You're done."

Sarah could no longer feel her arms or legs. Numbness washed over her as the room around her dimmed into blackness. At that moment, she felt an unexpected peace—a release. She was free.

The guard, pumped with rage, raised his boot high above her motionless head, preparing to deliver a crushing blow. It was a strike meant to do more than break her—it was meant to end her. But as his boot came crashing down, his body betrayed him. A muscle spasm, sharp and sudden, wrenched his leg mid-motion. He stumbled, his boot barely missing her head. With a strangled cry, he grabbed at his calf, his face contorting in agony as his muscles seized with a pain too intense to bear. He collapsed to the floor, writhing, clutching his leg in desperation.

It took him quite a while to recover, the pain radiating through his body, leaving him shaken and trying to straighten his leg. Eventually, he forced himself to stand and staggered out of the cell, the door slamming shut behind him with a deafening finality.

The silence that followed was heavy, oppressive. Sarah lay still, her body unmoving as the sound of the guard's limping steps faded into the distance.

But as the minutes passed, the question hung in the air—would she rise again, or had God finally set her free from her battered, broken body?

"The Mark of Allegiance"

The line outside the government facility stretched for blocks, a slow-moving serpent of anxious faces and shuffling feet. Armed guards stood at regular intervals, their silent presence a stark reminder of the gravity of the day's proceedings. The city, once vibrant, now lay under a heavy veil of uncertainty. Hushed conversations buzzed through the crowd, mingling with the uneasy silence of those who understood that their lives were about to change forever.

James and Emily stood near the back of the line, their expressions as tense as the others around them. The facility ahead loomed, cold and unwelcoming—a structure of steel and glass, with banners of the Global Faith Initiative draped over its entrance. The symbol—a stylized globe encircled by a laurel wreath—had become an oppressive reminder of the new world order imposed upon them since the Unifier's speech.

As the line inched forward, the murmured conversations ebbed and flowed, interspersed with nervous glances at the guards and the facility ahead.

"I heard they scan your whole body," a man ahead of them muttered to his companion. "They say the mark is like a microchip, embedded right under the skin."

"That's just rumors and lies," came the sharp reply, loud enough to draw uneasy looks. "Are you one of those Christians spreading this nonsense? It's just the new financial system—your bank account, your ID, even your medical records. We need it, or we won't be able to buy anything. They're not injecting us. My neighbor said it's just a new ID card. It even takes the place of your driver's license."

Emily squeezed her father's hand, her knuckles white. "Dad, I don't know if I can do this," she whispered, her voice trembling. "I don't want to have a chip injected into me. I remember Pastor Daniels talking about that." Her voice trailed off.

James glanced at her, his heart aching at the fear in her eyes. He felt it too, gnawing at his insides like a relentless predator. But they had come too far to turn back now. "We'll figure it out," he said, though the words felt hollow even to him. "Just... stay calm. We'll figure it out." The phrase had become the default response to every crisis, a way to skirt around the harsh truths they faced, an attempt to mask the reality they were too afraid to confront.

As the line moved slowly forward, they could see the facility's entrance more clearly. People walked through turnstiles, one after another, receiving a card or something before being directed to a large room hidden from view.

James watched, his mind racing. Was the card just a new form of ID, as the man had said? Or was there something more sinister at work? His thoughts were interrupted by a stern voice.

"Do you have your social security card and photo ID?" a clerk asked, her tone mechanical, without a hint of warmth.

"Uh, yes," James stammered, quickly fumbling for his documents. Emily offered hers as well, her hand trembling slightly as the clerk moved down the line.

People were leaving through a door far to the right, many with expressions of relief, others visibly upset, probably from the hassle of it all. James turned to Emily, offering what he hoped was a reassuring smile.

"It's going to be fine, Emily."

She forced a smile in return, though it didn't reach her eyes.

When their turn finally came, James's heart pounded in his chest with a ferocity that made it hard to breathe. They stepped inside, leaving the warm sun behind as they entered the cold, sterile facility. The air was heavy with the sound of footsteps and hushed voices, an almost surreal atmosphere that made it feel like they were walking through a nightmare.

A clerk motioned them forward. "Names?" she asked, her tone flat, disinterested.

"James Marshall, and my daughter Emily Marshall," he replied, trying to keep his voice steady.

The clerk typed something into her computer, then handed them each a small tablet. "Enter your social and sign at the bottom," she instructed.

James hesitated, his hand hovering over the tablet. He knew this was more than just a formality. Signing here meant agreeing to be part of the system—a system that would bind them in ways he wasn't sure he fully understood.

But what was the alternative? Refusing to sign would cut them off from everything—bank accounts, food, medicine, even basic existence. They would be outcasts, marked for refusal to conform.

"This is not an agreement or anything like that. You're just signing into the system and recording that you showed up," she barked. "Now sign it—there are people behind you."

The clerk inserted a card into the tablet, tapped a few keys, and then handed it to James. She did the same for Emily. "Head through the door into the hall," she said, gesturing vaguely.

"Dad..." Emily's voice was barely a whisper, heavy with fear. He could see the tears welling in her eyes as she clutched the card.

"I was reading Revelation yesterday..." her voice trailed off.

James knew what she was thinking. This wasn't just about survival—it was about their faith, about staying true to what they had always believed. Pastor Daniels had preached about this for years, and now it felt like those warnings were coming to life right before them.

James could see the fear in Emily's eyes, and he felt the same unease creeping over him. He took a deep breath and tried to sound certain, even though doubt lingered in the back of his mind.

"Emily, listen," he said, his voice low but urgent. "This can't be the Mark of the Beast. Remember what Pastor Daniels preached? He said we won't be here when that happens. We will be taken up before the tribulation. You know the rapture happens first, right? We're not even going to face that kind of choice."

Emily's eyes remained wide with confusion, and James struggled to reassure her, and himself.

"He always said we don't need to worry about the mark because we asked Jesus into our hearts, remember?" James continued, trying to sound more confident than he felt. "Maybe... maybe this is just a test. Or maybe we misunderstood, but it can't be the real thing. Pastor Daniels was certain about that. He was clear. Jesus is coming back to take us away."

James paused, his voice faltering. "I mean, I can't believe God would let us go through the real Tribulation."

Emily's gaze softened a little, but the fear was still there. "But what if he was wrong, Dad?" she whispered. "What if this really is it?"

He swallowed hard, fighting off a wave of doubt. "I don't know," he admitted, "but we have to believe we weren't misled all these years. It's the only thing that makes sense right now."

They walked through the doors together, directed to a row of tables. "Sit at the first one that opens up," a clerk ordered.

"The Weight of Allegiance"

James and Emily sat at the cold metal table, a sterile tablet resting before them. The room buzzed with low murmurs as others filled the seats at adjacent tables, each holding their new identity cards. A sense of dread hung in the air, heavy and suffocating.

A clerk approached, pushing a small cart. She stopped at their table and handed a second tablet to Emily. Without so much as a glance, the clerk spoke in a flat, mechanical voice, "Insert your new identity cards into the slots on the tablets. These are your new ID cards. Without them, you can't access anything—bank accounts, food, housing. Nothing. You'd better memorize the number, because if you lose it, it could take months to replace, and without it, you don't exist in the system."

James picked up the card, turning it over in his hands. The number was long, a jumbled mess of letters and numbers, but what stood out was the prefix. It began with BENRASHA, the name of the Unifier, followed by a string of characters that looked like an abbreviation of their U.S. state, county, and other identifiers he couldn't make sense of.

Emily stared down at her own card, her face pale. "Dad... this doesn't feel right."

James glanced around, noticing others doing the same—examining their cards, trying to process the enormity of what they were being asked to accept. The clerk continued her monotone explanation.

"You'll need to enter your personal information and answer a few questions. The system will use it to update your records and create your profile for the new global database. Afterward, you'll need to read and agree to the terms, which pledge your allegiance to the Global Faith Initiative and the Unifier."

Emily's breath froze in her throat. "Pledge allegiance... to the Unifier?"

The clerk didn't blink, her words like rehearsed lines. "Yes, to the Global Faith and its leader. This is part of the new order. You've seen the announcements. Now, insert your cards and get started."

The tablets flashed to life as they inserted their cards. Immediately, a series of probing questions appeared on the screen. They were asked about their religious beliefs, their financial situation, and their political views. Some questions were vague, others uncomfortably personal. James felt a knot tightening in his stomach as he answered each one, knowing that this information was no longer just data—it was control.

The last screen appeared, an agreement filled with legal jargon and phrases that turned his blood cold. The text pledged their allegiance to the Global Faith Initiative and declared their loyalty to Ben Resha, the Unifier. James's pulse quickened. They were signing away their faith, their beliefs, their identity—everything that had once been sacred.

"They had to have planned this," James whispered, his voice strained. "All of this... the cards, the tablets, the workers. It's only been a week since his speech, but they've been setting this up for months. Years, even."

Emily stared at the tablet, her fingers trembling above the screen. "I can't do it, Dad. I won't." Tears welled up in her eyes as she shook her head. "I won't betray Mom like this. She'd never agree to this. She'd rather die. Dad, if this is not the Mark, it is just as bad."

James closed his eyes for a moment, his heart aching. He knew Emily's faith was strong, and her loyalty to her mother's memory even stronger. But the consequences of refusal were too great. "Emily... please. We don't have a choice. Without signing, we'll lose everything. We won't survive in this new world."

She shook her head fiercely, her voice choked with emotion. "I don't care. I can't. I won't."

James leaned in, his voice dropping to a harsh whisper. "You don't have to mean it. Just sign the damn thing. We'll figure it out later. But right now, we need to stay in the system. Please, Emily, for both of us. This is not the Mark. It can't be. You remember what Pastor Daniels said."

Her refusal was written on her face, her lips trembling with the words she couldn't say. "I can't, Dad. Something in me is screaming, telling me not to sign it."

James stared at her, torn between fear and desperation. Finally, with a heavy sigh, he turned to his own tablet and pressed his own trembling hand to the screen, signing the agreement with a touch that felt like sealing his fate. The tablet beeped in approval.

Then, in one swift motion, before Emily could stop him, he reached over and pressed her hand to the screen, signing her name.

The tablet flashed, confirming the signature.

Emily gasped, her eyes widening in shock. "Dad! How could you?"

James clenched his jaw, his heart breaking as he turned away. "We'll figure it out," he whispered, but his words felt hollow. The deed was done.

They sat there in heavy silence, the weight of their decision pressing down like an immovable force. There was no turning back.

"Countdown"

Bruce sat on the edge of his cot, his fingers tapping against his thigh in a slow, steady rhythm. One Mississippi... two Mississippi... three Mississippi. He counted the seconds in his head, over and over, just like Lance had suggested. Without a watch, it was the only way to measure time, to make sure he moved when the moment came. When the key was in his hand, he would count out thirty minutes—that was one thousand eight hundred seconds—and then slip out. He had practiced this over and over. But now, as he sat waiting, doubt gnawed at the edges of his mind.

The minutes dragged on, each second feeling heavier than the last. The dim light flickered from the small light above him, casting shadows that danced with every shift as he nervously waited for the key. He clenched his fists, focusing on the rhythm of his breathing. Twenty-two Mississippi... twenty-three Mississippi. His mind began to wander, questioning if this would really work. He had trusted Lance, trusted that the plan was solid, but where was he?

Bruce's pulse quickened as the moments stretched into what felt like an eternity. He replayed Lance's words in his head: I'll give you the key, then you wait exactly thirty minutes, and after that, you make your move. But Lance hadn't shown.

The air in the prison felt thick, oppressive. Something was off. The usual routine of the guards had shifted. There was a tension in the air that Bruce could feel, a subtle shift in the way the guards moved—faster, more urgent. He strained to hear past the thick walls, his heart pounding in his chest.

Whispers traveled through the cells, faint yet insistent, creeping into his ears. He couldn't make out the words at first, but then, like a wave, it came.

"Someone's dead... a prisoner..."

"Did you hear? One of the guards killed her..."

A cold chill ran down Bruce's spine. He leaned closer to the bars, trying to catch more of the hushed voices.

"A woman... killed by one of the guards..."

His heart sank, and for a moment, he couldn't breathe. Sarah. The thought hit him like a punch to the gut. His chest tightened as panic began to claw its way through him. Could it be her? Was Sarah the woman they were talking about? He gripped the bars so tightly his knuckles turned white. The idea lodged itself in his mind, refusing to let go.

"Did you hear which one?" a voice whispered from two cells down.

"I don't know... I just know it was a woman. One of the guards lost it."

Bruce's head swam. He tried to push the thoughts away, tried to tell himself it couldn't be her. Not Sarah. But the whispers carried a weight, and each passing second without an answer felt like it stretched into forever.

He sat back on the cot. The sound of his heartbeat filled his ears. He was supposed to be focused, counting the seconds, waiting for the key. One thousand eight hundred seconds. But his mind was elsewhere now, torn between the ticking time and the dreadful possibility that Sarah— fiery, defiant Sarah—was gone.

The stir among the guards grew louder, footsteps heavy in the corridors, voices sharp with tension. But Lance... Lance never showed.

"Satan Takes Control"

The air in the infernal chamber buzzed with an energy, both sinister and intoxicating. Shadows danced along the stone walls, flickering, as though they, too, were eager participants in the dark proceedings. At the head of the gathering stood Satan, his towering figure casting an ominous presence over the assembly of demonic generals. Even the mightiest of the demon commanders, beings of immense power and dread, seemed small and insignificant in his presence.

Satan was no angel. He was a cherub, a creature, far more ancient and powerful, with a form that embodied both beauty and terror. He had wings, unlike those of the fallen angels around him. His wings were not merely decorative; they radiated an elegance and authority that marked him as superior. Ezekiel's words rang true: "You were the anointed cherub who covers... perfect in beauty" (Ezekiel 28:14-15). Those wings, with their divine craftsmanship, allowed him swift and unmatched movement in battle, a trait that angels could not boast, for they bore no wings.

The room quieted as Satan's deep, resonant voice filled the air. His piercing eyes surveyed his generals—demons that had spread chaos across the earth. War now engulfed the globe, and they reveled in the destruction they had wrought.

"It is time," Satan began, his voice low, yet commanding. "The world burns. Nation rises against nation. The wars have spread like wildfire, and humanity is breaking under the weight of the conflict we have stirred." His lips curled into a sinister smile, as the generals nodded in agreement, their twisted faces alight with satisfaction.

Satan's wings, majestic and terrible, unfurled slightly as he spoke. "But now, we enter the final phase." His gaze darkened, and the very air in the chamber seemed to grow heavier. "I will now enter the vessel we have prepared for so long—Ben Reshan."

He reveled in recounting his past triumphs. "Do you remember, my generals, how I entered Judas?" His voice rose, filled with twisted pride. "I betrayed the Son of God with a kiss. I had Him beaten, scourged, and nailed to a cross. I had Him killed!" His laughter filled the chamber, but the faintest tremor of uncertainty crossed the face of one or two demons who had witnessed the ultimate consequences of that betrayal.

The murmur of approval spread like a dark ripple through the gathering, but one demon's thoughts strayed to a moment in the distant past. Judas, the demon recalled, a shadow of doubt creeping into its mind. When Satan entered Judas, it had backfired. Yes, Judas had betrayed the Messiah, but what had that ultimately accomplished? The demon shuddered, remembering the terrifying truth: Jesus had been crucified, but through His death, He had risen. He had conquered mortal death. That resurrection had sealed their defeat, and worse, it had granted weak, fallen men the power to overcome death, as well.

Now, fear gnawed at the demon's core. Jesus is coming for us, it thought, its mind swirling with dread. This plan—Satan possessing Ben Reshan—what if it only made things worse? What if, in the end, they were unwittingly hastening their own destruction?

"And now," Satan continued, brushing away the past failure with sheer arrogance, "Reshan has been groomed from birth. Every step he has taken has been guided by our hands—his rise to power, his wealth, his influence. It is by our work that the nations bow before him. And now, I will step into him, and the world will be mine."

The demons roared in approval, but beneath their shouts, one could still sense the unease that lay hidden in the hearts of a few. They feared the coming of the One who had already triumphed over death, and they knew that this time, their master's overconfidence might again bring about consequences none of them were prepared to face.

For now, however, Satan's mind was set. Ben Reshan, the man who had been shaped by demonic influence since childhood, would be his vessel. The time had come for Satan to take full control and wield his power on earth as never before. The ultimate plan was in motion.

Unseen by most in the room, a shadow of doubt lingered, but for now, war and chaos reigned supreme. And in Satan's eyes, that was victory enough.

7

MARK UNSEEN

"Silent Allegiance"

The market buzzed with the sounds of daily life, yet an air of unease seemed to linger in the crowd. Stalls, lined with fresh fruits, vegetables, and processed goods, stretched out beneath the shadow of sleek digital terminals. The once-familiar clink of coins and rustle of cash had vanished, replaced by the quiet hum of transactions initiated by the mere swipe of a card or the entry of a number.

James watched from a distance, his eyes tracing the movements of shoppers, each one walking up to the clerk and producing a small, sleek card. Some held the card up proudly, as if it were a badge of honor. Others, though, approached the counters with a weary tension, as if they were navigating a system they barely understood.

A woman stood at one of the terminals ahead, nervously fumbling in her pockets. She turned to her husband, who was holding their daughter's hand, panic flashing across her face.

"I... I can't find the card," she stammered, her voice shaking. "It must have slipped out somewhere."

Her husband's face drained of color, and he immediately fished his phone out of his pocket, dialing home. "Check the drawer next to the fridge," he said into the phone, his voice tight with urgency. "I wrote it down there."

Minutes felt like hours as the woman stood frozen, her hand trembling at her side. The clerk behind the counter tapped impatiently, waiting for the number. When the call finally ended, the man spoke quickly, reading off a string of digits.

The clerk frowned, pausing before entering the number into the system. The moment she did, a photo of the woman appeared on the screen, her image clear and unmistakable. The clerk glanced from the photo to the woman standing in front of her, nodding in quiet approval. "Alright. It matches. You're good to go."

Relief washed over the couple, but the fear remained etched on their faces as they hurriedly gathered their purchases. James watched as they left, a cold shiver running down his spine. The system was airtight—no one could buy or sell without their card or number. It was efficient, yet it was a system that ruled over them all, demanding not only submission but active participation in their own subjugation. Losing that number meant losing everything. It was life itself.

James and Emily sat with Pastor Daniels in the dim light of the underground church, the weight of the world pressing on them like a suffocating fog. They described what they had seen at the market—the new system, the cards, and how everything was controlled by the digital transactions. James explained how people had to sign an agreement, pledging allegiance to the new global religion and the Unifier, just to receive their card and access basic necessities. It was clear to all of them now: this wasn't just a new financial system or technological advance—it was something far more sinister. Something spiritual.

Pastor Daniels, leaning over an open Bible, spoke with a voice heavy with conviction. "This isn't the first time people have been marked. Remember Ezekiel's vision? God commanded that a mark be placed on the foreheads of those who grieved over the sin and abominations in Jerusalem. It was a spiritual mark, invisible to the naked eye, but seen by God."

He paused, his eyes lifting slowly to meet James and Emily's. "I always thought the mark in Revelation would be clear, something we could physically see. But now... now I'm starting to think I was wrong." His voice trembled slightly, the weight of his admission sinking in. "I see it differently now."

He leaned back, his eyes searching their faces for understanding. "The mark may not be visible to us, but God had shown it to John in his vision in a way he could make it known to us. It could be a mark of the heart, a spiritual sign of allegiance—a mark only God can see. I thought it had to be on the right hand or the forehead, something that couldn't be missed. But I realize now that the real mark doesn't need to be seen by our eyes. You said the people in the market said they were told to memorize the number if they lost the card. Remembering the number would explain the vision of the forehead, and holding the card fits the vision of the hand." He trailed off, the realization settling heavily.

His gaze shifted downward, then back to them, his voice lowering. "It's not just the card or the number that marks them—it's the choice they made to get it. The moment they signed that pledge, the moment they swore allegiance to the system and its leader, that's when they were marked. Their decision to surrender their faith, to place their trust in the

Unifier instead of Christ, sealed it. They may not bear a visible mark, but spiritually, they've aligned themselves with the Antichrist."

He looked at James and Emily with a deep sorrow in his eyes, as if carrying the burden of his past teachings. "It's the same with us. Christians are marked by God through faith and obedience. The world can't see it, but God knows who we belong to. And now, I understand that the Mark may not be what I said it was, not a visible symbol, but they are marked by pledging their loyalty to Satan through this system."

He paused, as if overwhelmed by the gravity of his revelation. "I thought I understood Revelation, but I see now that the mark was never meant to be something obvious. It's always been about the heart. And now I realize how many I may have misled." His voice broke as he finished, the air thick with the weight of his words.

James's face paled as Pastor Daniels' words sank in. His voice wavered as he spoke, the weight of his guilt pressing down on him. "But I... I signed it, Pastor. I signed the agreement. And not just for me—I used Emily's hand to sign it for her too. What have I done?" His hands trembled as he looked down, the gravity of his actions nearly overwhelming him.

Emily, her eyes filled with anguish, leaned forward, her voice rising in frustration. "But it says in Revelation that the mark will be in the hand and the forehead! That's what I read, Pastor! I didn't see any mark when Dad made me sign it, so how can this be the same thing? How can it be the mark if there's nothing there?"

Pastor Daniels, keeping his calm, gently closed the Bible before him. He leaned in, his voice steady but urgent. "Emily, let me try again. What John saw in his vision wasn't necessarily a physical mark like we would expect. It was a vision given to him to reveal the truth about the future. How else could John understand that people were being spiritually marked, set apart by their allegiance to the Antichrist? The vision of the number in the hand represented people physically holding the card with the number on it. When John saw the number in the forehead, it symbolized how people would memorize and retain that number in their minds, making it a part of their very thoughts and identity. When you and your father signed that agreement, it wasn't just a formality. You swore loyalty, not to a system, but to a man, to a leader who carries the number of the Antichrist. Ben Rashan!"

He paused, letting the gravity of his words sink in. "You didn't need a visible mark because that signature was the act that aligned your heart and mind with him. That's what John saw, people pledging their lives, their souls, to something other than God, and in doing so, being marked. The card, the number, the name Ben Rashan..."

Emily's lip quivered as tears welled up in her eyes, the realization hitting her like a tidal wave. She shook her head, standing up and backing away, her voice cracking with the weight of her pain. She turned to her father and raised her voice. "I didn't want to sign it... I knew it was wrong. But you—you grabbed my hand. You made me sign it."

Her sobs broke through as she collapsed to her knees, her hands covering her face. "I didn't want to, I didn't want to. I told you something inside of me was screaming, 'Don't sign it! "She said, her voice dropping to a whisper as the guilt and anguish consumed her.

James's heart shattered as he watched his daughter crumble before him. His own tears flowed freely as he knelt beside her, placing a trembling hand on her shoulder. "I thought I was protecting you, Emily. I didn't understand... I'm so sorry."

James wept, the enormity of it all sinking in. He had been thinking about the pledge he signed, the way he was entered into the system, carrying the number in their hand and their minds. The scripture echoed in his mind: "He causeth all, both small and great, rich and poor, free and bond, to receive a mark in their right hand, or in their foreheads." Revelation 13:16.

The world had expected a physical mark—something obvious, something unmistakable. But that wasn't how it worked. The number, the card, the memorization of that number—it was all about control. Once the number was assigned, the system had them.

Pastor Daniels flipped to John 8:44, reading aloud before he could stop himself. "You are of your father, the devil, and your will is to do your father's desires." He paused, his face darkened by the weight of the words. "I'm sorry, I should not have read that to you," he said, then continued. "Jesus spoke of those who would follow Satan, and now, they're being marked. Not with something physical, but with something more binding. They've pledged their allegiance, and Satan has claimed them. They're his children now." Pastor Daniels cursed himself in his thoughts. Why did I tell them that? I am making it worse for them.

Emily's face was pale, her eyes wide with fear. "But it's just a card... it's not a real mark," she whispered, clinging to a sliver of hope.

Pastor Daniels shook his head slowly. "It doesn't matter if we can see it or not. Just like God's mark on His people is spiritual, this mark is Satan's—a mark that only Heaven can see, but it binds the soul all the same. You've given their allegiance to get the number, and in doing so, they've become children of the father of lies. Just as Jesus said, 'You are of your father, the devil.'"

Again, Pastor Daniels was shocked at the harsh words he spoke.

James's face turned red, his fists clenched tightly by his sides. He felt a surge of anger that had been building since the realization of what he'd done. He could no longer hold back.

"You know what, Pastor?" he said, his voice rising. "I trusted you! I trusted everything you taught us, and that's why I signed it. You told us the pre-tribulation rapture was a guarantee. You made it clear that we wouldn't be here for any of this—that the mark would be something visible, something we'd have no doubt about. But now you're telling us that I've given my soul to Satan?"

Emily flinched at the harshness in his tone, but James couldn't stop. He pointed an accusing finger at Daniels, his voice seething with betrayal. "You preached there would be a great deception during the end times. You told us that even the elect could be deceived, if that were possible. You said it wasn't possible. You warned us about those who would mislead the faithful. But you never once thought that it could be you, did you? You're the one who deceived us, Pastor! You told us this could never happen, that we'd be raptured out before any of this started. Now look at where we are. Because of what you said, I took the mark, and I made Emily take it too!"

Tears blurred James's vision, his anger giving way to a wave of deep regret. He dropped to his knees, burying his face in his hands. "I never thought it would be like this. I was just trying to protect her... but I ended up dooming us both."

Pastor Daniels' shoulders slumped under the crushing weight of James's accusations. His voice was barely audible as he responded, "James, I never meant to deceive anyone. I was convinced of what I believed, and I thought it was true. But maybe... maybe I was the one who was deceived all along."

James looked up, his anger mingled with desperation. "You were more than deceived. You were the one who led us into this deception. You told us not to worry, to be calm, and now we're trapped."

For a moment, the room was silent, the tension thick enough to cut. Then James's expression shifted. He took a deep, shaky breath, trying to steady himself. "I have to forgive you, Pastor. I knew not to sign it; there was a voice inside of me screaming too, screaming not to sign it. I made the easy choice. I used you as an excuse. I signed the papers. I knew in my gut it was wrong, but I did it anyway. I was weak, and I just wanted to believe what you said because it was easier than facing what would happen if I didn't sign."

Daniels' eyes were filled with sorrow, a deep sadness that seemed to age him in an instant. "I don't know what to say... I'm so sorry."

Daniels placed his hand over James's, his voice barely above a whisper. "I... I'm..." He tried to speak, but the words wouldn't come. His voice broke, and he fell silent, overcome by the gravity of what he had done. What he caused.

James and Emily slowly rose, their faces etched with exhaustion and sorrow. Without another word, they left the dimly lit room, the weight of their shattered faith heavy on their shoulders. The door clicked shut behind them, leaving Pastor Daniels alone in the stillness, swallowed by the silence that followed.

As the minutes stretched, the reality of what had transpired settled over Daniels like a suffocating blanket. His shoulders slumped, and he felt a wave of nausea rise within him. How many? The question battered against his mind, relentless and merciless. How many people had I misled? How many had taken the mark, believing it could not be the mark of the beast because of what I preached?

The room seemed darker now, the shadows deeper, as if the very walls bore witness to his failure. He pressed his hands to his face, trying to hold back the tide of emotions threatening to overwhelm him, but it was futile. Tears broke free, hot and bitter, streaming down his cheeks as he collapsed to his knees, his strength gone.

"God... Oh God, what have I done?" he cried, his voice hoarse and broken. His words echoed in the emptiness, a desperate plea that seemed to fall flat in the stale air. For the first time in years, Daniels felt the full weight of his own arrogance—a pride that had blinded him, that had kept him from even considering the possibility that his interpretation could be wrong.

He had been so certain. He had spoken with such authority, with such confidence, never allowing room for doubt, never humbling himself before the mysteries of prophecy. He had preached the pre-tribulation rapture as an absolute certainty, convinced that believers would be spared from the horrors of the tribulation. He had been adamant that the mark of the beast would be obvious, undeniable, and unmistakable. But now, he saw his pride for what it was—arrogance masquerading as faith.

His body shook with deep, heaving sobs, each one wracking his frame like a physical blow. "I thought I was helping them, guiding them," he whispered, his voice trembling. "But I led them into darkness. I was so sure, so sure..." His words trailed off as the crushing realization hit him anew. "I never even considered that I could be wrong."

He fell prostrate on the cold floor, his face pressed against the unforgiving concrete. "Forgive me, Lord," he begged, his voice choked with desperation. "Forgive me for my pride, for my arrogance, for failing to approach Your Word with humility. I thought I understood Your plan, but I was blind—blind to my own ignorance, blind to the truth."

The memories of his sermons flooded back, each one laced with the confidence that now felt like poison. He had warned of the dangers of false teachings, of deception, but he had never thought to question his own understanding. He had been so quick to dismiss other interpretations, so quick to label them as misguided or heretical. And in doing so, he had shut out any possibility that God might have been trying to show him a different perspective.

His chest tightened with a grief that felt too large to contain. "How many souls, Lord? How many are lost because of me?" His voice broke again, barely audible. He pounded the floor with a clenched fist, not out of anger, but out of a soul-deep anguish that words could not express. "I led them astray. I led them straight into the enemy's hands."

For years, he had dismissed warnings from others who suggested that the church might actually endure the tribulation, that believers would face persecution before the end. He had scoffed at interpretations that implied suffering instead of escape, convinced they were misguided. "I was so certain," he whispered, the words like a confession torn from his soul. "I was so certain we'd be gone before it all started... and that certainty led them to take the mark."

The room was silent, save for his ragged breaths and quiet sobs. He felt utterly alone, stripped of the confident preacher's facade he had worn for so long. But beneath the weight of his remorse, there was a glimmer of something else—a raw, painful honesty that he had never allowed himself to face.

"I should have been humble, Lord," he wept, his words now coming in a steady flow of repentance. "I should have approached prophecy with an open heart, knowing that I am just a man, flawed and limited in my understanding. I let pride guide me instead of Your Spirit." He paused, his face wet with tears, his voice breaking with sincerity. "I thought I was defending the truth, but I was only defending my own beliefs."

He lay there for what felt like an eternity, his heart laid bare before God. The weight of his failures pressed down on him, and he did not try to escape it. He welcomed the crushing sorrow, knowing it was the only honest response to the depth of his mistakes.

"I can't change what I've done," he whispered, his voice barely audible now. "I can't undo the harm, the deception. But please, God, show me mercy. Show me how to make this right, if it can be made right. I can't carry this alone."

In that moment, something shifted within him. It wasn't relief—far from it—but a strange, painful sense of clarity. He had spent his life trying to understand the mysteries of God's Word, but he had forgotten the most essential truth of all: humility before the Almighty. He had treated prophecy like a puzzle to be solved, a certainty to be grasped, rather than a divine mystery to be approached with reverence and awe.

His voice fell to a whisper as he offered his final plea. "Lord, help me to be humble from now on. Help me to listen, to seek Your truth above all else. I have failed You, but I beg for Your mercy. Not for my sake, but for theirs—for all those I led astray."

For the first time, he felt a strange, painful sense of release—a release not from the consequences of his actions, but from the blinding pride that had ensnared him for so long. He would carry the weight of his mistakes, but now he would carry it with the humility that he had so desperately lacked.

"Let me be a warning, Lord," he prayed, his voice soft but resolute. "Let my failure be a lesson to others. If nothing else, use this broken vessel to show the danger of pride and the necessity of approaching Your Word with humility. I don't deserve it, but I ask for Your grace."

He lay there, exhausted and empty, but also strangely at peace. The repentance was not complete—it never would be—but it was genuine, raw, and real. It was the first step on a path that would be long and painful, but one that was finally rooted in truth.

"Have mercy, Lord," he whispered one last time, his voice barely audible. "Have mercy."

And then, in the stillness of the dimly lit room, Pastor Daniels remained alone—broken, repentant, and truly humbled. He realized now that prophecy held many possible interpretations, each one beyond his human certainty. The true meaning had been clear only as it unfolded, revealed by God in His timing. Before the God he had failed to fully comprehend, Daniels wept, finally understanding that divine truth could not be confined to his limited understanding.

"The Awakening"

Sarah's eyes fluttered open as the harsh brightness above her pierced through the fog in her mind. Her body was stiff and cold, her muscles unresponsive. She couldn't move. Panic surged through her veins as she struggled to lift even a finger, but nothing obeyed her will. Her breath came in shallow gasps, her chest tight with fear.

The room was sterile, almost painfully white, with harsh fluorescent lights glaring down from the ceiling. The gurney she lay on was cold beneath her, the thin hospital gown barely a barrier against its chill, but she could not feel it. Machines beeped softly around her, their monotonous rhythm a cruel contrast to the storm raging inside her mind.

Her throat tightened, her pulse quickened. She tried to scream, but no sound escaped her dry lips. Why couldn't she move? Her mind raced, flooding with terrifying possibilities. Had the guard's assault broken something inside her? Was this how she would spend the rest of her life—trapped in her own body, helpless?

Tears welled up in her eyes as she fought to keep from spiraling into despair. "God... please, help me," she whispered silently, her soul reaching out in desperation. She had been through hell, but this... this felt like the end.

As the tears spilled down her cheeks, Sarah's thoughts tumbled back to the moment everything had snapped. The stress, the constant abuse, the isolation—it had been buried deep inside. That day, she panicked and reacted in a way she hadn't thought herself capable of. It was as though every ounce of rage, every bit of hurt she had buried deep inside, came rushing to the surface in one explosive moment when she saw the guard taking Rebecca out of the re-education room. She had screamed at the guards, cursed at them, and defied them.

And then the Taser. The electric current had ripped through her body, sending her crumbling to the ground in convulsions. She remembered the searing pain, the darkness closing in. After that, there had been nothing but cold and fear. And now, here she was—paralyzed and broken, lying on this gurney like a corpse waiting to be claimed.

A sob escaped her as she thought back to when they first placed her into her cell. She had been terrified, her body aching from falling to the floor and the effects of the Taser, her spirit shattered. But it was in that cold, empty cell that she had finally reached the end of herself. In that moment of complete brokenness, she had a real, soul-shaking come-to-Jesus moment. She had cried out to Him, not with words, but with the raw, desperate need of her heart.

And He had answered.

The peace that flooded her soul that day had been unlike anything she had ever known. It wasn't the peace of freedom or safety—it was deeper, more profound. Even as her body bore the marks of abuse, her spirit soared with a freedom that no cage or captor could take from her. She had felt truly alive, even in the midst of hell.

Now, as Sarah lay paralyzed, fear began to creep back in. Her flesh, her human weakness, wanted to take control. Her heart raced, her mind swirling with dread. But she couldn't go back to that place of fear, that prison of anxiety. Not after her mind and spirit had tasted a peace that defied understanding.

It was in her cell, that first day she reached out as never before: "God... Holy Spirit..." Her silent prayer rose from the depths of her soul, her tears flowing freely. "Please... I need You. I can't do this alone. I'm begging You, Lord, fill me with unbreakable faith. Make me stronger than my fear, stronger than my flesh. Take control of my heart, my mind, my body. I need You..."

In that cold, sterile moment, her mind rebelled. A flood of doubt and fear surged through her, threatening to drown the fragile peace she was reaching for. What if there was no way out? What if she was abandoned, alone in this place of torment? Her heart pounded in her chest, a desperate rhythm that mirrored the chaos in her soul. "God... where are You? Have You left me here?" she thought, the words barely forming in her mind, fragile as glass.

The silence in the room seemed deafening, pressing in on her, squeezing her heart. For a moment, she felt nothing—just the crushing weight of despair. But she held on, a single thread of faith tethering her to the hope she had once known.

In that moment, something shifted. It wasn't dramatic or loud. It wasn't a sudden bolt of lightning or an audible voice. It was something much more intimate—a presence, a warmth that filled the room that filled her very soul. The fear, the panic—all of it began to fade. She felt the Holy Spirit, as personal and real as if He were sitting beside her, gently wrapping her in a love that was stronger than anything she had ever known.

Then, in the stillness, it came. At first, it was barely perceptible, like a whisper carried on the wind, a warmth she couldn't explain. Slowly, it grew, a presence so gentle yet so overwhelming, it was as though a light had pierced the darkness surrounding her. It wasn't in the room; it was inside her.

As the warmth filled her chest, Sarah's breath **stilled for a moment,** the tension in her muscles slowly releasing. Her tears flowed freely now, but they were no longer tears of fear—they were tears of surrender. "I can't do this alone," she whispered, her heart breaking open. And that's when she felt it—the unmistakable presence of the Holy Spirit, like a river of peace flooding every corner of her soul.

The fear hadn't disappeared, but it was swallowed by something far greater. It was as if the weight of her burden had been lifted from her shoulders, replaced by a peace so deep, she couldn't find words to describe it. The very presence of God enveloped her, filling every crack and crevice of her broken spirit.

And then came the joy.

It started softly, like the first light of dawn after the darkest night. It didn't make sense—not in this place, not in the middle of such pain. But it was there, growing brighter, more powerful, until it became overwhelming. The joy was so pure, so consuming, it took her breath away. She wasn't just alive—she was alive in Christ, more than she had ever been.

Tears of gratitude streamed down her face as her chest heaved with silent sobs. She was loved. She was held by the One who had promised to never leave her. The joy was not of this world—it was the joy of knowing she was His, no matter what this place did to her body, no matter what tomorrow held.

For the first time in her life, she felt truly alive. More alive than she had felt before the camp. She was loved, cherished, and held by the Creator of the universe. A joy bubbled up within her, so overwhelming it made her weep. Not with sadness, but with pure, unfiltered joy.

In the joy her thoughts shifted to the day she had met Bruce. She remembered the way he had looked at her, the confusion in his eyes. He had seen something radiating from her—a peace and joy that didn't belong in a place like this. He had been drawn to her, unable to explain why.

But Sarah knew why. It wasn't her—it was God. The Holy Spirit flowed through her, a river of life in a wasteland of despair. And Bruce, lost in his own fear and anger, had felt it. That day, when their eyes met through the bars of her cell door, something inside him shifted. He needed something he didn't have, though he didn't fully understand it yet. As they talked, he was changed by the presence of the One who had given her peace, in a place where there was no peace. Sarah spoke words of truth his ears had never heard before, and in that moment, he simply believed. The presence of the Spirit was strong.

Sarah felt that same presence now, as she lay on the gurney. Her body might be paralyzed, but her spirit was more alive than ever. She wasn't afraid anymore. The Holy Spirit was with her, and that was enough.

"Thank You, Lord," she whispered silently, her tears drying as the overwhelming love of God filled her soul. "Thank You for reminding me who I am. I'm Yours, and no matter what happens to me, You will never leave me."

As Sarah rested in that truth, she felt a subtle tingling in her fingers, then her toes. Slowly, ever so slowly, she began to regain feeling in her body. Though her body remained still, she could feel the paralysis slowly loosening its grip, as if the very presence of the Holy Spirit was flowing through her, gently restoring her. Every subtle shift in sensation felt like a deliberate act of grace, a quiet miracle unfolding within her. She wasn't fighting to regain control—He was granting it, piece by piece. As she surrendered herself completely to His will, she gained control. The warmth of God's presence surrounded her, and she knew that no matter what came next, she would face it with unshakable faith.

"Blast"

Pastor Daniels walked the narrow alleyways of the old downtown area, his heart heavy but resolute. The towering courthouse, with its weathered bricks and faded grandeur, loomed over the surrounding streets. It was a symbol of authority and justice, but also a reminder of a world that was slipping away. He moved quietly, his hands buried deep in his worn coat, blending in with the homeless men and women scattered throughout the area.

They had always been his people—the forgotten, the lost. Over the years, Pastor Daniels had spent countless hours with them, listening to their stories and sharing in their pain. Many nights, when the world seemed too heavy, he found solace among them, where titles and status meant nothing. They knew him not as a preacher, but as a friend, a man who brought them food, blankets, and hope. Now, in the madness of the unfolding world, he found safety in their midst.

He had been on the run for weeks, hiding in plain sight. The authorities were looking for anyone who refused to bow to the new system, and Pastor Daniels was high on that list. The underground church he now led had become a lifeline for those holding onto their faith, and the basement where they gathered had been a sanctuary—hidden and safe, for now.

Here among the homeless, he felt an odd sense of belonging. These were people who had no ties to the new world order, no cards or numbers to speak of. They lived on the fringes of society, and for them, nothing had really changed. The system didn't care about them—they were ghosts in their own city.

Pastor Daniels nodded to a man sitting against a wall, his face shadowed by the brim of a filthy hat. "Good to see you, Rev," the man said, his voice gravelly but warm. "Word's been goin' round that things are gettin' worse out there. But here, it's just the same old struggle, ain't it?"

Daniels quickly raised a finger to his lips, signaling the man to be cautious. The title "Rev" was a dangerous giveaway, and he couldn't afford to be identified as a pastor in this environment. After a brief pause, Daniels smiled weakly and crouched beside him. "It's getting bad, Roy. Real bad. But God's still with us. We've just got to keep faith."

Roy laughed bitterly, shaking his head. "Faith? That's all some of us got left. But you... you still got hope. And that's somethin'."

Before Pastor Daniels could respond, a sudden roar filled the air. The sound was so deafening, so violent, it felt like the earth itself was being ripped apart. A blinding flash erupted from the courthouse steps, followed by a massive explosion that shook the very ground beneath them. Daniels was thrown sideways, crashing into the side of a building. His ears rang, the world around him spinning as screams filled the air.

He forced his eyes open, his body trembling from the impact. Blood trickled down from a gash on his scalp where his head had slammed into the wall. The courthouse—a symbol of authority—was now a smoldering ruin, its front reduced to rubble, engulfed in flames. Debris was scattered in every direction as thick clouds of smoke billowed into the sky. Bodies lay strewn across the street—men, women, children— all victims of the blast. Some were eerily still, lifeless, while others writhed in agony, their desperate cries for help blending with the chaos around him.

Daniels pushed himself to his knees, blood dripping onto his coat. His vision blurred, but he could still make out the wreckage and the wounded. His heart raced as he saw the familiar faces of those he had spent years ministering to—the homeless who had become like family to him. They were among the casualties, some dead, others clinging to life.

"No... no..." he whispered, crawling toward the nearest person, an elderly woman named Agnes, who had once shared her last piece of bread with him. Her body lay crumpled, her eyes vacant. He could barely breathe as the pain of loss twisted in his chest.

He reached another man, hands shaking as he touched his shoulder. "Hang on. Stay with me," he urged, but the man's eyes were already glazed over, his soul embracing freedom.

Pastor Daniels' hands were stained with blood, his own grief threatening to consume him. But he couldn't stop. He had to help.

"Pastor..." a voice rasped weakly behind him. He turned to see Roy, clutching his side, blood seeping through his fingers.

"Roy!" Daniels rushed to him, pressing his hands over the wound, trying to stem the flow of blood. "Just hold on. We're gonna get you out of here."

But before he could do anything more, the wail of sirens pierced the chaos. Red and blue lights flashed in the distance as police vehicles and emergency teams raced toward the scene. His heart sank. The authorities were coming—and they were looking for him.

Roy coughed, his grip on Daniels' arm tightening. "You gotta go, Rev. They'll take you in if they find you."

"No, I can't leave you like this," Daniels argued, tears welling in his eyes.

"You ain't got no choice," Roy wheezed, his voice weak but resolute. "This place ain't safe no more. You're a marked man, Pastor. If they catch you here..."

Daniels froze, the reality of the situation crashing down on him. He had to leave. If they found him now, he'd be arrested—maybe worse. But how could he abandon these people? How could he turn his back on them when they needed him most?

His mind raced as he scanned the wreckage, the police closing in. He couldn't stay. Not now.

With a heavy heart, he made a decision. He pressed his hand to Roy's wound once more, praying over him. "Lord, keep him safe. Protect him. Please."

Roy gave a weak smile. "I'll be alright. Get goin', Rev."

Pastor Daniels quickly raised a finger to his lips, signaling the man to be cautious.

"Oops, sorry, Rev," Roy whispered, realizing his mistake. "Sorry."

Daniels smiled faintly, but his eyes were heavy with concern. Reluctantly, he rose to his feet, casting one final, sorrowful glance at the devastation around him. The faces of the dead and wounded would haunt him, but he knew he had no choice. Pulling his hood over his head, he slipped into the shadows, moving swiftly through the alleys. If they arrested him, he'd lose his chance to continue helping those on the streets—and the believers who still depended on him.

The sound of the sirens grew louder as the police arrived on the scene, and Daniels could hear their shouts as they searched the area. The wounded were being helped, too.

He slipped down a side street, his heart pounding in his chest, knowing he had narrowly escaped. But the pain of leaving behind those he loved, those who had trusted him, weighed heavy on his soul. The rider of the red horse had brought more than just death and destruction to his city—he had unleashed chaos, igniting old tensions, fanning the flames of hatred, and turning neighbor against neighbor. What once had been a place of uneasy peace now teetered on the edge of war and madness. The courthouse, once a symbol of order and authority, now lay in ruins, a stark reminder that no place was safe from the spreading violence.

Pastor Daniels could feel the darkness closing in, the fear and distrust that crept through the city like a poison. The red horseman had ridden into their lives, sowing division, and the result was carnage on every street corner, every home, and in every heart. The world was unraveling, and the madness threatened to consume them all.

As he fled through the darkened streets, Pastor Daniels prayed for strength, for protection, but most of all, for guidance. He knew that the forces behind this destruction were more than mere human conflict—something spiritual had shifted, and now, more than ever, he needed to be the shepherd his people deserved, even if it meant sacrificing everything. He prayed for wisdom, for the courage to stand against the rising tide of violence, even as the world around him was falling apart.

The rider of the red horse had delivered his blow, and now it was up to those who still believed in the power of faith to hold the line, to resist the madness, even as war threatened to engulf them all.

"A Narrow Escape"

Emily's voice rose, frustration bubbling over as they walked briskly down the dimly lit hallway toward their apartment. "Dad, why won't you let me come with you to the underground church in the basement? I'm not a child! I have the right to be there!"

James clenched his jaw, his hand gripping the strap of the bag slung over his shoulder. "Emily, it's not safe for you. I've told you that a thousand times. I can't risk you getting caught."

Her steps quickened to keep pace with him. "Risk? I'm already at risk! We all are! If they find out you've been going, they'll come for both of us. I need to be with other believers, Dad. I need to—"

They rounded the corner, and Emily's voice cut off abruptly as they came face-to-face with Mrs. Kincaid, an elderly woman who had lived in their building for years. Her gray hair was pinned back neatly, and she clutched a grocery bag in one hand, her expression one of shock and suspicion.

"Church? What church?" she demanded, her voice sharp, eyes narrowing as she looked between them.

James froze, his heart pounding in his chest. "Mrs. Kincaid," he stammered, forcing a nervous smile. "It's, uh, not what you think."

The old woman stepped closer, her face tight with alarm. "Did I hear you say church? Are you talking about one of those illegal gatherings?

130

You know the government's banned those! It's dangerous—nothing but trouble!"

Emily's heart raced, and she shot her father a panicked glance. "No, no, Mrs. Kincaid, we weren't talking about that. I was just, uh, telling Dad about a documentary I watched—about old churches. You know, back when they were still legal." She laughed awkwardly, but the sound was hollow, desperate.

Mrs. Kincaid's eyes narrowed even more, her grip tightening on the grocery bag. "A documentary? Hmm..." She looked them over, suspicion etched deep in the lines of her face. "You young ones are too bold for your own good. Don't go playing with fire. There are eyes and ears everywhere, and I won't tolerate anything that spreads hate."

She stepped closer, her voice lowering to a conspiratorial whisper, her breath sour with age. "You know, I've seen others in this building disappear for less than that. It starts with talk of religion, of church, and then—poof!—they're gone. You'd be wise to keep your mouths shut. People are watching, and some of us aren't afraid to report things that look suspicious."

Mrs. Kincaid glanced around the hall, as if expecting someone to emerge from the shadows, before fixing her cold gaze on Emily. "And I'm always watching."

James nodded quickly, trying to maintain a calm demeanor. "Absolutely, Mrs. Kincaid. We wouldn't dream of doing anything that could get us in trouble. It was just a conversation about a documentary, nothing more."

The old woman stared at them for a long, uncomfortable moment, her lips pressed into a thin line. "Hmm," she muttered again, before turning to walk down the hall, casting one last glance over her shoulder.

James grabbed Emily's arm, steering her toward their apartment door. They walked the last few steps in silence, their earlier argument replaced by a suffocating tension. James fumbled for his keys, his hands shaking as he unlocked the door and hurried them both inside.

The door slammed shut behind them with a loud, abrupt thud. Both of them stood there for a moment, frozen, barely daring to breathe. Emily's face was pale, her hands trembling.

"We were so careless," James muttered, running a hand through his hair. "What if she reports us?"

Emily swallowed hard, her eyes wide with fear. "I didn't mean to... I wasn't thinking."

"I know," James replied softly, pacing the room. "We've got to be more careful. One slip, and they'll be knocking on our door."

Emily hugged herself tightly, her back pressed against the wall as she slid down to the floor, her mind spiraling into panic. "What if she tells someone, Dad?" Her voice trembled, barely above a whisper. "What if they come for us? We can't go into hiding yet. What if Mom gets released, and we're hiding?" Tears welled in her eyes as she shook her head, the weight of fear almost unbearable. "We have to stay here. I'm so stupid! Stupid! Stupid! It's all my fault for arguing with you about church!"

James exhaled slowly, but the heaviness in his chest remained. He knelt beside her, his hand hovering near her arm, hesitant to touch her, unsure how to calm her spiraling thoughts. His voice was thick with concern, guilt gnawing at him. "Emily, we have to stay calm. That's all we can do now. Pray she doesn't say anything. Pray God protects us. And keep an eye out for anything that might be a sign she's reported us." His words hung in the air, heavy with dread.

Silence swallowed the room, wrapping them in a suffocating fog of anxiety. The walls seemed to close in on them as the weight of how close they were to disaster settled heavily on their hearts.

8

WORLD ABLAZE

"Fire from the Sky"

The world seemed to hold its breath, the stillness of night broken by the sudden roar of violence that erupted across three coasts of America. Lurking below the surface of the Pacific, Atlantic, and Gulf, submarines—unseen, unknown—launched their payloads. The missiles streaked through the night sky in deadly arcs of fire, each destined for a different target—strategic, precise, and catastrophic.

Onlookers stood frozen as the first missile struck a major military installation on the West Coast, obliterating the base in a blinding flash. The fiery explosion spread out in waves, engulfing everything in its path. Within seconds, fires erupted across the surrounding forests and towns, choking the air with thick, black smoke. Panic surged through the streets as people ran, their terrified screams echoing through the burning ruins. Sirens wailed, but it was too late.

At the same moment, the East Coast trembled beneath the impact of a missile that ripped through the heart of a major port city. Ships were blown to pieces in the harbor, their remnants sinking into the water. The skyline lit up like a second sun as buildings crumbled, collapsing into piles of rubble. Firestorms spread rapidly as the city became a battlefield of chaos, with people screaming for mercy that would never come.

In the South, the Gulf Coast faced its own reckoning as the third missile struck. Refineries exploded in fiery plumes that lit up the night like a hellish beacon, black smoke blotting out the stars. Flames danced across the skyline, consuming everything in their path, while terrified families fled their homes, seeking shelter where none could be found. In the distance, demons moved unseen, feeding on the fear, twisting the minds of those in positions to respond.

The devastation didn't end with the missile strikes. Across the nation, chaos spread like wildfire, fueled by an unseen, sinister force. Enemies of America—nations that had long schemed for its downfall—had successfully infiltrated the country. They sent waves of sleeper agents, slipping through the southern border under the guise of immigrants. But these individuals weren't seeking safety or refuge; their mission was purely one of destruction. These were no ordinary rioters; they had been carefully placed, biding their time, waiting for the signal to act.

The missile attack, though unexpected by them, was taken as an omen, a divine cue to commence their plan. Though uncoordinated in the physical realm, the timing was no accident—spiritually, it was perfectly synchronized. Demonic forces, long whispering into the hearts of men, now unleashed their full power, fueling the hatred and chaos. Fires ignited in cities across the land, consuming entire neighborhoods. Streets once alive with the hum of daily life were now battlefields.

Looting, violence, and death spread like a plague, turning America's proud cities into war zones. The demons, who had fanned the flames of hatred for years, reveled in the destruction, watching with glee as the country descended into madness.

Phones went down. Power grids collapsed. Social media feeds vanished, leaving only static and silence. The once vibrant world of communication, news, and connection fell into darkness, leaving people isolated in their fear and confusion. It was as if the very lifeblood of society had been severed.

In the midst of this chaos, demonic forces fed hungrily on the despair. Invisible but ever-present, they whispered lies into the ears of the broken, fanning the flames of hatred and division. Violence was no longer just a physical act—it had become spiritual warfare, with the world teetering on the brink of total destruction.

James stood frozen in his living room, the news report flickering across the screen in front of him. His heart pounded in his chest as the scenes of destruction unfolded before his eyes—fires raging, buildings crumbling, and people screaming. He could barely process what he was seeing. America, the land he had known his entire life, was being torn apart.

Emily sat on the couch, her knees drawn to her chest, her eyes wide with fear. "Dad... what's happening?" Her voice was small, almost childlike. "Is this it? Is this the end?"

James didn't answer right away. His mind raced with the enormity of what was happening. He had felt it coming—this darkness that had been creeping over the world—but he hadn't imagined it would strike with such devastating force. He could feel the presence of evil in the very air, thick and oppressive.

"We've been attacked," he finally whispered, his voice shaking. "I am afraid this is only the beginning."

Emily's eyes filled with tears. "But... what are we supposed to do? How can we survive this?"

James sank onto the couch beside her, putting his arm around her shoulders. "We can't fight it, not like this. But we can pray. We can trust that God will protect us, that He has a plan even in this madness."

Emily shook her head, tears slipping down her cheeks. "But what if He doesn't, Dad? What if we don't make it?"

James tightened his grip on her, his own fear threatening to overwhelm him. "We'll make it," he said, though the words felt hollow. "We have to believe."

As the power flickered and the screen went black, James and Emily were left in the suffocating silence of their apartment. Outside, the sounds of sirens and distant explosions filled the night, but inside, the world seemed to have stopped.

In the darkness, they could only cling to each other, knowing that the world they had known was gone, and something far more dangerous had taken its place.

"The Second Seal Fulfilled"

Rebecca tossed and turned in her sleep, her mind trapped in a maelstrom of images too vivid to ignore. The heavens shifted in her vision, and the thunderous sound of hooves echoed across the firmament, reverberating through the spiritual realms like a drumbeat heralding calamity. Her breath quickened as the scene unfolded, drawing her deeper into its grasp.

The Rider of the second horse loomed before her, a crimson figure of terror astride a blood-red steed. His hollow gaze swept over the earth below, where chaos reigned unchecked. The ground burned, cities crumbled, and nations raged, their cries of anguish rising like smoke into the heavens. The clash of steel and the relentless percussion of explosions had become the earth's new heartbeat.

Rebecca could feel the weight of it all—the despair, the rage, the grief, as if it pressed down on her chest, suffocating her. The Rider's massive sword, gleaming with an unholy light, swung with brutal precision. Each arc severed the fragile bonds of peace that once held humanity together, unraveling harmony into violence. Blood ran in rivers across battlefields, and the anguished cries of the suffering became a deafening symphony of despair.

Above the carnage, demons reveled in the destruction. Their laughter echoed through the spiritual realm, feeding hungrily on the hatred and bloodshed that spread like wildfire. The Rider was their champion, the force driving humanity's descent into chaos. His task was not merely to oversee destruction, he was its architect, ensuring that no corner of the earth escaped his wrath.

Rebecca's gaze followed the Rider as he surveyed his work. Alliances lay in ruins, kingdoms toppled, and even the mightiest empires had succumbed to internal strife. The red horse pawed the ground, its breath steaming in the cold air of the darkness, restless for more. Yet the Rider remained still, his empty eyes fixed on the horizon, waiting. The time was near for his successor to take the stage.

Rebecca turned her eyes upward to a distant light. She was in an instant in the light. She saw Jesus holding the scroll sealed with seven seals. Rebecca's heart ached as she felt the heaviness of His heart as He looked at the scroll He held. She could feel the tension in the heavens and the earth alike. The second seal had been broken, and the Rider of War had unleashed his fury. But the scroll remained unsealed in its entirety, and the third rider waited.

The Lamb's hand moved toward the third seal.

Rebecca's eyes shot open. Her body trembled as she gasped for air, drenched in sweat. The thin blanket clung to her as she lay there, heart pounding, her chest tight with lingering fear. The images burned into her consciousness—the crimson Rider, the destruction, the demons feasting on hatred. Every detail felt more real than a dream, more vivid than memory.

She pressed her hands to her face, trying to steady her breathing. The understanding weighed heavily on her, this was no ordinary nightmare. It was a vision, a revelation of the great tribulation. The seals were breaking. The world, already fractured, was unraveling into chaos foretold long ago.

Rebecca turned onto her side, now understanding the visions. She lay in still, exhausted silence.

"A Cry in the Dark"

The power suddenly went out, and Rebecca sat up in the darkness. The air hung thick and unmoving, suffocating in its stillness. The hum of machinery, once constant and reassuring in its familiarity, had vanished. No fans whirred, no equipment buzzed. Not even the faintest breeze moved through the bars of the heavy steel doors. The camp felt as though it had been sealed off from the rest of the world—cut off from light, from sound, from hope.

It was the silence that unnerved her the most. A silence so deep, so absolute, it pressed down on her chest like a great weight. The air was thick with the scent of sweat, fear, and despair, amplifying the sensation of being buried alive. Somewhere, far off, the distant echo of footsteps rang out, slow at first, deliberate, like a predator stalking prey. Then voices—a panicked exchange between guards—reached her ears, barely discernible at first. She strained to listen.

"Get to the front gate—now!" one voice hissed, breathless.

The footsteps grew faster, more frantic, until they seemed to scatter in all directions, growing fainter and fainter until there was nothing but silence again. Absolute, terrifying silence.

The air inside the camp was heavy, almost smothering, thick with the stench of despair and the agony of broken spirits. Rebecca sat alone in her cell, the rough stone walls pressing in on her like the weight of her suffering. Her body trembled with exhaustion, her once-strong frame now frail from weeks of malnutrition and abuse. Her knees were drawn to her chest as she huddled in the farthest corner, her body instinctively trying to make itself as small as possible, as if disappearing could somehow offer relief.

Her hands, raw and calloused, gripped the thin, filthy blanket that had done little to keep her warm during the freezing nights. Her lips moved soundlessly, her throat too dry and her spirit too shattered to form the words she longed to speak. It had been days—no, weeks—since she had last felt God's presence, since she had last prayed and truly believed He was listening.

The silence was overwhelming, pressing in on her like the weight of the stone walls. With no sounds of machinery or voices, it was as if the entire camp had been abandoned, as if she were the last soul left, but she knew better. She knew they were still out there—watching, waiting.

Her head dropped to her knees as she began to shake, the tremor starting deep within her bones and spreading outward. She couldn't hold on much longer. The silence, the stillness, it felt like it was closing in on her. She longed to cry out, but her voice had abandoned her days ago, just like her hope.

Tears welled in her eyes, hot and thick, as she stared blankly at the barred door, invisible in the surrounding blackness. Yet somehow, she could still feel it—the iron bars, not just trapping her body, but imprisoning her soul. The darkness around her seemed to echo her despair, wrapping itself around her like an oppressive shroud.

"I can't... I can't do this anymore." The words slipped through her cracked lips, barely more than a whisper in the oppressive darkness, so faint that even she wasn't sure if she had spoken them aloud.

Rebecca leaned her head back against the cold stone, her heart pounding with fear and hopelessness. "Where are You, God?" she whispered, her voice cracking with desperation. "Have You abandoned me? Have You forgotten Your promise? I can't... I can't feel You anymore."

The tears came harder now, uncontrollable, her body shaking with sobs. She had tried—tried so hard to be strong, to endure, to hold onto her faith. But the days had stretched on endlessly, each one darker than the last, filled with the torment of isolation and the relentless cruelty of her captors. The beatings, the interrogations, the constant threats against her life—they had worn her down to the point where she no longer recognized herself.

Her lips moved again, forming a prayer that felt weak, almost futile. "Jesus, please..." she breathed, the words barely more than a sob. "Please, help me. I don't have any strength left. I can't do this anymore. I can't keep holding on. If You don't save me, I'm going to break. I'm going to fall apart, and I don't know how to get back up."

Her body slumped forward, her forehead pressing into her knees as she wept, her sobs echoing in the empty cell. "Please, God, don't leave me here. I don't know how much longer I can survive this..." Her voice faded into broken whispers as her prayer became a raw, aching plea. "I need You. I need You to save me. Please... please..."

For a moment, there was nothing but silence, her tears soaking the rough fabric of her prisoner's clothes. The darkness around her seemed to close in, smothering any remaining sliver of hope. And then, just as she felt she might drown in her despair, a voice—soft and urgent—cut through the stillness.

Rebecca's eyes were pressed into her knees, her body shaking with silent sobs, when something in the air shifted. Slowly, almost unwillingly, she lifted her head. A sharp, blinding light pierced the darkness, so intense that it seemed to carve through the void itself. She recoiled, the sudden brightness gripping her with a fear so raw it felt like a physical force wrapping around her chest. The light wasn't a beacon of hope—it was oppressive, cold, and unnatural, casting twisted shadows against the stone walls of her cell.

For a heartbeat, she froze, terror seizing her, her breath faltered. Her mind raced, unable to understand if this was another cruel trick or something more sinister.

Then, through the stillness, a soft, sweet voice broke the silence, barely more than a whisper.

"Rebecca..."

Her heart lurched. She blinked rapidly, blinded by the light, and strained to see—but there was nothing. Just the voice.

"Rebecca..." The voice came again, gentle yet urgent, reaching out to her like a thread of warmth in the cold, repressive darkness.

The light that had pierced through the blackness slowly lowered, no longer blinding but softening, illuminating the cold, cracked floor beneath her. Rebecca's heart still raced, the terror gripping her chest slowly loosening its hold. Her eyes adjusted to the dim glow, the oppressive darkness around her lifting like a crushing shroud.

As the light spread, something shifted in the room. The walls, the shadows—everything felt different. It was as if the very air had changed. The ambient light, or something almost otherworldly, seemed to fill the cell, bringing with it a strange stillness. Her breath came in shallow, uneven gasps as she tried to steady herself.

Then, through the haze, she saw it.

Standing at the edge of the shadows, just beyond the bars of her cell, was a figure—barely visible, as if clinging to the darkness that still filled the hallway. Rebecca blinked, her mind struggling to comprehend what she was seeing. For a moment, she thought it might be another illusion, a cruel trick conjured by the darkness. But as her vision sharpened, disbelief washed over her, followed by a flicker of hope so fragile she almost couldn't bear it.

The silence in the room was broken by a sound—soft, fragile, yet filled with a tenderness that pierced through the darkness. It wasn't a voice of command or force, but something sweeter, something that carried a weight of love. The sound wrapped around Rebecca's heart, drawing her back from the edge of despair.

"Rebecca... Rebecca..."

Her name, whispered to her like a prayer. The word slipped through the shadows, almost too delicate to be real, yet it reached her like a lifeline. Rebecca blinked, her breath catching in her throat, as if the very sound was pulling her from the abyss. The voice—loving, familiar—echoed in her soul, its sweetness filling the air and pushing back the crushing weight of hopelessness.

Slowly, trembling, she lifted her head. The figure moved forward, emerging from the edge of darkness and into the light that was reflecting off the floor. Rebecca's heart pounded in disbelief as the figure took shape before her, bathed in the glow of the soft beams of light bouncing off the stone floor.

It was Sarah, standing there with a flashlight in her hand, her face streaked with dirt and tears, but her eyes shining with something so powerful it made Rebecca's heart swell. Sarah's voice, so gentle yet filled with a strength Rebecca had never seen, whispered her name again.

"Rebecca... I'm here."

The sight of her friend, alive and standing before her, hit Rebecca like a wave. Tears welled up in her eyes, her entire body trembling with an emotion she hadn't felt in so long—hope. Real, undeniable hope. Her chest tightened, her breath shaky as the disbelief slowly gave way to overwhelming joy.

"Sarah..." The name fell from her lips, trembling, barely able to hold the flood of emotions coursing through her. It was as if every prayer she had whispered, every plea for mercy, had been answered in this single, breathtaking moment—encapsulated in a word, in a name: Sarah. She had feared, in her darkest hours, that she would never see her again, that the relentless shadows had swallowed her whole. But now... here she was. Sarah took another step forward, the flashlight in her hand casting a soft glow across her face, illuminating her tear-streaked cheeks and tired eyes. Her expression was a mixture of joy, relief, and exhaustion, but in the depths of her gaze, there was something else—something unbreakable.

Rebecca gasped, the sound of her own voice startling her. "Sarah..." she whispered again, but this time, it wasn't a question. It was a cry of joy, of wonder, of gratitude. The word came out stronger, filled with more emotion than her frail body had the strength to express.

The two women stood there, staring at each other through the dim light, through the bars, neither daring to move, as if afraid the moment would vanish like a dream if they did. Tears spilled freely down Rebecca's cheeks, her body quaking as the weight of her suffering began to lift, replaced by the pure, undeniable reality that she wasn't alone.

Rebecca's mind raced, struggling to comprehend the reality before her. Her breath faltered, unable to speak or move as Sarah stood there—alive. The mix of pain and determination in her friend's face only deepened the miracle of this moment. It felt impossible, like a dream she had prayed for in the darkest of nights but never truly believed would come.

"Sarah..." she said again, louder, though her voice cracked. She tried to push herself up, but her limbs felt impossibly heavy, too weak to respond. All she could do was stare at Sarah, the woman she had thought she'd lost forever, the flood of relief and joy nearly overwhelming her.

Tears streamed down her cheeks, hot and unrelenting. She had begged for this moment, but now that it was here, she didn't know how to grasp it. It felt too real—yet so fragile, like the slightest movement would shatter it and send her spiraling back into darkness.

Sarah stood there, her own face streaked with tears, lips trembling as she finally stepped forward, pressing her hand against the cold iron bars.

"Rebecca... Are you okay? Can you walk?" Sarah's voice was laced with urgency, but underneath, there was something tender—a desperate hope that Rebecca would answer.

Rebecca gasped, her heart pounding as disbelief gave way to a rush of emotion so strong it stole her breath. Her body trembled, weakened by suffering, as she struggled to grasp the reality of Sarah standing there, alive, reaching out to her. She opened her mouth, trying to respond to Sarah's questions, but the words caught in her throat.

Tears filled her eyes, a single shaky breath escaping her.

"Sarah..." The name came out, not as a question, but as a cry of gratitude too powerful for words. Her voice trembled, carrying the weight of every unspoken prayer, every desperate plea for this moment.

Then another sound—a deep masculine voice "Rebecca..." Bruce's voice low and deep, his broad figure towering beside Sarah, his hands steady as he held something in his grasp.

A man's voice? She instinctively recoiled in fear, unable to place it. It sounded foreign to her ears, distant, as if it belonged to a dream rather than the cold, unbearable reality of the cell. Who is this? She wondered, her mind sluggish from exhaustion, her heart unable to fully grasp what was happening. The voice was too soft, too gentle, and too real. Fear gnawed at her—could this be yet another cruel trick?

But then, something stirred deep within her, beyond reason or understanding—something that hadn't moved in what felt like years. It was as if her spirit, buried beneath layers of grief and suffering, recognized the voice before her mind could catch up. She heard, or perhaps felt, a whisper deep in her soul. "This is him. The man you prayed for."

A fragile but persistent sense of certainty bloomed within her, a whisper from her soul telling her that this—this—was the one sent by God, the answer to her desperate prayers in the darkest of nights. She had cried herself to sleep, praying for a man she didn't even know. She had wept for his sufferings, and now, here he was, God's answer, standing before her.

Bruce held the key in his hand and slid it into the lock. The lock clicked, the sound echoing through the stone walls like a distant thunderclap, reverberating through the cell and breaking through the layers of hopelessness that had long weighed Rebecca down. It was real—Bruce had turned the key. The door, the barrier that had kept her bound and beaten for weeks, was about to yield.

Sarah pushed the door open and dropped to the floor, pulling Rebecca into a fierce embrace, her arms wrapping tightly around her. "Oh my God, Rebecca," Sarah cried, her voice breaking as she held her friend close.

Rebecca said "I thought we lost you. I thought... I thought..." She couldn't finish her sentence, her own tears falling freely as she buried her face in Sarah's shoulder.

Rebecca clung to her, her body shaking with sobs as the reality of the moment finally sank in. "Sarah... I didn't think I'd see you again. I thought it was over. I..." She choked on the words, her voice trembling with a mixture of disbelief and overwhelming relief.

Bruce stepped into the cell, his voice soft with emotion. "You're safe now, Rebecca... well, almost. We're getting out of here," he said, his deep voice steady but tinged with urgency. He placed a gentle hand on her shoulder, firm and reassuring. Then, taking her hand in his strong grip, he helped her to her feet and guided her toward the door. He took a deep breath. "Let's do this," he said, and followed her out the door.

Sarah swiftly followed behind, her footsteps quick and determined.

Suddenly, Rebecca froze, her body trembling as she turned and clung to them, overwhelmed by the moment. The weight of her suffering, so heavy for so long, slowly began to lift. She had prayed for a miracle, for a way out, and here it was, God had answered her prayers in the form of her dearest friend and a man she did not know, but for whom she had cried out in her prayers to God.

"Thank you," Rebecca whispered, looking into Bruce's eyes, her voice cracking with emotion as she lifted her gaze upward. "Thank you, Lord..."

"A World Unraveling"

The city had become a battlefield, teetering on the edge of madness. What had begun as protests, a mix of political unrest and desperation, had devolved into something far darker, something far more sinister. The explosion at the courthouse had been the breaking point, sending shockwaves not only through the physical streets but through the hearts of men. In an instant, all hell had broken loose. The blast ripped through the air like a harbinger of doom, the shockwave fueling the fires already burning in the souls of the angry and the lost. It was no longer about demands for justice; the lines between right and wrong, peace and terror, had dissolved into ash.

Activists, once motivated by calls for change, were now indistinguishable from the shadows of those who had infiltrated their ranks, agents of chaos, driven by nothing more than the desire for destruction. In the crowd, it was impossible to discern who fought for righteousness and who harbored darkness. The lines blurred as violence surged, swallowed by flames that devoured the city's soul. The explosion at the courthouse became a rallying cry for anarchy, and with it, the spirit of violence was unleashed, a beast untethered.

The streets pulsed with anger, confusion, and fear, the night illuminated by the eerie glow of overturned cars and burning buildings. Shouts ricocheted between high-rises, blending with the sickening cacophony of smashing glass and gunfire. The courthouse, once a symbol of law and order, now lay in ruins, its debris scattered like the shattered hopes of the city. But it wasn't the surface-level destruction that sent a chill through the streets—it was the sinister undercurrent, the unseen manipulation driving the chaos. Something darker moved beneath the violence, stirring hatred, twisting minds, and feeding on the despair that gripped the people like a vice.

Demonic forces, invisible to human eyes, moved freely among the rioters, whispering into the hearts of those who led the attacks. Their voices were like poison, feeding into the darkest fears, twisting intentions, and turning frustration into madness. In the heart of the mob, demons swirled like a storm, urging them toward violence, spurring them on to attack the very systems keeping the city alive.

The power plant stood on the edge of town, a hulking fortress of steel and concrete. It had provided energy for the entire region, a lifeline to homes, businesses, and security systems—everything that kept the modern world running. But tonight, it was a target.

The mob descended upon the plant with an almost primal fury. What began as chants for change quickly morphed into screams of destruction. A group broke away, determined and armed. Their faces, concealed beneath hoods and masks, showed no hesitation as they tore through the outer gates, setting fire to anything in their path. Explosions rocked the air, sending shockwaves through the night. The plant's security forces, overwhelmed and unprepared, had no chance to stop the wave of destruction.

The first fire ignited, crackling in the darkness, sending plumes of black smoke into the sky. Sparks flew as the rioters targeted the transformers, striking at the very heart of the city's power grid. Lights across the skyline flickered, then died. Block by block, the city plunged into darkness, the hum of electricity replaced by the low, sinister growl of unrest.

Then as the city was swallowed by darkness, the camp became a target.

"The Camp Under Siege"

A second wave of attackers broke off from the main chaos, their eyes set on the facility that loomed just beyond the city limits. The camp, already a place of torment and broken spirits, now faced something even more dangerous—a force that didn't come to free the prisoners, but to tear the place apart from the outside in.

The gates of the camp trembled under the force of the crowd. Metal groaned as the mob threw themselves against it, battering rams and makeshift explosives chipping away at the barrier that had kept so many trapped within its walls. Their screams mixed with the clang of metal, and the darkness seemed to pulse with the rhythm of their assault.

In the shadows, demons moved, feeding off the frenzy, their twisted forms lurking just behind the activists, urging them on. The attackers didn't care about the people inside—Rebecca, Sarah, and the others. To them, the camp was just another symbol to destroy. The voices of hatred and destruction swirled in their minds, drowning out any thought of mercy.

Inside the camp, panic spread like wildfire. Beyond the walls, the city was swallowed by darkness—an ominous void where the once-vibrant skyline had disappeared. But inside the camp, it was a stark contrast, bathed in blinding, unnatural light. The floodlights and spotlights—powered by the camp's backup generators—cut through the night, casting harsh beams across the grounds, making every corner visible, exposing every shadow. The brightness was disorienting, almost oppressive, a glaring reminder of the chaos that was storming the gates.

Guards scrambled, their voices frantic as they barked orders into radios, the air thick with the scent of fear. Their faces were pale with terror, eyes darting to the gates as the mob outside grew bolder. From within the safety of the light, they could see the wave of attackers, relentless and violent, smashing against the camp's gates. The sound of metal groaning under the force of the mob's assault echoed through the grounds.

For now, the camp remained illuminated, a beacon of defiance in the midst of a city plunged into chaos. But that light, that brief illusion of control, was fragile.

The moment the gates gave way, the mob surged forward, their cries of victory mingling with the grinding of metal and the sound of heavy footsteps pounding across the concrete. Within minutes, they located the generators, massive machines that hummed with power, casting the last vestiges of light across the facility.

With ruthless efficiency, they descended on the generators, ripping through wires and smashing controls. One by one, the blinding lights flickered, then died. As the final light blinked out, the camp was swallowed by the same darkness that had consumed the city, leaving both prisoners and staff alike vulnerable and exposed to the terror that had breached their walls.

"The Last Key"

Bruce and Sarah had freed Rebecca, but the tension and events leading to that moment are worth telling, a moment that had shaped everything that followed. To truly understand the depths of Bruce's quest, let us go back to that critical night when Lance showed up with the key.

Lance's footsteps echoed down the darkened corridor, his flashlight casting flickering beams of light against the cold stone walls as he ran. The camp was in chaos—he could hear the distant shouts of guards and the rising roar of the mob that had broken through the gates. The power was out, the generators down. Radios had crackled with warnings of potential violence, but now the threat was no longer distant. It was here.

He cursed under his breath as he tightened his grip on the flashlight, the cold weight of the key in his pocket a constant reminder of the promise he had made. He had planned to give Bruce the key at 7:30 in the morning, thirty minutes before his shift ended. But now, everything had changed.

Lance weaved through the corridors, the sounds of guards rushing in the opposite direction filling his ears. They were moving to fend off the mob that had breached the camp, but Lance had only one focus, Bruce.

Finally, Lance reached the familiar cell. Bruce was there, waiting in the dark. His broad frame was barely visible in the thin beam of light as he approached the door.

"Lance?" Bruce's voice was low but steady, the edge of urgency unmistakable.

Lance was breathless as he pulled the key from his pocket. "The mob's broken through the gates," he said, his voice tight with the weight of what was happening outside. "Generators are down. It's all going to hell out there."

Bruce's eyes were sharp, though the darkness made it hard to see his full expression. Lance hurried on, knowing there wasn't much time. "I was supposed to bring you the key earlier, at 7:30, but…" He hesitated, then forced himself to continue. "It's Sarah. She's why I didn't show up earlier."

Bruce's face stiffened. "What happened?"

"They beat her," Lance said quietly, "so severe they nearly killed her. She was in the med center. I wasn't sure she'd make it… but then… I don't know how to explain it, Bruce. She just… she recovered. Like nothing I've ever seen."

Bruce's hands clenched into fists, his jaw tightening as he absorbed the words. His heart was pounding, the thought of Sarah in that state fueling the fire inside him.

Lance swallowed hard, his voice becoming urgent. "Listen, we don't have time. This is your chance. Get out now, before everything collapses." He pressed the key into Bruce's hand, the cold metal almost burning against Bruce's palm in the tension of the moment.

146

"I've already scouted the path. You remember where the infirmary is? Three turns from here. On the last one, take the corridor to the med center. Sarah's in one of the medical cells—third on the left after the final turn. Don't lose count, Bruce." Bruce nodded, his mind already running through the route in his head. His pulse quickened, but he kept his voice calm. "I'll get her. I won't fail."

Lance gave a quick nod, urgency written across his face and handed him his flashlight. "Good. Go fast, and be quiet. They're everywhere."

Bruce stood, his heart thudding as he prepared himself for what lay ahead. Lance's words echoed in his mind—this was his chance, and he wasn't going to waste it.

"Godspeed, brother," Lance whispered. He had never used the phrase before, but somehow it flowed off his lips with power and purpose. Gripping Bruce's shoulder for a moment, he released it, and Bruce gave him a look of deep gratitude. Flashlight in hand, Bruce turned and hurried away into the darkness, heading to find Sarah.

Lance stood there in silence, the words still lingering in the heavy air, swallowed by the pitch-black darkness around him. He could hear the distant roar of the mob, the echoes of chaos drawing closer. For a moment, he remained frozen, feeling the weight of what he had just done—handing over the key, handing over hope. His heart pounded, not just with fear, but with the uncertainty that hung like a shroud over everything.

He let out a slow, steady breath, but the stillness was short-lived. The urgency of the moment pressed down on him. He turned, his hands reaching out into the void, fingers brushing against cold, rough stone as he began to feel his way blindly forward. Each step was tentative, each movement deliberate, as if the darkness itself were trying to hold him back.

The sound of chaos grew louder with every step. Shouts, the clash of metal, the faint crackle of fire, it all mixed with the oppressive silence of the camp's deadened power. But what unnerved him most wasn't the noise; it was the spiritual weight pressing on him, the unmistakable sense that this battle was not just of flesh and blood. There was something darker here, lurking, feeding on the violence.

He pushed forward, the fear gnawing at him, his flashlight flickering weakly as if it too sensed the coming storm. But Lance couldn't turn back. He couldn't retreat, not now. Somewhere ahead, the mob was tearing through the camp, and with every passing moment, the line between life and death grew thinner. He had chosen his side—he had given Bruce the key, and now he had to face whatever was waiting for him in the chaos ahead.

Lance's throat tightened, his heart heavy with the knowledge that, while Bruce searched for Sarah, he was heading into the heart of destruction. His footsteps, though soft, felt like they echoed endlessly in the void, a reminder that he was walking into the eye of a storm.

9

UNRAVELING

"Manipulation and Chaos"

In the darkened halls of power, Ben Reshan stood before the screens that flickered with the images of world leaders, his hands clasped behind his back. His once-charismatic aura was overshadowed by the malevolent presence within him, his mind no longer his own. The whispers of Satan, dark and commanding, echoed through his thoughts, twisting his words, guiding his every move.

In moments of rare clarity, Ben's mind would flicker back to life, allowing him to briefly grasp the full horror of what he had done. The faces of the leaders he had deceived swirled before him, haunted by the terror he had planted in their hearts. It wasn't just the words he had spoken—it was the darkness that controlled him, using his voice to turn nations against one another.

Ben Reshan stood alone in the dimly lit room, the world outside his window spiraling into chaos, and yet within him, a darker storm raged. He gripped the edge of the desk, his knuckles white with tension as the cacophony of voices in his head rose and fell like a relentless tide. His breath came in short, shallow bursts, the weight of invisible chains tightening around his chest. Something was wrong—deeply, horribly wrong—but every time he tried to grasp it, the thought slipped away like smoke between his fingers.

It was Satan's voice he heard most often, no longer subtle whispers coaxing him into decisions, but a roaring torrent, commanding and drowning out his own thoughts. Ben was no longer sure where his will ended and Satan's began. Every choice felt like it wasn't his own.

"You know what to do," Satan's voice thundered, twisting around his consciousness like a vise. The power should have felt intoxicating, but it filled Ben with a hollow dread. This was everything he'd been promised—power, dominance, control over nations—and yet, something inside him recoiled. Was any of it real? Was any of it his?

And then, just as suddenly, Satan would vanish. Ben would collapse into the stillness, Satan's presence withdrawing as he tended to other parts of the world, orchestrating his grand design elsewhere. During these moments of respite, Ben would feel fragments of himself return, a glimmer of his own thoughts peeking through the fog.

"What have I done?" The question haunted him, but there was never time to answer.

Satan always left one of his demons in his place—twisted beings who slid into Ben's consciousness like poison. The demon that possessed him now was subtler than the others, its grip loose, almost lazy. That made it worse. The demon's inattention allowed Ben's own thoughts to surface more often, and in those fleeting moments of lucidity, the horror of his actions crashed over him.

It was during these lapses that Ben felt the full weight of what had been done in his name. He saw the faces of world leaders, twisted with fear, men he had manipulated with threats and promises of power. He had ordered nations to attack each other, fueling conflict with well-placed lies, whispered paranoia, and false promises of protection.

"Why?" he whispered, his voice trembling, barely audible. But the demon ignored his cries, allowing Ben's confusion to fester, and his guilt to deepen.

The faces of leaders he had manipulated with his words swirled before him. He had incited madness in their minds. It wasn't just his words that had driven them to madness; it was the dark spirits that had crept into the hearts of the world's leaders. "Your neighbor is planning to destroy you. Preempt the attack." The command had left Ben's lips, but it wasn't his voice—it was the voice of the demons, the voice of Satan himself.

As he spoke, the demons under Satan's control seized the minds of those leaders, corrupting them from within. His commands and manipulations were eagerly received, as those spirits whispered fear and paranoia into the hearts of leaders, generals, and men of influence, twisting their thoughts and igniting suspicion. The leaders believed every lie, their frantic calculations guided not by reason, but by the pernicious forces that had taken root in their souls.

Ben had turned nations against each other, not with mere words, but with the dark presence he carried—the presence that spoke through him, sending orders to the demons lodged deep in the minds of the powerful. He had seen the fear in their eyes, the desperation, the helplessness, as the demons clouded their judgment and stripped away their will. They acted as if their hands were tied, as if war were inevitable. In moments of clarity, he could relate to their fear and helplessness.

Satan, a vile creature, had used him as a conduit to sow destruction. They couldn't be his words. They couldn't be, but he was complicit.

Satan relished the chaos, feeding off the destruction Ben had unleashed. He reveled in the suffering and war, especially when he had succeeded in turning the world's attention against Israel. Ben had watched it happen, his words twisting truth and lies until entire nations were consumed by hatred.

"Turn them all against Israel," Satan growled, his voice like a venomous hiss slithering through Ben's mind, feeding him instructions. "Their destruction will be your victory."

Ben's heart raced as the command settled deep within him. The weight of Satan's words clung to his soul, tightening its grip around him like an iron vice. He felt the familiar surge of power from Satan's influence, yet with it came a gnawing dread, what was happening, a shadow of doubt creeping into his thoughts.

The words cut through Ben like a blade. He had once believed in his mission, had once thought he was bringing order to a broken world. But now he saw the truth—he was nothing more than a puppet, his strings pulled by dark forces he couldn't control.

"This isn't me." The thought slipped through his mind, fleeting yet powerful, as the demon's grip momentarily loosened. He could see the wars he was igniting, the devastation he was bringing. It used to sicken him, but now, more often than not, he accepted it.

But as soon as the thought surfaced, the demon tightened its hold, pulling him back into the shadowy depths. The weight of his choices, the rituals he had performed for power, and the promises he had made to the darkness hung heavy in the air. The fight within him was slipping away, as was the man he used to be. He had become a vessel for Satan's plans, and though he still caught glimpses of his former self, the darkness was winning.

He had reached out to this—he had summoned it.

There was a time when Ben had known exactly what he was doing, fully aware of the price he would have to pay. In his thirst for power, he had performed the ancient rituals—dark, forbidden rites that had been whispered through the ages. He had prepared the altar, gathered the necessary sacrifices, and recited the incantations that would open a gateway to the dark powers. His voice had echoed in the hidden chamber, trembling with anticipation and fear, but unwavering in its purpose. He wanted power, at any cost. Even the price of his own soul.

The air had grown thick and oppressive that night, the shadows around him twisting unnaturally as if alive. He had felt it then, the presence of something ancient, something vile, answering his call. It had been a moment of triumph, his heart racing with the knowledge that he had broken through the veil and reached the powers of darkness. He had invited them into his life, into his mind, into his soul. He had wanted it all, the wealth, the influence, the absolute authority over nations. He had been willing to give up everything for it.

Now the cost was being extracted.

The demon that controlled him had been waiting for that moment, that one act of surrender when Ben had fully opened himself to the forces of hell. Now it spoke through him, used him like a puppet, twisting his thoughts and desires to serve Satan's greater purpose. Even now, as it manipulated his every move, there were moments—fleeting, agonizing moments—where Ben would surface from the depths of darkness, gasping for air, realizing what he had done.

"This isn't me," he whispered, his voice barely audible against the oppressive weight of the demon's influence. He wanted to believe it wasn't, that somewhere deep within, there was a part of him that could still fight, that hadn't been consumed by the darkness.

But he knew the truth.

He had made his choice. He had sacrificed his soul on that altar, and now the demons would never loosen their grip.

Nations had fallen. Wars had begun. And Ben—Ben Reshan, the Antichrist—was at the center of it all. And yet, in his heart, he still clung to the hope that there was something left of himself, something that could resist.

But as Satan's plan neared completion, those faint glimmers of hope that had once surfaced grew ever dimmer, swallowed by the all-consuming darkness that had claimed him. Resignation seeped into his soul like a slow poison. The fight was gone. Now, he found himself yielding more willingly, surrendering to the inevitable.

"I have heard whispers," Ben said, his voice low, smooth, almost hypnotic as he spoke to a prime minister on the screen. "Your neighboring country... they are amassing weapons, preparing for an invasion. You must act swiftly before they strike you."

The prime minister's face paled, uncertainty flashing in his eyes. "We haven't seen any indication—"

"You haven't," Ben interrupted, his eyes gleaming with cold calculation, "because they have hidden their plans well. But I have friends in high places. They have informed me of the impending threat. You cannot afford to wait."

Fear took root in the prime minister's heart, and Ben smiled inwardly. It was always fear. The demons whispered in his ear, feeding him lines, stoking the fires of paranoia among the leaders of the world.

Across the globe, similar conversations played out. Ben, and world leaders, with the unseen guidance of the Rider of the Red Horse, turned nation against nation, spreading war and discord with ease. Promises of power and riches kept many in line, while threats of annihilation brought others to their knees.

Behind closed doors, world leaders spoke in hushed tones, driven mad with paranoia and ambition. Their greed, their lust for power, and their desperation to secure their own survival blinded them to the true nature of their actions. They were all pawns in a much larger game, a game orchestrated by forces far beyond their understanding.

But Ben knew. In his brief moments of lucidity, he saw it, the destruction he was sowing, the wars he was igniting. It had once sickened him, but now he accepted it. The darkness surged over him, within him, choking his conscience. He would become the puppet once more, a vessel for Satan's plans.

Each day, the world moved closer to total collapse. The Rider of the Red Horse, unseen by human eyes, rode through the streets of nations, fanning the flames of conflict. Ben watched, controlled, manipulated by the very being who had crafted his rise to power. The chaos would only grow, and the world was none the wiser.

In the shadows, Satan reveled in his victories, his influence reaching every corner of the earth. He smiled, knowing that soon, all eyes would turn against Israel. The final pieces were falling into place, and as nations fell to war, he prepared for the next phase of his plan.

The world would burn. And Ben Reshan, the puppet of darkness, would be its harbinger.

"A Narrow Escape"

The cold stone walls seemed to press in as Rebecca, Sarah, and Bruce made their way down the narrow corridor. Their footsteps were cautious, a soft echo in the oppressive silence of the camp. Rebecca's heart pounded in her chest as she cast glances at the other detainees locked in their cells. Shadows flitted across the faces of men and women, pale with fear, eyes wide with terror. They huddled in corners, too afraid to move.

"We can unlock your doors," Bruce whispered urgently, his voice barely carrying through the suffocating silence. He motioned to the key Lance had handed him, the metal cool in his palm. "You don't have to stay here."

But the prisoners shrank back, shaking their heads. One man, his voice hoarse and barely audible, muttered, "No... they'll come for us... we'll be killed..."

Rebecca's throat tightened, her chest heavy with the weight of their fear. She reached out, her fingers grazing the cold bars. "Please, we can get you out..."

"No." A woman's voice, cracked and broken, came from the corner. "Leave..."

For a moment, Rebecca wanted to argue, to plead with them to take this chance at freedom, but the look in their eyes—the despair, the certainty of their fate—stopped her. They were already lost.

"Let's go," Bruce said firmly, pulling her back. Time was slipping away. They couldn't afford to waste another second.

They moved silently through the shadows, heading toward the back of the building where Lance had told them the wire fence had been spliced. Every step was a gamble, every corner turned a risk. The air was thick with tension, an airless weight pressing down on them as they neared the exit.

Then came the sound they had dreaded, footsteps.

Bruce motioned for them to press against the wall. His eyes were sharp, his body tense as the footsteps drew closer. The shadow of a guard loomed ahead, his hand on his baton, eyes scanning the corridor. Rebecca felt her pulse spike, her body frozen in fear. Sarah clutched her side, her breath ragged with pain.

In a blur of motion, Bruce lunged forward. He was silent, lethal, moving with the precision of a man trained for moments like this. His hand clamped over the guard's mouth as his other arm locked around the guard's neck in a chokehold. The guard's eyes widened, struggling for breath, but Bruce's grip was unrelenting, a grim focus in his gaze.

Rebecca watched in horror as the guard's struggles slowed, his body going limp as he fell unconscious. Bruce let him drop silently to the ground, checking his pulse. "He's alive," Bruce whispered, his voice strained but steady. "Let's move."

They reached the back of the building, the wire fence ahead barely visible in the dim light. The spot where Lance had cut the wire was there, barely noticeable, the thin splice holding it together. Sarah squeezed through first, the wire scraping her arms as she pulled herself through. Rebecca came next, her face contorted with pain as she struggled to follow. She was bruised, battered, dehydrated—her body weak from days of torment.

"I… I can't," Rebecca gasped, her strength faltering as she tried to push through the narrow opening.

"Yes, you can," Bruce urged, his voice low but brimming with an intensity that sliced through the exhaustion dragging her down. His eyes locked onto hers, steady and relentless, as though he could transfer his strength into her with sheer willpower. "Come on, Rebecca, we don't have a choice anymore. We're too far in now to stop. Just push through this, and I'll take care of the rest." His grip on her arm was firm, grounding her, but there was something else beneath his calm exterior— a quiet, desperate urgency. "You're not alone. I'm right here with you."

With a final, desperate push, Rebecca made it through, collapsing on the other side. Bruce followed swiftly, his broad frame barely fitting through the gap. He scanned the area, the tension in his muscles never easing. They had made it out, but they weren't safe yet.

"The guards… they don't just take your freedom," Bruce muttered, his voice tight with disgust. "They take everything after processing— your clothes, your shoes, your dignity." His eyes darkened with anger as he recalled the guards, laughing and making crude remarks as they sifted through the personal belongings of the women. They'd pull out the undergarments, holding them up like trophies, mocking the prisoners with rudeness and sneers, some stuffing them into their pockets.

"They tore through everything," Bruce said, his voice tightening with disgust. "Whatever they didn't want, they dumped at a charity drop-off. I've been there… I had no choice but to help them. I watched them discard what was left—stuff they didn't care to steal. It's just a few blocks from here, behind an old grocery store." He paused, eyes scanning their surroundings. "We need to stay out of sight. We'll find something there—clothes, shoes—anything so we don't stand out in these jumpsuits."

Sarah felt a shiver run down her spine, imagining the guards rifling through her belongings, their cruel laughter as they handled her intimate items with disrespect. The thought of their rough hands invading her privacy sent a chill through her, but Bruce's words provided a sliver of hope.

"If we can just get to that drop-off," she whispered, her voice wavering, "maybe we can find something, blend in, and find a safe place."

Rebecca's heart ached as she thought of everything they had been stripped of, the sense of humiliation and loss heavier than the filthy prison garb clinging to her skin. But they had no choice. She squeezed Sarah's hand, whispering softly, "Maybe we can get to Emily and James."

The idea seemed fragile, like a thin thread they were desperately clinging to. Yet it was enough to push them forward, enough to keep them moving.

They slipped through the alleyways, sticking to the shadows. Every sound made Rebecca flinch, everything felt like a potential threat. The roar of the mob echoed from the other side of the camp as they moved deeper into the darkness. There it was, the drop-off, hidden behind a grocery store, just a few blocks away. Urgency hung in the air; time was running out, and they were still exposed. The guard must have come to by now, but Bruce had blinded him with the flashlight. He didn't see their faces, but they wouldn't have long. The guards would be occupied with the rioters for now, giving them precious moments to slip away.

They reached the drop-off, their breath catching in their throats. Clothes, shoes, bags, everything was dumped in careless piles. Rebecca sifted through the mess, her hands trembling.

As they sifted through the discarded clothes, a mixture of emotions churned within Rebecca. Each piece of fabric felt like a reminder of what had been lost, of the identity stripped from them. The smell of sweat, dirt, and old memories clung to the air. Bruce moved methodically, but Rebecca's hands trembled, brushing past jackets and shoes that once belonged to people like her, people who had been reduced to nothing but a pile of discarded belongings.

Suddenly, in the dim light at the edge of a streetlamp's reach, something caught her eye. Her heart skipped a beat. Could it be? She moved closer, her pulse quickening as she caught a glimpse of something familiar. There, lying half-buried beneath a worn coat, was her purse.

With a gasp, Rebecca dropped to her knees, frantically digging around the pile. Her fingers grazed the rough edges of her shoes, her clothes—rolled together, even her bra—but her panties and wedding ring were gone. "I found mine," she whispered, her voice barely audible as she clutched her belongings, her fingers tightening around the fabric like a lifeline.

Relief, mingled with a strange sense of violation, washed over her. Though she had found what was hers, the small, intimate loss reminded her of just how much had been taken.

Bruce and Sarah were searching too. Bruce found something that fit him quickly, slipping into a plain shirt and pants, his movements quick and deliberate. Sarah was slower, her body weakened by the abuse she had suffered. But with Rebecca's help, she found her clothes too, the familiar fabric bringing a small, fragile comfort.

The odds of finding their clothes in the chaotic mess felt impossible, but as Rebecca knelt, clutching her belongings, Sarah glanced up at the stars, her heart swelling with gratitude. The moment was small, but to her, it felt like divine intervention. With a quiet, trembling voice, she whispered, "Thank you, Lord. I know it was you. I needed this little comfort." Tears brimmed in her eyes as she held onto the fleeting sense of peace in the middle of the chaos surrounding them.

Sarah and Rebecca crept behind the drop-off container, hidden in the shadows. The pile of discarded items piled and scattered around were a symbol of everything they had lost. Trembling, they slipped into their own clothes, the feel of the soft fabric almost foreign to their battered skin. They searched and found a faucet with a hose at the back of the store. Their hands shook as they turned the faucet, using cold water to wash away days of dirt and blood.

They washed their hair under the icy flow of water from the hose, gasping as the cold stung their skin. The water streamed down in rivulets, carrying away the grime of captivity, if only for a moment. With no towels, they dried their dripping hair on extra soft garments they had scavenged from the pile, the fabric gentle against their tender scalps. Sarah's fingers trembled as she wrung out her hair, still knotted and unyielding, but it felt cleaner, lighter. It wasn't much, but it was enough to remind them they were free.

Sarah and Rebecca struggled with the tangles in their hair, their fingers trembling as they tried to ease through the knots. Every tug sent sharp pain through their bruised scalps, the sensitive skin raw from the beatings and lack of care. Sarah winced, her eyes watering as she fought against the stubborn mats. Their hair seemed to rebel with each stroke. After several agonizing minutes, they both gave up. Defeated, they shared the soft brush they had found and straightened what they could, smoothing only the top layers. The pain was too much, both physically and emotionally, and with each tug, they were reminded of the deep humiliation they had endured.

Exhausted beyond words, Sarah leaned heavily against the cold wall, sliding down until she sat on the hard ground. The brush slipped from her hand, hitting the concrete with a sharp clatter. Every part of her body ached, bruises beneath the new garments burning against her skin, but it was her mind that suffered the most. The dull throb in her head was nothing compared to the ache in her soul. Thoughts collided violently, everything they had endured, the fear tightening around her chest, and the uncertainty of what lay ahead.

Her life, as she knew it, was gone.

She closed her eyes, the weight of loss pressing down on her, suffocating her spirit. Her fingers dug into the soft fabric she wore, a fragile comfort in the face of overwhelming pain. The enormity of it all crushed her, leaving her drained, questioning how much more she could bear.

Her eyes were closed, but the sound of Rebecca and Bruce sliding down the cold wall beside her pierced the silence. It wasn't just exhaustion, they were all unraveling, their bodies broken and minds battered. Rebecca's breath was labored as she settled next to her, and Bruce sat on the other side. They leaned toward her, their shoulders barely touching. For Sarah, the contact was grounding, a quiet reminder that she wasn't alone in this nightmare. The weight of their shared ordeal pressed down like a tangible force. In the stillness, the unspoken fear of not surviving hung heavy in the air. No words were needed; the silence between them was thick with shared pain and fragile hope, binding them in a moment of raw vulnerability.

Bruce pressed his shoulder gently into Sarah's, the contact sending a jolt of electricity through him. He had every reason to resent her, she was the one who had dragged him into this nightmare. Yet, now, something deeper stirred within him. Sarah had also been the one who freed him, the one who gave him hope when he had none. The warmth of her shoulder against his was a quiet reminder of their shared fight. His heart, once hardened by years of discipline, softened as he glanced at her bruised face and damp hair.

Bruce's fingers twitched as though he wanted to reach out but hesitated, unsure of what this moment truly meant. His thoughts were a jumble, anger at their situation, gratitude for her resilience, and an unexpected tenderness. He stayed silent, the weight of their ordeal binding them more than words could.

Bruce hesitated, then shifted and placed his hand close, barely touching Sarah's leg. She instinctively leaned into him, needing his strength.

The three of them sat in silence, the weight of their shared suffering heavy. Bruce's hand moved and rested gently on her leg, while Rebecca reached out and took Sarah's hand in hers, holding it tenderly. Sarah felt the warmth and roughness of Rebecca's fingers, a comforting reminder of their bond. The quiet connection between the three of them was stronger than words—a silent promise to keep going. Both Rebecca and Bruce leaned into Sarah, offering each other strength. The night air hung heavy with exhaustion, bruised bodies, and broken spirits, yet a fragile thread of resilience held them together. No words were needed—just the stillness of three people bound by a desperate fight for survival, leaning on each other for what remained.

"Closing In"

The patrol cars hummed softly in the early morning silence, their lights casting brief flashes of red and blue across the street. The air was heavy with tension as the officers gathered near the trunk, their breath visible in the cool dawn air. One of them, Officer Hartman, flipped open a worn folder, the creases in its edges hinting at the frantic pace of the investigation. "The old woman at 418," he began, his voice low and steady, "she says they should still be in their apartment. They do not leave until around 8:00." His finger traced over the names Emily and James. The spouse Rebecca has already been sent to the camp. "Her tip's solid." Hartman studied the pictures of Emily and James stapled to the report. Rebecca's picture was in the folder loose. It fell to the sidewalk. He picked it up studying it.

The second officer, Lyons, shifted uneasily. "People are turning on each other left and right. We should approach with caution. Last thing we need is to underestimate anyone."

Hartman nodded, his gaze sharpening. "This city's gone to hell. Everyone's desperate. But we've got a job to do. In and out—clean."

As the group moved toward the building, their footsteps muted on the wet pavement, the distant sound of city chaos reached their ears— the shouts of rioters, the hum of unrest growing as the city crumbled under the weight of fear and distrust. The apartment towered ahead of them, dark and unassuming, but the sense of looming danger was always present.

Sarah, Bruce, and Rebecca crept up behind a rusted dumpster, their breaths shallow as they watched two officers. Bruce squinted as one of the officers, while rummaging through his file, accidentally dropped a photograph. It fluttered to the ground, just out of their line of sight. Bruce leaned forward, straining to see, but before he could make anything out, the officer stooped and hastily stuffed the photo back into the file. Rebecca tugged at Sarah's sleeve, and they ducked out of sight, retreating into the shadows as the officers entered the apartment.

The old woman stood at her window, her frail figure framed by the dim light from inside, casting her in silhouette. A twisted smile crept across her lips as she spotted the police entering the building below. Her bony fingers traced the windowsill, her heart swelling with a perverse sense of pride. "Told 'em... too many haters in the world," she muttered under her breath, her voice rasping with age and spite.

The knock came, right on time, just as she knew it would. She shuffled over, her feet dragging against the floor, and opened the door with deliberate slowness. One of the officers stood before her, his eyes scanning her with a mixture of impatience and indifference. Her hand clutched the doorframe, knuckles white as she basked in her self-importance.

"I saw them," she croaked, her voice filled with grim satisfaction. "Last night. They haven't left. I've been watching."

The officer's eyebrow lifted slightly, waiting for more.

"They always come out this way," she continued, her trembling finger pointing down the hall. Her eyes gleamed with malice as she imagined Emily and James being dragged away. There was no doubt, no remorse, only the chilling certainty that she had done her duty, protecting the neighborhood from whatever imagined threat they posed. To her, this was justice. To her, she was purging the world of what didn't belong.

The morning air inside the apartment was tense. Emily and her father, James, moved about quietly, careful not to disturb the fragile peace that cloaked them.

James poured coffee, his eyes flicking toward Emily, who was packing her school bag. They were trying to act normal in a world that was anything but. The knock at the door came abruptly, shattering the delicate calm, freezing them both in place.

James glanced at the clock, his brow furrowing. "Who would be knocking at the door this early?" he muttered, suspicion creeping into his voice.

Panic flashed across Emily's face, and she sprinted to the window. Pulling back the curtain just enough, she saw the unmistakable markings of a police car parked outside. Her breath clung to her throat. "Dad, it's the police," she whispered, her voice trembling with dread.

James, struggling to remain calm, took a deep breath. "I'll answer it," he said. "I'll get them inside. When I make a move, you run out the door. Don't go the way we always do. Understand? Don't look back, just run as fast as you can."

Emily nodded, her heart racing as she stepped into the shadows of the room. James crossed the small living room and opened the door, subtly twisting the lock back into the locked position. "Officers," he greeted them with a friendly smile, his voice steady despite the tension crackling in the air. "Come on in, no need to stand in the hallway."

The officers hesitated for a moment, then stepped inside. They walked past James, who nearly closed the door but kept it ajar. With deliberate casualness, James moved deeper into the room, drawing them further from the entrance. "Can I offer you something to drink?" he asked.

Hartman cut him off, "We're here to bring you and your daughter Emily in for questioning."

James didn't flinch. "My daughter was brought in yesterday. They picked her up from school, and I was upset when she wasn't released," he said with convincing calm.

Hartman's face showed suspicion mixed with confusion. James gestured toward the desk, saying, "I have the form from the school." He walked toward the desk, rummaging through papers. The officers followed him, circling around the furniture and momentarily losing sight of Emily's hiding spot.

Distracted, the officers glanced at the pile of papers. It was the only opportunity James needed.

"Go!" he shouted.

In one swift motion, James shoved Hartman into the other officer, sending them tumbling. He vaulted over the sofa, and Emily darted out like lightning. James followed, pulling the door shut behind him. They bolted down the hall, his long strides keeping pace with her.

At the corner of the hallway, they turned sharply left—away from the old woman's door.

They hit the stairs, taking them two at a time, their hurried footsteps echoing in the stairwell. Emily's breath came in ragged gasps, but she pushed herself harder, knowing they couldn't afford to stop. Behind them, the officers struggled to their feet, but when they reached the door, it wouldn't open. James and Emily knew the trick to deal with that troublesome lock. It cost the officers precious seconds.

When the officers finally got through, they reached the end of the hall, but Emily and James were nowhere in sight. The old woman, hearing the commotion, opened her door.

"They always leave this way!" she shrieked, pointing frantically down the opposite hall.

The officers, misled by her certainty, charged in the wrong direction as Emily and James burst out into the alley, the cool morning air hitting their faces. They didn't stop running.

The officers burst out of the apartment building, Hartman in the lead, his radio already in hand as he barked into it. "This is Hartman. The Marshalls resisted arrest—James and Emily Marshall are on the run. We need immediate backup at the scene!"

Rebecca, crouching behind the rusted dumpster with Bruce and Sarah, heard his words. Her breath froze in her throat, and she gasped before she could stop herself. Bruce shot her a sharp look, too late. Hartman's head snapped in their direction.

He motioned silently to his partner, signaling for him to circle around the left side of the dumpster while Hartman himself moved right. Rebecca's heart pounded in her chest hoping he did not hear her.

Hartman crept closer, his steps deliberate, the barrel of his gun raised. He rounded the corner and stopped dead when he saw them huddled there.

Remembering the woman's picture in the folder he exclaimed in surprise "Rebecca Marshall?" Hartman's weapon trained on her as the weight of the situation settled over them like a crushing wave. "Raise your hands. All three of you. Slowly."

Bruce raised his hands first, his expression fierce but calm, trying to calculate their next move. Sarah, trembling, followed his lead, her hands shaking as she lifted them above her head. Rebecca stared at the officer, her breath shallow, heart hammering in her chest as she slowly raised her hands as well. Her mind raced, but no plan seemed feasible. They were going back to the camp of hell and torment.

Hartman's partner came around the other side, his hand resting on his holstered weapon, his eyes locked on Bruce. They were trapped.

Hartman took a step forward, eyes narrowing as he reached for his radio again. "This is Hartman. We've got three I bringing in, one of them I believe is Rebecca Marshall."

Suddenly, in a burst of desperate adrenaline, Bruce lunged forward, knocking Hartman's arm to the side just as the officer pulled the trigger. The gun fired, the shot ricocheting off the metal of the dumpster as Sarah let out a sharp scream. Bruce tackled Hartman, sending him crashing into the ground. The other officer scrambled for his gun, but Rebecca reacted in the same instant.

"Run!" Bruce yelled, struggling with Hartman on the pavement.

Rebecca shoved the officer backward with both hands, sending him stumbling with a startled grunt. Without missing a beat, she grabbed Sarah's arm and yanked her forward, their feet pounding the asphalt as they bolted toward the alleyway. Behind them, the officer regained his footing and raised his weapon, taking aim.

Bruce, with a swift kick, sent Hartman's gun skittering across the pavement and, in an instinctive move, struck the second officer from behind. In one fluid motion, he disarmed him and dashed into the alley, buying them the precious seconds they needed to gain distance.

Rebecca's legs burned as they sprinted, her vision blurring from the sheer panic that surged through her body. Behind them, Bruce was back on his feet, running just a few steps behind. Rebecca yelled, fighting to catch her breath, let's get to the place where all the homeless live.

The sound of heavy boots echoed behind them as the officers gave chase. Their shouts of "Stop!" rang out in the air, but they kept running, turning sharply down a narrow side street.

The camp came into view, hidden behind a makeshift fence of broken pallets and discarded tarps. The figures of the homeless, cloaked in shadows, watched their approach. Rebecca's lungs screamed for air, her whole body protesting the effort, but they couldn't stop now. Sarah was falling behind, Bruce aiding her.

"Help us!" she cried, her voice desperate as they neared the edge of the camp.

One of the older men, his face weathered and eyes sharp with understanding, stepped forward. He didn't need to be told what was happening. "This way," he rasped, jerking his head toward a gap between two crumbling buildings.

Rebecca, Bruce, and Sarah darted through the narrow passage, running between the walls. Behind them, the officers struggled to keep up. "They went this way!" Hartman's voice called out, the sound of his boots drawing nearer.

The homeless man shuffled forward, blocking the passage just as the officers arrived, panting and furious. "Which way did they go?" Hartman demanded, his eyes wild.

The man shrugged, giving them nothing but a blank stare. "Ain't seen nothin'. Nobody came through here."

Hartman cursed under his breath, his frustration boiling over, but he hesitated, unsure whether to trust the old man or not. Rebecca, Bruce, and Sarah crouched in the shadows, their breath shallow as they pressed themselves into the dark recesses of the narrow alley. The officers paced outside the camp, their radios buzzing with updates, but the trail had gone cold.

10

HEARTS AND HUNGER

"Desperation"

Pastor Daniels sat alone in his room at the back of the underground church, his hands clasped together as if in prayer, but his thoughts were far from prayers. His mind churned with doubts, fears, and unspoken struggles that threatened to swallow him whole. The dim light of the single flickering lamp cast long, eerie shadows that danced across the cold, bare walls, mimicking the unrest in his soul. The underground church had never been large, but now it was empty, emptier than ever before. The silence wasn't just the absence of people; it was an unyielding weight that grew more suffocating with each passing day.

It had been weeks since he had seen more than a few brave souls daring enough to seek refuge here. The crackdown was relentless against Christians, especially those who refused to align with the new world doctrine, they were being hunted, persecuted, and silenced. Most of the congregation had vanished into the shadows, hiding in fear, desperate not to lead the authorities back to him. They were afraid that a single misstep, a single visit to the underground church, would be enough to bring disaster to their beloved pastor. Fear had fractured the once-close community, leaving him isolated in the very place meant to provide sanctuary.

Daniels pressed his palms together more tightly, as if the physical act could somehow bring him closer to God in this moment of overwhelming despair. But his mind was adrift, tangled in a web of emotions too complex to sort through. The loneliness cut deeper with every hour spent in this hollowed-out room, and worse, the rising fear that perhaps they were losing—losing the battle, losing faith, losing everything they had fought so hard to protect.

His thoughts drifted, unbidden, to Sarah. There it was again, the flicker of something deep, unshakable, that shouldn't have been there. It gnawed at him, a feeling he couldn't quite name, and it terrified him more than the threat outside the church doors. She was younger than him, and yet, she was constantly on his mind. Why now? In the middle of chaos, in the midst of everything crumbling around him, why were these emotions tormenting him?

Guilt washed over him, thick and overwhelming. He wasn't supposed to feel this way. Not now. Not ever. And yet, despite his best efforts to bury the feelings, they rose unbidden, making his heart ache in ways he wasn't prepared for. He squeezed his eyes shut, trying to pray for relief, but the prayer never came.

Sarah clouded his mind. The image of her face was as vivid as ever—strong, yet vulnerable. He clenched his fists, feeling ashamed of how his heart quickened when he thought of her. She was so much younger, and his position as a pastor only magnified the struggle, the guilt. What kind of man allowed these feelings to surface, especially now? He scolded himself, trying to push the thoughts away, but it was impossible. His feelings for Sarah were undeniable, and that terrified him.

The loneliness, the isolation, and now this, emotions he had no business feeling, especially when the world was unraveling. He bowed his head, but the prayer still wouldn't come. Instead, an empty ache gnawed at him, the kind that left him questioning everything. He was afraid—not just of what was happening in the world, but of the turmoil inside himself. Sadness enveloped him, and he wondered what had happened to Sarah in the camp. The last he had heard, the camp was attacked and almost overrun, but then the military dispersed them. Was she still in the camp, being tortured, or worse?

Suddenly, a loud banging at the door cut through the oppressive silence, jolting Pastor Daniels upright. His heart leapt into his throat. He froze, every muscle tensing. Was it the authorities? Had they finally found him? The pounding continued, harder now, more intense. He stood, his legs heavy as lead, and made his way up the stairs toward the door. His breath was shallow, his mind racing. If it was them, he had only moments to escape through the back.

But then he heard it, a voice, frantic, familiar.

"Pastor Daniels! Please, please! It's Emily! Are you here? Please!"

Daniels' heart stopped, recognition flooding him. "Emily?" He rushed to the door, hearing her voice, strained and panicked. He hesitated, still fearing it might be a trick. But her desperate pleas broke through his caution.

"Please, Pastor Daniels! Open the door!"

With trembling hands, he unlatched the lock and swung the door open. Emily stumbled inside, followed by James, both of them breathless and wild-eyed. James slammed the door behind them, locking it again in one swift motion before doubling over, hands on his knees, gasping for air. Emily collapsed against the wall, clutching her side, her face pale, her breath coming in shallow bursts.

Daniels stood frozen for a moment, his mind struggling to catch up with what was happening. He moved toward them, instinctively placing a hand on Emily's shoulder. "What happened? Are you hurt?"

James straightened up, still panting heavily. Sweat dripped from his forehead, and he wiped it away with the back of his hand. His voice was hoarse, ragged. His throat burned from running and breathing the cold air. "They're after us. We barely made it here."

Emily, still trying to catch her breath, nodded frantically. Her eyes were wide, fear radiating from her. "The police... they were at our apartment. We had to run; they almost got us." Her voice cracked, and she pressed her hands to her face, fighting back sobs. "We didn't know where else to go."

Daniels' stomach dropped. The authorities were closing in, just as he had feared. "What if they were followed?" he thought. He guided them away from the door, the weight of the situation pressing down harder with each passing second. He had to get them to safety, away from the door, as if that would protect them from the danger.

"This way," he urged quietly, leading them toward the makeshift sanctuary below. The underground church was nothing more than a dim, hidden room beneath the building, but it was all he had. He guided them down the narrow stairs, his heart pounding in his chest, feeling the danger creeping closer with every step.

They collapsed onto the thrown together benches, still struggling to breathe. Their fear filled the room. James leaned his head back, closing his eyes, his chest heaving as he tried to recover. Emily curled into herself, her arms wrapped tightly around her knees, trembling uncontrollably.

Daniels knelt in front of them, his concern overwhelming the questions racing through his mind. "What happened?" he asked, his voice low but urgent. "Tell me everything."

James shook his head, as if trying to shake off the terror clinging to him. "They came to the apartment," he said, his words clipped and uneven. "A woman in the apartment tipped them off. They knew we were Christians. We barely made it out before they could arrest us."

Emily's voice was barely a whisper. "We ran... we didn't stop. I thought we weren't going to make it."

Daniels' heart tightened in his chest. He had known the risks, known that the authorities were starting to gather Christians like them, but hearing it firsthand—seeing the fear in their eyes—made it all the more real.

"You're safe now," he said softly, though the words felt hollow. Could anywhere truly be safe anymore?

But he had to believe it, for their sake. He had to protect them, no matter what it cost. He looked at them both, seeing the exhaustion etched into their faces, the sheer terror that had chased them here.

Pastor Daniels got them some water, and when they finally recovered, they sat together, trying to figure out what to do next.

Pastor Daniels took a deep breath, running a hand through beginnings of a full beard as he glanced between Emily and James. They looked completely drained—fear had taken its toll, and the weight of it pressed heavily in the room. Daniels sank onto the bench across from them, his shoulders sagging as the reality of their situation settled over him.

"No one's come to the church in weeks. They're all too scared." He paused, his voice thick with unspoken sorrow. "I can't blame them. It's not worth the risk anymore."

James wiped his forehead with his sleeve, still catching his breath. "What do we do, Pastor? Where do we go from here?"

Daniels sighed, looking around the small, darkened room that for a brief time been a sanctuary of hope. "I don't know," he admitted quietly. "I don't have the answers anymore." His voice wavered with the weight of failure, but he pressed on. "I'm barely hanging on." He hesitated, glancing toward the back of the church. "I tried to buy food, but it's nearly impossible now. The whole city's rationed and you have to have the new card. I've been getting by with help from the homeless."

"The homeless?" Emily asked, her voice weak but curious.

Daniels nodded, his gaze distant. "Their numbers have been growing rapidly. People are fleeing their homes, their lives—forced to live out on the streets. Hiding where no one thinks to look. They've been helping me when they can. Showing me where find scraps, old cans of food, whatever I can find. But even that's drying up."

He leaned forward, his elbows resting on his knees as he stared at the floor. "The world is unraveling, and the worst part is... no one seems to care. The new regime... they've convinced people that this is just a transition, that it's necessary for peace. But what's really happening is control—control over everything. Food, freedom, faith. It's all slipping away."

James shook his head, his jaw tight. "How long do we have before they come for us? Before they find this place?"

Daniels didn't answer right away. He looked up, his eyes dark with a mixture of dread and determination. "We'll hold on as long as we can. But we need to be ready. They're hunting us, and they won't stop until they've wiped us out or forced us to submit."

Daniels shifted, looking at Emily. "We'll figure out a plan," he said softly. "But for now, you need to rest. Both of you. We will figure out how to get food"

Emily nodded weakly, leaning her head against her father's shoulder. The fear had drained her, but in this small moment of respite, she allowed herself to close her eyes, just for a moment, trusting that they were safe. For now, it was enough.

James leaned forward, still breathing heavily, as he spoke in a low, urgent tone. "Daniels, I still have my cards. So does Emily. We can buy food. We've got enough in the account, but..." he hesitated, glancing at his daughter. "Using them would be like sending a beacon straight to the authorities. They've got us flagged, and the moment we make a transaction, they'll track us."

Pastor Daniels nodded, his expression grim. "They'd have you within minutes if you used those cards. But if we don't find a way to get food... well, hiding is one thing, but starving to death is another."

Emily's eyes darted nervously between the two. She could see the weight of the decision crushing them. "So... what do we do?" she whispered, her voice tinged with desperation.

James rubbed the back of his neck, frustration etched in every line of his face. "We need to get the money out, or food somehow. I was thinking... maybe we don't use it ourselves. What if we got one of the homeless to make the transaction? Maybe pull out cash from an ATM? They wouldn't think twice about someone like that, would they? I would share it with them."

Daniels frowned, deep in thought. "Maybe. But even pulling cash from an ATM could raise red flags if they've got the account flagged. Still, if we're careful enough..." He trailed off, tapping his fingers on the bench, his eyes dark with consideration. Suddenly, Daniels' expression changed "That won't work. Things have changed. You can't get cash anymore. You can only use the cards. Everyone has to turn in cash and it will be put on their card."

169

Daniels said finally. "I'm hungry, I am going to go out and see what I can find. Do you want to go? We will have to be careful."

Emily held her breath, fear flickering in her eyes as she recalled their narrow escape. She gripped her father's arm tightly.

James took her hand, giving it a gentle squeeze. "Alright," he said, his voice firm. "We head to the homeless area, and see what we can find. We'll keep a low profile."

Daniels nodded, rising to his feet. "Let's go. No sense in."

The three of them crept out into the cool air, sticking to the shadows as they made their way toward the area where many of the homeless had gathered. The streets were eerily quiet, save for the distant sounds of sirens and the occasional rumble of vehicles passing through the deserted city. Tension hung thick in the air.

But as they neared the homeless encampment, James suddenly stopped in his tracks, pulling Emily and Daniels down into a crouch. His eyes were wide, locked onto a small group of officers—Hartman and his partner, standing among at least eight more officers, scanning the area. Their radios crackling faintly as Hartman spoke into it.

James strained to hear, his heart pounding, but it was Emily with her sharp hearing who caught the fragments of conversation. Her eyes went wide as she gasped, clutching her father's arm. "Dad… they're looking for Mom!" she whispered, her voice trembling. "They're searching for Rebecca Marshall."

James' face tightened, a storm of fear and determination flashing in his eyes. He turned to Daniels, his voice barely audible. "We have to find her first. Now!"

They moved cautiously, circling around to approach the encampment from the other side several block behind. The fear gnawed at them with every step, the weight of the officers' presence like a shadow looming over them. But they couldn't leave without finding Rebecca. She was out there, somewhere among the scattered souls trying to survive.

They began asking around quietly, trying to blend into the shadows of the camp as they searched for any sign of her. Every face they passed seemed to carry the same worn expression—tired, broken, lost. But they kept moving, their hearts heavy with dread, knowing the authorities were just steps away.

James whispered to Emily, his voice thick with urgency. "We will find your mom and get her out of here. Whatever it takes."

There were so many people—too many, all desperate, huddled in groups or alone, scattered across the filthy street like discarded remnants of lives once lived. Emily's heart began to race as they moved through a narrow alley. Everywhere she looked, there were faces, hollow, sunken eyes staring back at her from behind piles of boxes and tattered blankets. She swallowed hard, suddenly aware of how out of place they were. She had just taken a hot shower yesterday morning, getting ready for school, her hair clean and brushed. She wore decent clothes, far too clean for this world of grime and despair. She felt... exposed.

A prickling sensation ran up the back of her neck, the unmistakable feeling of eyes on her. Emily glanced around, trying to appear calm, but the growing paranoia gripped her tighter with each step. Everyone was watching. She could feel it. Each face she passed seemed to turn toward her, as if their desperation could see through her, see the difference, the privilege she still clung to, despite everything that had fallen apart.

James sensed it, too. He felt her anxiety like a ripple in the air, the way her pace quickened, her breath shallow and uneven. He tugged her closer, trying to be reassuring, but the paranoia was seeping into him as well. It was hard not to feel it, the weight of hundreds of eyes, the sense that the world was closing in on them. They were losing focus, their mission slipping away as fear gnawed at the edges of their resolve.

James' eyes darted back and forth, unable to shake the creeping sense that they didn't belong here. Everyone around them was broken, desperate, clinging to what little they had left, crates, dirty blankets, and boxes filled with their last few possessions. Some of them had their arms draped protectively over their meager belongings, their gazes sharp and suspicious. Were they staring at him? Judging him for having more?

Suddenly, it felt like they weren't just being watched, they were being marked. James' grip on Emily tightened as his mind raced. How could they have been so careless? If they could have dressed differently, acted differently. Their clean clothes, their obvious discomfort, it was like a beacon in this sea of despair. The fear closed in around him, making it hard to think, hard to breathe.

Every movement around them seemed deliberate now, every pair of eyes seemed to follow their steps. He tried to keep moving, tried to push through the rising panic, but it felt like they were walking into a trap, as if the walls of the alley were closing in.

Yet, Pastor Daniels seemed oblivious to it all. He strode ahead, his eyes scanning the crowd for any sign of danger, but his focus was on the distance, on the faces he'd seen a hundred times before. He didn't feel the tension pressing down on them; he didn't sense the rising dread that threatened to choke Emily and James. This was his world. He had worked with these people for years, ministered to them in their pain and loss. To him, this was home, but to James and Emily, it was a nightmare, a living, breathing mass of fear and suspicion that seemed to tighten around them with every step they took. What Emily and James were feeling wasn't just paranoia, it was a warning, a visceral instinct they couldn't ignore. Yet, Pastor Daniels remained oblivious, focused ahead, unaware of the danger looming closer with each passing moment.

The alley grew narrower as they continued, the air thick with the stench of decay and hopelessness. Trash littered the ground, discarded bottles, torn rags, and bits of food decaying. People crouched along the sides, watching, waiting. Emily's skin prickled with the growing certainty that they weren't going to make it through. The stares were no longer passive. Now it felt as though every set of eyes bore into her, judging, angry, desperate for what she had. They wanted her card she thought.

She couldn't stop her hands from trembling, her breath coming in shallow, panicked gasps. James felt it too, his heart hammering in his chest, his grip tightening around her arm as if he could shield her from the unspoken threat surrounding them.

"Daniels..." James muttered under his breath, but the pastor was too far ahead, his eyes locked on something in the distance.

The alley felt like it was closing in on them. Every step brought Emily deeper into a world that seemed foreign and terrifying, as if every set of eyes was watching, waiting for her to stumble. The tension had her heart in a vise, and she could barely breathe. The stench of rot and filth clung to the air, mixing with the sounds of quiet whispers and shuffling bodies. James walked ahead, tense, but trying to remain calm. Pastor Daniels had stopped, scanning the crowd, Emily and James walked up behind him.

Suddenly, from the shadows, there was movement, a figure in a dirty, torn hoodie lunged from the side, hands outstretched. Emily barely had time to react before cold fingers gripped her arm, yanking her back. A shriek pierced the air, and in a panic, Emily recoiled, trying to pull away. The figure clung to her, and they both tumbled to the ground in a blur of tangled limbs and frantic motions.

"Emily!" James shouted turning around, his voice sharp with alarm as he was caught off guard by the chaos. Pastor Daniels turned quickly and started to run to her aid, but just as he moved, another figure, wild-eyed, hunched, charged toward Pastor Daniels.

"Pastor!" James called, his voice laced with fear. Daniels spun around, eyes wide, only to see the second attacker barreling toward him with a desperate intensity.

The air crackled with tension, confusion blurring reality as the scene unfolded in flashes of panic and motion. Emily struggled on the ground, fear gripping her heart, her mind racing as she fought to free herself. The alley erupted with murmurs and movement, the homeless crowd stirring as if sensing the violence that was breaking out.

"Let go of her!" James shouted, rushing forward, his mind racing with fear and instinct.

Suddenly, the figure holding Emily screamed, "Emily! Emily! It's me!" The voice cracked with desperation, raw and familiar. "It's your momma!"

Emily froze. The world seemed to tilt as she realized the person in the ragged, dirt-covered hoodie clinging to her wasn't an attacker, but her mother, Rebecca. "Mom?" Emily whispered, her heart hammering against her chest. Tears brimmed in her eyes, the horror of the moment shifting into a new, unbearable reality. Relief. Joy.

Rebecca, disheveled and weak, clung to her daughter, sobbing into her shoulder. "I thought... I thought I lost you..." Her voice broke, trembling with emotion.

As the reality of the moment sank in, James turned toward Pastor Daniels. The man charging at him skidded to a halt, breathing heavily. "Pastor Daniels, it's me, Sarah." Her voice, though raspy from exhaustion, was unmistakable. She stood trembling, her body weakened from days of hardship, but there was no mistaking the love in her eyes.

Daniels, frozen in disbelief, blinked as if trying to clear the fog in his mind. "Sarah?" he whispered, his voice cracking with emotion. His mind struggled to reconcile the ragged woman before him with the Sarah he had longed to see for so long. His heart skipped, guilt and confusion swirling inside him.

From the shadows, Bruce emerged, his tall figure rising from the debris, his eyes locking onto Pastor Daniels with urgency. "It's okay," he said, his voice rough but edged with relief. "I was helping them find you."

James stood stunned, staring at the unexpected reunion unfolding before him. Pastor Daniels, still shaken, approached Sarah, his heart pounding. "What happened to you?" he asked, his voice barely above a whisper. Tears already forming in his eyes.

Rebecca, still holding Emily as if she might disappear, wiped away her tears with trembling fingers. Her voice broke as she whispered, "I prayed for you every single day... I never stopped believing God would unite me with you again. Thank you Lord..."

"I thought I'd never see you again," Sarah whispered, her eyes locking with Daniels', and for a moment, the world outside the alley faded.

James gently helped Rebecca and Emily to their feet, and the three of them fell into a tight embrace, their arms wrapped around each other as if letting go would shatter the fragile moment. Tears flowed freely, their hearts bound by the overwhelming relief, love, and their answered prayers that had brought them back together.

Their embrace tightened, as a sudden shout shattered the moment. "There they are!" The sound of heavy boots pounding against the pavement echoed down the alley. The police, now in full pursuit, rushed toward them, voices crackling through the radios. "We've located them! They're all here!" The officer's frantic hollering sent a chill down their spines as they broke apart.

"Famine"

The underground church was cold and damp, lit only by a few flickering candles that cast long shadows on the stone walls. Rebecca leaned back against the wall, feeling the cold seep into her bones as she took a deep breath, trying to steady her racing heart. The adrenaline was still coursing through her veins, but now, in this brief moment of safety, exhaustion began to take over.

James sat beside her, his head in his hands, while Sarah and Bruce huddled near the small group of candles, whispering to one another. Emily, silent and wide-eyed, clung to her mother's side, while Pastor Daniels stood at the center of the room, his expression distant, as if he was deep in prayer.

For a moment, no one spoke. The weight of their escape from the alley pressed down on them.

"I didn't think we'd make it," Bruce finally muttered, breaking the silence. His voice was low, filled with disbelief. "They are everywhere... those police..."

174

"They are," Sarah agreed, her voice steady but shaken. "It felt like the whole city was closing in on us."

Rebecca nodded, her mind drifting back to those frantic moments in the alley. The police had been closing in, their shouts and boots echoing through the narrow streets.

Then, the woman, an old, familiar face from the streets—had appeared. Her presence had been a sudden burst of hope in the chaos. She had called out to Pastor Daniels, pointing them back to a narrow side alley they had missed in their panic.

"Run, Pastor! Run!" she had yelled, her voice sharp and commanding, despite her frail appearance.

The old woman, standing like a sentinel, yelled, "Everyone, get up. Now. Block the alley!" Homeless men and women, once invisible to the rest of the world, rose up at her command. They formed a wall, a human barrier that blocked the police's path, giving Rebecca, Sarah, Bruce, and the others just enough time to slip away.

It had been the only reason they made it to the underground church. Without those people, those forgotten souls, they would have been caught.

"We owe them everything," Rebecca said quietly, glancing at James. "That woman, the others, they didn't have to help us, but they did."

James lifted his head, nodding in agreement. "They put themselves in danger for us," he said, his voice heavy with gratitude. "People we didn't trust... or even understand."

A wave of guilt crashed over him as he spoke. Just hours before, as they had walked through the homeless encampment, James had felt nothing but fear. The gaunt, watchful faces, the murmured voices, the sense of being out of place, it had unnerved him. He'd clutched Emily's arm, his paranoia growing with each step, sure that they would be marked as outsiders, as targets. He had expected hostility, not help.

"I was afraid of them," he admitted quietly, his voice thick with remorse. "When we walked through the camp earlier, I thought... I thought they were a threat. But I was wrong. They saved us."

Rebecca squeezed his arm, her eyes filled with understanding. But it was Pastor Daniels who spoke, his voice steady and calm. "Fear does that to all of us, James. It blinds us to the people around us, makes us see them as threats rather than what they really are—our brothers and sisters, even in the darkest places."

James lowered his head, the weight of his misjudgment heavy in his chest. He had doubted the very people who had risen to protect them. And now, that truth was hard to bear.

"God sends help when we least expect it," Pastor Daniels continued, his deep voice breaking through the tension in the room. "We can't always understand His ways, but we must never doubt His providence."

Rebecca felt the weight of everything she had endured pressing down on her, her body trembling with exhaustion. It was as if her strength was slipping away, her limbs heavy and unresponsive. She turned to James, her voice weak. "Is there somewhere I can lay down?"

Concern flickered across his face as he nodded. "Come with me," he said softly, guiding her to a small pallet tucked away in a back room. She sank onto it, the thin bedding a welcome relief, and closed her eyes, letting the tension begin to release from her weary body.

Rebecca drifted into a deep, dreamless sleep at first, her body giving in to the exhaustion that had weighed her down for so long. The pallet beneath her offered little comfort, but it didn't matter. Darkness wrapped around her like a blanket, pulling her deeper into oblivion. Then, without warning, the void shifted, giving way to a vision so vivid it felt as though she had been transported to another realm.

The heavens darkened as the scroll in Jesus' hands unrolled further. Standing sovereign and unshaken, He reached for the third seal, His movements steady and deliberate. Tension rippled through the celestial realm, an almost tangible stillness as creation seemed to hold its breath. Then, with a crack like the shattering of the earth's very foundation, the seal broke, and the sound reverberated across realms.

A commanding voice rang out, resonant and clear, filling the expanse like the blast of a trumpet.

"Come and see."

A shadow stirred against the backdrop of the heavens, moving with a sinister grace. Emerging from the darkness was a new rider astride a horse as black as the abyss. The black steed moved soundlessly, its presence suffocating and cold, as though it carried the weight of despair itself.

The rider, cloaked in shadow, held an ancient set of scales in his skeletal hand. They teetered precariously, the balance shifting with each motion. The scales gleamed faintly, not as instruments of justice but as harbingers of scarcity, weighing out the fragile survival of the world below.

As the black horse moved forward, a voice, hollow and foreboding, echoed across the Earth, "A quart of wheat for a denarius, and three quarts of barley for a denarius. And do not harm the oil and the wine."

The meaning struck Rebecca in her spirit, Famine had come. The world would now know hunger on an unimaginable scale. Prices would soar, food would vanish, and the desperate would give their lives for the smallest scrap of sustenance.

Rebecca's vision shifted, and she was thrust into the heart of the devastation.

Markets once brimming with abundance stood eerily empty, their stalls stripped bare. Coins clinked in trembling hands as crowds jostled for the meager rations left behind. The cries of hungry children filled the air, their mothers clutching them tightly, hollow-eyed and desperate. The rich, once secure in their wealth, now stared helplessly at the rising cost of survival.

The rider of the black horse moved swiftly through cities and villages, unseen by human eyes but leaving ruin in his wake. The scales he carried tipped further and further, a mocking reminder of the imbalance his presence wrought. The rich hoarded what little was spared, oil and wine, but even their opulence was hollow. Gold could not fill their bellies, and their luxury became meaningless as starvation closed its grip on the earth.

Rebecca's heart ached as she witnessed the devastation. The scenes played out before her like an endless, haunting nightmare. The weight of the vision pressed on her chest, a suffocating reminder of the fragility of human existence.

Suddenly, the vision began to fade, and Rebecca awoke with a sharp intake of breath. Her body trembled as her mind scrambled to process what she had seen. She shifted, clutching the blanket close. She could hear the others talking from down the hall.

She couldn't explain it, but in her spirit, she knew there was hope in the middle of this chaos. Though her heart still mourned the world's suffering, she felt a flicker of hope deep within.

Rebecca lay back against the thin pillow, staring at the ceiling as she whispered a prayer. The vision's weight lingered, but so did the peace, grounding her for the trials yet to come.

"The Orchestration"

Ben Rashan stood in the heart of his inner sanctum, surrounded by walls lined with maps, and reports stacked on his desk. The maps were marked with red zones representing the devastation caused by his policies. The hot setting sun cast long shadows and bathed the room in a deep crimson glow, accentuating the sharp lines of determination etched into his face. His mind churned under the weight of his decisions, choices he believed were saving the world but were, in truth, leading it toward ruin.

Rashan had ascended to power with a vision: to save the planet from the ravages of climate change, to restore balance between humanity and the Earth. The world had rallied behind him, captivated by his charisma and his message of peace with nature. They worshiped at the altar of his doctrine, an ideology that placed the Earth, "Mother Gaia" at the center of all life. The cost, he promised, was necessary for the survival of the planet.

But as Rashan made his decisions, he didn't know he was being used. Satan's whispers filled his mind, each thought twisting further from the truth, yet Rashan saw only righteousness in his path. He believed he was the savior of Earth, while behind the scenes, the Rider of the Black Horse was at work, bringing famine to the world through the very policies Rashan enforced.

He rummaged through the papers, where new reports of drought and crop failure were in red, one after the other. His chest tightened with the pressure, but his resolve never wavered. "It's for the greater good," he muttered to himself, eyes narrowing. "We must reduce carbon emissions, at any cost."

The first step in his grand design had been to wage war on CO_2, labeling it the enemy of the planet. Rashan's policies restricted CO_2 emissions to nearly zero, shutting down industries and forbidding the burning of fossil fuels. What he didn't understand was that CO_2 was part of the natural design. Plants, crops, everything that sustained life, depended on it. The more carbon dioxide in the air, the more bountiful the harvests. But Rashan, in his zealotry, saw CO_2 only as pollution. And so, the very essence that sustained the Earth's greenery was being stripped away.

As carbon levels fell, so did crop yields. Fields once brimming with golden wheat and lush vegetation began to wither under the strain of unnatural conditions. But Rashan, blinded by his crusade, interpreted the failing crops as a need for even more drastic measures.

The ban on animal livestock followed swiftly. "Cattle and chickens," Rashan declared at a global summit, his voice firm and unyielding, "are damaging the environment. The methane they produce is killing the planet. We must limit animal agriculture." And so, with a single sweeping motion, cattle farms were shuttered, meat production was outlawed in many regions, and even chickens, once a common staple, were deemed harmful to Mother Earth. The world's food supply dwindled further.

In their place, Rashan proclaimed a new global standard for protein. "Insects," he declared, "will be the sustainable answer for human health. Crickets will become the primary source of protein, manufactured into all forms of food." His voice carried a cold certainty as the decree spread worldwide. Beneath the surface, however, the true horror was revealed.

As Satan possessed Rashan, a cruel and twisted laughter echoed through his mind, like the shadow of death. "God's creation, once abundant with fields of golden grain, providing bread for all mankind," Satan gloated with venomous delight, "will now be reduced to crawling insects. The very soil that gave life will now bear corruption. I will pervert what was once pure, twisting creation into a mockery of its former self, a haunt of filth and wickedness. Let them feast on the lowest of the earth, for I will strip them of the blessings they once took for granted."

Fossil fuels, the lifeblood of agriculture, were outlawed entirely. Farmers could no longer use machinery to tend to their crops. "We must return to the land," Rashan insisted. "To the old ways, using only the power of our hands and the strength of the sun." But without the power of machines, vast fields of crops went untended. Harvests rotted in the fields, and the world's agricultural systems ground to a halt. Rashan praised the reduction in CO_2, unaware that the lifeblood of humanity, food, was disappearing before his eyes.

The famine that had begun in whispers was now spreading like wildfire. People were starving. Yet Rashan, manipulated by the dark forces he didn't understand, pressed on. His mind was captivated by the delusion that this was all necessary for the planet to heal.

The final blow came with the geoengineering programs, Rashan's most ambitious project. To counter the warming of the Earth, his scientists implemented a process known as stratospheric aerosol injection (SAI). By releasing reflective aerosols into the stratosphere, they aimed to block portions of the sun's rays and cool the planet. However, they failed to anticipate the resulting chaos. As the upper atmosphere cooled, the Earth's surface temperature plummeted, leading to severe crop failures and the contraction of the planet's crust.

Tectonic plates, once held in balance, began to shift unnaturally. Earthquakes ravaged cities, and dormant volcanoes suddenly awakened, spewing ash into the sky, further blocking out the sun. The world shuddered, not under the weight of human pollution, but under the weight of human arrogance.

Rashan watched the reports roll in, the data cascading down the screens, volcanic eruptions, massive earthquakes along fault lines, and the cooling temperatures that had gone far beyond what had been predicted. His advisors whispered concerns, but Rashan silenced them with a wave of his hand. "This is temporary," he declared, though his voice wavered ever so slightly. "The Earth is resetting. This is a new beginning."

But the new beginning was one of death and starvation.

Farmers, now without access to water and unable to grow crops in the rapidly cooling climate, were mandated to reduce their already dwindling water usage. Reservoirs were rationed strictly for the elite, leaving the common people with nothing. Desperate faces appeared on the screen of his phone, a mother clutching her starving child, entire villages withering away to dust as crops failed, and nations teetering on the brink of collapse.

And yet, Rashan continued.

"The Earth must be saved," he repeated, his eyes hollow as Satan whispered sweet reassurances into his ear, filling him with false purpose. "We are on the right path."

The rider of the black horse rode through the world, and famine covered the earth like a shroud. Where Rashan thought he was healing the planet, he was in fact unleashing death. Fields were empty, storehouses barren, and even the wealthy began to feel the grip of hunger. Markets, once bustling with trade, were ghost towns, their shelves picked clean. Desperate people, starving, began to turn on each other. Society unraveled as hunger gnawed at the souls of men.

Rashan believed he was steering humanity toward a brighter future, but he was a mere pawn in Satan's grand design. Yet more frequently, he felt an unsettling sense that he was being used, as if his decisions were laced with evil. He told himself it was merely the burden of leadership, a natural consequence of bearing the weight of the world. But each move he made, intended to protect the Earth, became a tool of destruction.

Meanwhile, the shadow of the black horse loomed ever larger, the scales tipping relentlessly toward famine.

The famine that swept the earth was not God's wrath, but the result of man's arrogance and Satan's deceit. In their blind pursuit to save the planet, men like Ben Rashan, manipulated by the lord of the air, twisted the balance of creation, bringing ruin instead of restoration. The ban on livestock, misguided environmental policies, and reckless tampering with nature unleashed devastation. This famine was not divine punishment, but the inevitable consequence of human pride and the evil allowed to flourish, as Satan reveled in turning God's creation into a wasteland of suffering. The seals were simple prophecies, foretold before the foundation of the world. As mankind wages war against God's creation and His people, the true wrath of God draws ever closer because of their arrogance.

11

GLOBAL DEATH

"The Refuge Beneath"

Rebecca entered the room quietly, her steps deliberate as she tried to shake the heaviness of the vision that still lingered in her mind. Her nap had been anything but restful. She wanted to talk about her dreams, but felt the weariness of the others in the room, their unease an undercurrent to all the day's events. Taking a seat in the corner she decided to keep her dreams to herself. She folded her hands in her lap and listened as the tension in their voices filled the space.

It didn't take long for the conversation to turn grim.

Sarah looked over at Pastor Daniels, her face pale and vulnerable. "How long can we keep running? They're going to find us eventually. What if they find us here?"

Pastor Daniels sighed, his shoulders slumping slightly under the weight of their situation. "I don't know how long we have," he admitted. "But what I do know is that we're not running just to stay hidden. We're running to buy time, time to gather, time to pray, and time to prepare. This fight isn't against the authorities, not really. It's against the powers and principalities working behind them."

Rebecca felt the weight of his words settle into the room like a lead blanket. It wasn't just a physical battle. It never had been. This was a spiritual war—a war for their souls.

Emily, who had been silent until now, finally spoke, her voice soft and filled with uncertainty. "What if they catch us? What if... what if this is it?"

James wrapped an arm around her shoulders, pulling her close. "They won't catch us," he said, though Rebecca could hear the uncertainty in his voice. "We'll keep moving if we have to. We'll stay ahead of them."

Rebecca glanced at James, the same doubt gnawing at the back of her mind. How many more escapes could they make before the authorities finally caught them? She could see the fear in everyone's eyes, the exhaustion etched into their faces. It truly was a miracle they had made it this far. But how many more miracles would they need?

Pastor Daniels was right, though. This wasn't just about staying ahead of the authorities—it was about standing firm in their faith, no matter the cost.

The room fell silent again as the weight of the situation pressed down on them. Rebecca closed her eyes, drawing in a deep breath. They were safe, for now. But tomorrow was another battle. Another test of their endurance and faith.

For what felt like an eternity, no one moved. The soft flicker of candlelight painted shadows on the cracked walls, a reminder that they were living on borrowed time.

Finally, it was Bruce who broke the silence, his voice low but filled with conviction. "I haven't told you all much about myself," he began, glancing around the room. The others stirred, their tired eyes now fixed on him.

"I was lost, for a long time. I didn't believe in anything." Bruce paused, his gaze falling on Sarah, who sat close to him. "But then... I found Sarah. She brought hope into my life when I didn't think there was any left. Because of her, I found my faith in Jesus. I found a reason to fight, a real purpose."

Sarah's eyes softened as she looked at him. There was a connection between them, something quietly growing, though neither had spoken of it. Bruce shifted, the weight of his words heavy in the small room.

"And now we need to get to work," he said, his tone sharpening as he addressed the group. "The city's managed to restore power in some areas, and now it's reached here. I can't stand the thought of us just sitting around, huddled without light or heat. My father... he was an electrician. I learned a few things from him. I might be able to jump the meter outside and get power flowing back into this place—we just need to find it."

He turned to Pastor Daniels, determination etched on his face. "We can't live on candlelight forever. We need to make this place livable for the women, for all of us. They deserve some comfort after everything they've endured. They've already suffered through a living hell."

His eyes flicked briefly toward Sarah as he spoke, and for a moment, the bond between them was undeniable. He felt something stirring inside him, a growing affection, though she was older than him by at least fifteen years. It didn't matter. There was a connection, and he knew she felt it too. His gaze softened with compassion as he turned back to Pastor Daniels. "We need to make this place better for them."

Pastor Daniels nodded, listening closely. "What else do we need?"

"Water," Bruce said decisively. "Is there a meter we can turn on? We are hiding here, but if we're going to survive, we need more than just a dark room and candles. We need water, and we need food."

Daniels glanced around, rubbing his chin thoughtfully. "I haven't checked for a water meter," he admitted. "But you're right. We'll need to start looking for supplies. We can't survive on hope alone."

Bruce looked toward Rebecca, who had been quiet during the conversation. "We need to get into your apartment. Is there anything there we could use?"

Rebecca hesitated, biting her lip. "I left my apartment over a month ago when they took me to the camp. I don't think it's safe to go back."

Bruce nodded, considering his options. "We will see if we can get in your apartment tonight. And you, Pastor? Do you still have a place we could sneak into for supplies?"

Pastor Daniels looked down, regret darkening his features. "I haven't been back to my place since the crackdown started. They were looking for me, and I barely escaped. But the church... I have food there, stockpiled for when we used to do distributions. I was afraid to go back, but maybe now we don't have a choice and it may not even be there."

Bruce's eyes brightened at the mention of food. "Good. We'll need that. The three of us—me, James, and you, Pastor—we'll go out tonight. I'll see what I can do about the power and water, and we'll scavenge what we can from your church."

The weight of his words sank into the room. They could not just hide. They had to act, had to prepare, because the darkness around them was closing in fast. The air was tense, but beneath it, there was a faint spark of hope, something tangible they could cling to.

"How far is the church from here?" Bruce asked, his voice steady as he began mentally preparing for the night ahead.

"Not far," Pastor Daniels replied. "But it'll be dangerous. The authorities are tightening their search."

Bruce cracked a small, determined smile. "Everything's dangerous now. But we can't sit around waiting for miracles. We need to make our own."

Pastor Daniels smiled, his eyes softening. "We are God's miracles, Bruce. And He works through us."

Hours passed in focused silence, broken only by the sound of hushed conversation and the scrape of objects being moved. Bruce worked steadily, his brow furrowed in concentration as he carefully bypassed the broken connection left by the removed electrical meter and restored power to the building. The soft hum of electricity felt like a small victory, but they kept the lights off in areas visible from outside to avoid detection. They only lit the spaces below with no windows, and any window was carefully covered to prevent any light from escaping their new hidden home.

"We've got power," Bruce said quietly, a faint smile tugging at the corners of his lips. "But no lights where they can be seen from outside."

James gave a nod of approval, still preoccupied with his own task of clearing space. Sarah, though exhausted, had helped Rebecca bring in blankets and pillows they'd retrieved from their apartments, and hopefully we can get more supplies from Pastor Daniels' church. They had found an old cart and a couple of dollies, and though the trek had been grueling, they'd managed to bring back a few mattresses—enough to make the place feel less like a refuge and more like a home. The musty smell of the underground lingered, but with the fresh linens and makeshift beds, it no longer felt like they were merely hiding—it felt like they were surviving.

Bruce wiped his hands on his shirt, glancing toward Sarah, who caught his eye and gave a small smile in return. His heart stirred. The bond between them had grown, and while he knew she was older, it didn't matter. There was something about her presence that grounded him, gave him strength he hadn't known he needed.

"We need water next," Bruce said, turning to Pastor Daniels, who had been deep in thought. "Is there a meter somewhere we can turn on?"

Daniels frowned, scratching his chin. "It should be around the back, in the alley. It might be locked, but if we can cut the lock, we should be able to get it working…"

Bruce nodded, determination setting in. "We'll check it out. I don't want the women here without running water. They need comfort. We all do."

Rebecca, overhearing him, looked up, her eyes filled with appreciation. "Thank you, Bruce."

Bruce shrugged, trying to hide the warmth in his chest. "It's what we need to do. We've made it this far. No point in giving up now."

As they worked, Bruce's mind churned with practical details. They couldn't stay cut off from the world forever. They needed supplies, information, and a way to know what was happening outside without exposing themselves to the authorities.

"We need more supplies," Bruce said, looking at James and Pastor Daniels. "Not just food and water, but intel. We need to know what's going on out there."

Daniels nodded in agreement. "There's food stockpiled at the church. I haven't dared to go back since the crackdown, but now… we'll need to."

"And phones," Bruce added. "We'll remove the SIM cards, that way they can't trace us. When we sneak out, we can use free Wi-Fi spots to download news, both from the government and the underground sites."

"We left the phones at the apartment," James said. "I'll get them."

The plan was already taking shape in Bruce's mind. He, James, and Pastor Daniels would head out tonight. He would check on the power and water meters, and then they'd gather what they could from the church after getting the phones. It would be risky, but it was necessary.

"We can't stay cut off forever," he murmured, more to himself than to the others. "We need to know what's coming."

Pastor Daniels placed a hand on his shoulder. "And we will. Tonight, we'll go together. But remember, Bruce—we're not just making our own miracles. We're part of something bigger. God can guide us."

Bruce smiled faintly, the weight of their situation pressing on him, but the resolve was clear in his eyes. "How far is the church from here, Pastor?"

"About twenty minutes, if we move quietly."

Bruce nodded. "Good. Let's get this place set up. Then we move."

The sense of purpose hung in the air as they finished preparing the underground hideaway. For now, it felt like they had reclaimed a small corner of the world, away from the chaos and violence that roiled outside.

"Pale Horse"

Rebecca sat alone in the back room, the dim light from a single crack in the boarded window barely illuminating the sparse space. She perched on an old wooden box, her hands gripping the edge as if steadying herself against the weight of her thoughts. She had sought this solitude to think, to make sense of the visions and dreams that had consumed her.

Her mind raced as she pieced together the fragmented images, the breaking seals, the riders, the escalating chaos. They weren't just dreams, they were a puzzle, each piece woven into the next. A deep stirring moved in her spirit, a sense that these revelations were connected, forming a larger picture she was only beginning to understand.

Rebecca closed her eyes, drawing a long, trembling breath. She concentrated, willing herself to remember every detail, every word, every image etched into her consciousness. As the memories sharpened, a sudden, overwhelming force gripped her. It was as if she were ripped from her body, hurled through space and time at an incomprehensible speed. Colors and shapes blurred around her, and the sensation of weightlessness was replaced by an unshakable pull, drawing her into yet another vision she had yet experienced.

Jesus stood before the scroll, His movements steady, deliberate. His hand reached out again, fingers pressing lightly against the fourth seal. Despite the calmness of His actions, there was a weight in His gaze, a deep understanding of what was to come. Without a sound, the seal was torn away.

A chilling wind swept through the unseen realms, carrying with it an eerie silence. Then, a voice, hollow and cold, pierced the stillness, "Come."

From the shadows, the Pale Horse emerged. Its color was ashen, lifeless, a hue of decay and finality. The Rider upon it was a skeletal figure cloaked in shadows, a void where life had never been. Unlike the other riders, there was no banner, no weapon, no symbol of conquest or balance. This was Death, and behind him followed Hades, a creeping darkness that consumed all in its path.

The Pale Horse moved silently, its hooves brushing the ground with barely a sound, yet each step left a trail of rot and desolation. The air grew colder as light itself seemed to retreat, replaced by an oppressive void. No cry or clash of armies heralded his arrival, only the crushing weight of finality that seemed to seep into her as she looked in, as if ice flowed through her veins.

Rebecca felt the truth of the vision settle deep within her. This was no act of divine wrath but the culmination of humanity's own self-destruction. The unchecked hatred, greed, and violence of the world had emboldened the powers of darkness, granting Death the strength to march unopposed. This was the natural end of a world that had rejected the light.

A voice, heavy with authority, echoed across the heavens, "Power was given to them over a fourth of the earth, to kill with sword, with hunger, with disease, and by the beasts of the earth."

Rebecca's heart wrenched as she witnessed devastation in the Rider's wake. There were no battles, no armies clashing, only the silent, unrelenting advance of Death. Disease swept through streets like an invisible tide, leaving bodies where they fell. Starvation hollowed out entire nations, their lands barren and lifeless. Even the beasts of the earth turned against humanity, driven mad by the collapse of the natural order.

Rebecca gasped, her eyes snapping open as she was wrenched back into the dark room. Her heart pounding as if it might break free. The visions lingered, vivid and unrelenting, burned into her mind. Her body trembled as tears streamed down her face, and she leaned forward, wrapping her arms around herself.

She knew and felt the dread in knowing that the great tribulation was no longer a concept, it was here. It was real, unfolding in agonizing detail in her visions, in the world.

Rebecca sat in the silence, her whispered prayer trembling in the oppressive air.

"Triangle"

Pastor Daniels sat alone in the dimly lit room, his hands clasped together in prayer. No words came to his lips, but his heart was heavy, laden with feelings he couldn't reconcile. Sarah's image lingered in his mind—her face, her resilience, and the inner light that drew people to her. It was a light he admired, a beacon of hope in the darkness of their struggles. But he couldn't ignore the growing sense that his admiration had become something deeper, something not right for a man in his position.

He remembered moments shared during ministry, when Sarah's eyes softened at his words and a silent understanding seemed to pass between them. It was a spiritual connection—at least it had been. Now, as he watched her closeness with Bruce develop into something more, a different kind of ache filled his heart. It was no longer just admiration but a longing he had tried to suppress.

Sarah and Bruce had been through hell together. Bruce had risked his life to save her from captivity, deepening a bond that Daniels knew he couldn't match. The look in Bruce's eyes when he was near her was tender, even protective, and Sarah seemed to lean on him in ways she hadn't leaned on anyone before.

Daniels felt the tension growing within him. It wasn't just the danger from the authorities that weighed on him; it was the guilt of feeling something he couldn't allow. He found himself glancing at Sarah not as one of his flock but as a woman—a woman who stirred emotions he never intended to feel. Each time he encouraged Bruce to support Sarah, he told himself it was for the best. This was God's will, he reasoned. But as he continued to push them together, the guilt deepened, mingling with the pain of watching her move further away.

Sarah sensed something was different. Daniels had become distant, less personal, and it confused her. She had once harbored feelings for him, simmering quietly beneath the surface. His sudden withdrawal felt like rejection, stirring confusion and a sense of abandonment she struggled to suppress. At times, she found herself staring at Daniels when he wasn't looking, her heart aching with the confusion of mixed signals. She wanted to confront him, to demand an answer, but fear of the truth held her back. Daniels' inner conflict was becoming clearly visible.

Feeling the weight of his own struggles, Daniels agreed to join Sarah and Bruce as they stepped out into the chilly night air. The streets were quiet, with only the distant hum of the city breaking the silence. Sarah, carrying a bag of canned goods, led the way, her resolve evident despite her exhaustion. Bruce walked beside Daniels, occasionally glancing at him as if to gauge his state of mind.

When they reached the encampment, the familiar sight of makeshift shelters came into view—tattered tents and cardboard lean-tos that lined the alleyways. The people there, huddled against the cold, greeted them with cautious hope, recognizing the trio who often brought both sustenance and a sense of compassion.

Daniels felt a sense of duty rise within him, mixed with the lingering turmoil he couldn't quite shake. He forced himself to focus on the task at hand, approaching the nearest group of people to talk with them and pray and see if he could help them in any way.

As he knelt beside an elderly woman, he tried to focus on prayer, on the work he had committed his life to. The woman's frail hand reached out, resting gently on his. "You've been running," she said, her voice filled with certainty. Her gaze was sharp, penetrating. "But not from the enemy—from what God's placed in your heart."

Daniels was startled, but he managed to maintain a composed expression as the woman continued speaking.

"There was once a shepherd," she began, her voice low but filled with conviction. "He watched over his flock faithfully for many years, guiding them through storms and keeping them safe from wolves. Among his flock was one sheep, special and dear to him, one he had cared for with great tenderness. But as time passed, a new shepherd came—one strong, bold, and willing to face the dangers of the wilderness to protect that same sheep.

"The first shepherd saw the bond growing between the new shepherd and the sheep, and it pained him. He began to retreat, telling himself that this was for the best. After all, the new shepherd was strong and capable. The sheep seemed content, safe in his care. But the first shepherd's heart was heavy, because deep down, he loved the sheep dearly. He simply didn't believe it was right to let his feelings show, so he kept them hidden, convincing himself that it was God's plan for the new shepherd to take over."

Daniels listened intently, his brow furrowed. "What happened to the first shepherd?" he asked quietly, confusion evident in his voice.

The woman looked at him, her eyes piercing. "He struggled, unsure if he should reveal his true heart. But tell me, Pastor, if God brings love into a man's heart, is it right to hide it—even from the sheep he loves most?"

Daniels opened his mouth, uncertain how to respond. Before he could say anything, the woman leaned closer, her voice barely above a whisper.

"The sheep," she said, "she is standing right beside you, and you are the first shepherd."

He looked up at the woman standing next to him. He could tell by the way she looked at him, she heard what the woman said.

Her words lingered in the air like a thunderclap, resonating deep within Daniels' heart. It felt as if the very ground beneath him had shifted, leaving him unsteady. He wanted to dismiss it, to treat it as another test of his resolve, but something in the woman's voice—a haunting blend of truth and urgency, refused to let him push it aside.

Was this truly God's plan? Or was it the longing of his own heart, a desperate desire cloaked in divine purpose?

Sarah, standing right next to him, felt a rush of emotion swell within her as the old woman's story unfolded. Her heart leaped at the parable of the sheep and the shepherd, every word resonating as if pulled from her own soul. This was their story, hers and Daniels'. But when he looked up at her, their eyes connected as she turned toward him, searching for a sign of recognition in his eyes, her hope collided with confusion. Daniels remained still, his expression unreadable, as if he hadn't truly heard what had been spoken.

Disappointment washed over her like a cold wave. Did he really not understand? Did he not feel the same fire that was burning inside her? The silence between them was unbearable, and Sarah felt tears sting her eyes as she turned away, retreating to the safety of darkness.

That night, Daniels sat alone, the dim flicker of a candle his only companion. He preferred a candle at times like this. It gave him peace. He stared into its flame, lost in the storm of his thoughts. He felt torn apart, the words of the woman still echoing like an undeniable truth. This wasn't the sharp, commanding voice of divine revelation he had always imagined. It was softer, gentler, like the clearing of a morning fog after a long, restless night.

It dawned on him slowly, painfully. His love for Sarah wasn't a temptation to be shunned, nor was it just an earthly desire he needed to suppress. It was something deeper, a love forged not just in passion but in shared purpose, sacrifice, and a faith that had grown stronger with every trial.

For the first time, he allowed himself to feel the full weight of it, to acknowledge the longing that had been buried beneath his pastoral duty. He realized that God's will wasn't always delivered with the force of conviction but sometimes whispered through the stillness of an aching heart. And as he closed his eyes, a single tear escaped down his cheek, the floodgates of his heart opening to a truth he could no longer deny.

When he saw Sarah again, there was a subtle shift. He did not rush toward her, nor did he allow his emotions to overwhelm him. Instead, he approached with caution, acknowledging the love in his heart but recognizing that their connection needed time to evolve.

Sarah's eyes met his, a mixture of longing and uncertainty lingering within them. This time, Daniels did not retreat. He reached out slowly, gently taking her hand in his, and she allowed it. The moment was tender but restrained—filled not with immediate passion but with the promise of something deeper.

"Whatever this is," Daniels said, his voice low but heavy with the weight of his struggle, "we have to let God guide it. I don't know what He has planned for us, if anything at all. But I know one thing—I can't keep pushing you away. Not anymore. It doesn't feel right; it feels like I'm fighting something that's meant to be."

Sarah sucked in a sharp breath, her eyes filling with tears she could no longer hold back. She searched Daniels' face, as if trying to grasp the depth of his sincerity. Then, slowly, she nodded. There was no dramatic embrace, no rush of passion, just a quiet, raw understanding that they would have to navigate this carefully. Love and duty were fragile forces that needed to be balanced, and both knew that the path ahead would be uncertain.

Later that night, Daniels sat alone in his room, his head resting heavily in his hands. A deep ache filled his chest, mingled with frustration. Why does it have to be so complicated? He thought, wrestling with his conflicting emotions. He could still see the tears in Sarah's eyes, but he couldn't forget the pain in Bruce's either.

Bruce. The man who had risked everything for Sarah, who had faced death to protect her. Daniels had seen the connection between them, a bond forged through survival and shared suffering. It was real, and it had pained Daniels deeply to watch it grow. He had encouraged it, believing it was God's will. He had praised Bruce's strength and new faith, trying to convince himself that it was best for Sarah.

But now, as Daniels faced the truth of his own feelings, he felt a bitter regret. He had pushed Sarah and Bruce together, thinking he was doing the right thing. Instead, he had created a situation that was not only uncomfortable, but cruel. He had led Bruce to hope for something that could never truly be, all while hiding his own love behind a mask of selflessness.

Daniels leaned back, the weight of guilt pressing down on him. It wasn't fair to Bruce, he realized. The man deserved honesty, not manipulation disguised as sacrifice. As much as it hurt, Daniels knew he had to make things right, not just with Sarah, but with Bruce too.

He took a deep breath, feeling a tentative resolve begin to form within him. He couldn't erase the mistakes he'd made, but he could be honest going forward. He could approach this with humility, acknowledging both the love he had for Sarah and the pain he had unintentionally caused. It would not be easy, love never was, but it was the only way to honor God's will and restore some sense of integrity to his heart.

"Lord," he whispered into the darkness, "help me make this right. Help me love her the way You intended, without hurting anyone else along the way."

Daniels lingered in the silence, feeling the weight of his prayer settle over him. But he knew that prayers alone wouldn't resolve the tangled web he'd created. He had to act; he had to be honest with Bruce.

He took a deep breath, trying to summon the courage that was eluding him. Rising from his chair, he felt a surge of determination, a clarity that cut through the haze of confusion. He couldn't keep hiding the truth. Bruce deserved to know.

With trembling hands, Daniels moved toward the door, his footsteps slow but deliberate. He reached for the handle, his heart pounding in his chest. He could already imagine the confrontation: Bruce's confused eyes, the inevitable pain in his face, the fragile hope that would shatter the moment Daniels spoke.

But this was the only way to make things right, wasn't it? To stop the lies, to own up to his mistakes? Daniels' fingers tightened around the cold metal of the doorknob, his jaw set. This has to be done, he told himself, willing the fear away.

He opened the door a crack, but his legs felt like lead. A wave of nausea rose up, his stomach twisting at the thought of Bruce's expression when the truth came out. He closed his eyes, trying to push past the knot of dread in his chest.

How can I tell him?

His hand dropped from the doorknob, his shoulders slumping. He couldn't do it—not now, maybe not ever. The fear of Bruce's pain, of seeing the betrayal in his eyes, was more than Daniels could bear. His heart felt heavy, crushed by his own cowardice.

"I'll do it tomorrow," he whispered, his voice breaking. But even as he said the words, he knew they were empty. He was stalling, hiding behind the safety of postponement. Deep down, he knew he would never have the courage to speak the truth.

Daniels turned back into the room, closing the door softly behind him. He sank to his knees, his chest heaving with silent sobs. I'm a coward, he thought bitterly. A hypocrite hiding behind the guise of righteousness.

Days passed, and the words he needed to say remained unspoken.

"The Cards"

Daniels and Sarah had been talking about moving forward together, exploring the fragile beginnings of a relationship that had been long denied. Sarah was eager, pushing to close the distance between them, but Daniels was determined to go slowly. He wanted to be certain it was truly what Sarah needed, and yet, beneath his caution, he had to restrain his own desire. He wanted to move as fast as she would allow, but he held back, letting patience govern his steps.

Despite Daniels' failure to confront Bruce, the atmosphere was charged with the lingering tension of unspoken words. Bruce, perceptive as ever, had noticed the shift between Daniels and Sarah. He'd seen how Sarah, once open to his reassurances, had started to pull away. The change hurt, more than Bruce wanted to admit, but he kept it buried beneath a mask of quiet resilience.

As Daniels and Sarah entered the living area, they were laughing softly, trying to find a moment of lightness amid the darkness of their reality. Bruce was in the room, his back turned as he organized supplies. At the sound of their laughter, he stiffened, his hand pausing mid-motion. When he turned around, his face was tight with a mixture of confusion and hurt.

The laughter died instantly. Sarah's expression shifted, a mix of guilt and uncertainty clouding her eyes. Sensing the tension, she gave Daniels' hand a brief squeeze before letting go, her fingers lingering for a second longer than necessary. Daniels felt the loss of her touch acutely, but his attention was drawn back to Bruce, whose gaze was now fixed on them.

Daniels met Bruce's eyes, feeling the weight of the unspoken pressing down like a vice. It was a look filled with questions, none of which Bruce voiced. The silence between them was awkward, laden with the heaviness of what had been left unsaid.

Desperate to shift the focus, Daniels cleared his throat, forcing his voice to adopt a tone of business-like urgency. "We need to try using the cards anyway. If we can still get cash, maybe we can use it on the underground market. Maybe they have not completely transitioned." he said, his words coming out steady but strained, as if he were battling the turmoil within. "James, Emily—find an ATM far from here. Withdraw whatever you can before they trace us. Bruce, can you go with them? Be a lookout."

The request felt hollow, more like a means to evade the tension than to address the immediate need. But the damage was already evident.

Bruce's expression tightened, a painful mix of betrayal and reluctant acceptance crossing his face. He stood still for a moment, as if weighing whether to respond. Then he gave a small nod, his jaw set, the muscles in his face hardening as he turned back to his task.

Daniels watched, a sinking feeling in his chest. He knew this small nod wasn't agreement—it was resignation. The unspoken words hung heavy in the air.

Sarah's eyes darted between the two men, her heart aching with the realization that the bond they had all shared was fracturing, not from violence or external danger, but from the choices made in pursuit of love. She wanted to reach out to Bruce, to offer some comfort, but her feet stayed rooted, it would make it worse.

The air in the room was thick with unresolved emotions, and Daniels knew that no amount of practicality could fill the void that now existed between them all.

James hesitated, glancing nervously at Rebecca before opening his mouth to respond. But before he could speak, Rebecca's voice cut through the room, sharp and demanding. "What cards?" she asked, her eyes narrowing.

For a moment, there was a stunned silence. Daniels' heart sank, the realization of his mistake hitting him like a blow. The room seemed to freeze, the air thick with tension as the weight of the revelation settled over them all.

Rebecca's voice broke the silence, low and edged with concern, her eyes locked on James. "James... what cards?" she asked, her voice trembling. "What kind of cards?" The words cut through the air, filled with a mix of rising fear and distress.

James stood paralyzed, his eyes wide with guilt and uncertainty. He tried to form a response, but the words stuck in his throat. Rebecca's confusion slowly morphed into dread, her gaze burning with unanswered questions. "Tell me! What cards, James?" she demanded, her voice cracking.

Emily, who had been standing quietly, suddenly began to cry. Her sobs broke the silence like a dam bursting, and she collapsed onto a nearby chair. "It wasn't my choice, Mom!" she cried, tears streaming down her face. "Dad, he made me do it. I didn't want to sign anything, but he grabbed my hand and forced me."

The room seemed to spin for Rebecca. Her chest tightened, her breath coming in ragged gasps. She stared at James, her eyes wide with disbelief, a mix of shock and anger simmering beneath the surface. "You did what?" she demanded, her voice breaking, raw and hoarse. "What did you force her to sign? What did you sign?"

She froze, her mind struggling to piece together the implications. But James's face gave him away, his averted eyes, the sag of his shoulders, the guilt etched into every line of his expression. The truth hit her like a punch to the gut. She knew, deep down in her soul, exactly what he had done.

James flinched as Rebecca's fists struck his chest, her blows more desperate than violent. Her face was twisted with unbridled rage, tears streaming down her cheeks. "What have you done?" she shrieked, her voice cracking under the weight of her grief. "Have you doomed my baby? I survived torture, the camps, everything, just to hold onto the hope of seeing her safe. And you, her own father, you killed her!"

Rebecca's fury eventually gave way to exhaustion, her strength faltering. Her hands shook uncontrollably, her sobs turning into broken, anguished cries. She ran to her room, fell on her bed, burying her face in the pillow. The living area felt colder, emptier, as if the very walls absorbed the pain that hung in the air.

James stood motionless, his body trembling. He felt the sting of Rebecca's words like physical blows, each one driving deeper into his heart. Tears streamed down his face, but he had made no attempt to defend himself. He deserved every bit of her anger, and he knew it.

Walking into the room he said "Rebecca... I'm sorry," his voice barely audible. But his words felt hollow, insignificant against the magnitude of what he had done. He sank to his knees, unable to bear the weight of his own betrayal any longer.

Emily, still sobbing, walked in and reached out hesitantly toward her mom, her hand hovering just above her mother's back. "Mom... please," she pleaded, but Rebecca remained unmoving, her body racked with silent convulsions.

Daniels, having watched the scene unfold, felt a deep sense of failure. He had tried to lead them all, to protect them, but now it felt as though he had led them straight into ruin. He stood in the doorway, wanting to comfort Rebecca, but the intensity of her grief kept him rooted in place.

"I never meant for this to happen," James choked out, his voice filled with remorse. "I thought... I thought it was the only way. I was just trying to keep us all alive."

Rebecca's sobs quieted, but her voice was laced with bitterness as she finally spoke. "Alive? You call that being alive? You've taken everything, James. Everything."

The room fell silent, the echoes of Rebecca's words lingering in the heavy air. Daniels felt tears pricking at his own eyes, a sense of helplessness washing over him. He had witnessed so much suffering, but seeing the disintegration of love and trust before him was almost unbearable.

James, still on his knees, whispered one final, desperate plea. "Please, Rebecca… don't shut me out. I know I've screwed up, but I still love you. I always have."

But Rebecca's response was empty, her voice devoid of hope. "You had my love, James. You had everything. And you destroyed it."

The whole basement settled into a mournful quiet, the gravity of what had transpired settling over the group like a thick fog. There was no easy resolution, no comforting words to bridge the chasm that had opened between them. Only the sound of quiet weeping and the unspoken realization that something had broken beyond repair.

12

BURDEN OF KNOWLEDGE

"The Final Reduction"

Ben Reshan's plan was unfolding precisely as Satan had whispered to him in the darkest hours. It was no longer enough to exert control through influence and policy. Now, it was time to actively shape the world's population, to bring about what he and his elite advisors had called "the Final Reduction."

The reports on Rashan's desk grim, exactly as expected. Starvation was already sweeping through vast swathes of Africa, parts of Southeast Asia, and even pockets of Europe. The world's resources had been purposefully choked by the restrictions his policies had imposed, policies that, on the surface, appeared to be for the "greater good." But the truth was much darker. The planet, his advisors claimed, could only support a fraction of its current population. Sacrifices were necessary. The weak would fall so that the strong could survive.

Ben's eyes flickered as the voice in his mind spoke again. "Eliminate the unnecessary. This is your mission." It was Satan, filling Ben's heart with a cold resolve. Every decision had been guided by the forces that controlled him, and now, the culmination of those choices was at hand. The corporate powers and world governments had already fallen in line, blinded by promises of wealth and stability. Ben knew they were nothing but pawns, unaware of the true game being played.

"The food rationing will intensify," Ben murmured, his voice detached. "Abortions, already government-sponsored, will be mandatory in certain zones. And medical care... Only those who are still deemed productive will receive any form of treatment." He paused, staring at the screen as a city's power grid flickered out, a deliberate act of control. "Those who refuse will face starvation. It is simple."

One of his advisors nodded, the flicker of doubt in his eyes quickly extinguished. "Shall we prepare the next wave of population control measures?" the man asked, hesitating briefly before continuing. "You mentioned a... final phase."

199

Ben's lip curled. The advisor knew nothing of what was truly at stake. "The viruses," Ben began, the words rolling off his tongue with an eerie calm, "are in development. We will ensure they are released in the third world first—places no one will notice. It will spread. Millions will die before we find a 'solution.' It's inevitable." He said it so casually, as if the loss of life was no more than a statistic, a number to be adjusted.

But behind his cold exterior, Satan reveled in this moment. He whispered lies into Ben's ear. "This is how you please me. This is how you destroy God's creation, the very beings He loves." The joy Satan took in watching humanity unravel was undeniable, a twisted delight in watching God's image-bearers fall victim to the manipulation.

Satan summoned his Commander. When he arrived he issued his next orders. "Release the demons who control earth's beasts," he commanded with authority. "Let them stir the beasts. Begin in the wild places, and then move closer to the cities. We need fear to grip their hearts."

Across the world, in places where humans had once felt safe, the natural world turned against them. Sharks began attacking coastal swimmers without provocation. Wild animals, which had once fled from human presence, now prowled cities. Packs of wolves and large dogs hunted down anyone they encountered. Bulls, wild boars, and even docile creatures became aggressive, driven by a dark force unseen but undeniably present.

As his power reverberated across the globe, Ben Reshan murmured the name "Satan," a strange peace settling over him as he stood in the chaos he had orchestrated. He had accepted his role completely, a willing instrument of destruction. "Your will be done."

"Denial and Revelation"

Rebecca sat across from Pastor Daniels, her face pale, her hands trembling. The soft hum of the old fluorescent lights blended with the silence, contrasting with the heavy tension between them. The lights flickered occasionally, casting long shadows across the room, but it wasn't enough to break the weight of the moment.

"Pastor," she began, her voice barely above a whisper, "they took the mark, but they're not marked."

Daniels' expression softened with a mixture of sorrow and understanding. He leaned forward slightly, his hands clasped in his lap. "Rebecca, the mark... it's not just physical. It's spiritual." He paused for a moment, letting the weight of his words settle. "James and Emily... they signed the agreement, even though their spirits screamed not to."

Her eyes searched his for hope, but there was none. Pastor Daniels took a breath, choosing his words carefully. "The moment they turned away, when they signed their allegiance, even though they knew it was wrong—that was when they accepted the mark. It's recognized by God and Satan alike." His words hung heavily in the air, the truth of them like a dagger to her heart.

Rebecca felt a numbness wash over her. "But... it's not visible. There's no mark on them."

Daniels shook his head. "It doesn't need to be. It's about what lies within, where their hearts turned. The mark is spiritual, just as scripture says God's people are marked. They are aligned with Satan, and recognized by God." He paused, letting the weight of his explanation sink in. "It's not just about survival or signing some document. It's about where their trust lies—and in that moment, they chose the world."

Rebecca, eyes wide with desperation, grabbed his Bible from the table and hurried back to her bed. She searched frantically through the pages, her fingers trembling as they flipped through verse after verse, trying to find some loophole, some passage that would release her husband and daughter from the condemnation they had brought upon themselves.

And then, she found it. Her breath hesitated as she read the words that seared into her mind: "If anyone worships the beast and its image and receives its mark... they will drink the wine of God's fury." She couldn't believe what she was seeing. There was no escape.

Her heart shattered as the realization fully settled in. "They'll die," she whispered, tears spilling from her eyes. "They've lost eternal life."

That night, Rebecca withdrew into herself. She avoided James and even Emily, unable to face them, unable to comprehend what they had done. The pain was too much—her whole world was crashing down, and the people she had survived for, her family, were now marked for death.

James tried to approach her, his steps slow and unsure as he entered their small room. But Rebecca didn't look up. She sat on the edge of the bed, the Bible open on her lap, but her eyes were distant.

"Rebecca," he called softly, but there was no response. His heart ached as he stood there, unsure of how to reach her. He tried again, stepping closer.

But she didn't even turn. "You need to leave," she said quietly, her voice cold and distant. "You can't stay here."

James froze, his breath taken away. "What? Rebecca, please, we need to talk about this."

She finally looked up at him, her eyes filled with pain and betrayal. "There's nothing to talk about. You made your choice when you signed that agreement. You chose to betray us, betray God."

James stood there, helpless, as Rebecca's words cut through him like a knife.

"I thought I was protecting us," he whispered, tears forming in his eyes. "I didn't know..."

Rebecca's voice cracked as she yelled, "You killed my baby!" Her grief spilled over into anger as she pointed toward the door, her face flushed with rage. "Get out!"

James, overcome with guilt and sorrow, felt the floor fall out from under him. He had lost everything, the love of his life, the trust of his family. Numbly, he turned and left the room, the sound of Rebecca's sobs echoing through the small space.

He had no choice but to sleep elsewhere, banished from her presence, the woman he had sworn to protect.

As James walked out of the room, the weight of Rebecca's words still crushing his chest, he nearly stumbled upon Emily, who stood frozen in the hallway. Her eyes were red, wide with disbelief, her body stiff, as if her very soul was anchored to the spot. Tears streamed down her face, unchecked, her expression a mix of fear, sorrow, and something he couldn't quite name, perhaps a silent plea for understanding, for forgiveness.

James slowed his pace but didn't stop, the shame of what he'd done too overwhelming to face her. He couldn't bear to look into her eyes, to see the reflection of his own failure as both a father and a protector. He wanted to say something, anything, but no words came.

As he passed her, the air between them was thick with unspoken pain. Emily didn't move, her tears the only sign of the storm raging inside her. Her lips parted slightly, as if she wanted to call out to him, to make him stop, to ask for answers. But she couldn't bring herself to utter a word.

James, for his part, couldn't afford to stop. Each step felt heavier, as though the ground beneath him might crumble at any moment, yet he kept walking. The silence between them screamed louder than any confrontation ever could. He left her standing there, alone, her tears falling silently onto the cold floor.

"The Melt"

Bruce checked his surroundings as he slipped out of the underground hideout, his eyes scanning the deserted street. The cold, quiet air felt wrong, almost too still. He pulled the phone from his pocket, heading down the alley toward the place he had spotted a free Wi-Fi hotspot. His footsteps echoed off the walls as he quickened his pace. It was too risky to go out, but they needed information, now more than ever.

After a few minutes, he reached the edge of a public park, its benches empty and abandoned. He tapped into the Wi-Fi, letting the phone connect to a secure network. Quickly, he downloaded the app Pastor Daniels had mentioned, one designed to pull news from restricted or hidden sites without detection. His fingers moved rapidly across the screen, downloading articles, videos, anything he could find.

As the files began to populate the phone, he froze, feeling the weight of the world crashing onto his shoulders. His pulse quickened, a cold sweat beading on his forehead as the realization of what he was reading sank in.

"New Plague Spreads from Africa to Europe, China, and New York in Days."

His heart raced as he read the details. This was no ordinary outbreak. The virus, they claimed, had originated from a remote lab experiment in a small African country funded by world powers. The virus had mutated at an alarming rate. It carried the DNA of Ebola, spliced into a common respiratory virus, something as harmless as the common cold—until now. The reports were graphic, describing how victims' organs began to break down inside their bodies, blood pooling in their lungs, and how their skin blistered as if they had been burned from the inside out. It was terrifying.

His stomach churned as he read about the speed at which the virus spread, jumping continents in mere days, moving faster than any plague in modern history.

Back at the hideout, Bruce rushed inside, his face pale. He found Pastor Daniels and James sitting at the small table in the corner. The tension in the room was thick as they worked in silence. Without saying a word, Bruce placed the phone on the table, the screen glowing with the news headline.

"Look at this," he said, his voice shaking.

Pastor Daniels squinted at the screen, leaning closer as he read. His expression darkened, and James, sitting beside him, rubbed his forehead in disbelief.

"Is this real?" James asked, almost hoping it wasn't true.

Bruce nodded, but his voice trembled as he began to explain what he had read, the weight of the information overwhelming him. "When they first discovered it, they called it Corona-1745a. It had already wiped out three entire villages before anyone knew what it was, completely destroying them. The doctor who first found it—who risked everything to bring a sample to the WHO, died five days later." He paused, his breath catching in his throat, as the horror of it all sank in. "But it's worse now, and the media is calling it ... The Melt."

His hands shook slightly as he continued. "Everyone who gets it... they don't just die. They suffer. Their organs melt inside them. Blood fills their lungs. Their skin blisters like they've been burned from the inside. It's horrific—no one survives. So far, everyone who's caught it has died in agony."

The room fell into an uneasy silence as Bruce spoke, the gravity of the situation clear in his eyes. "And now... it's spreading. Fast. Europe, India, China, and now New York. It's moving quicker than anything we've ever seen, and there's no way to stop it."

Daniels sat back in his chair, his hand covering his mouth as if trying to process the gravity of what he was seeing. "This is no accident," he muttered, his voice low. "This... this is prophecy come to life, this has to be the rider of the Pale Horse."

James looked at him, confusion flickering in his eyes. "You mean... from Revelation, the Bible?"

Daniels nodded. "It's the fourth seal in Revelation. Death followed by Hades." He looked down at the table, his mind racing. "I had my suspicions during the last pandemic... COVID. The way it spread, the fear, the chaos—none of it felt like a natural plague. It wasn't from God. It was created in a lab by men, and that's when I knew that this... this was not of God, but the rider of the pale horse, using man, to create their own destruction. I never preached on this theory. It seemed too farfetched."

"The Pale Horse," Bruce whispered, confused. "This virus... pale horse?"

"This is bad," Daniels continued, keeping his train of thought, his voice heavy. "This is a virus born from man's manipulation. They've taken something from the natural world, something that spreads so easily, and spliced it with something horrific. They're playing God, and now... Death will spread across the earth."

The room fell silent, the weight of Daniels' words suffocating.

"They've conquered the church," Daniels said, breaking the silence, his voice hollow. "That has to be the first horseman of Revelation. The world governments are destroying each other, piece by piece. War... war is everywhere. Nations are at each other's throats. That has to be the rider of the second horse, war. And now, people can't buy food without pledging allegiance to the new order. Food shortages, crop failures—people are dying of starvation. That's the third rider, famine."

"Third World countries are starving," James added quietly. "They're being denied food aid. Thousands, if not millions, are dying. The livestock are being slaughtered or seized, as meat is being outlawed, and no one can buy food unless they sign their loyalty. This famine is intentional."

Daniels leaned forward, his voice rising with conviction. "This is all prophecy fulfilled—the first seal was to conquer God's people, the second seal was war, and the third famine. We've watched it all unfold, one rider after another. Now the Pale Horse is here. Death has come!"

Bruce shook his head in disbelief. "This virus... I was reading the articles, it's like nothing we've ever seen before. It's melting people from the inside. And the animals—animals are attacking and killing people everywhere"

"It's the demons," Daniels interrupted, his voice hard. "Satan has to be the cause, manipulating the beasts. Animals that once feared humans are now attacking. Sharks, wolves, even pets. It's all connected. In the New Testament, is said that a legion of demons entered a herd of pigs and made them run off a cliff. So, I guess it is possible to make them attack people."

A tense silence fell over the room as they realized the full scope of what was happening. It wasn't just an isolated plague, a freak event. This was evil. This was Death itself, followed by Hades, attempting to claim souls before they find God.

At that moment, Sarah and Emily, who had been standing in the doorway, finally spoke.

"We heard everything," Sarah whispered, her voice trembling. "Is this... is this the end?"

Daniels looked up, his face filled with sorrow. "No, not yet. This is the Tribulation and it has been getting worse and worse for two-thousand years. The world is suffering because of the evil unleashed by man, spurred on by shadows, shadows of evil. But God will have enough of this evil eventually. At some point, God will pour out His wrath on those who have destroyed His creation and His people."

Emily stepped forward, her voice barely audible. "So what do we do now?"

Daniels' gaze softened as he looked at the two women, his heart aching for the fear he saw in their eyes. He wanted to offer more comfort, to tell them everything would be okay, but the truth weighed heavily on him. The reality of what was unfolding around them—prophecy in motion—was undeniable. He had always believed in God's plan, but watching it unravel in such a painful and terrifying way was more than he could have prepared for.

"We survive," he said softly, his voice steadier than he felt. "We stay faithful. We endure... and we help everyone we can." His words carried conviction, but deep within, he wrestled with the knowledge that this suffering was only the beginning. He wished he could shield them from the worst of it, but that wasn't within his power.

As silence settled around them once again, he could feel the weight of his responsibility pressing down. Had he had been chosen to lead these people through darkness, to carry the burden of guiding them through a world falling apart? All he could offer was faith. It had to be enough—because it was all they had left.

"The Depth of Despair"

In the back room, Rebecca sat alone, her body hunched over, her hands limp in her lap. Days had passed, yet she had refused to talk to anyone. She had shut herself away from the world, from her friends, and even from Emily. She barely ate the food Sarah brought her, picking at it listlessly before pushing the plate away. Her once-bright eyes were hollow now, lost to the darkness that had consumed her thoughts.

She had scoured the Scriptures, desperate to find something—anything—that would give her hope for Emily and James. But nothing. Every verse she turned to only deepened her despair. She had slowly come to terms with the reality of it. Emily and James were lost, marked, their fates sealed. Her prayers, her pleas for mercy, had fallen on deaf ears.

Then came the anger.

It had started with James, a quiet rage toward him. His decision, his betrayal—it was unforgivable. But soon, that anger spread like wildfire, consuming every part of her soul. She lashed out at God with a fury she didn't know she was capable of. How could He? She had cried out to Him in the camps. She had begged Him for deliverance, for reunion with her family, and He had answered. Only to snatch it all away again. It was beyond cruel.

The bitterness swelled inside her like a tidal wave, and she felt herself drowning in it. She had trusted God, had given Him everything, and in return, He had given her nothing but heartbreak. The God she had believed in—His mercy, His love—felt like a lie now. How could He claim to be good, to be just, when this was His answer?

I prayed, she thought bitterly, her hands trembling in her lap. I prayed every day in that hell, begged for a miracle. You answered, only to take them away. How is this fair? How is this love? The questions were endless, spiraling through her mind, each one driving a wedge further between her and the God she had once clung to. A God that was her only hope, had turned into a thing of scorn.

As she sat there, lost in her fury, the door creaked open. Sarah stepped inside, holding a small glass of water in her hands, her footsteps cautious as if walking through a minefield.

"Rebecca," Sarah said softly, approaching the bed, her eyes filled with concern.

But Rebecca didn't look at her. The fury that had been simmering inside her rose to the surface like a volcano about to erupt.

"Why?" Rebecca's voice shook, barely above a whisper. "Why would God do this to me? Why would He answer my prayers, only to tear it all away? Why would He... how could He be so cruel?"

Sarah set the glass of water down on the small table by the bed and reached out to touch Rebecca's shoulder. "He isn't cruel," she whispered. "He loves you, Rebecca. I know it hurts, but—"

"No!" Rebecca's voice exploded, pushing Sarah's hand away, her anger finally spilling over. "Don't tell me He loves me! Don't you dare say that!" She stood up, trembling, her hands clenched into fists at her sides. "You have no idea what I've been through. You can't possibly understand what God has done to me! I cried out to Him in that camp, over and over. And He answered. He brought me back to them—only to take them from me again. He hates me!"

Tears streamed down Sarah's face, but she stayed quiet, not knowing how to console her friend.

Rebecca's voice cracked as she continued, her words drenched in bitterness. "I trusted Him. I believed in Him, and this is what I get? I begged Him to save my family, and now they're marked for death. My own husband, marked by Satan. Emily, my daughter... lost. And you want to stand there and tell me He loves me?"

Sarah tried to speak, her heart breaking for Rebecca. "It's not what you think—God hasn't abandoned you. We just don't always understand His plan—"

"Get out!" Rebecca screamed, her voice raw and filled with rage. She pointed toward the door, her whole body trembling. "Get out! Go away! Leave me alone. You can't understand, Sarah! You have no idea what God has done to me."

Sarah's face crumbled with sorrow, but there was nothing more she could say. Rebecca was drowning in her anger, her grief consuming her like a fire that refused to be extinguished.

Without another word, Sarah turned and left the room, closing the door softly behind her. She leaned against the wall outside, tears streaming down her cheeks as Rebecca's sobs filled the silence. Her heart ached for her friend, who was so lost in her pain and anger. Sarah felt helpless, powerless to pull Rebecca from the darkness that had consumed her.

She slid down the wall, her knees pulling into her chest. Looking upward, her eyes filled with uncontrollable tears, she whispered a desperate plea, her voice trembling.

"God, please... have mercy on her. Don't let her drown in this. She needs You, even if she can't see it right now. Please... don't let her go."

The words left her lips like a prayer caught between hope and heartbreak. She could do nothing more but entrust Rebecca's soul to the only One who could truly save her from the storm within. And as the tears rolled down her face, Sarah remained there in the hallway, pleading silently for mercy, for comfort—for her friend to find her way back to God.

"Valley of Shadows"

Daniels paused, his hand resting on the edge of the worn wooden table. The sound of Rebecca's shouting and sobbing shook the underground refuge just moments before, her anger cutting through the walls like thunder. He closed his eyes for a moment, saying a quiet prayer for her, for strength in this dark time. When the sounds from Rebecca's room finally subsided, he made his way down the narrow hallway, toward Rebecca's room.

As he reached the doorway, his heart sank. There, sitting on the cold floor, her knees pulled to her chest, was Sarah—his Sarah, the newly confirmed love of his life. She sobbed silently, her body trembling as tears streamed down her face. The sight of her there, so broken by everything happening around them, twisted his heart. In his mind, the joy they had only just discovered together—the pure, overwhelming love—felt distant, stolen by a world spiraling into despair.

He stopped in front of her, his heart breaking at the sight of her. His voice was barely above a whisper, trembling with the weight of everything unsaid. "Sarah…"

Her tear-filled eyes lifted to meet his, and in that instant, it was as though the world outside ceased to exist. The pain, the fear, the chaos— they all faded in the presence of the man standing before her. She felt lost, like a ship caught in a storm, and yet, here was her anchor. In him, she found the one thing that felt solid, the one place she could breathe.

She wanted nothing more than to escape—escape this cruel reality, the crushing weight of everything that had gone wrong. She just wanted to be with him, to hold onto the one thing that still felt right, the one thing that still made sense. His presence was her refuge in the middle of the storm, and she clung to that, desperate for a reprieve from the darkness closing in around her.

Slowly, her trembling hand reached up, and his warm fingers enveloped hers. The simple touch ignited a sense of safety she hadn't felt in so long. Gently, as though afraid to break the fragile moment, he helped her to her feet, his hand never leaving hers. In that fleeting moment, all that mattered was him, and for a second, she was no longer drowning.

Daniels sat beside her on the makeshift bed, their shoulders touching as they both sat in silence for a moment, trying to find some peace in the midst of the chaos outside.

Sarah wiped her eyes and whispered, "Rebecca… she screamed at God. She said… horrible things. Part of me wants to believe they're not true. But… I don't know anymore, Tim. How can I believe God is good when all of this is happening? How can I trust Him when it feels like He's abandoned us?"

Her voice cracked, the raw emotion spilling out as she spoke. The weight of Rebecca's words, her own doubts, and the despair of the world seemed to settle on her shoulders all at once. She was being crushed. She looked at Tim, searching for answers, for some kind of reassurance.

He took a deep breath, his heart aching for her. He let her words linger in the air for a moment, not wanting to rush into an answer. Finally, he spoke, his voice gentle and understanding.

"Rebecca... she's grieving. Right now, it's as though James and Emily have died. She's going through the stages of grief, Sarah, and she's in the thick of it—the anger, the disbelief, the pain." He paused, turning toward her, his hand resting on hers. "This is a long, hard process for her. We just need to be there for her every step of the way."

Sarah nodded, though her eyes remained distant. "But it's so hard... seeing her like that. Seeing her hate God."

"I know," Daniels whispered, his voice soft but firm. "But she's in the valley right now, the valley of shadows. It's a place she has to pass through. We can't rush her out of it, we can't fix it for her. She needs to feel it, to process it. But we don't leave her there. We stand with her."

Tears welled up in Sarah's eyes again as she listened to him. "But how do we help her when she's so angry? How do we keep her from falling apart?"

"We stay patient," Daniels said, his gaze steady. "We stay caring. God is with her, even if she can't feel Him. Christ is in us, Sarah. He's with her through us. We're His hands, His heart, in this moment. And she needs that more than anything."

Sarah leaned her head on Daniels' shoulder, her body relaxing just a little, the tension releasing in the presence of his calm voice. She closed her eyes, letting the words settle. It wasn't easy, but it made sense. Rebecca wasn't lost, she was just walking through the darkest part of the journey. And they would be there, waiting, when she came through the other side.

They sat there for a long time in silence, the weight of the world outside falling away for just a brief moment. Sarah pressed her head into his shoulder, her tears finally slowing as his presence calmed her racing thoughts. She could feel his hand gently running through her hair, the tender rhythm of his fingers offering her the comfort she so desperately needed.

Tim turned and kissed the top of her head, the simple gesture speaking volumes. In the midst of the chaos surrounding them, here, in this quiet moment, there was peace. It was as if the love between them—newly discovered and still fragile—was a light in the darkness. Together, they shared a connection that went beyond words, a bond that could not be broken by the turmoil around them.

For a moment, the storm outside ceased to matter. It was just the two of them, in a world where love and faith still held meaning. Sarah closed her eyes, sinking into the warmth of Tim's embrace, feeling the steady rise and fall of his chest as he held her close.

In his arms, she found the peace she had been searching for. And in that peace, there was love—unspoken, but undeniably present. They stayed there, pressed together, hearts aligned, knowing that whatever came next, they would face it together.

"The Burden of News"

The main room, once filled with the sound of praise and prayer, now rearranged to serve as their living room. Emily, James, and Bruce sat together in silence, the only sound the occasional muted beeping from the three phones Bruce had managed to download news on.

Bruce scrolled through the screen, his brow furrowed as he read the grim headlines aloud. "More deaths reported in the wake of the new plague. Famine sweeping through the developing world. Entire regions are collapsing into chaos. No end in sight."

He stopped for a moment, glancing over at Emily and James. The two of them sat quietly, the tension between them obvious. There was a deep sadness in their eyes, an unspoken burden that weighed them down. Bruce shifted in his seat, unsure of what to say next.

"They're calling it 'The Melt,'" he murmured. "It's spreading faster than anything we've seen before. It's like the whole world is unraveling."

James rubbed a hand across his forehead, staring down at the floor. "Pastor Daniels was right... this is more than just coincidence. This is prophecy coming to life."

Emily remained silent, her hands clenched in her lap. She had hardly spoken since her mother had pushed her and her father away. Her eyes flickered to the doorway, watching as Pastor Daniels led Sarah to her room, her fragile form clinging to him like a lifeline. There was something unspoken in the way they moved together, something she couldn't quite put into words. There was in Bruce's eyes, a shadow of longing that passed briefly, unnoticed by the others.

Bruce cleared his throat, trying to shake the feeling of loss that gripped him. "I think I'll head back out. See if I can get more news." His voice was quieter now, filled with an uncertainty that none of them could ignore.

James glanced up at him, his expression hard to read, but he nodded. "Be careful, Bruce."

Emily echoed the sentiment, her voice soft but hollow. "Yeah... just be careful."

Bruce stood, pocketing the phone. He could still feel that unsettling pang of jealousy when he saw Sarah lean into Daniels, but he pushed it down. They needed him out there, to gather as much information as he could. With a short nod, he slipped out of the room, leaving Emily and James alone.

The silence between them was thick, awkward. James shifted uncomfortably in his chair, glancing at his daughter but unsure of what to say. He wanted to comfort her, to ease the tension that had grown between them, but the words wouldn't come.

Emily broke the silence first. "She won't talk to me."

James looked at her, his heart aching. "Your mom?"

Emily nodded, her gaze dropping to her hands. "She won't even look at me. I think... I think she's mad at me. Maybe she blames me for what happened."

James swallowed hard, the guilt rising in his throat like bile. "She doesn't blame you, Emily. It's... it's not your fault."

"But it is," Emily said, her voice cracking. "I signed it, Dad. I took the mark. Mom... she can't even look at me. How can she forgive me when I can't even forgive myself?"

James reached out, his hand trembling slightly as he placed it on hers. "I made the choice, Emily. I thought we were doing the right thing, protecting us... but I was wrong. I was wrong."

Emily's tears fell silently, but she didn't pull her hand away. For the first time in days, she allowed herself to be consoled by her father. The pain between them was deep, but for a moment, they found a small thread of comfort in their shared sorrow. Life was still too hard to bear.

James squeezed her hand gently, his voice low. "We'll get through this. Somehow. We'll find a way."

Emily nodded, though the weight of her guilt still pressed heavily on her. They sat there together in the dimly lit room, the distant sound of footsteps echoing down the hallway as Bruce slipped out into the night.

"Needing More News"

Bruce moved quickly through the darkened streets, keeping to the shadows as he made his way back to the Wi-Fi hotspot. His mind raced with the events of the day, with everything Pastor Daniels had said about the riders of the apocalypse, with the way the world seemed to be spinning out of control. He thought of Sarah and Daniels, of the love they had found amidst the chaos, and for a fleeting moment, he wondered if he would ever find the same.

The park was eerily quiet when he arrived, its benches empty, the trees casting long, haunting shadows across the ground. Bruce crouched near the spot he had used earlier, tapping into the Wi-Fi signal once more. The phone connected, and immediately, a flood of new headlines appeared on the screen. War, famine, disease—it was all spiraling out of control, faster than anyone could have predicted.

Bruce's fingers hovered over the screen, but a sinking feeling washed over him. He had returned to the same Wi-Fi hotspot—just like before. His mind raced, recalling the first time he had come here, the risks he knew were involved. He had felt eyes on him even then, but desperation for information had overridden his caution.

Now, standing in the dark once again, it dawned on him—this was a mistake. A critical one. He froze, and a cold sweat broke out on his forehead. How could I have been so careless? he thought, the weight of his error settling in his gut like lead. In his rush to help the group, to bring them more news, he had ignored the golden rule of survival: never return to the same place twice.

Fear twisted in his chest as he realized the depth of his error. They could be watching this place. And now, had he walked into their trap?

The latest headlines on the screen grabbed Bruce's attention, and his heart sank even further. War, famine, plague—the world was unraveling. What good am I really doing? he thought bitterly. He had set out hoping to help, to gather crucial information for their group, to protect them. But now, all he had accomplished was putting himself—and possibly all of them—at risk. He had to leave, now.

As he slipped the phone into his pocket, a noise caught his attention—a soft rustling behind him. Bruce's heart pounded in his chest as he turned, feeling the world close in on him. Flashlights cut through the darkness. All of the beams converged on his face, blinding him.

Police.

They moved quickly, across the park, their footsteps heavy on the ground. Bruce's pulse raced as he scanned for a way out, but there was none. The trees were too thin to hide him, the streets too open to run. The noose had tightened around him, and there was nowhere to go.

He broke into a run anyway, but the officers surrounded immediately. His heart thundered in his ears as he realized his carelessness in returning to the same location.

The faces of the others flashed in his mind: Sarah, Daniels, James, Emily. What would they do—what would happen to them? The weight of responsibility pressed down on his chest like a vice. He had promised himself that he'd be useful, that he'd be a protector. But now, as Officer Harman yelled, "Put your hands behind your head and lock your fingers together," the world closed in, and all he felt was helplessness. I've failed them. The thought echoed in his mind, tormenting him as he was ordered to the ground and his hands were cuffed behind his back.

Would they even know what had happened to me? Would they know I had been arrested, or would they think I had turned me back on them and fled? He swallowed hard, his mouth dry with fear. I failed them. An officer pressed his face into the ground as he whispered under his breath, "I'm sorry, God.

13

HOW MUCH LONGER

"End of the Shadows"

The low hum of electricity buzzed through the hideout, casting a stark reminder of how fragile normalcy had become. Rebecca sat in a chair near the soft glow of the single lamp, her Bible open on her lap, though the words on the page blurred before her. The power had returned, but inside her, a different kind of darkness still reigned.

Pastor Daniels stood at the edge of the room, watching Rebecca's fragile form. She hadn't spoken much in the past week, and the weight of her silence pressed on everyone, but no one more than him. He knew the shadows she carried were deeper than the loss of light—they were a loss of hope.

"Rebecca," Daniels finally said, his voice soft, careful. He moved closer, his footsteps muted against the hard floor.

She glanced up at him, her face pale, dark circles beneath her eyes from nights spent pleading in prayer. Her lips trembled as she opened her mouth to speak, but no words came. When she finally did, her voice was a whisper, heavy with the burden of what she had been carrying.

"Pastor... I've been asking Him... I've been begging Him to change it, to take it all back." Her eyes welled up with tears, the pain so raw it seemed to tremble in the air around her. "Why didn't He stop them?" Her voice broke, the sobs she had been suppressing now shaking her small frame.

Daniels sat down beside her, his expression etched with sorrow and understanding. He didn't speak immediately. Instead, he let the silence between them settle, knowing that sometimes the deepest wounds needed space to breathe before they could heal.

Rebecca's hands gripped the edges of her Bible, her knuckles white. "I prayed," she whispered, the words barely audible. "I prayed for them... that He would protect them, protect their hearts. Why couldn't He make them see?" Her voice cracked as her tears began to fall freely. "Why couldn't He make them choose Him and not sign for the card?"

Daniels' heart clenched as he watched her break under the weight of it all. He reached out, placing a gentle hand on her shoulder. "Rebecca... He heard your prayers. He hears them still."

"But then why?" she interrupted, her voice rising, frustration and anguish mingling together. "Why didn't He stop it? Why didn't He stop them from signing their souls away?" The intensity in her eyes was wild, desperate. "They're lost now... forever. My family, my daughter..."

Daniels leaned closer, his voice calm yet carrying the weight of truth. "God gave us all free choice, Rebecca. And in His love, He could not force them. They had to make that decision on their own. I don't think it is fair."

Tears streamed down Rebecca's face as she listened, her chest heaving with sobs. "I don't understand," she cried. "I don't understand why He let this happen."

"It's hard to understand," Daniels replied, his voice steady, but his own eyes glistening with unshed tears. "And it's okay to question... to not understand. But you must know, Rebecca—God loves you. And He loves them. He didn't want this to happen. He gave them the choice because true love allows freedom. But they were deceived."

Rebecca stared at him, her breathing ragged, as the truth of his words settled over her. Her sobs slowed, but the grief in her eyes remained as deep as ever. She slumped forward, her head dropping into her hands. "Why does it feel like He's punishing me?" she whispered. "Why does it feel like He's abandoned me?"

Daniels gently pulled her toward him, and she leaned against his chest, sobbing quietly. "He hasn't abandoned you," Daniels murmured. "He's right here. He's been with you through every cry, through every plea. And He's not leaving."

For a long time, Rebecca stayed in his comfort, letting her tears flow freely. Her body shook with the release of all the pain she had bottled inside, and Daniels held her, offering her the only comfort he could in that moment.

"I want to believe you," she whispered after some time, her voice soft and weak. "I want to believe He's still with me... that He still cares. But it's so hard."

"I know," Daniels replied gently. "It's a process, Rebecca. A hard one. And sometimes, it feels like the darkness will never lift. But it will. You're not alone. You have us. You still have James and Emily. And you have Him. Even in the shadows of the valley you are in."

Rebecca didn't reply, but a quiet acceptance seemed to settle over her. She wasn't healed, not yet. But the storm inside her had calmed, if only for a moment. As the tears subsided, an exhausted silence followed.

Daniels remained beside her, his heart heavy for her pain. He felt the weight of her grief, the silence thick between them. After a while, Rebecca spoke again, her voice flat, drained of all the fight it once held. "I'm so tired, Pastor. I don't even know what to feel anymore. I've prayed... I've pleaded... and now, I just don't have anything left."

Her voice was hollow, as if the fight had drained every ounce of her energy. She stared blankly ahead, the lines of her face etched with deep sadness. Rebecca's body sagged as though the weight of the world had finally crushed her spirit. The bargaining had ended, and now the numbness of depression set in, cold and quiet.

Daniels let the silence stretch between them for a long moment, knowing that pushing her for more words would be futile. He reached out, covering her hands with his, the warmth of his touch anchoring her to the present. "You're not alone," he whispered again, his voice full of compassion. "We'll carry this together."

Rebecca closed her eyes, leaning into his words but still feeling so far from any sense of relief. She wanted to believe it—to cling to the hope that had once been the center of her life. But now, all she could feel was the vast emptiness of everything that had been taken from her.

Eventually, she nodded, though it was more of a gesture of surrender than agreement. "I don't know how to climb out of this, Pastor," she admitted, her voice barely audible. "I feel so... lost."

Daniels squeezed her hands gently. "You don't have to climb out all at once," he said softly. "Just take it one moment at a time. One day at a time. We'll walk through this together, Rebecca. God is here, even when we can't see Him in the darkness. He's still holding onto you, and so are we."

She exhaled a long, shaky breath, the tension in her shoulders slightly easing. "I'll try," she whispered, though the uncertainty still lingered.

"That's all you need to do," Daniels reassured her. "Just keep trying. And when you can't hold on, we'll hold onto you."

Rebecca's eyes glazed over, a mixture of exhaustion and sorrow still clinging to her, but the edge of despair had dulled. She nodded again, this time with just the faintest spark of willingness to accept the comfort being offered.

The room fell into a heavy silence once more, but this time it was not quite as unbearable. They sat together, the quiet hum of the powered lights buzzing above them, a testament to the fragile normalcy that had returned.

She accepted the silence, leaning into it, the weight of everything resting like a shadow but no longer entirely suffocating her. She whispered, "I will be fine."

Daniels took that as a signal and quietly left the room.

"Heart of Hartman"

Bruce sat in the cold, steel chair, his hands resting loosely in his lap, though the tight cuffs around his wrists dug into his skin. The interrogation room was empty, sterile, the faint hum of the overhead light the only sound to keep him company. Why do the lights always seem to hum? he thought, mildly annoyed. Even in a place like this, the world around him continued its indifferent rhythm. His heart pounded in his chest, but he remained still, his head bowed slightly, eyes half-closed as if deep in thought. In reality, he was praying. Not loudly, not in any way that would betray the quiet desperation running through him, but inwardly, seeking strength for what he knew was coming.

Lord, give me the words. Give me strength. I know you're with me, and I trust You.

The door creaked open, pulling Bruce's attention upward. Officer Hartman entered, his expression a mask of professionalism, though something in his eyes seemed harder than Bruce had expected. He carried a file, no doubt containing everything the authorities thought they knew about Bruce and his escape with the two women.

Hartman didn't sit right away. Instead, he stood by the door for a moment, studying Bruce with an intensity that made the air feel heavy. The officer finally moved to the table, pulling out the chair opposite Bruce and sitting down with a slow deliberation. He opened the file, flipping through the pages before looking up.

"You know why you're here," Hartman said, his voice calm, measured.

Bruce nodded but said nothing. The silence stretched between them like a taut wire.

"We know about your escape," Hartman continued. "You helped two women—Sarah and Rebecca, was it? You took them with you." His eyes locked onto Bruce's, probing for any sign of weakness. "Where are they now?"

Bruce's heart raced, but outwardly he remained calm. He had prepared for this, the questioning, the pressure. But even still, he found himself offering another silent prayer. Help me, Lord.

Hartman leaned forward, narrowing his gaze. "They were dangerous, weren't they? They refused to cooperate, didn't they? That makes them an enemy of the state. You know that, don't you?"

Bruce shook his head, feeling his pulse quicken. "They weren't dangerous," he said, his voice steady but filled with emotion. "You don't understand. They were going to kill Sarah for her faith. She wasn't a threat; she just refused to give up what she believed in."

Hartman's brow furrowed in confusion, as if trying to reconcile what he was hearing with the hardline protocol he had been taught. "Refusing to comply with the state—refusing to pledge—is a threat, Bruce. It's rebellion."

Bruce leaned forward, locking eyes with Hartman. "She wasn't rebelling. She was standing for something bigger than any of us. It wasn't about refusing the state, it was about refusing to deny her God. She wasn't a danger to anyone."

Hartman paused, his stern expression faltering just slightly. "You expect me to believe that? You think faith excuses treason?"

"No, I'm telling you that faith is the only thing that gave her strength to stand against a system that was taking everything from her," Bruce said, his voice unwavering. "She believed in something that made her stronger, and they were going to kill her for it."

His voice was low, almost persuasive, as if trying to lure Bruce into a trap. "Tell me where they are, and this doesn't have to get worse for you."

Bruce felt a cold knot of fear tighten in his stomach, but he shook his head slowly. "No."

Hartman frowned, leaning back in his chair. "No? You realize the consequences of protecting them, don't you? You're facing charges of aiding enemies of the state. That's treason."

Bruce swallowed, his mouth dry. "I saved them from being killed. They were going to kill Sarah—just for her faith. Because she believed."

Hartman scoffed, shaking his head. "Believed in what? A God that abandoned this world? You're telling me you risked everything for someone who was marked for death by their own hand?"

Bruce's heart ached, but he knew he couldn't back down. He leaned forward, the chains rattling softly against the table as he locked eyes with Hartman. "You don't understand. They weren't the enemy. Sarah... she was innocent. They wanted to kill her because she wouldn't renounce her faith. I couldn't let that happen."

Hartman's eyes hardened. "I don't care about her faith. I care about the law."

Bruce's gaze never wavered. "But that's just it. The law isn't justice. It's evil." He paused, his voice gaining strength as he spoke. "When I met Sarah, something changed in me. She shared her faith with me, and I saw something I hadn't seen in years—hope. Purpose. It wasn't just a religion to her. It was love, peace, something I never had."

Hartman shifted uncomfortably in his seat. "Stop." He held up a hand as if to cut Bruce off, but Bruce pressed on, his voice filled with conviction.

"I didn't believe at first either. But she showed me a way to live that was more than just survival. More than just following orders. I felt it," he glanced at the man's name tag" Officer Hartman. I felt that peace when I simply believed what she was saying." Bruce's eyes softened as he saw a flicker of something in Hartman's gaze—a crack in the hardened exterior.

For a split second, Hartman's mind drifted. Unbidden, memories of his mother flooded back, vivid and sharp. He remembered sitting in church with her as a teenager, the way she would sing with such joy, her hand resting gently on his shoulder. He had felt something back then—a pull in his spirit, something that stirred in him every time he heard the sermons. He had felt a fire for God, active in the youth group, excited to live out his faith. When his mother died, all of that died with her. He had blamed God. He had buried the pain and locked it away, refusing to step foot in a church again.

Hartman blinked, snapping back to the present. Bruce was watching him intently, and it took a moment for him to realize how far his thoughts had wandered.

Bruce's voice was softer now, gentler. In his spirit he felt something for Hartman "I know you've felt it too, haven't you? That pull? That love? Maybe you don't want to admit it, but it's still there. God hasn't given up on you, even if you've turned your back on Him."

Hartman stiffened, the walls around his heart slamming back into place. He shook his head, trying to regain control of the conversation. "This isn't about me," he said tersely. "This is about you betraying the law."

Bruce didn't flinch. He met Hartman's gaze head-on. "I won't betray them. I can't. I saved them from evil, and I will not send them back to it."

Hartman's chest tightened at Bruce's words. He felt something stir inside him, something he hadn't allowed himself to feel in years. Compassion. Understanding. He knew what it was to try and protect someone from a world that felt too dark, too broken. But more than that, he knew what it was to feel like God had abandoned you—and yet, here was this man, risking everything for the same faith he had turned away from.

A long silence stretched between them, the weight of Bruce's words sinking deeper into Hartman's heart. Slowly, Hartman let out a breath, his resolve softening.

"I get it," Hartman muttered, almost more to himself than to Bruce. "I... I understand."

Bruce watched him, hope flickering in his eyes.

Hartman stood, pacing for a moment before finally stopping in front of Bruce. His tone was quieter now, less authoritative. "Look... I'll ignore the request to send you back to the camp. I'll make up some excuse. But..." He hesitated, glancing away before locking eyes with Bruce again. "The truth is... I need to talk to you more about this. About what happened."

Bruce blinked, surprised by the shift. "You'll keep me here?"

Hartman nodded, his voice tight with emotion he wasn't ready to show. "For now. But don't get any ideas. This is still an interrogation. I just... I need to understand more."

As Hartman turned to leave, Bruce whispered a quiet prayer of thanks, his heart full of gratitude, but was there still hope for Hartman, and for others.

And in that moment, Bruce knew that even in this dark place, God was still working.

"The Cry for Justice"

Rebecca lay on the bed in her makeshift room, her world heavy, thick with the weight of her grief. She stared at the low ceiling, her eyes burning from tears that refused to fall. James and their daughter had taken the mark. The thought gnawed at her soul, leaving her hollow and numb.

She turned onto her side, clutching the blanket against her chest as her mind churned. The visions that had plagued her for so long now took on new clarity. They were not random, they were linked, each a part of a greater story unfolding over the centuries. She shut her eyes, trying to quiet the storm within, but the images came rushing back, blinding, relentless.

A deep stirring rose in her spirit, a pull she couldn't resist. She concentrated on the visions, forcing herself to remember every detail, every whisper of divine revelation. Suddenly, it was as if she were being hurled from her body.

The heavens stood still. A sacred hush fell over the expanse as Jesus again stood before the scroll, His hand resting on its surface. His eyes, deep pools of sorrow and resolve, traced the ancient document sealed with divine purpose. This was the fifth seal, its breaking a moment that carried the weight of eternity.

Around Him, the angels knelt in reverent silence. They dared not speak or move as the prophecy, long hidden, was about to be revealed. The scroll bore the history of rebellion, both human and angelic, and its unsealing would unleash truths too profound to comprehend. Jesus, steady and deliberate, pressed His hand against the seal.

The sound of its breaking reverberated across the heavens, a brilliant light erupted from the scroll, illuminating the celestial realm with a holy flame. From the light emerged the souls of those who had been slain, the martyrs of more than two thousand years of tribulation and persecution. They were clothed in the righteousness of Christ, their faces marked with both the pain of their deaths and the glory of their reward.

Their voices rose as one, a cry that pierced the heavens: "How long, O Lord?" Their plea echoed with sorrow and longing. "How long before You judge and avenge our blood on those who dwell on the earth?"

Rebecca's mourning increased as she witnessed their cry, her spirit overwhelmed by the anguish and hope mingled in their voices. These were not just the apostles and early saints, these were souls from every age, men and women who had died for their faith, refusing to deny Christ in the face of unimaginable suffering. From the first martyrs to those in her own time, their blood cried out to God.

Jesus closed His eyes, their agony reflected in His expression. He had walked with them through their trials and held them through their deaths. Now, as their souls cried out to Him, He reached into the light of the scroll and drew out robes of purest white.

With infinite tenderness, He presented the robes to the martyrs. "Rest a little longer," He whispered, His voice filled with love. "The time is coming, and it will not delay. But first, the full number of your brothers and sisters, who will also be killed as you were, must be completed."

Rebecca's heart ached as she watched. The martyrs, though still longing for justice, were filled with peace as the robes wrapped around them, a symbol of the purity and victory they had gained through their suffering. They rested beneath the altar, their souls clothed in glory, waiting for the final fulfillment of God's plan.

Rebecca's eyes slowly opened, as she was pulled back to her dark, lonely room. She lay motionless, her body had no desire to move, the vision vivid and sad. The weight of what she had seen pressed on her like a crushing tide.

Tears welled in her eyes, her despair deepened by the knowledge that the tribulation was not yet over. The cries of the martyrs echoed in her spirit mixing with her own loss. She had to find the strength to endure, even if her heart felt too broken to bear it.

"Embracing the Storm"

Pastor Daniels' heart was heavy with the weight of Rebecca's sorrow. The air in the hideout felt thick, oppressive, as though her grief had seeped into the very walls. He paused in the hallway, running a hand over his face, his own emotions threatening to overwhelm him. He had walked with her through the darkness, absorbing her pain, carrying the burden alongside her, but now... now he needed someone to share his own burden.

He needed Sarah.

His steps were slow as he made his way through the narrow corridors, the dim light casting long shadows that danced with the flickering power. The buzzing hum of the light grated on his already frayed nerves. He had expected this—he had always known that helping someone through the valley of shadows would drain him—but it didn't make it any easier. He needed to find her.

Finally, he saw Sarah in the small room that she had made her own. She was sitting on the edge of the makeshift bed, her hands clasped together, staring off into space, lost in thought. There was something fragile in the way she held herself, and yet, just seeing her there brought a flicker of warmth to his weary heart.

"Sarah," he whispered, stepping into the room.

She looked up, her eyes softening as they met his, but there was something clouding her gaze—something he hadn't noticed before. A shadow of guilt, perhaps, or regret.

"Tim," she murmured, standing as he approached.

Without a word, he drew her into his arms, pulling her close. He held her tightly, as if trying to bridge the emptiness that had lingered since leaving Rebecca. The warmth of her body seeped into him, easing the cold ache that had settled deep within his bones. Sarah rested her head against his chest, her breath soft and steady, matching the rhythm of his own.

For a few precious moments, they stood in silence, letting the weight of their past struggles dissolve in each other's embrace. It wasn't just comfort—it was a sense of home, the kind that could only come from working through the feelings together and finally finding peace in the love they had built.

"I talked to Rebecca," Tim finally said, his voice a low murmur. "She's... she's slipping into a deeper depression now. She's moving into the next stage of grief. Acceptance will come, but right now... she's going to need you. I encouraged her to reach out, but it's going to be hard. She's trapped in her sorrow, and she might not reach out on her own."

Sarah nodded against him, her breath soft on his chest. "I'll try to talk to her," she whispered. "But... I'm scared, Tim. What if I say the wrong thing? What if she pushes me away?"

Tim pulled back slightly, looking down at her. "She needs you, Sarah. She needs all of us. And she'll come through this, I know it. But you have to be there when she's ready. Depression is... it's a valley. We can't pull her out, but we can walk beside her."

The room fell into a comfortable silence, but there was a tension between them now, something unsaid lingering in the air. Sarah pulled away from him, walking across the small room. Her back was to him, but he could see the way her shoulders tensed, the way her hands trembled at her sides.

"Bruce never came back," she said suddenly, her voice barely above a whisper.

Tim's heart clenched at the mention of Bruce. He had been avoiding the thought of him, avoiding the weight of his absence. "I know," he replied quietly. "We haven't heard anything…"

Sarah turned, tears glistening in her eyes. "Tim… I think it's my fault."

He stepped toward her, confusion crossing his face. "What do you mean? How could it be your fault?"

Her voice broke as she spoke, the guilt she had been carrying for days spilling over. "I… I think Bruce left because of me. Because I hurt him. I created this… emotional tie to him. I let him care for me, I let him feel close to me. And then I…" She swallowed hard, her voice trembling. "I hurt him, Tim. When I chose you, I hurt him, and I think that's why he left. I pushed him away."

Tim's heart ached for her. He reached out, taking her hands in his. "Sarah… this isn't your fault. Bruce made his own choices. You didn't force him to leave."

"But what if I did?" she whispered, her voice thick with emotion. "What if I broke something in him? He cared about me, Tim. And I hurt him. He probably felt like there was no reason to stay, no reason to fight, because I wasn't… I wasn't his."

Her tears fell freely now, her body trembling with the weight of her guilt. Tim pulled her into his arms, holding her close as she wept, her face pressed against his chest.

"Sarah, listen to me," he said softly, his hand stroking her hair. "You didn't do anything wrong. You followed your heart. And Bruce… he knows that. He made his own choices, and whatever happened to him out there, it wasn't because of you."

Sarah clung to him, her sobs quieting but her heart still heavy. "I don't want to hurt anyone," she whispered. "I never wanted this."

"You didn't hurt anyone, Sarah," Tim whispered back. "You've only ever tried to love, to help, to care. And that's why I love you. That's why we're here together."

For a moment, the world outside seemed to fade, and it was just the two of them, their hearts intertwined in the quiet space they had created. Tim gently pulled back, lifting Sarah's chin so her tear-streaked face met his gaze.

"I love you," he said, his voice thick with emotion. "And I'm here. No matter what happens, I'm here with you."

Sarah's eyes searched his, and in that moment, something shifted inside her. The guilt, the sadness—it didn't disappear, but it no longer consumed her. She felt something deeper, something stronger—love, unyielding and raw, coursing through her veins.

Without a word, she reached up, her fingers brushing against Tim's cheek, tracing the line of his jaw. Her touch was soft, tentative at first, but then something within her broke free. She leaned in, her lips finding his, kissing him with a hunger she hadn't realized she was capable of. Her hands slipped around his neck, pulling him closer, the warmth of his body flooding her with an emotion she couldn't control, didn't want to control.

Tim responded, his arms wrapping around her waist, pulling her closer, their kiss deepening with each passing moment. Sarah's hands moved through his hair, her touch urgent, desperate. She had needed this—needed him.

She broke the kiss for a moment, her breath heavy, her eyes filled with a fiery intensity. Then, without hesitation, she pressed her body against his, pushing him back onto the bed. Tim's heart raced as he fell backwards onto the mattress, Sarah's weight on top of him, her lips finding his again, kissing him with a passion that ignited every part of her being.

The world outside didn't matter. The pain, the guilt, the uncertainty—they all faded into the background as Sarah lost herself in the moment, in him. She kissed him again and again, her hands running down his chest, every touch sending waves of emotion through her. This was her release, her way of finding something solid, something real in the midst of the chaos.

Tim's arms wrapped around her, pulling her close. Their lips met again, slower this time, the kiss deepening as they lost themselves in each other. They held on, the weight of their shared pain and their love mingling in every touch. Time slipped away as their hands explored, their bodies pressed together, trying to hold on to this brief moment of solace.

Every kiss, every embrace, was a way to speak what words couldn't express—how desperately they needed this, needed each other. Sarah poured all her remaining energy into the passion between them, her hands running through Tim's hair, her lips tracing the edge of his jaw, his neck.

But eventually, exhaustion overtook her. With a soft sigh, she let herself collapse against him, resting her head on his chest. She could hear the steady rhythm of his heartbeat, and for a moment, it was the only thing that mattered. The room fell into a peaceful silence, broken only by the sound of their labored breathing, still catching up from the intensity of the moment.

Tim's hand gently stroked her hair, his fingers trailing along the back of her neck. Her skin was no longer just warm—it was burning, flushed with the fire of passion that still coursed through her. The heat radiated between them, an undeniable reminder of the intensity they had shared, wrapping them in a blanket of closeness and raw emotion.

Neither of them spoke for a while, content to simply feel the rhythm of each other's breaths, the connection that pulsed between them, as the heat of Sarah's body pressed firmly against his.

Finally, Tim broke the silence, his voice a soft murmur, as if he were thinking aloud. "I haven't seen Anthony since I went underground. I need to find him…" His words trailed off, the weight of the moment making him hesitate. He shifted slightly beneath her, the burning heat of her body still clinging to him, drawing her attention in ways that made his heart race.

"Sarah…" he began, his voice trembling not from fear, but from the overwhelming emotions swirling inside him. "Will you marry me?"

Her heart seemed to pause for a brief moment, caught between the echo of his words and the blazing warmth that still spread through her, making every inch of her body feel alive, ignited. She didn't need to think. The answer had been written in her heart long before this moment, as sure as the fire that still simmered beneath her skin.

"Yes," she whispered, her voice barely audible, as if the word had found its way to her lips on its own, carrying a quiet, undeniable sense of peace. It felt natural, like something that had always been meant to be.

A smile spread across both their faces, the joy of that simple word—yes—filling the room with a lightness that danced over the intensity of their connection. It wasn't a grand moment, it wasn't loud or ceremonious, but it was perfect. After a quiet pause Sarah lifted her head off of Tim's chest and looking into his eyes with a questioning look "Who's Anthony?"

"Anthony's a pastor," he said with a gentle grin, a touch of humor breaking through the emotion, the heat between them was still intense. "I can't officiate my own wedding, you know."

For the first time in what felt like forever, they laughed softly, the sound mingling with the steady beat of their hearts, the moment alive with both passion and peace.

14

SHAKEN

"Restoration"

Rebecca sat on the edge of her bed, the dim light of the underground room casting long shadows across the walls. The weight of her grief still lingered, but there was something different in the air—a quiet resolve settling in her heart. After more than a week of being lost in the darkness of her depression, something inside her had shifted. She had prayed, screamed, and begged God to change things, but none of it had eased her pain. Now, she understood: she couldn't change the past. She couldn't undo what had happened. But she could choose how to move forward.

It was time to forgive. It was time to heal.

James. Emily.

They were all she had left, and despite the pain, she needed them. She had shut them out, but now, sitting in the silence, she realized that she didn't want to lose them again. Her heart ached at the thought of what she had put them through, the bitterness that had consumed her, the anger she had taken out on them.

With a deep breath, Rebecca stood, her legs shaky but determined. She walked out of her room and down the narrow hallway, her footsteps echoing in the quiet refuge. The weight of the conversation she was about to have hung heavy on her chest, but she knew it had to be done.

She found James sitting alone in the small common room, his head in his hands. He looked up as she approached, surprise flickering across his face. Rebecca hesitated for a moment, but then the flood of emotions overtook her. Tears welled up in her eyes as she stepped toward him.

"James," she whispered, her voice breaking.

He stood quickly, his eyes wide with concern. "Rebecca..."

"I'm so sorry," she sobbed, her tears falling freely now. "I'm sorry for pushing you away. I'm sorry for blaming you. I... I don't want to lose you. I need you."

James was stunned, his heart swelling with relief and sorrow all at once. He closed the distance between them in an instant, wrapping his arms around her tightly. Rebecca melted into his embrace, her sobs shaking her small frame as she clung to him.

"I'm sorry too," James whispered, his voice thick with emotion. "I thought I lost you, Rebecca. I didn't know how to fix it. I'm just... I'm so glad you're here."

They stood there, holding each other as if the world outside had disappeared. It was a fragile moment, but it was real, and it was healing. Slowly, Rebecca pulled back, wiping the tears from her eyes.

"Come with me," she said softly, taking his hand and leading him back to her room. They sat together on the bed, and for the first time in what felt like forever, they talked—really talked. They talked about everything they had been through, the pain of their choices, the fear that had driven them apart, and the hope that still flickered somewhere deep within them. Rebecca's voice trembled as she spoke, but there was a newfound strength in her words—a determination to move forward, to survive together.

"I was so angry," Rebecca admitted, her eyes fixed on her hands as she twisted them in her lap. "I didn't know how to handle it, and I took it out on you and Emily. But... I don't want to live like that anymore. I want us to heal. I want us to be a family again."

James nodded, his own voice thick with emotion. "I understand. I was scared too, Rebecca. I thought I'd lost you after everything that happened in the camp. When you escaped, I thought we'd be free. But the pain we brought with us... it felt like we were still prisoners."

Rebecca's eyes welled up with tears again, but this time, they weren't tears of despair. "I forgive you, James," she whispered, her voice breaking. "And I forgive Emily too. I just... I want us to be whole again."

As if summoned by her mother's words, Emily appeared at the doorway, hesitant and unsure. She had heard their voices from down the hall and had been drawn to the sound of her mother's soft voice, something she hadn't heard in what felt like a lifetime. She stood there, her heart pounding in her chest, afraid to intrude but desperate for the warmth of her family again.

Rebecca looked up, her eyes meeting Emily's across the room. In that moment, all the walls that had been built between them crumbled. The anger, the bitterness—it all fell away. All that was left was a mother's love for her daughter and a daughter's need to feel that love.

"Emily," Rebecca whispered, her voice filled with longing.

Emily didn't wait. She ran across the room and threw herself into her mother's arms with such force that Rebecca was knocked back onto the bed, her breath catching as Emily clung to her. The joy that filled the room was overwhelming, the heaviness of the past weeks lifting as they held each other. Emily's tears flowed freely as she hugged her mother so tightly it was as if she were afraid to let go.

"I'm sorry, Mom," Emily cried, her voice muffled against her mother's shoulder. "I'm so sorry."

Rebecca stroked her daughter's hair, her own tears falling. "It's okay, sweetheart. It's okay. I love you. I never stopped loving you."

James, who had been watching quietly, was overcome with emotion as well. He moved closer, wrapping his arms around both Rebecca and Emily, the three of them tangled together in a heap of love, forgiveness, and relief. They stayed that way for what felt like hours, the tension and pain of the past melting away in the warmth of their embrace.

As the tears subsided, they found themselves lying on the bed together, Emily nestled between her parents, her head resting on mother's chest. James lay beside Rebecca, his arm draped over both of them. There was peace in the quiet that followed, a peace they hadn't felt in so long. It was as if, for the first time, they could breathe again.

"We're going to make it," Rebecca whispered, her voice barely audible. "We have to. We have each other."

James nodded, pressing a kiss to her forehead. "We'll get through this. Together."

Emily smiled softly, her heart finally at ease as she lay nestled against her mother. For the first time since the escape, she felt safe. She looked up at her parents, her eyes filled with hope. "What do we do next?"

Rebecca sighed, glancing at James before answering. "We keep going. We survive. We take care of each other."

"And we find Bruce," James added quietly, his brow furrowed in concern. "He saved you. We can't just leave him out there."

A shadow passed over Rebecca's face at the mention of Bruce, but she nodded. "We owe him everything. We'll find him, somehow."

The three of them lay there, wrapped in each other's warmth, the weight of the world still pressing down on them, but no longer unbearable. They had found each other again, and that was enough— for now.

Tim and Sarah had gone out for the day, not saying much about where they were headed, though it was likely they had ventured to the homeless area in search of Bruce. They had done this before, quietly slipping out without explanation, their unspoken worry for Bruce always hanging in the air. Sarah blamed herself. When they returned, however, the usual tension in the hideout felt different, quieter. The house seemed empty, not a sound from Rebecca or Emily. But as they walked down the dimly lit hall, soft, joyful laughter echoed through the walls, a sound so unexpected it stopped them in their tracks.

It was Emily's laugh.

Tim and Sarah exchanged a look before hurrying toward the room, wondering what could have caused such a shift in the air. When they reached the doorway and peered inside, what they saw took them by surprise. There, on the bed, were Rebecca, James, and Emily, all lying together, tangled in each other's arms, smiles lighting up their faces. The sorrow that had weighed them down for weeks seemed to have lifted— at least for this moment.

Rebecca noticed them standing in the doorway, her eyes softening with gratitude. She carefully untangled herself from Emily's embrace, though she hesitated as if not wanting to break the moment. Sitting up, she met Sarah and Tim's gaze with something close to peace.

"Thank you," Rebecca said quietly, her voice filled with emotion. "Thank you for loving me, even when I didn't deserve it."

James sat up beside her, his hand resting protectively on Rebecca's back, his brow creased with concern. "Where were you?" he asked, the worry clear in his voice. "We were worried."

Sarah smiled softly, stepping forward as she held up her hand, her ring finger catching the light. The small, simple band glittered, and for a moment, the room was filled with a different kind of lightness.

"Introducing Mrs. Sarah Daniels," she said with a laugh, her cheeks flushing with joy.

The room erupted into shock, then laughter. Rebecca, almost knocking James off the bed in her eagerness, scrambled to her feet and rushed toward Sarah, pulling her into a tight embrace. "Oh, Sarah!" she cried, her voice trembling with emotion. "I'm so happy for you."

Tim stood in the doorway, smiling as he watched his new wife and Rebecca embrace. For a moment, the worry that had filled their lives seemed to fade, replaced by joy, love, and a sense of family that had been missing for so long.

"How did it happen?" Emily asked, her eyes wide with curiosity as she sat up, leaning into her father.

Sarah beamed, looking at Tim. "He asked me, and I just… knew. It felt right." She paused, laughing softly. "He couldn't wait any longer, I guess."

Rebecca squeezed Sarah's hands. "I'm so happy for you both. You deserve this."

They sat down together, the energy in the room light and filled with hope. For a while, they talked about the engagement, about the happiness that had bloomed between Tim and Sarah despite the darkness around them. The moments of joy felt like a balm, a brief respite from the endless worry.

But as the conversation quieted, as it always did, the subject shifted to Bruce.

"What do we do about Bruce?" James asked quietly, his brow furrowing. "He hasn't come back, and no one's heard from him. It's been too long."

The joy in the room dimmed as they all shared the same thought—the same worry. Bruce had been the one to who saved them, the one who had risked everything. Now he was gone.

"We can't just leave him out there," Tim said, his voice serious. "But we also don't know where to start. We've checked the homeless areas. We've asked around, but…" he shook his head, "it's like he vanished."

Silence fell over the room, the weight of the unknown pressing down on them. Rebecca looked at Emily, then at Sarah, her eyes filled with concern.

"We need to keep looking," Rebecca whispered. "We owe him that much."

They all nodded in agreement, their thoughts heavy with worry and uncertainty. The joy from moments before had given way to a somber reality. Bruce was gone—somewhere—and until they found him, there would be no peace.

"Heart of Truth"

Later, as the dim light of evening settled over the city, Rebecca found herself unable to shake the feeling of unease. Her thoughts kept returning to the earlier hints of change in Sarah's demeanor, the subtle joy beneath her guarded exterior. The sense of something left unsaid nagged at Rebecca until she couldn't bear it any longer.

Determined to understand, Rebecca made her way to Sarah's room, knocking softly before stepping inside. She found Sarah sitting on the edge of her bed, lost in thought.

"Show me your ring," Rebecca said quietly, her voice both curious and cautious.

Sarah looked up, a hint of surprise in her eyes. Slowly, she extended her hand, her fingers trembling slightly as she revealed the simple band on her finger. It wasn't ornate, but its meaning was clear and profound.

Rebecca's eyes widened, darting between Sarah's face and the modest ring. "You... got married?" she asked, her voice a mix of disbelief and concern.

Sarah nodded, a soft smile tugging at her lips. "Yes, we did."

Rebecca's brow furrowed, her thoughts clearly racing. She took a deep breath, her voice dropping as she spoke. "Sarah... isn't this all a bit too fast? I mean, after everything you went through in the camp, and then what happened with Bruce... I just—I'm worried about you. This feels like one of those war-time weddings, you know? People grasping at something hopeful because of the chaos around them."

Sarah's smile faded, her expression shifting to one of understanding. "I know it might seem that way," she admitted quietly. "I understand why you'd think that."

Rebecca leaned forward, her eyes filled with genuine concern. "You're vulnerable right now, Sarah. You've been through hell—more than anyone should have to endure. I saw you clinging to Bruce for comfort, and now, marrying your pastor? I just don't want you to mistake the need for security for love."

Sarah's eyes glistened, and she reached out to take Rebecca's hand. "I hear you, Rebecca. I do. And if I were in your shoes, I'd probably be saying the same thing."

Rebecca searched Sarah's face, her own expression softening. "You've been so strong, but I know the wounds are still there. I don't want you to make a decision that you might regret later."

Tears brimmed in Sarah's eyes, but there was a steadiness in her voice. "You're right—I am vulnerable. I've been hurt, I've been scared, and I've leaned on people in ways I never thought I would. But this... this isn't about filling a void. It's not about safety or trying to replace the past."

Rebecca's grip tightened around Sarah's hand, her voice laced with both worry and love. "Then what is it, Sarah? Help me understand."

Sarah took a moment, her gaze drifting as she gathered her thoughts. "When I was in that camp, I prayed for a way out, but more than that, I prayed for a reason to keep going. Tim—Pastor Daniels—was a part of that answer. It wasn't just his kindness or his protection; it was the way he believed in me when I couldn't believe in myself. He saw me as more than a victim, more than someone broken. He saw me as someone worthy of love, and that's something I never thought I'd find again."

Rebecca's eyes softened, her defenses slowly crumbling. "I know he's a good man, Sarah. I've seen that. But are you sure you're not rushing this just to escape the pain?"

Sarah shook her head gently, her voice steady. "No, it's not about escaping. It's about embracing what's real, what's here. We didn't plan this. We didn't rush it. It was more like... a slow realization that grew into something we couldn't ignore. And yes, maybe the timing seems sudden, but it feels right. It feels like it's what God intended all along."

Rebecca's lips trembled, and she wiped a tear from her cheek. "I just want you to be happy, truly happy. You deserve that, after everything."

Sarah leaned closer, her voice filled with warmth. "I am happy, Rebecca. For the first time in a long time, I feel like I'm not just surviving—I'm living. Tim and I have worked through this, and we've done it together. This isn't a decision made in desperation; it's one made with hope."

Rebecca nodded slowly, her eyes searching Sarah's face one last time. "If you're sure... then I'll trust you. Just know that I'll always be here for you, no matter what."

Tears finally spilled over Sarah's cheeks, and she pulled Rebecca into a tight embrace. "I know," she whispered. "And that means everything to me."

They held each other for a moment, the weight of past suffering mingling with the lightness of newfound hope. It was a silent promise between them—one of love, understanding, and the courage to move forward, even when the path was uncertain.

"The Unseen Trail"

Officer Hartman sat in the dimly lit room of his modest apartment, the soft glow of his computer screen reflecting off his face. Bruce's phone—no, it was James' phone, actually—sat in front of him on the desk. He had spent hours combing through its contents, scrolling past old messages, photos, apps, and anything that might give him a clue about the whereabouts of James, Rebecca, and Sarah. His mind buzzed with a need for answers, but the task felt maddeningly tedious.

Hartman exhaled slowly, rubbing his eyes in frustration. The answers had to be in there somewhere. He just had to keep digging.

He scrolled through the phone's settings, checking for anything out of the ordinary. Finally, he came across a saved list of passwords. It was nothing unusual, just a string of mundane services James must have used. But it was when Hartman ventured into the map app that something caught his attention.

He navigated through the settings of the app, searching for anything that might give him a clue. Then, he found it—a small, hidden section of stored locations. It appeared that the phone had logged the last place it was used before Bruce was captured. His pulse quickened as he opened the map screen showing the location.

The location that popped up was the park where they had captured Bruce. Hartman leaned closer, his eyes narrowing as he searched through the timeline. The phone had stored Bruce's location when it connected to the public Wi-Fi hotspot, but Hartman needed more. He scrolled further back to see the phone's history prior to that day.

For a moment, it was blank—no data, no traces of movement. They must have removed the SIM card, Hartman thought, as there were no logs from the time they had gone underground. But as he scrolled back further, he found something. A familiar address—a location James had frequented before everything went south.

Hartman clicked on the address, his breath catching. It was their old apartment. That's where they had last been before removing the SIM he thought. But something else caught his attention. He scrolled further, watching the digital footprint of James' movements—work, the store, school. Then, something stood out. An address downtown, logged several times over a period of weeks. It wasn't a store or an office. It was an abandoned building.

Hartman's heart raced as he jotted down the address, then searched it on his computer. It was a run-down, forgotten structure, boarded up and neglected. But James had gone there—more than once.

"I bet that's where they are," Hartman muttered under his breath, a grin forming as the pieces started to come together.

Without wasting another second, he jumped up, grabbed his coat, and headed for the door. He was going to the station to confront Bruce. He finally had something—a lead. He wasn't going to let it slip through his fingers.

"Breaking Point"

Bruce sat on the cold, hard cot in his cell, staring blankly at the floor. His heart was a constant drumbeat in his chest, anxiety gnawing at him as the threat of being sent back to the camp loomed over him like a dark cloud. The camp—where he had escaped with Sarah and Rebecca, where he had seen things that no one should ever witness. Would he survive if they sent him back? Would they make an example of him for daring to escape? The thought alone made his hands tremble.

Suddenly, the clanging of keys rattled through the still air of the cell block. Bruce's eyes darted to the door, and he saw Officer Hartman standing there, his face unreadable. A guard approached, unlocking the barred door and letting Hartman in. Without a word, Hartman motioned for the guard to leave them alone. The guard hesitated for a moment but eventually stepped back, the door shutting behind him with a loud clang.

Hartman didn't speak at first, just stood there, his presence unsettling. Bruce remained on the bed, his back stiff, and his hands clenching the edge of the thin blanket. The silence was thick, oppressive, but Bruce wasn't one to wait for answers.

He began to speak, his voice low but steady. "I've been thinking... about everything. About God, about faith. Even in this cell, I feel Him with me. There's something bigger than all of this, Officer. Something you can't control with handcuffs or laws." His words hung in the air as he glanced up at Hartman. "You can't lock away faith."

Hartman, who had been standing still, seemed to waver slightly. His jaw clenched, but he didn't interrupt.

Bruce continued, his voice taking on a softer, more reflective tone. "I know you feel it, too. I can see it in your eyes. Maybe you're trying to forget, but faith—it doesn't leave you. I can see it in your eyes, you remember it, don't you? What happened?"

Hartman's expression hardened for a moment, but then, something flickered in his eyes—a memory, perhaps. He blinked, his face momentarily softening as Bruce's words stirred something deep inside him. He remembered his mother, how her faith had once been the center of their lives, how he'd felt so alive when he was younger, sitting in the pews beside her. And then... her death. The anger. The rejection of everything he once believed in.

But Hartman quickly shook the thoughts away, snapping back to the present. He cleared his throat, cutting through Bruce's speech. "That's enough," Hartman said gruffly, his voice tight. He paused, drawing in a breath before speaking again. "I'm not here to talk about faith. I'm here to talk about this." He reached into his pocket and pulled out the phone—James' phone. He held it up, his eyes narrowing as he turned it slowly in his hand.

Bruce's stomach dropped. His throat tightened as Hartman began to speak again, this time slowly, methodically, as if trying to build a case.

"I've been searching through it. I went through the settings, the apps, everything." Hartman's tone was calm, but there was an edge to it. "I found the list of saved passwords, tracked the last places it connected to Wi-Fi. And then, I went deeper." He paused, watching Bruce's face for any reaction. "I found the map app. I saw where James went. The last place this phone connected was in that park where we captured you."

Bruce remained silent, his body tense, his mind racing. He could feel where this was going.

"But I didn't stop there," Hartman continued, his voice growing colder. "I went further back. Saw all the places James had been before that. Work, the store, places that don't matter. But there was one location... downtown." He smirked slightly, watching Bruce's reaction closely. "An abandoned building. He went there more than once."

Bruce's heart pounded in his chest, but he kept his expression neutral, refusing to give anything away.

Hartman stepped closer, his eyes narrowing. "That's where they are, isn't it? James, Rebecca, Sarah—they're hiding there."

Bruce's pulse raced, but he still said nothing. His fists clenched tightly at his sides, his knuckles turning white.

Hartman's voice dropped lower, more menacing. "I'm going there. I'm going to bring them in. You can't stop this, Bruce."

Bruce's voice broke, raw with desperation. "Hartman, please, don't do this," he pleaded, his eyes wide and frantic. "You know what they did to Sarah... they tried to kill her once, and they will this time. And

Rebecca—she escaped with Sarah. If you turn them in, you're sentencing them both to death."

Hartman's face remained cold, his eyes devoid of sympathy. "They are the law now, Bruce. They are justice. No one will kill them. They'll be taken in and shown the truth—helped to understand that they need to be part of the new unity, the new peace."

Bruce's desperation turned to anger. "Peace?" shot back. "You call that peace? You know damn well it's not about unity. It's about submission. They'll break them, Hartman. You'll be killing them—don't you see that?"

Hartman's gaze hardened. "I'm not killing anyone, Bruce. I'm saving them from themselves."

The two men stood locked in a tense silence, the air between them heavy with unspoken words. Bruce's hands trembled, the rage building inside him like a storm. "If you walk out that door and hand them over, you're no better than the ones you swore to fight against."

Hartman took a step back, shaking his head slowly. "I don't expect you to understand, Bruce. But I'm going to get them—all of them."

With that, he turned toward the barred door, his intention clear.

In that instant, Bruce's mind raced, his heart pounding in his chest. He remembered the training he'd undergone, the countless psychological evaluations meant to prepare him for impossible choices. One question had haunted him more than any other: Would you be willing to kill if it meant saving innocent lives? His instructors had drilled it into him: sometimes you have to choose the lesser of two evils. It wasn't about what was right—it was about what was less wrong.

One scenario they used to force him to grapple with this harsh reality flashed before him now, vivid and relentless: What if a Nazi officer was about to take fifty children to a concentration camp? The answer was clear, even if it was brutal: stopping that officer—no matter the cost—was the lesser evil.

The rationalization struck him like a lightning bolt. Stopping Hartman was not just a choice—it was a necessity. The horrors that awaited Sarah and Rebecca, the monstrous system that would consume them, were far worse than taking one life to save them. It was not murder. It was preventing a greater evil.

That rationale released what was restraining him. The thought of Hartman capturing Sarah and Rebecca, dragging them back to the horrors of the camp—he couldn't allow it. It was as if a dam had burst, unleashing a torrent of rage that he had tried desperately to contain. In that moment, his faith collided violently with a primal urge for vengeance, a darker instinct rising up within him. All the self-control he'd worked to build was suddenly consumed by a single, terrifying clarity: to save them, he had to stop Hartman, no matter the cost.

Something snapped inside Bruce. The thought of Hartman capturing them, dragging Sarah and Rebecca back to the horrors of the camp—he couldn't let it happen. It was as if a dam inside him burst, releasing all the rage he had tried to contain. In that moment, his new spirit of faith clashed violently with the primal urge for vengeance, and the darker side of his flesh overpowered the restraint he had worked so hard to cultivate.

His body moved on instinct, propelled by raw survival. In one fluid motion, Bruce surged to his feet, every muscle tense with urgency. He launched himself at Hartman, his training taking over as he executed a rapid series of Jeet Kune Do strikes. It wasn't just about defense—it was the unbridled release of a fury that had been building since the camps.

Hartman had no time to react. Bruce's fist connected squarely with his chest, sending him reeling back into the cell bars with a loud clang. The impact was harsh, but Bruce's rage kept him moving, driven by a desperation that had consumed him more than he wanted to admit.

As Hartman collapsed to the ground, Bruce's assault continued. Fists and knees crashed against the officer's body, fueled by a mix of fear, anger, and the overwhelming need to protect those he loved. But with each strike, a different kind of pain tore through Bruce—a deep, inner struggle between the man he had been and the man he wanted to be.

For a brief moment, he felt a surge of shame beneath the rage, a realization that his actions were driven by his own carnal nature rather than the spirit he had been striving to follow. Yet, he couldn't stop. The instinct to destroy what threatened Sarah and Rebecca was too powerful, too primal. The officer's head snapped back against the cold concrete floor, and his hands scrambled in vain to protect himself.

The rawness of Bruce's attack was not just about Hartman; it was about everything Bruce had suffered and witnessed. The darkness he had tried to bury had risen up, reminding him that he was still flesh, still fallible, still prone to the old ways of violence.

Suddenly, the sound of footsteps echoed down the hallway. The guard heard the commotion and was sprinting toward the cell, his keys jangling as he ran. "Hey! Hey!" the guard yelled as he unlocked the door and stormed inside.

Bruce had Hartman pinned to the floor now, his hands wrapped tightly around the officer's throat, squeezing with a terrifying intensity. Hartman's face turned red as he struggled to breathe, his eyes bulging in panic. The guard drew his weapon, shouting, "Let him go! Step back now!"

But Bruce didn't let go. He continued to tighten his grip, his vision narrowing as his rage consumed him. He couldn't let Hartman take them—he had to protect Sarah and Rebecca. The guard's voice was drowned out by the sound of his own heartbeat pounding in his ears.

The guard had no choice. His finger squeezed the trigger, unloading his clip into Bruce's back. The shots echoed in the small cell as Bruce's body jerked with each impact. But even then, he didn't release Hartman right away. His grip remained tight for a few agonizing seconds, and then... slowly, his fingers loosened. His body slumped forward, collapsing onto the floor beside Hartman.

Hartman lay there gasping for air, dazed and shocked, his hands clutching his bruised throat. The guard rushed to his side, pulling him up and away from Bruce's lifeless body. The cell door clanged shut as the guard locked it, even though there was no need—Bruce was gone.

The guard helped Hartman to his feet, guiding him out of the cell block and into the hallway. Hartman leaned against the wall, still coughing, his throat raw and aching. The guard looked at him, wide-eyed. "What the hell happened in there?"

Hartman shook his head, struggling to find his voice. After a few painful coughs, he finally managed to speak. "He... he just snapped." His voice was raspy, barely audible. He rubbed his bruised throat, wincing at the pain.

The guard looked back toward the cell, his expression grim. "I didn't have a choice."

Hartman nodded weakly, his mind racing. He had gone into that cell thinking he had control, thinking he could break Bruce. But now, as he stood there, shaken and bruised, he realized how wrong he had been.

"The Final Number"

All of creation trembled. A single shockwave, like the first note of a divine symphony, rippled through the fabric of existence. It started small, almost imperceptible, yet in a heartbeat, it reverberated across galaxies, shaking the foundations of both heaven and earth. The air seemed to vibrate with an unseen energy, as if time itself paused for an eternal second, sensing the gravity of what had just occurred.

In the heavenly realm, a sudden stillness swept over the angels, who were once engrossed in the tasks of eternity. Their bodies, mid-flight, stilled, their voices silenced in reverence and awe. Their gazes lifted toward the Throne of God, where the glory of the Lord shone brighter than ever before, as though anticipating what was to come. Their very beings resonated with the power of the shockwave as it passed through them, filling them with a sense of urgency, excitement, and something else—completion.

At the created center of the cosmos, fallen angels, twisted and darkened by rebellion, also felt the tremor. Panic spread like wildfire through their ranks, a deep, foreboding sense that something monumental had shifted. They looked around the earth, their eyes narrowing with fear and rage. Somewhere, amidst the shadows of humanity, something had changed, something final. And they knew that time—their time—was slipping away.

Satan, who had momentarily left Ben Rashan to oversee other pieces of his diabolical plan, stopped cold in the midst of his dark work. He felt it—the shift, the change, the undeniable call. His blackened heart twisted in fury and fear as he realized what it meant. Without hesitation, he surged through the spiritual realm, racing back to the body of Rashan, his vessel, to regain control. He would need every ounce of his power now. The end was closer than he had thought.

The shockwave surged through dimensions, traveling faster than light, faster than time itself. Like a symphony building to its crescendo, the ripples harmonized with each other, gaining strength as they approached the very throne room of Heaven. Then, at the apex of it all, as the energy collided with the throne of God, a voice—strong, ancient, and filled with authority—rang out from one of the living creatures who guarded the Throne.

"The number is complete!" the creature proclaimed, its voice like the sound of many waters, powerful and resonant. The declaration swept through heaven with such force that even the stars seemed to brighten in response. The angels, once still, burst into joyous exclamations, as they cried out in praise. The final piece of God's grand plan had fallen into place, and now, everything was set into motion.

The chain reaction did not stop there. The divine energy, now with purpose, began its return journey, flowing back through the corridors of creation, down from heaven, past galaxies and realms unseen, back to the world of men and fallen angels. The energy quickened, like a melody rushing toward its final chord, descending toward the source, the moment, the heartbeat of change.

There, in a dimly lit prison cell, amidst the clatter of metal and the stench of death, the source was found.

Bruce lay lifeless on the cold, hard floor, his body still, blood pooling beneath him where the bullets had ripped through his flesh. The guard had already locked the door, Hartman stood in disbelief, nursing his bruised throat, staring down at the lifeless man lying on the cold floor of the cell. Something far greater than death had just occurred in that small, dark room.

As Bruce's last breath escaped his lungs, and his heart beat for the final time, the man—the real man, the one reborn by the power of God through faith—departed from the body of flesh. He was the last. The final one. The number was now complete.

In that moment, Bruce became more than a body. He became the fulfillment of the divine plan. His act of love and sacrifice—his pure, selfless determination to protect Sarah and Rebecca from evil—was not in vain. It was an act of pure faith and total surrender, a sacrifice that echoed the very heart of the Gospel. And it was enough. It was more than enough.

Bruce's spirit, fully conscious, floated free from the body that lay crumpled on the floor. His vision, once clouded by the limitations of flesh, was now clear, as if he were seeing with the eyes of his soul for the first time. He looked down, seeing both the physical and spiritual worlds with perfect clarity. The scene below him seemed small, distant, as if it belonged to another existence. The cold, sterile cell. The crumpled body. The shock on Hartman's face. It all felt insignificant in the grand scheme of what was happening.

As Bruce looked at his own lifeless form, he wasn't afraid. Instead, he felt more alive than he ever had in his life. He was weightless, filled with a sense of peace that transcended anything he had known before. The chains of fear, pain, and doubt had fallen away, and in their place was joy, love, and pure connection to the divine.

He could feel the presence of God surrounding him, embracing him, welcoming him home. As Bruce lingered in the prison cell behind, he understood. His life, his death, his sacrifice—it had all been part of something far greater than himself.

He was the last one. The final soul to complete the number. The martyrs who had cried out for justice, the saints who had suffered for their faith—all of it was culminating in this moment. The stage was set for what would come next.

Bruce smiled, more alive than ever. He was free, and the world around him—though still gripped by darkness—was now about to be shaken to its core.

"Sixth Seal"

Rebecca lay in her bed, the blanket pulled loosely over her as the soft, rhythmic breaths of James sleeping beside her filled the room. The weight of recent days still hung over her, though it felt less oppressive now. The grief over James and their daughter taking the mark lingered, but it no longer consumed her. Instead, a quiet, inexplicable sense of relief had begun to bloom within her. She had wept for Bruce countless times, but now she found herself oddly at peace. She couldn't explain why, but her heart no longer ached for him.

There were faint shadows from a distant light filtering down the hall through the cracked door. She stared at the ceiling, her mind heavy with thought. Sleep tugged at her, pulling her into a deep stillness, and before long, the edges of her vision blurred, giving way to something extraordinary.

She was no longer in her room but standing in a realm of radiant glory. The throne room of Heaven stretched endlessly before her, vast and resplendent, alive with movement and charged with electric anticipation. Angels rushed in from all creation, their forms glowing with holy light, their voices a symphony of praise.

At the center of it all stood Jesus, the Lamb of God, holding the scroll in His hands. His eyes, luminous with divine love, gleamed with an excitement tempered by solemnity. The scroll, ancient and full of the history of men and angels, both past and future, was gripped with reverence and authority. Around Him, the hosts of Heaven erupted in praise: "Worthy is the Lamb! Glory to the King!" Their voices rose in a crescendo that vibrated through Rebecca.

Rebecca's spirit felt both small and overwhelmed, yet deeply comforted as she fixed her gaze on Jesus. His presence radiated a peace and joy so profound it washed over her, filling her with a sense of belonging and reassurance. She felt her earlier worries for Bruce dissolve entirely, replaced with an unshakable certainty that he was held securely in the arms of the Savior. Why she knew this, she couldn't say, but the peace in her heart was undeniable.

Jesus raised the scroll above His head, His posture that of a victorious King, yet His eyes spoke of a Savior's tender love. The praises grew louder, the worship of the angelic host shaking the throne room until, suddenly, the Lamb lowered the scroll back to His chest. Silence fell, rippling outward across the multitude like waves.

Then, a voice like the sound of a thousand thunders filled the expanse. It was the voice of the Father, raw and overwhelming, vibrating with unimaginable power. "I AM," He declared, shaking the very foundations of Heaven. The cherubim bowed low, their wings covering their faces, and emerald light radiated from the throne, bathing all in a shimmering green hue.

"The time has come," the Father proclaimed, His words both terrifying and glorious. "The great day of the Lord. A time of fear and trembling for all that is evil, but a time of redemption for those who are mine." His voice filled the universe, reaching into the deepest realms of existence.

Rebecca's heart swelled as she watched Jesus step forward, scroll in hand. His excitement was tempered with the weight of His task, but His joy at the redemption of His people could not be hidden. With steady hands, He broke the sixth seal.

A resounding crack reverberated through the heavens, and the scroll unfurled further, revealing the next stage of God's plan. The skies of the earth below grew dark, the sun blackened, and the moon turned blood-red. The stars trembled, mountains crumbled, and the powerful of the earth fled in terror, crying out for the rocks to hide them. Yet in the midst of this upheaval, the people of God stood in peace, knowing their ultimate deliverance had come.

Rebecca felt the weight of this vision settle into her soul. Though the world trembled and chaos reigned, the Jesus was victorious. His authority, His love, and His justice were undeniable. As the angels erupted in worship once more, she felt a deep, unshakable peace within herself, a reassurance that God's plan was perfect.

Rebecca awoke slowly, the warmth of the vision lingering. James stirred beside her but didn't wake, his soft breathing a comforting rhythm in the quiet room. For the first time in what felt like ages, Rebecca felt no fear, no pressing grief. The peace she had experienced in the throne room of Heaven stayed with her, a steady presence that seemed to fill the cracks in her weary heart.

She didn't know what tomorrow would bring, but for now, she rested in the assurance of the God's love, the certainty that His plan was unfolding as it should. With her worries for Bruce laid to rest, she closed her eyes, as sleep gently reclaimed her.

15

GATHERING

"The Quiet Before"

The early morning darkness held the hideout in a comforting embrace. It was about 6 a.m., the world above still, as if time itself had paused. Everyone inside was sound asleep, unaware of what was unfolding on the grand stage of history, unaware that the tides of destiny had converged in this very moment.

Emily was nestled under a heavy blanket, her breathing soft and steady. She had fallen asleep with a smile still faintly lingering on her lips. After what felt like an eternity, she had spent the day in her mother's arms—talking, laughing, feeling the warmth of a bond rekindled. Her heart had been so full that even in her sleep, the happiness seeped into her dreams. There were no nightmares tonight, just the soothing memories of her mother's embrace.

James lay beside Rebecca, curled up against his wife, holding her close. His dreams flickered between the joy of what they had rekindled and the uncertainty of what the future held. Somewhere in the tangled images of his slumber, he saw Emily and Rebecca laughing together, their faces radiant. But he also felt the shadow of fear, the same fear that had haunted them since they escaped—the fear that their fragile peace could be shattered at any moment.

Rebecca, exhausted from the emotional roller coaster of the past few days, slept deeper than she had in weeks. Her body was still, but her mind swirled with half-formed dreams—images of the camp, the cold nights, the desperate prayers for survival. Even in her sleep, she clung to the peace she had felt in her family's arms, afraid that at any moment it would slip away, like water through her fingers. She had forgiven, she had accepted, but the scars still lingered. Even in this fragile calm, fear was in the shadows ready to pounce.

In another room, tucked away in the safety of the basement, Tim and Sarah lay together, lost in their own small world. Newlywed, they had longed for this closeness, this sacred bond that had finally become theirs. Their hands intertwined, their bodies pressed together as if they could shield each other from the darkness that lurked just beyond the walls.

They were safe here, hidden from the evil creeping through the world above, but only for now.

None of them knew that the very fabric of the universe was stirring, that the culmination of history had arrived at this precise moment. A great shift had occurred in the heavens, a shockwave reverberating through all of creation. But here, in the quiet hideout, the only sounds were the soft breaths of those sleeping.

They had no idea that while they rested, while they clung to each other in the small pockets of safety they had formed, the world outside was changing forever. The convergence of prophecy, destiny, and divine intervention had arrived, and soon nothing would ever be the same.

But for now, in this fleeting moment of peace, they slept—unaware that the storm was about to break.

"Every Eye Sees"

Far above in the heavenly realm, in the sacred throne room, Jesus stood in the center of the hosts of heaven, His presence radiating power and light more brilliant than the sun. A deep silence had settled upon the assembly, the weight of eternity pressing in. His eyes, filled with both love and righteous fire, swept across the gathered multitude of heavenly beings. Then, with a voice that resonated through the entire cosmos, He spoke.

"The hour of redemption is at hand," He declared, His voice like the sound of many waters. "Let us gather My elect, the Church, My bride, from the four corners of the earth, for the appointed time has come."

As the words left His lips, the throne room erupted in a chorus of praise, but Jesus, with resolute purpose, turned and descended from His place at the right hand of the Father. The heavenly hosts parted before Him, bowing low as He passed. All of creation seemed to hold its breath as the moment all of history had awaited began to unfold.

With every step, the atmosphere seemed to tremble, and as He left the throne room, He crossed into the realms beyond time and space. In an instant, He descended through the heavenly realms, His radiant form cutting through the fabric of existence.

He arrived above Jerusalem, the city where His blood had been shed for the salvation of mankind. It was the ninth hour of the day—3 p.m., the very hour when He had once cried out, "It is finished," and gave up His spirit on the cross. Now, at the same hour, He returned, not in suffering, but in glory.

His presence filled the sky above the ancient location of the temple, His form brighter than the sun, yet no one was blinded by His brilliance. Instead, every eye on earth was drawn to Him. The sky seemed to bow before Him, clouds swirling toward Him as if forming a pillar beneath His feet, exalted above all creation. Power and authority radiated from Him, stretching out to cover the surface of the earth. Darkness fled before Him, demons screeching as they were forced into hiding, unable to withstand the purity of His light.

Every eye saw Him, just as He had promised centuries before. People ran outside in shock, thousands pointing their phones toward the sky, live streaming the event in disbelief. News organizations quickly set up cameras, broadcasting the image of Jesus standing in the clouds over Jerusalem. The words He had spoken to His disciples were now fulfilled: "Every eye shall see the Son of Man coming in the clouds with power and great glory."

He raised His right hand above His head, and the world seemed to hold its breath. The air grew still as all of creation paused, waiting. Then, Jesus motioned downward from the heavens, a gesture of divine command. In response, the archangel Gabriel descended from the heights, clothed in robes of pure white, shining with the same brilliance as his Lord. Gabriel carried in his hand a golden trumpet, adorned with engravings of divine truth, inscribed long before the creation of heaven and earth.

Jesus, His eyes aflame with holy fire, turned to Gabriel and gave the command. "Sound the call," He said, His voice reverberating through the skies.

Gabriel raised the trumpet to his lips, and from the trumpet came a mighty blast—a sound that echoed through all of creation, a call that reverberated across the heavens and the earth. The blast was so powerful it seemed to shake the very foundations of existence, awakening the sleeping dead and announcing to the living that the time had come.

Jesus spread His arms wide, the authority and glory of His presence filling the entire earth. Gabriel, his mission complete, fell back behind Jesus, his trumpet now silent.

Then, Jesus motioned again, this time calling forth the commander of heaven's armies—Michael, the archangel. Michael appeared in golden armor, reflecting the light of Jesus with a brilliance that dazzled the heavens. His presence was awe-inspiring, his form radiating the strength and authority that only the leader of the angelic hosts could possess.

Jesus looked upon Michael and gave him a single command: "Go, gather My elect."

Without hesitation, Michael raised his hands high above his head. His golden armor shimmered, reflecting the brilliance of Jesus' light like a thousand suns. With a single, powerful motion, he thrust his hands downward and out, his voice ringing out like the clash of swords, echoing through the heavens with a command that shook the very foundations of creation:

"Hosts of heaven! Go forth and gather the elect of the Lord! From the ends of the earth to the highest heavens—bring them to Him who reigns forever! Let none be left behind! Let the redeemed be gathered to the Lamb!"

The thunder of his words reverberated through the skies, and at once, the legions of angels obeyed, descending with unstoppable force, their light streaking across the heavens as they went forth to fulfill the divine command.

Instantly, a column of angels descended from the farthest reaches of the heavens, moving so fast they appeared as a blur of light. The column of radiant beings shot downward, to a point directly above Michael, then fanned out in all directions, spanning the horizon as far as the eye could see. The mission was clear—gather the elect, the chosen of God, from the four corners of the earth.

People across the globe stood frozen in shock and disbelief, their hearts racing as they witnessed the unimaginable. Millions of angels moved across the earth like flashes of lightning, entering homes, cities, and villages. They were gathering the faithful, those who had remained true to the name of Christ, and those whose lives had been redeemed by the blood of the Lamb.

The scene was a symphony of divine order and power. The angels swept down with precision, moving through the nations as prophesied in Scripture: "He will send out His angels with a loud trumpet call, and they will gather His elect from the four winds, from one end of the heavens to the other."

Those who witnessed it could hardly believe their eyes. Many fell to their knees, weeping, some in awe, others in terror, for they knew the time of judgment had come. As the angels gathered the elect, the world trembled, for the great and terrible day of the Lord had arrived.

"Transcended"

Bruce floated above his lifeless body, not ready to leave, bound by some unspoken connection to the earthly shell lying below him on the cold cell floor. His spirit lingered, hovering, until a powerful sound pierced through him—the blast of a trumpet, more than a sound, it was a force that vibrated through his very soul. The energy coursed through him, reigniting his being, pulling him down from the air.

He hit the ground—but there was no pain. Instantly, he jumped up, disoriented for a moment. His gaze darted to where his dead body had been. It was gone. There was nothing. He blinked, stretching his arms out, twisting them slowly. His skin, once marred by wounds and the scars of a harsh life, was now flawless. Perfect. Not a scratch, not a blemish, not even the tattoos remained. A soft glow radiated from him, casting light against the dim cell walls.

"My God," Bruce whispered to himself, his voice trembling with awe. He looked down at his clothes—pure white, seamless, flowing like they were made of light itself.

Turning toward the barred door, he saw Officer Hartman and the guard staring at him, their faces frozen in shock. Their wide eyes reflected the brilliance of the glow emanating from Bruce.

"Did you hear it?" Bruce's voice shook with disbelief. "The sound of a horn?" His mind reeled as he tried to process what had just happened. "I... I was floating above my body, and then I just... fell back into it. Now..." He held his glowing arms out to them. "Look at me."

Hartman swallowed hard, still processing. "I heard it," he murmured, his voice distant, like he wasn't sure of his own words. "Then... there was a light. Blue. It came from your cell, like a flash. We ran here, and then... you."

Suddenly, a brilliant figure appeared beside Bruce, as if stepping through the very fabric of the wall itself. The angel's light matched Bruce's, but with a divine intensity that made the air vibrate. The angel, looking like a man in his thirties, radiated authority. His voice was calm but urgent.

"Christ has returned. You must go meet Him in Jerusalem," the angel commanded, his gaze locking onto Bruce with purpose.

Bruce blinked, confusion swirling through him. Hartman and the guard stood paralyzed, the reality of the situation crushing every rational thought they tried to cling to.

"How?" Bruce stammered, turning back to the angel. "How do I get to Jerusalem?"

The angel's eyes were calm, patient. "Just go."

251

"But how?" Bruce asked, desperation rising in his voice.

"Just go. Now," the angel repeated, his voice firm as he extended his hand. Without hesitation, Bruce took it, and in an instant, they ascended through the ceiling. They flew, up and up, until they hovered above the station, above the city.

Bruce's heart raced, but not from fear—from exhilaration. The sky opened before him, and as he turned his gaze eastward, a radiant light curved across the horizon. The light wasn't just filling the sky—it was illuminating everything below it. Trees, buildings, rivers—they all shimmered with a divine brilliance. It felt as though the entire earth was waking up.

"Follow the light," the angel said. "I have more to gather." He shot down like lightning, darting through the building below.

Bruce hovered in the air, suspended in awe. A woman, led out by the angel, shot past him, heading toward the east, toward the light. Bruce glanced around and noticed, for the first time, dozens of angels—maybe hundreds—darting around, guiding others, each person glowing like Bruce, filled with the same unearthly light.

It all felt so natural, so effortless. With a rush of excitement and purpose, Bruce launched himself eastward, soaring higher and higher. The sensation was overwhelming—pure freedom. He was no longer bound by fear or pain or confusion.

He was alive—more alive than he had ever been.

As he flew toward the source of the light, all his worries melted away, his mind and spirit wholly focused on the radiant glory that awaited him in Jerusalem.

"Awakened"

As Bruce ascended higher into the sky, the brilliance of the light that radiated from the East intensified, engulfing everything in its path. Below him, the cities and towns were stirring, their streets now filled with people glowing like him—people who had been resurrected. Everywhere he looked, the once lifeless were now alive, radiant, proclaiming a message that thundered in every heart and mind: Jesus has returned.

The air buzzed with energy, and Bruce felt it—like a symphony playing across the heavens, resonating through every corner of creation. Below him, on the ground, the once broken world was in upheaval.

People were rushing out of their homes, gathering in the streets, staring in awe at the glowing figures walking among them.

On social media, the frenzy had erupted almost instantly. Phones, tablets, cameras—everything was being pointed toward the sky and the newly resurrected people. Live streams and videos flooded the platforms. The hashtags began trending at breakneck speed: #JesusReturned, #SecondComing, #RaptureNow. Every social media platform became a witness to the unfolding event. Just as every eye was seeing Jesus in the clouds, they were seeing those transformed to be eternal, like Him.

News organizations scrambled to make sense of it all, some broadcasting live from the streets where people were pointing upward, their faces pale with awe. Reporters, at a loss for words, simply held their microphones as the glowing figures walked past, proclaiming the good news.

"Jesus has returned," one resurrected man shouted as he walked through a crowded square, his voice filled with a joy that resonated through every person around him. "The King of Kings has come!"

Camera crews zoomed in on the radiant figures, unable to look away. From the busy streets of New York to the markets of Tokyo, from the deserts of the Middle East to the plains of Africa, people were gathering, witnessing the same phenomenon.

The whole world was watching.

Television screens in homes, malls, and airports displayed the same scenes: glowing figures walking through the streets, proclaiming the return of Jesus with fervent joy. "It's real!" one news anchor stammered on a major network, his normally composed demeanor cracking under the weight of the moment. "The whole world is witnessing what was foretold."

Phones rang and buzzed. Text messages flew between friends and families, many asking the same thing: Are you seeing this?

Some watched in fear, others in disbelief, and many in pure, unbridled joy. Crowds gathered outside to witness the unfolding event firsthand. In some places, people fell to their knees, overwhelmed by the sight of the glowing figures walking among them.

Bruce continued to soar, the light pulling him toward Jerusalem. The cities below were aglow with people filling the streets. Some called out in joy, while others wept, their hands lifted toward the sky. The world was no longer just watching. It was changing before their eyes.

As he flew, Bruce could hear the echoes of proclamation from those who had been raised.

"The Lamb has returned."

"The King is here!"

"The time has come for all things to be made new."

"Every eye will see Him," a resurrected woman declared as she stood in front of a news camera, glowing with a light not of this world. "The Son of Man comes in the clouds with power and glory!"

The reporters stood frozen, unable to even ask questions, as the entire planet bore witness to the fulfillment of ancient prophecy.

The whole world watched as heaven and earth collided, and Bruce—along with the countless others—rushed toward the King.

"Left Behind"

Across the globe, the air was thick with awe and confusion. The dead had risen—those who had been in Christ, resurrected, filling the cities and streets with their glowing presence. The news broadcasts were flooded with images of them, the resurrected, walking among the living. But something wasn't right.

Christians who were still alive began to panic. They had been waiting for this moment—the return of their Savior—but why hadn't they been changed? How could it be that those who had already passed on were transformed, yet they themselves remained as they were, untouched by the transformation they had long anticipated?

In homes, churches, and streets, confusion spread like wildfire. Hands raised to the heavens, pleading for answers. Questions filled the air, desperate cries mingled with the undeniable glory of the resurrected walking among them.

"I don't understand!" one man shouted, his voice trembling. "Why haven't we changed? What's happening?"

Another, a woman clutching her Bible to her chest, whispered, "Did we miss it? Are we being left behind?"

The fear was overpowering, rippling through the hearts of those who had been waiting, trusting, believing. Had something gone wrong? Had they failed somehow?

In the midst of this confusion, all eyes turned to the heavens once more. Above Jesus, who stood in the clouds all His radiant glory, Gabriel appeared, rising above him once again. His face, focused, glowed with heavenly light as he hovered above the Son of Man.

In one swift motion, Gabriel brought the golden trumpet to his lips once again.

The world seemed to hold its breath as this was broadcast and streamed for the world to see.

And then, the trumpet sounded.

A blast so mighty, so powerful, it reverberated through every corner of creation. The earth quaked, and the heavens trembled as the second trumpet blast filled the air. It was louder, stronger, and it pierced through every heart, every soul. The sound spread like a wave, washing over the living, sending a jolt of divine energy through their very beings.

Across the world, Christians who were alive began to feel the change. Their bodies, once burdened by mortality, were now being transformed in an instant. It was as if a light had ignited from within them, spreading to every cell, every fiber of their being.

One by one, those who were alive and remained were changed, just as they had hoped for, just as the Scriptures had promised. Their skin began to glow, their hearts pounding with the overwhelming sense of divine power coursing through them.

In the midst of a live broadcast, a news anchor had been speaking to her viewers, trying to keep them calm. She was reporting on the bizarre phenomenon of the resurrected walking among them when, suddenly, she felt it—the transformation.

Her breath strengthened as her body began to glow with radiant light. The camera zoomed in as she raised her hands, now glowing with the same brilliance as the resurrected had moments before.

"Oh my God..." she whispered, her eyes wide with realization. "It's happening."

She glanced around the newsroom, seeing some of her colleagues beginning to change as well. Her voice caught in her throat as she remembered the very Scripture she had been taught as a child, now unfolding before her eyes.

With tears streaming down her face, she looked into the camera, her voice trembling but full of awe. "The dead in Christ will rise first," she whispered, quoting 1 Thessalonians 4:16, "and then... then we who are alive and remain will be changed... will be caught up together with them in the clouds..."

Her voice broke as she gazed down at her glowing hands. "This is it... this is the promise."

An angel appeared beside her on camera, urging her to head to Jerusalem. She responded by flying up and off screen.

The world watched in stunned silence as millions across the globe were transformed before their very eyes. Social media exploded with images of people changing, their bodies glowing with the same light that had filled the resurrected moments earlier. The once confused and fearful Christians were now radiant, their joy unspeakable.

In the midst of the chaos, one figure stood still, glowing with the same light. Her phone, clutched tightly in her hand, trembled slightly, but her face—radiant and full of peace—held the camera steady. She was a Christian video blogger, a social influencer, someone who had always shared her faith online, but nothing could have prepared her for this moment.

Her hands moved almost instinctively, pulling up her live stream, and within seconds, she was broadcasting to her thousands of followers. The screen blinked, and her face filled the frame, glowing brighter than the light behind her.

"Hey, everyone," she began, her voice filled with awe. "I don't know if you're seeing this yet, but if you're watching, if you're out there..."

Her voice cracked with emotion, but she quickly gathered herself. "I don't even know how to explain it. I just... I need you to see. I need you to believe. This is real. This is what we've been waiting for."

She turned the camera briefly, showing the glowing figures walking through the streets behind her, proclaiming the return of Jesus. Then, she brought it back to herself, her face illuminated, her breath catching as tears began to well in her eyes.

"In the blink of an eye," she whispered, her voice trembling. "Just like Scripture said. We've been changed. All of us. I... I don't even know how to describe it. My body, my soul—I feel it. We've been transformed."

She paused, the weight of her words sinking in, as more viewers began to flood her stream. The comments section exploded, but she didn't read them. She couldn't. She was too caught up in the moment.

"I know it sounds impossible, but I feel like... like I was just standing here, and then all of a sudden, I felt this blast of light, then I heard a trumpet... and I was changed." She lifted her hand to the camera, showing her flawless skin, glowing with the same light that had enveloped her. "I was changed in a twinkling of an eye. Just like the Bible said."

Her voice grew stronger, more passionate. "This is it. Jesus has come back. I know some of you didn't believe, but you can't deny this anymore! Every eye is seeing Him. It's not just some fairytale. It's happening right now!"

She wiped a tear from her cheek, her smile growing even as her voice cracked with emotion. "I know some of you are scared. I know this is overwhelming. But this—this is the best day ever! He's here. He's gathering His church. The King has come, and nothing will ever be the same."

Behind her, the sky glowed brighter, the light continuing to spread across the earth, and her followers watched as history unfolded.

"This is what I've been telling you about," she continued, her voice steadying, her eyes glowing with hope. "Jesus is real. He's here. And if you're seeing this—if you're feeling it in your heart—don't wait. Don't hesitate. He's calling you. This is your moment."

She paused, her voice softening as the emotion welled up inside her again. "You don't have to be afraid. He's not here to condemn you. He's here to save you. Just believe. Just trust Him. He's everything we've ever needed."

She looked directly into the camera, her heart spilling over with love and urgency. "The world is watching. The whole world is seeing. But you—right now, if you're hearing this, you can be part of it. He's calling His church, His bride. Come to Him. He's waiting for you. Don't miss this."

As she spoke, her viewership continued to climb, the comments pouring in from all over the world, but her focus remained on the message. This was it. This was the moment she had always known would come, but never imagined it would be this real.

"He's here," she whispered, her final words before ending the stream. "He's here."

James began to toss and turn in his sleep, his dreams filled with an uneasy sense of dread. Dark shapes loomed in the recesses of his mind, fear crawling through his subconscious. Then, in the midst of his turmoil, a sharp sound cut through the fog—a trumpet blast. His eyes flew open, and he rolled onto his back, staring into the shadows of the room. A faint light filtered in from a single lamp left on in the living area, casting long, faint shadows against the walls.

Beside him, Rebecca stirred, her brow furrowing as she tugged the blanket up tightly around her neck, seeking comfort in its warmth. James lay still, his heart racing, his mind spinning with thoughts of their future. Could they survive this? What would happen to them, to Emily? Time slipped away in the stillness, but his thoughts wouldn't rest.

Time passed, then, there it was again—a sound, distant yet unmistakable. A trumpet, or perhaps a horn, its tone clear and ringing through the silence of the night. James froze, his breath catching in his throat as his pulse quickened. The air felt heavy, as if the world itself was holding its breath.

Suddenly, the room filled with light—bright and blinding his eyes that were adjusted to the dark. James turned, blinking in confusion.

"Rebecca?" he whispered.

But before he could ask, Rebecca bolted upright, her eyes wide with shock. The light... it was coming from her. Her body glowed with an ethereal brightness, casting a soft, radiant glow that illuminated the entire room.

"What's happening?" Rebecca gasped, her voice trembling as she pushed the blankets away, turning her hands, her hands glowing.

Just then, footsteps echoed down the hall, and Sarah burst into the room, with Pastor Daniels close behind her. They, too, were glowing, their bodies radiating the same brilliance that enveloped Rebecca.

James sat frozen in place, his eyes wide as he watched them. "What is this?" he stammered, his voice barely a whisper.

Pastor Daniels, though glowing with an otherworldly light, carried an air of calm authority. "It's happening, James. The trumpet... it's the call. The dead will rise, and then the living will be transformed. This is the moment we've all been waiting for."

Tears welled up in Rebecca's eyes as she looked down at her glowing hands, her heart swelling with both overwhelming joy and dawning confusion. She turned to James, her face filled with a mixture of disbelief and sorrow. "James, I... you haven't changed," she whispered, her voice trembling with heartbreak. Her hand reached for his, her touch light but full of meaning. "I had hoped, I had pleaded... oh my..." Her voice broke, the weight of reality crushing her last thread of hope.

James looked down at himself. His skin was still the same—unchanged, untouched by the brilliant transformation that had overtaken Rebecca, Sarah, and Pastor Daniels. A lump formed in his throat, his heart sinking as the realization hit him. He wasn't like them. He wasn't glowing.

"It is my own fault," James murmured, his voice thick with pain. "I knew it was wrong. I'm sorry."

Rebecca turned to him, her hands reaching for his, but before she could speak, a brilliant figure appeared in the room—an angel, glowing brighter than them all. He stood with an air of urgency, his presence commanding yet gentle.

"Rebecca, Sarah, Tim," the angel said, his voice calm but firm. "You must leave. The hour has come, and Christ is waiting for you in Jerusalem. You are called to gather with the elect."

Rebecca's eyes widened, her grip tightening on James' hands. "I can't leave him," she cried, shaking her head. "I can't leave James and Emily. Please, I can't do this without them."

The angel's expression softened, but his resolve remained unshaken. "You must go. The time has come. He is waiting."

James, though his heart was breaking, knew what had to be done. He looked into Rebecca's eyes, his voice steady despite the pain. "You have to go, Rebecca," he said, his words heavy. "I will take care of Emily... you have to go. We will be okay. I will take care of her for you, I promise."

Rebecca shook her head, tears streaming down her face. "I can't leave you and Emily!" she sobbed, clinging to him. "I can't lose you both."

Suddenly, the air shifted, and a familiar presence filled the room. Bruce appeared, he had flown back, flying in from above, his body radiating with the same brilliance as the others. His face was filled with joy, his spirit renewed.

"Bruce!" Sarah cried, running toward him and embracing him in a hug. Bruce grinned and held her tightly, whispering his thanks for all she had done, for helping him to believe.

But Bruce's eyes quickly shifted to Rebecca, who was still arguing with the angel, pleading not to leave James. He stepped forward, his face filled with compassion.

"Rebecca, you have to trust. You have to go," Bruce said softly, his voice calm but insistent.

Before anyone else could speak, Emily walked into the room, her steps slow. James looked up, his heart rose to his throat as he saw her.

"Awe, Emily..." he whispered, his voice thick with emotion.

All eyes turned to Emily. She was glowing. The light radiated from her, just like the others. Rebecca stared in shock, her hands trembling as she reached out to touch her daughter.

"But... but you signed for the mark," Pastor Daniels stammered, his voice filled with confusion. "You signed the agreement."

The angel stepped forward, his voice filled with authority. "She did not agree in her heart. She did not sign her name. She was spared."

The angel then turned to James, his gaze piercing. "He did."

James' eyes filled with tears, and without hesitation, he pulled Emily and Rebecca into a tight embrace. He held them close, his body trembling with the weight of his guilt and love. "I'm so sorry," he whispered, his voice cracking. "I'm so, so sorry."

Rebecca and Emily clung to him, tears streaming down their faces. It was a moment of forgiveness, a moment of healing, but it was also a moment of goodbye.

"You have to go," James whispered, his voice barely audible. "Go, all of you. You have to go."

Rebecca kissed his cheek, her tears soaking into his skin. "I love you," she whispered.

"We love you," Emily added, her voice filled with sorrow and peace.

With heavy hearts, they pulled away from James, and one by one, they began to ascend, their glowing forms lighting up the room. The angel watched them go, and soon, they were gone—leaving James alone in the darkness.

The lights of his life were gone.

"Last Lights"

James lay in bed, struggling to process what had just happened. Suddenly, James was startled by a crash from the living area. The noise cut through the eerie silence, snapping him out of his fog. His heart pounded as a flickering light seeped into the bedroom. What now? Still groggy and emotionally drained, he swung his legs off the bed, trying to shake the exhaustion clinging to his every muscle. As he stepped into the dim hallway, he was suddenly blinded by a sharp, glaring light.

"Freeze! Raise your hands above your head!" a voice barked. James froze in place, instinctively raising his hands. The brightness burned into his retinas, making it impossible to see, but the voice was unmistakable. It was Officer Hartman.

James let out a long, weary breath. He had no fight left in him, no strength to resist. His world had already crumbled. What could Hartman do that hadn't already been done? Without a word, he stepped toward the kitchen table, each step heavy with the weight of everything he had lost. He slumped into a chair, his hands falling heavily onto the table. His spirit was crushed, his will hollowed out.

Hartman, realizing James posed no threat, clicked off his flashlight, leaving only the soft amber glow of the dim table lamp to wash over them both. The silence stretched as Hartman moved slowly, deliberately, taking a seat across from James. For a long moment, neither spoke.

Hartman was the first to break the stillness, his voice more measured than usual. "Where are Rebecca and Sarah?" he asked, his tone laced with something unfamiliar—concern.

James stared down at his hands, barely recognizing the man they belonged to. He felt so distant from himself, like a mere shell. "They're gone," James muttered, his voice raspy. "They... they were taken. They just flew away." He glanced up at Hartman, expecting disbelief, but Hartman simply nodded, as if he knew.

"They were glowing. It was surreal," James continued, his voice breaking. "I watched them... I watched them leave, and I stayed behind. I was left behind."

Hartman's gaze softened, his rigid exterior faltering. "Bruce... he's gone too, James. I saw him go." His words hung heavy in the air, and for the first time, there was no authority in his tone, only a strange sort of sadness.

James blinked, his exhaustion turning into disbelief. "Wait... what? What do you mean, Bruce was here? You saw him too, when?"

Hartman swallowed, his throat tight. "It's hard to explain. One moment, he was dead, shot by one of my men... and the next, he... he wasn't. He was back, alive—different. Glowing, just like you said Rebecca and Sarah were. He said something about hearing a trumpet, and then... he flew. Right through the walls. It was... it was insane." His voice trailed off, as if he couldn't believe his own words, but the truth was undeniable.

James felt his pulse quicken. So that's what had happened to Bruce. "I wondered," he muttered under his breath. "I saw him, Hartman. He came back. He could not help me, he left just like the others. They left me behind." His voice trembled with a mix of awe and sorrow.

The two men sat there in silence, both trying to wrap their minds around the impossible. For Hartman, it was a collision of everything he had known and everything he had refused to believe. For James, it was the harsh reality of being left behind, of watching everyone he loved ascend into something beyond his reach.

Hartman leaned forward, his elbows resting on the table. "I'm not taking you in," he said quietly. "I didn't tell anyone about this place." There was a pause, and James caught a glimpse of something human in Hartman's eyes—compassion, maybe even regret.

James's body trembled, the weight of it all finally crashing down on him. His head sank into his hands as sobs racked his chest. "I can't do it," he choked out, tears spilling freely. "I can't go on. They're gone. My wife, my daughter... they're gone." His voice broke again, deeper this time. "I was supposed to protect them... I failed. I don't even know why I'm still here."

Hartman's expression shifted, the stoic officer giving way to the man beneath the uniform. He had been trained to handle violence, resistance, and defiance, but this... this kind of brokenness, he didn't know how to respond. He reached across the table, hesitating before placing his hand on James's arm. "You're still here because... there's a reason, James. I don't know what it is, but there has to be a reason."

James looked up, his tear-streaked face filled with disbelief. "A reason? What reason could there be?" He shook his head, his voice thick with anguish. "Why would God let me stay behind while they were taken? Why?"

Hartman had no answers, no comforting words that could fix the wreckage James was trapped in. But he stayed there, in the silence, his hand still resting on James's arm as the weight of the world pressed down on them both.

"Order in the Skies"

The cabin hummed with the low murmur of passengers as the jetliner cruised through the clear, blue sky. Somewhere over the Atlantic, the mundane flight turned extraordinary in a heartbeat. It began with a glow—a gentle, golden light that seemed to come from nowhere, filling the cabin and casting a soft brilliance over the seats and walls.

A young man seated by the window, wearing a hoodie and jeans, felt the warmth of the light first. His hands began to glow as if some hidden fire had ignited within him. Startled, he looked down to see his clothes shimmering, transforming into a radiant white robe. A gasp escaped him at what he saw.

"Jesus... He's come," he whispered in awe.

A woman across the aisle gasped, her hands trembling as her body, too, began to radiate. She clutched her heart, tears spilling down her cheeks as she realized what was happening. "It's Him. The Lord has returned," she cried out, her voice breaking with emotion.

Whispers spread through the cabin, turning quickly to shouts. "Jesus has come!" someone yelled from the back. Panic and confusion rippled through the rows as some passengers began to glow, their clothes transforming into pure white garments. Faces that were once filled with fear and tension softened into expressions of peace and joy. But not everyone understood.

"What's happening?" a man in business attire stammered, pulling at his tie as if it were choking him.

Nearby, a mother clung to her child, both of them enveloped in the same holy light. The child smiled, eyes wide, while the mother wept tears of joy. "He's come for us!" she exclaimed, holding her glowing son tightly.

The young man by the window, his body no longer bound by the laws of nature, felt a pull deep within his chest. Slowly, as if he were lighter than air, he rose from his seat. His feet left the floor, and the passengers around him stared in disbelief as he floated upward.

"I'm not bound by gravity!" he exclaimed, his voice filled with wonder.

Gasps filled the cabin as others realized what was happening. One woman crossed herself and whispered a prayer as the young man moved effortlessly through the cabin, his body glowing brighter by the second. He drifted toward the window, and in a moment that defied explanation, he passed through the solid wall of the plane as though it were nothing more than a shadow.

Outside the plane, he was surrounded by the brilliance of the sky, with the world below reduced to a miniature landscape. He soared alongside the jet, the wind rushing past him, and he laughed—a sound of pure joy.

In the cockpit, the pilot and co-pilot were still adjusting to their own transformations. Both men had felt the shift, their uniforms replaced with radiant white suits. They sat in stunned silence for a moment, glowing with the same light as many of the passengers.

The cockpit door swung open, and the flight attendant rushed in, her face pale but her eyes wide with shock. "Captain," she began, her voice trembling, "the passengers... some of them are glowing, and one of them—he's outside the plane!"

The co-pilot leaned toward the window, squinting against the brightness outside. Sure enough, there was the young man, floating effortlessly alongside the aircraft. "It's true," he whispered, glancing at the pilot.

The pilot rubbed his temples, still reeling from the overwhelming events. He stared out the window, then shifted his gaze to the horizon.

A light—a brilliant, all-encompassing light—wrapped itself around the far reaches of the earth, drawing him in. It was unmistakable. "That's it," he said quietly. "We need to go."

The co-pilot nodded, both men feeling the pull toward the light in the east. "Autopilot's on," the pilot said, standing up from his seat. "We can make it."

The flight attendant blinked in disbelief. "Wait, what? You're leaving? We're still mid-flight!" Her voice cracked as she watched the two glowing men move toward the cabin door. "You can't leave! We're thousands of feet in the air!"

Ignoring her, the pilot and co-pilot walked through the plane, both glowing with heavenly light. They paused for a brief moment, their faces peaceful, and then, with a single leap, they too passed through the fuselage, leaving the plane behind.

The flight attendant screamed, rushing back to the cockpit in a panic. She stumbled into the controls, her heart racing as she realized the two men in charge of the flight were gone.

Outside, the pilot and co-pilot soared through the air, drawn toward the bright light on the horizon. But before they could move any farther, a figure descended from the heavens, shimmering with divine power. It was an angel, and his presence stopped them in their tracks.

"Stop!" the angel's voice thundered, powerful and commanding. His arms spread wide, blocking their path. "The God of all creation is not a God of chaos. You must return to the plane. You have a responsibility to land it safely. If you leave them, their blood will be on your hands."

Both men hesitated, glancing at each other. "But… the light," the co-pilot stammered.

The angel's eyes narrowed. "The light will be there. Your mission is not yet finished. Go back. Land the plane. Then you will be free to join the others."

Their shoulders sagged under the weight of the angel's words. They knew he was right. Without another word, the pilot and co-pilot turned back toward the distant jetliner, flying alongside it and re-entering the cockpit just as effortlessly as they had left.

Inside, the flight attendant nearly fainted when they appeared again. "I—what…? You left! I thought—"

The pilot, his voice now calm and resolute, slid into his seat. "We're landing this plane," he said, reaching for the radio. "Tower, this is flight 738. We're declaring an emergency landing request."

The radio crackled with static, and a voice replied, "You're not the first to request an emergency landing. Stand by for instructions. You'll be queued with the others. Hold your course and prepare for descent."

The cockpit was filled with the sound of overlapping radio calls, all from different aircraft requesting emergency landings. The magnitude of what was happening began to sink in, but the pilot kept his focus. He glanced at the co-pilot, who nodded.

"Let's get these people down safely," the pilot said as they prepared for their descent.

In the cabin, passengers watched through the windows, still in awe of the scene outside. The young man who had floated out was now flying alongside an angel, their conversation a mystery, but the peace that radiated from them was undeniable.

As the plane began its slow, careful descent, the glowing passengers held onto their faith, knowing that the God who called them was a God of order, love, and divine purpose.

"The Dance of Redemption"

Sally lay in bed, the same bed that had held her captive for more years than she cared to count. Paralyzed from the waist down, she felt the weight of her confinement pressing down harder than ever. The ringing in her ears—the constant, oppressive noise that dulled her hearing—was especially loud today, an almost unbearable reminder of her frailty. She closed her eyes and took a trembling breath, willing herself to find comfort in the sound of Tyler's sweet voice drifting in from the next room, even though she could barely make out his words. Her heart ached for the simple closeness she longed for but couldn't reach.

Suddenly, through the ringing, a new sound broke through. A distant trumpet blast, unlike anything she had ever heard, sharp and triumphant, cut through the noise in her head. Sally's eyes flew open in surprise, and for a brief, breathless moment, the ringing stopped completely.

Then, in a heartbeat, it was gone. Completely gone.

For the first time in years, silence filled her ears. Real silence. But it didn't last long. As her senses sharpened, Sally heard the soft ticking of the clock on table next to her bed—something she hadn't been able to hear for years. She could even hear the gentle rustle of the curtains swaying in the breeze. It was as if the world had suddenly come alive around her, every sound a miracle.

Then came the light.

A gentle glow filled her bedroom, not the harsh light of day, but something warmer, more profound. She sat up, her body feeling lighter than it had in years, and watched as the light grew brighter. It wasn't coming from the windows—it was coming from within the house, as if the very air was aglow with something divine.

"Sally..." The voice was soft, gentle, but clear. It was Tyler. But this time, his voice was perfectly clear, each word pristine as if it were part of a symphony. Her heart quickened, her breath catching in her throat.

Tyler stepped into her room, but he wasn't the same boy she had tucked into bed night after night, helping him with his words, struggling to understand him through his speech delays. Now, he stood in the doorway, bathed in that same warm light, a radiant figure glowing with glory. His face was serene, and for the first time, his features were not marred by effort. He spoke effortlessly, his voice ringing like music.

"Mom," he said softly, smiling as he entered. "You're glowing."

Sally's breath caught as she looked down at herself. Her frail body, once weakened by years of disability and pain, was now radiating with the same light as her son. Her hands, which had always trembled with weakness, were steady, shining with strength. And her legs—her legs!— she could feel them again. The ache, the fatigue, all of it had vanished.

Tyler, who had helped her for so many years, instinctively moved toward her bed as he always had, preparing to gently assist her into her wheelchair.

"Here, Mom, let me help you," he said, holding out his glowing hand. His voice, strong and steady, was no longer hindered by the struggle to form words. It flowed freely, easily, and Sally's heart swelled at the sound of it.

For years, Tyler had been her strength, lifting her into her wheelchair, guiding her through the simple acts of life. She smiled, her eyes filling with tears, but these were not the tears of exhaustion or frustration she had known for so long. These were tears of joy, of release, of freedom.

Sally shook her head gently and winked at her son. "No, sweetheart," she said, her voice warm and clear, free from the weight of pain. "Not today."

And with that, she did something she hadn't been able to do in years. She jumped to her feet—quickly, effortlessly—and stood before Tyler, beaming with joy. The weight that had held her down for so long was gone. She wasn't just standing; she was alive, fully alive, and her entire being pulsed with new strength.

Tyler's eyes widened in astonishment. He stared at his mother, speechless for the first time in this new life, his lips trembling in awe.

"Dance with me," Sally said, laughing through her tears as she reached out and pulled him into her arms.

Tyler, no longer the hesitant boy who struggled to form words, smiled wide and bright. The mother and son embraced in the middle of the room, twirling gently at first, but soon spinning faster, their feet moving lightly across the floor as they laughed with pure, unfiltered joy.

The room was filled with light, and as they danced, it seemed as though they were floating, free from the bounds of the world they had once known. Tyler held his mother close, and Sally, with tears streaming down her cheeks, marveled at the feeling of his strong arms around her. For so long, he had been her support, guiding her when she couldn't guide herself. Now, they were equals—no, more than equals. They were glorified.

"Where did you get that beautiful gown?" Tyler asked, his voice full of childlike wonder as they danced. He gazed at her white robe, radiant and pure.

Sally smiled, looking down at herself, at the gown that seemed to shimmer with the very presence of heaven. "I don't know," she said, her voice filled with awe. "But it's a gift. A gift from Him."

The light in the room intensified, and as they twirled, an angel appeared beside them, hovering just above the ground. He was radiant, and his presence filled the room with even more warmth and peace.

"Sally," the angel said, his voice gentle yet firm. "It is time. Come, both of you. The Lord is waiting for you in the clouds."

Sally paused, her heart swelling with the realization of what was happening. She looked at Tyler, his eyes glowing with the same divine light, and her heart brimmed with gratitude.

But before she took the angel's hand, she turned to him with a smile. "Can we walk down the street together first? Just for a moment?" she asked, her voice soft. "We have never walked side by side."

The angel nodded, understanding in his eyes. "Yes, you may. Take your time, and then you will join the others."

Sally grinned through her tears and took Tyler's hand. Together, they stepped out of the house, out into a world that was no longer broken or marred by pain. The air itself seemed to hum with life, and as they walked down the street, hand in hand, mother and son, they knew that this was the beginning of something far more beautiful than they had ever imagined.

They would go together to meet their Savior, but for now, they savored this moment—this moment of pure joy and freedom—as the light of heaven wrapped around them like an embrace.

16

THE FINAL CALL

"Ascend"

The sky above Jerusalem was filled with light, radiating from Jesus, standing majestically on a pillar of clouds. His brilliance illuminated the horizon as far as the eye could see, and all around Him, the elect gathered. They hovered in the air, their bodies transformed, glowing with the same ethereal light as their Savior. Faces were turned toward Him, eyes wide with awe and excitement, their anticipation gripping. This was the moment they had longed for—their King, their Redeemer, standing before them.

As far as the eye could see, the sky was filled with the redeemed, stretching from horizon to horizon. They floated in a breathtaking array, suspended in the air, their hearts pounding with the joy and wonder of what they were witnessing. Jesus, their King, their Savior, stood at the center of it all. His robe shimmered with a brilliance more dazzling than the sun, His eyes burning with a love that felt like it could encompass the whole universe.

For a moment, the world seemed to pause, the hum of the wind stilled, and even time itself seemed to hold its breath in reverence. Then, Jesus raised His hand, His eyes sweeping over His gathered people. The air thickened with a holy silence as every soul fixed their gaze on Him.

In that stillness, Jesus spoke.

"Come, follow Me," He said, His voice like the sound of many waters, reverberating through every heart. It was more than words; it was a command laced with love, and it filled the sky. Every ear heard Him, from the highest heaven to the farthest corner of the earth. "I have prepared a place for you."

He smiled, and the joy in that smile was enough to set every heart on fire. Then, with one powerful motion, Jesus pointed upwards, toward the open sky.

In an instant, He shot upward like a blazing star, rocketing into the heavens.

The elect followed, their spirits soaring as angels guided them from behind, ensuring none were left behind. They ascended in a magnificent column, rising higher and higher, their bodies carried not by wings but by the sheer force of divine will—the very power of God propelling them through the atmosphere.

The angelic armies followed close behind, with Michael closing their ranks, leaving Gabriel alone in the air over Jerusalem. The world watched as Gabriel lifted his golden trumpet to his lips one final time. The sound that followed shook both the heavens and the earth, a long, resounding blast that marked the end of one era and the beginning of another. The earth trembled beneath its power, and the sound echoed through every corner of creation.

As the last note of the trumpet faded, Gabriel launched himself upward, following the procession of saints into the sky. His light trailed behind him like a comet, streaking toward the heavens.

Those who had risen were not just traveling upward; they were traveling home. Higher and higher they soared, past the stars and into realms beyond mortal comprehension. The firmament opened before them, revealing the very throne room of God. The brilliance of heaven spilled over them like a waterfall of light, bathing them in glory.

There at the very center of it all, stood the throne of God, radiating a glory beyond imagination, surrounded by the living creatures, the elders, and an innumerable host of angels. As Jesus approached, the entire heavenly assembly erupted in a chorus of praise, their voices rising like a mighty roar, shaking the foundations of eternity itself.

The elect now stood in the throne room of Heaven, extending as far as the eye could see.

The uncountable multitude stood before the throne, their white robes gleaming like the purest light, with palm branches waving in their hands. The entire throne room radiated with the glory of God, the brilliance of His presence illuminating the vast assembly that stretched farther than the eye could see. The very air seemed to vibrate with the holiness of the moment.

Angels lined the expanse of heaven, their voices joining in unison with the multitude, singing praises that filled the atmosphere like a mighty symphony. Every sound was a note of perfection, blending into a magnificent harmony that reverberated through every corner of creation. The living creatures surrounding the throne cried out, "Holy, holy, holy is the Lord God Almighty, who was, and is, and is to come!" Their voices, like thunder, rippled through the air as the twenty-four elders fell on their faces before the throne, casting their crowns at the feet of the One who sat upon it.

Their voices rose in a unified declaration: "Salvation belongs to our God who sits on the throne, and to the Lamb!"

At the center of it all stood Jesus, resplendent in His glory. His presence commanded the reverence of the angels, the elders, and the living creatures. He approached the throne with grace and majesty, and as He did, a holy silence fell over the assembly. All eyes were on Him, the Lamb who had triumphed, the One who had purchased this multitude with His blood.

The elect, now clothed in white, stood in awe of their Savior. Many wept with joy, their tears sparkling like diamonds in the radiant light of Heaven. The overwhelming peace and love in the throne room engulfed them, erasing every memory of pain, fear, and death from their earthly lives.

They stood in the presence of the Almighty, where no darkness could dwell, where time held no meaning, and where the fullness of joy reigned forever. Heaven itself had come alive, and every soul knew, deep within their spirit, that they were finally home. This was the culmination of every promise, every hope, and every prophecy. They were in the presence of the King of kings, the Lord of lords.

As they gazed at the One seated on the throne, a wave of worship swept over the multitude, spontaneous and pure. Hands were lifted, and voices rang out in praise to the Lamb, for His great victory over sin and death. The throne room echoed with their adoration, filling eternity with the sound of worship that would never cease.

This was their moment—the moment for which they had longed, the moment for which all of creation had groaned. They were home, at the feet of their King, in the unshakable kingdom of God.

"And Heaven Rejoiced."

The air was electric with excitement, and Sarah could barely contain herself as she stood, her hand gripping Tim's tightly. Around them, as far as the eye could see, the elect were gathered before the thrones— glowing figures of all ages, races, and nations, their faces alight with awe. Angels moved gracefully among them, guiding, comforting, and ensuring that not a single soul was left behind. Before them, Jesus Himself stood in all His radiant glory, the very sight of Him filling their hearts with indescribable joy.

Sarah turned her head, her eyes wide with tears of happiness, and found Rebecca and Emily just behind them. The look of pure wonder on Emily's face made Sarah's heart swell even more. This was the moment they had longed for, prayed for, and now it was unfolding before their very eyes.

"Can you believe this?" Sarah whispered, her voice trembling with emotion. "We're here... we're really here with Him."

Tim nodded, his grip tightening on her hand. "I never thought it would feel like this. It's... it's more than real." His voice cracked as he spoke, his usual calm demeanor breaking under the weight of such overwhelming beauty.

Rebecca was quiet, her eyes locked on Jesus, as if afraid to blink and miss a single moment of His presence. Emily clutched her mother's hand, her voice small but filled with wonder. "Mom... it's really Him, isn't it? It's really Jesus."

Rebecca's voice was soft, choked with tears, as she nodded. "Yes, baby. It's really Him."

The crowd of the elect, now countless in number, swelled around them, a sea of believers, their voices lifting together in anticipation. Then, in a single, glorious moment, Jesus spoke. His voice echoed through the air, clear and majestic, resonating in every heart: "Well done, good and faithful servants."

The words sent a ripple of joy through the multitude, and suddenly, a great shout rose up from the crowd—praises and adoration that poured out from the very depths of their souls.

"Worthy is the Lamb! Holy, holy, holy is the Lord!"

Tim turned to Sarah, his face wet with tears, and without hesitation, they too joined the chorus. "Worthy is the Lamb!" Sarah shouted, her voice lifting with the others, her entire being filled with worship. Tim's deep voice echoed hers, and beside them, Rebecca and Emily's voices intertwined, crying out praises with tears streaming down their faces.

The sound of worship swelled, rising like a mighty wave, filling the air with a profound sense of unity and love. Sarah felt the vibrations of their praise deep within her very bones, and for the first time in her life, every trace of fear, every shadow of doubt, were completely swept away.

Palm branches were given to each of the elect, and they waved them in rhythm as their voices continued to lift in adoration, praising Jesus with hearts full of devotion.

Then, in a moment of divine majesty, Jesus ascended the steps to His throne at the right hand of the Father. With grace and authority, He took the scroll from the place where He had laid it upon the throne. Seated beside the Father, He held the scroll in His hands, and a solemn stillness fell over the multitude, blanketing them in reverent silence.

The atmosphere in the throne room shifted, growing heavier with an unspoken awareness. Every soul gathered understood the magnitude of what was about to unfold. The seventh and final seal—once broken—would unleash the full wrath of God upon the earth, and the fate of those left behind weighed heavily on the hearts of the redeemed. Their loved ones—those who had not yet believed, those who had rejected the truth, or taken the mark—would soon face the cataclysm that was prophesied.

A deep, reverent silence fell over the heavenly assembly, stretching out for what felt like half an hour. Time seemed to warp in the weight of eternity, and every being—angelic and human alike—held their breath in anticipation.

Jesus stood, His radiant figure towering above, the scroll in His hand. His eyes, once ablaze with divine love, now dimmed slightly, shadowed by the burden He carried. He gazed down at the scroll, at the final seal, His brow furrowed in deep contemplation. His hesitation was unmistakable, and the entirety of Heaven could sense the heaviness pressing on His heart. He knew what was coming. His omniscient mind held the horrors that would soon befall the earth, the suffering of those who had refused His grace, those who had persecuted His church.

The whole of creation waited, the tension in the air thickening with every passing second. The heavenly host stood motionless, the redeemed remained silent, their joy now mingled with sorrow for those still below. Sarah gripped Tim's hand tighter, her gaze shifting between Jesus and the faces of those around her. Tears welled up in her eyes, her heart aching for the loved ones who were about to experience the fullness of divine judgment.

For a moment, Jesus' hand hovered over the seal. His fingers trembled ever so slightly, as if the weight of the scroll itself mirrored the weight of His decision. The entirety of Heaven, it seemed, had paused in solidarity with Him, waiting for the moment when the heavens and the earth would be irrevocably altered.

Then, with the slightest movement of His hand, He placed His fingers upon the seal. A collective breath was drawn, every soul tensed as if bracing for impact. Jesus hesitated once more, His eyes closing as if in prayer, a deep sorrow etched upon His face.

Then, at last, He opened His eyes—filled with a resolute, divine authority—and broke the seal.

"The Heavens Shuddered."

The sound was more than thunder; it was the very voice of God reverberating through every fiber of creation. A roar so deafening, so cataclysmic, that it seemed to split the cosmos in two. The throne room shook violently, the floor beneath the feet of the multitude trembling as the seal was broken. The light from the throne intensified, blinding and consuming, as if the very glory of God were pouring out in judgment.

A windstorm erupted in the heavens, howling with the force of a thousand hurricanes, as the earth groaned in response. The stars flickered in terror, and the sun seemed to dim in mourning for what was to come. The living creatures around the throne covered their faces, and the twenty-four elders fell once again before the Lamb, casting their crowns in surrender to the awesome power that had been unleashed.

The silence of the throne room was shattered, replaced with the sound of Heaven itself groaning under the weight of divine wrath. Every soul in the multitude felt the earth trembling beneath them as the great abyss of God's judgment opened.

Angels aligned, shielding the elect from the sheer force of the event, while the sound of the seventh seal breaking rolled through the heavens like a great tempest. It was as if the very fabric of reality had been torn, the final barrier between God's mercy and His impending judgment now obliterated.

In that terrible and holy moment, all of Heaven understood: there was no turning back. The time for mercy had passed, and the full wrath of the Almighty would now descend upon the earth. A judgment that had been delayed for so long out of love was now unleashed, and the earth would tremble beneath its weight.

Rebecca's heart ached for James, the love of her life still on the earth, and for those who had chosen to reject God's offer of redemption. She thought of their faces—friends, family—people she had prayed for, wept for. They would face the fury of what was to be released. But amidst the sorrow, there was a sense of righteousness in the air. This was the day foretold—the day of justice.

And as the earth below quaked under the immense force of divine judgment, the multitude stood in awe of the Lamb, knowing that His justice was perfect, His timing exact, and His victory was eternal.

James sat in the dimly lit basement hideout, his hands trembling slightly as he held the phone Hartman had returned to him. He wasn't entirely sure why he'd reactivated it. Hartman had inserted the SIM card from his old backup phone, the one with a number he hadn't used in a while. Surprisingly, it still had service, though James didn't know how long that would last. A part of him knew it was risky—Hartman was probably tracking him, but he found he didn't care anymore. In fact, he appreciated the gesture. The phone, now active, gave him a sense of connection, something he desperately needed. Now, alone in the world, the isolation was crushing, and that was enough to make him turn it on.

For hours, James had scrolled through news feeds and video clips. The images were surreal, almost too much for his mind to grasp. People had captured footage of the unimaginable—of Jesus, radiant and majestic, standing on clouds, and the elect rising into the heavens. It was impossible to process, but he stared at the screen, trying to make sense of it all. The bright flashes of light, the blinding radiance. He searched the faces in the crowd, wishing he could find Rebecca and Emily. But the sheer enormity of the event made it impossible.

The whole world had seen it. It wasn't hidden in secret. Reports flooded the networks—some in disbelief, some in awe, others in panic. He felt a knot tighten in his stomach as the magnitude of what had happened began to sink in. His wife and daughter were gone, taken into the skies with the saints. And he... he was left behind. Alone.

Then, the ground beneath him lurched violently.

James grabbed the edge of the desk as the entire building began to shake violently. At first, it was a subtle tremor, like the distant rumble of thunder deep underground, but within moments, the shaking grew ferocious. The lights above flickered and swayed, casting erratic shadows across the room. A deep, guttural roar rumbled up from the depths of the earth, vibrating through the floor and into his bones.

Suddenly, a sharp jolt hit, throwing him off balance. The walls groaned under the strain, twisting and buckling as if the very building was being pulled apart. Glass shattered somewhere above him, sending shards crashing down, while the sound of bending steel beams filled the air like tortured metal screams.

Everything—furniture, books, and equipment—began to jump and skitter off shelves, vibrating violently before crashing to the floor in a chaotic chorus of destruction. The ground beneath him felt unstable, like it was rolling in waves. James could barely keep his footing as the tremors tossed him around. Cabinets toppled, spilling their contents across the room, and the ceiling above creaked ominously, threatening to collapse.

Each second felt like an eternity, the quake's fury growing more and more violent. The deafening cacophony of objects crashing to the ground merged with the terrifying roar from the earth below, making it impossible to think, let alone move. It was as if the entire world was unraveling, the ground itself rebelling against everything standing on it.

He stumbled to his feet, heart racing as the tremors grew more violent. A wave of panic surged through him, but there was nowhere to go—no escape from the earth's fury. Desperately, he made his way toward the stairs. Gripping the handrail for balance as the building quaked around him, he fought his way up from the basement. The walls groaned ominously, and each step felt like the ground beneath him was trying to shift away.

Bursting through the door at ground level, James stumbled into the open air. For a brief moment, the chaos inside the building seemed to ease, but outside, the true extent of the disaster was just beginning. The ground still shook violently beneath his feet, but it was the sky that caught his attention.

The atmosphere above was changing, darkening slowly as smoke and ash from volcanic eruptions on the horizon began to billow into the sky. Thick clouds rolled across the heavens like an approaching storm, but James knew this was no ordinary weather—this was the earth itself becoming violent. The ash drifted slowly at first, then faster, carried by winds stirred up by the chaos below.

Suddenly, flashes of light streaked across the sky as meteors began to burn through the atmosphere, falling sporadically like fiery rain. Some were small, disappearing with a quick flash as they disintegrated in the upper layers of the sky, but others were larger—much larger. James watched in horror as one blazing meteor, larger than any he had ever seen, plummeted toward the horizon. Its impact sent a shockwave through the air, and though it hit miles away, the ground beneath him trembled as though it had landed right at his feet.

He knew what was happening. The meteors weren't just falling harmlessly into the ocean or uninhabited land. They were slamming into cities, turning them into infernos in an instant. The earth groaned beneath the force of each impact, and volcanic eruptions sent even more ash and smoke into the sky, slowly blotting out the sun.

Instinctively, James knew he had to get away from the building. The structure groaned under the relentless shaking, and staying there felt like waiting to be buried alive. His heart pounded in his chest as he stumbled forward, his legs barely finding balance on the trembling ground. He sprinted through the debris-strewn street, dodging falling pieces of brick and shattered glass as the quakes intensified.

He needed higher ground—somewhere he could get a better view of what was happening and nothing could fall on him. His eyes scanned the landscape frantically, catching sight of a small ridge just beyond the ruined buildings in the park. Without thinking, he pushed himself toward it, muscles aching with the effort. The ground lurched violently beneath him, sending him stumbling, but he didn't stop.

As he neared the ridge, the shaking lessened just enough for him to scramble up the incline, grabbing onto rocks and branches for support. Reaching the top, he gasped for breath, his chest burning, but when he finally looked out across the horizon, the sight stole his breath all over again.

From this vantage point, he could see the full scale of the devastation. The distant sky had turned a sickly shade of gray, thick clouds of volcanic ash and smoke rolling in from the horizon like an unstoppable wave. Overhead, meteors streaked across the sky, their fiery tails cutting through the darkened air as they hurtled toward the earth. Every so often, one of the larger ones would crash into the ground, and though the explosions were far away, James could feel the reverberations through the very earth beneath him.

The horizon itself seemed to ripple, as if the land was writhing under the assault. Mountains in the distance belched thick plumes of smoke, their molten cores spewing fire and ash into the sky. The distant outline of cities was barely visible now, swallowed by the dark clouds rolling overhead. He could see nothing but destruction, and the realization hit him like a blow—there was no refuge left, no place safe for the fury was from the earth itself.

James could barely breathe as the atmosphere thickened with ash.

A deafening explosion rocked the ground as one of the meteors struck the distant horizon, its impact rivaling that of a nuclear bomb. The ground beneath him convulsed, and James could feel the shockwave even from miles away. The shockwave knocked him to the ground. Mushroom clouds of fire and ash erupted in the distance, the destructive force obliterating everything in its path.

Then another—closer this time. The sky lit up with blinding flashes as more meteors rained down from above. Each one struck with the force of a small apocalypse, reducing cities to rubble in mere moments. Skyscrapers crumbled like sandcastles beneath the weight of the impacts.

The earth itself seemed to fracture, splitting open to swallow entire buildings whole.

Mountains, once towering and unshakable, sank into the molten earth beneath the crust. The ground cracked like shattered glass, and the tremors didn't stop. They only grew stronger. Volcanoes, long dormant, suddenly erupted with explosive violence, sending plumes of smoke and ash into the sky. The horizon burned as rivers of lava flowed from the earth's wounds, incinerating everything in their path.

James could barely breathe, his lungs burned as he inhaled, the acrid taste of sulfur filling his throat. He pressed his sleeve to his mouth, trying to filter the smoke, but it was no use. The world was being consumed by fire. The sky—once filled with light—was now a swirling, apocalyptic haze of black and red.

The sun, which had shone so brightly just hours ago, was now obscured by the billowing clouds of ash. Darkness swept across the land, like a funeral shroud spreading over the earth. James couldn't tell day from night anymore; all he could see was the ever-encroaching blackness, a suffocating void swallowing the world whole.

The quaking finally began to subside, but the damage had been done. Cities had crumbled, mountains had fallen into the earth, and the landscape itself had changed. As the tremors faded into an eerie stillness, James rose to his feet and stood frozen, staring out at the ruined horizon in the distance to the west and the city around him.

He found a place to sit on the ridge, where he leaned against the trunk of an old oak tree. Hours passed, and the day was as dark as night. True night had come, but he only knew that because of the time displayed on his phone, which no longer had service. Then, through the thick veil of smoke, something strange caught his eye. The clouds overhead shifted slightly, revealing a faint, ominous glow. Slowly, the smoke thinned, and there, hanging in the sky like a grim harbinger, he could just make out the light of the full moon.

But it was no longer the pale, familiar orb he had known. Its light, filtered through the smoke, was red. It hung high in the sky, looking down on the devastated earth like a bloodstain in the heavens. Its color was deep red, as if dipped in blood—like the final warning to a world on the brink of annihilation. It cast an eerie, crimson light over the shattered land, illuminating the ruins with an unnatural glow.

James rose to his feet and stood in silence, his heart pounding in his chest. The moon seemed to stare back at him, a haunting symbol of the wrath that had only just begun. The world had changed forever, and he knew—deep in his bones—that this was only the beginning. With the final judgment still pending, there was no way to avoid facing God's wrath.

Suddenly, his phone chimed. There was cell service again, maybe powered by backup generators. The chime was from the social media account he had checked earlier. There was a message.

He opened the notification, and as the screen loaded, his eyes locked on the profile picture—seeing the face flooded his mind with memories from his past, a time before Rebecca. His loneliness was reaching for that picture, that face. Something stirred deep within him, a memory he had buried long ago, now unearthed in the midst of the chaos.

He hesitated for a moment, his heart pounding, staring at the name attached to the message. It was impossible, he thought. But there it was, undeniable and real.

With a trembling finger, James tapped on her message…

"Pressed"

Hartman had been sitting in his recliner when the first tremor hit. It was subtle at first, like a passing truck rumbling beneath the pavement, but then the floor beneath him began to heave violently. The building groaned, and Hartman instinctively grabbed the arms of his chair, his heart hammering in his chest. The shaking intensified, rattling everything around him—books fell from shelves, picture frames shattered, and the ceiling above cracked ominously.

Before he could react, the floor beneath him buckled, and his apartment walls seemed to cave inward. Hartman tried to stand, but a massive jolt sent him crashing to the ground. The lights flickered, and then, with a deafening roar, the entire building collapsed around him. He was plunged into darkness.

For a few terrifying moments, all he could hear was the sound of debris settling around him, the weight of the structure pinning him down. Dust filled his lungs, making it hard to breathe, and he could barely move. His legs were trapped beneath the rubble, and his left arm was pinned awkwardly under a wall framing. Panic gripped him as he tried to push against the debris, but it was no use. He was completely immobilized. The quaking continued as the sounds of the building continued to crumble around him.

He remembered his phone in his pocket. Hope surged in his chest, igniting a small flicker of relief. He tried to reach it with his free hand, but his arm was pinned too tightly against his body. Gritting his teeth, he shifted, trying to wiggle his fingers toward the pocket where his phone was nestled. Every movement sent sharp pain shooting through his ribs, like daggers piercing his side. The phone felt so close, yet impossibly out of reach. He grunted in frustration. He was helpless.

Then a thought hit him—voice recognition.

He'd set up the feature when he got the new phone, an iPhone. He set it up more out of curiosity than necessity, but he had never really used it. Now, in the suffocating darkness, he realized it might be his only chance. His heart raced as he tried to remember the right command. He wasn't sure exactly how to trigger it.

"Uh... phone?" he said hesitantly, his voice raspy from the dust choking the air around him. Nothing happened.

He coughed violently, dust settling in his lungs, and tried again, louder this time. "Phone, unlock!"

Still nothing.

Hartman let out an exhausted sigh, his body aching, the weight of the debris pressing down on him. His breath was shallow, his vision blurry from the dust and strain. He squeezed his eyes shut, willing the phone to respond.

Then, remembering the command, he said louder, "Hey Siri!"

There was a brief pause, then a soft chime. His heart leapt.

"Yes!" he whispered under his breath, the relief flooding through him.

"Call... call Tammy," he said quickly, his voice shaky.

But Siri's robotic voice replied, "I can't do that while your iPhone is locked. Try unlocking first."

Hartman froze. Of course—he hadn't unlocked the phone. His contacts and calling features were restricted while the device was locked. He cursed under his breath, frustration mounting. There was no way he could reach the phone physically to use Face ID or enter his passcode.

"Okay," he said aloud, trying to stay calm. "Hey Siri, unlock phone."

"I'm sorry, I can't do that," Siri responded.

Hartman's chest tightened with fear. His contacts weren't accessible unless the phone was unlocked. The realization hit him hard—without facial recognition, a passcode, or internet to sync his contacts, he couldn't make any calls.

"I can't do that while your iPhone is locked," Siri repeated.

Hartman's panic grew. His mind raced, trying to think of a workaround. He knew he was stuck without unlocking the phone, but there had to be a way. The frustration gnawed at him as the crushing weight of the rubble seemed to press harder with each passing second.

"Siri, call David!"

Same result.

"Call Mike! Call Lisa! Call Commander Scott! Call anyone!"

The same robotic response echoed back at him, unfeeling and cold. "I can't do that while your iPhone is locked."

Hartman's breathing became labored. He was trying everyone he could think of, but his contacts were out of reach. He hadn't dialed a number manually in years. Everything was done by contact name.

"Call 911!" he barked, out of sheer desperation.

"Dialing 911." A recording answered "Service not available. Please hang up and try again later."

He tried it over and over "Service not available. Please hang up and try again later."

Hartman slammed his head back against the debris in frustration. His lifeline was failing him. His contacts weren't accessible, his phone was locked, and he could only dial 911 and that service was down. He was stuck.

And then, through the fog of panic, a thought surfaced. He can't remember anyone's number, but, my old phone. He hadn't dialed it in years, but the number had been burned into his memory from giving it out. He knew it by heart.

It was a long shot, but it was all he had left.

"Hey Siri... dial 555, 867, 5303."

There was a pause, and for a moment, he thought nothing would happen. But then, the familiar sound of a dial tone echoed from his phone. His pulse quickened. One ring. Two rings. Three. It seemed to last forever.

And then, a voice came through the static, crackling but clear.

"Hello?"

EPILOGUE

"The False Light Rises"

The world, still reeling from the cataclysmic events—the great earthquakes, volcanic eruptions, and the devastating meteor shower—was now cloaked in a thick layer of ash and fear. Communications across continents had been crippled, and darkness seemed to cover both the land and the hearts of its people. Yet, in the midst of this chaos, a broadcast emerged, carried by whatever surviving means remained: satellite channels, emergency radio signals, and even hand-delivered messages to the most cut-off parts of the globe. The message came from a man claiming to speak truth, yet it was the voice of deception.

Ben Rashan, a figure who had risen to power, appeared on screens worldwide. His face, illuminated by a false light, was calm and composed as he began to speak. There was a terrible magnetism in his words, drawing people in as he spoke.

"The God of the Christians is a cruel and destructive force," Rashan declared with venom. "The so-called prophecies in their Bible—they foretold this. The shaking of the earth, the crumbling of mountains, the falling stars... They call this the wrath of God, but I tell you, it is the destruction of a tyrant."

His voice dropped, and with a deliberate sneer, he began to read from the Bible, his words dripping with scorn. "It is written, 'The earth will shake, and the mountains will crumble into the sea.' What are we to make of this? You saw it yourselves—the earthquakes, the crust fracturing, the mighty mountains sliding into the molten core below. 'Stars will fall from the sky'—this Bible says. You all witnessed the meteor shower with your own eyes. And 'the sky will be rolled up like a scroll'? We all saw the ash spread, turning the heavens into a veil of darkness, blotting out the sun. And the red moon—ah, yes, we all saw that too, didn't we? Blood red, its light filtered by the ashen sky, hanging over a world in ruin."

Rashan's eyes gleamed as he continued, his voice rising with a chilling conviction. "The Bible says the kings of the earth will hide in caves and in the rocks of the mountains. That happened, didn't it? The leaders of your nations fled to their underground bunkers like the cowards they

283

are. But I... I did not cry out in fear. I did not tremble when this day came, because I knew it was coming. I was prepared."

The audience—those left in the shattered remnants of cities and countries—listened with growing unease. There was truth in his words, but it was a truth twisted into something dark, something sinister. But, they yearned to hear more, to breathe it in.

"The Bible speaks of me," Rashan declared with a bitter smile. "I am the one whose names are written on its very pages, the Prince of the Power of the Air, the God of this World, the Angel of Light, the Morning Star. Yes... Lucifer. But I tell you this: they lie about me. I am not the enemy they make me out to be. I am the true Light Bearer. I am the one who brings freedom, not chains. I am not Ben Reshan, my name was altered as a child to be revealed on this day. I am Ben Rasha—not Ben Reshan. And my name, in the ancient language of my ancestors, when translated into Hebrew phonetically, is the number 666."

A shudder rippled through those listening, though many did not understand the full weight of the number. Yet the ancient prophecies now seemed to take on new meaning, and fear tightened its grip on many hearts.

"I was born for this time, prophesied in the days of old," Rasha said, his voice low and powerful. "My origins trace back to Jerusalem, to a time when my ancestors knew the truth—when they rebelled against the lies of Israel and the God they claimed to serve. My mother, a descendant of this world's keepers of the real truth had waited for generations. They knew this day would come. Her people despised the Jews for their betrayal, for losing their way. And I was born to reclaim what was stolen from us—the true power, the true light."

Rasha paused, letting his words sink in. "I am the one foretold in the ancient prophecies, but I am not the villain they want you to believe I am. I am the good Angel of Light. I am the one who will lead you into a new era—an era where you will no longer be slaves to the false god of the Christians. That god has tried to destroy us, but we will rise. We will have our vengeance."

A murmur began to rise from the people watching and listening. The world had changed forever in the wake of the disasters, but now something was unfolding.

"Israel," Rasha hissed like a serpent, "is the so-called apple of God's eye, isn't it? It is written, 'For thus says the Lord of hosts: After his glory sent me to the nations who plundered you, for he who touches you touches the apple of his eye.' (Zechariah 2:8). This God calls them His chosen people, His treasure, but look at what He has done to the world. Look at the chaos He has unleashed. The apple of His eye must be plucked out. His chosen people must be brought down."

The hatred in his voice was unmistakable as he turned his venomous gaze toward Israel and the remnants of the Church. "The time has come to punish God for what He has done. The people of Israel and anyone who calls upon His name! God wants us to face His wrath, but those who reach out to Him will face my wrath, our wrath. The wrath their god has caused us to rain down on them, wrath they deserve. The world is ours now, and I will be your god."

As the broadcast continued, Rasha began to demonstrate his power. In an eerie and unsettling display, he called forth signs and wonders, reminiscent of the plagues from the Book of Job. Fire fell from the sky, lightning struck on command, and violent storms whipped the landscape into chaos. People screamed, some in terror, others in awe, as Rasha proclaimed his dominion over the earth.

"This is only the beginning," Rasha promised, his voice echoing across the broken lands. "The God of the Christians may have tried to destroy us, but we will rise, and we will have our vengeance."

As the transmission ended, the world stood on the precipice of a new and terrifying era, where light was twisted into darkness and truth into lies. Rasha had declared himself the god of this broken world, and for those who remained, the final battle had only just begun.

"Coffee Shop Encounter"

The smell of freshly ground coffee fills the air, blending with the silence in the empty coffee shop. You find it odd that no one else is here today; there are usually a handful of people reading books in the back. After ordering a cup of coffee from the young lady behind the counter, you head to your cozy corner in the back, nestled between two book nook shelves. It feels like a world of its own—safe, secluded, a place where you can hide from the chaos outside. It's your refuge, where you sit in solitude, unnoticed, pretending for just a while that everything makes sense.

You sink into an old, worn chair that blends with the hodgepodge of mismatched furniture scattered among the shelves packed with well-read books. You set your cup of coffee on the side table and reach for the book you found on a bottom shelf the other day, carefully sliding it into the hidden nook behind the chair you love to nestle into. Your focus returns to the worn copy of Caught Up in the Tribulation, a book you've been trying to make sense of, though something about it still feels distant, unfamiliar, despite its well-known words. You turn the pages slowly, as if reading might reveal the answers you thought you already had.

From the corner of your eye, you notice a middle-aged woman enter the shop. She walks up to the counter and orders a cup of hot cocoa, then heads in your direction. You're aware of her but try to track her movements without looking directly at her. Her steps slow as she passes by the rows of shelves. She stops and looks at the books on the shelf next to you. Her gaze drops and lingers on the book in your hands. You wonder if she came in to finish reading the book, and now you have it. She smiles to herself, as if recognizing it. She stops, and you realize it's not you she's interested in—it's the book. But then you wonder, or is it me?

Maybe it was simple curiosity, or maybe it was something more, but you sense she couldn't just walk past.

"That's a good book," she says warmly, her voice gentle yet purposeful. She hesitates for a moment, then gestures to the chair across from you. "Mind if I join you?"

You blink, momentarily startled, but nod, unsure why her presence feels both unexpected and oddly natural. She sits down, her movements calm, as if she's done this countless times before. Her eyes glance down again at the book in your hands before meeting yours, her gaze filled with a quiet kindness, as if she already understands something about you.

"Do you like it?" she asks, nodding toward the book.

You shrug. "Yeah, it's... interesting. A bit intense, though."

She smiles knowingly. "Yeah, it can be. There's a lot in there. Sometimes, it's not so much about what's written as how it makes you feel, you know?" She leans back and relaxes in the chair across from you, her eyes scanning your face, reading something beyond your words.

You shift in your seat, feeling a little exposed, like she can see something in you that even you're not fully aware of. "I guess. I mean, I think I've got it figured out."

Her smile softens, but her eyes sharpen with a gentle yet undeniable intensity. "Do you?" she asks, her voice low, almost as if she's posing the question more to the universe than to you directly.

There's a pause. You can't place it, but something about her presence makes you feel unsettled. She isn't pushing or judging; it's as if she's waiting for something to click inside you, like she already knows there's more beneath the surface.

She leans in slightly, lowering her voice. "You know, sometimes we think we've got everything figured out. We think we know where the story is going, how it all ends. But then... we realize we missed something. Something important." She glances at the book again, her fingers lightly brushing the edge of the table. "What part are you at?"

You tell her, a little unsure of where this conversation is going but feeling compelled to keep talking. As you describe the scene in the book, her expression shifts slightly, as if she's seen it all before, but in a way you can't fully understand.

"You ever feel like that?" she asks after a pause, her voice quiet but deliberate. "Like you've got it all figured out, but something feels... off? Like maybe there's more going on than you can see?"

Her words hang in the air, unsettling in their accuracy. You swallow, trying to find a response, but something about her question hits closer to home than you expected.

She smiles again, softer this time, and nods as if she already knows. "I thought so. It's easy to think we've got it all under control that we've figured out the story. But sometimes, the real story isn't the one we thought we were reading." She gestures to the book, her voice gaining a little strength. "This story... it's not just about what's written on the pages. It's about what's happening in your heart, in your life. And trust me, the real story, the one you haven't seen yet, is far bigger than you realize."

You feel a strange tug inside you, like something deep within you is shifting. The way she speaks, the way she looks at you, makes you feel like she's seeing something hidden inside you, something you haven't even seen yourself.

"I've been there," she says softly, her voice tinged with an unmistakable sadness but also hope. "I've been where you are, thinking I understood everything, thinking I knew how it all worked. And then..." She looks down for a moment, gathering herself. "And then I realized how wrong I was. How lost I was, without even knowing it."

Her words pierce through the comfortable bubble of your solitude, and for the first time, you feel like you're truly seeing her, not just as a stranger, but as someone who has walked through something you're only beginning to understand.

She takes a deep breath, her gaze steady on you. "There's more to this story than you think. And I'd like to help you see it—if you're willing."

Suddenly, you feel something is not right, something is off, but you can't identify it. You look at her in the chair across from you and say, "Do I know you? What's your name?"

"I'm Rebecca," she says with a soft smile. "You don't know me, but I think you recognize who I am."

Her name strikes you like a bolt of lightning, a sudden grip tightening around your heart. Your eyes widen as the realization sinks in. You turn the book in your hands a glance at the picture on the cover, then back to her. She watches you calmly, her smile unwavering, as you struggle to mask the shock that's written all over your face.

She sits quietly for a moment, her thoughts moving like a slow current through everything written in the book you're holding, everything she had been through on its pages. How she had lost her focus and was led astray and it had caught her off guard. She had clung to those images for so long, but now, after everything she had lived through, she could see it with a new clarity.

Rebecca's eyes softened as she spoke, her gaze distant as though looking back on memories both comforting and painful. "You know, when I was a little girl in Sunday school, it all seemed so simple," she began, her voice warm with nostalgia. "I remember the teacher, Mrs. Robin, telling us about Jesus coming back in the clouds, and I could see it so clearly in my mind, Jesus, descending from heaven, all of us rising to meet Him, joy on everyone's faces. It was wonderful, uncomplicated. It was what the Scriptures said, without all the extra stuff people added later." She smiles faintly, the memory still alive in her heart.

"As a kid, it felt so real to me. The way it's written in the Bible, 1 Thessalonians 4:16-17, it's simple: 'For the Lord Himself will descend from heaven with a cry of command, with the voice of an archangel, and the dead in Christ will rise first. Then we who are alive will be caught up together with them in the clouds to meet the Lord in the air.'" Her voice trembled slightly, a mix of awe and sorrow. "It's a beautiful promise. I'd daydream about it, imagining that moment when the clouds would part, and we'd see Jesus coming. That's how I always understood it... until things changed."

She sighed, her hands tightening around the worn Bible she always carried. "In the 90s, I started hearing something new, a teaching that said Christians wouldn't go through the tribulation, any of it, that we'd be raptured before it started. I remember how everyone around me embraced it so quickly, as if it was fact. It gave us this strange sense of comfort, thinking we'd be spared from all the suffering. And not just that, but we'd never even have to worry about the mark of the beast. The pastors told us, 'Don't worry about it. You won't be here. You'll be safe with the Lord before any of that happens.'"

I had embraced what I was told, that I would be raptured and not go through the Tribulation, but now, after everything I had lived through, I can see it with clarity. "The sky," she whispers, as though seeing it unfold before her, "will be heavy, thick with the weight of what is coming." She looks down, the memories of what she had been taught rushing back. "For as long as I can remember, the church has talked about this moment, the visible return of Christ. We've pictured Him coming down in glory, the whole world watching, trembling in awe as He descends to gather His people. And yet... over time, something changed. The simple beauty of that moment, the straightforward promise, got tangled up in explanations that complicated what Scripture had plainly said."

Rebecca's voice grew stronger, more certain, as if the truth had settled in her bones. "They added something to the Bible. The idea that Christ would come back an extra time, that first He would come in secret, invisible to rapture His church, and then later return in the clouds for the rest. That wasn't part of what the church taught for almost two-thousand years. That idea, it felt strained to me, as though it was trying too hard to explain something that wasn't clearly written in the Bible. People created this idea out of a need to prove that Christians wouldn't have to go through the tribulation, that they would be spared from the suffering that Revelation foretells. But to believe that, you have to interpret scripture in ways that it was never meant to be stretched and twisted."

She shook her head, recalling the teachings that had once seemed so concrete, so comforting. "For centuries, the church held to what was clearly written: Jesus would return, visibly, with the sound of a trumpet, and we would be caught up to meet Him in the clouds. That's what 1 Thessalonians 4:16-17 says. It's a moment of majesty, of glory, not something done in secret. And Matthew 24 makes it even clearer, 'Then will appear in heaven the sign of the Son of Man, and all the tribes of the earth will mourn, and they will see the Son of Man coming on the clouds of heaven with power and great glory.' Everyone will see it. This is not a hidden event."

She paused, as though the weight of those words had grown heavier with time. "The idea of a secret rapture, of Christ coming quietly, only for the church to disappear while the rest of the world remains in confusion until He returns again... that's not what scripture says. People started believing it because they didn't want to face the idea that Christians would suffer through tribulation. But when you read the text simply for what it is, it's clear, Jesus comes back once, for all to see, and He gathers His people."

Rebecca's eyes shone with a mix of grief and certainty. "People have argued for so long that God wouldn't let His followers go through the tribulation, that He loves us too much for that. But if that's true, what do we say about the apostles? What about Peter, crucified upside down? What about the early Christians who were thrown to lions, and burned at the stake? Was God's love absent for them? Of course not. Tribulation doesn't mean God has abandoned us. In fact, it's in those times of suffering that our faith is refined. "The truth is, Daniel's vision of the final seven years for Israel pointed to Jesus. The first three and a half years were fulfilled through Jesus' ministry, and in the middle of those years, He was sacrificed for the sins of the world, putting an end to the temple sacrifices. The apostles then carried on, proclaiming the Gospel to Israel for the remaining three and a half years, until Stephen's death. His martyrdom marked the scattering of the church into Judea and Samaria, signifying the end of the Old Covenant and the beginning of the New Covenant, and the Church Age. The Gospel spread to the Gentiles, and tribulation began with the church's dispersion. This tribulation has continued and will grow more intense until Christ returns in the clouds to rescue His church."

Her hands, resting on the Bible in her lap, clenched slightly as she continues, her voice calm but firm. "James in the New Testament told us to consider it joy when we face trials, because the testing of our faith produces perseverance. The early church knew that suffering wasn't a sign of God's absence. It was part of the journey. And when you accept the reality that Christians will endure the tribulation, the whole narrative falls into place. We face tribulation, just as believers always have. It rains on the just and the unjust. And then, at the appointed time, Christ returns. He comes to gather His church, and then... God's wrath is poured out on the earth."

She looked up, her expression clear, resolved. "People want to believe that God will spare us from suffering, but they forget that the greatest love story ever told was written through suffering. Jesus Himself endured the cross for us. The apostles followed in His footsteps. Suffering isn't a sign of God's absence, but of His work in us, refining us for His glory. We are promised that we will overcome, not be spared.

Her voice softened as she continues, "When Christ returns, it won't be in secret. There won't be any confusion or speculation. The world will see Him coming in the clouds, with power and great glory. The trumpet will sound, and the sky will split open. And those who are His will be gathered to Him, the church united in His presence, in a moment that all creation has been waiting for."

Rebecca let out a slow breath, her eyes softening. "This is the promise you should hold on to—the visible return of Christ. It's not about secret events or hidden raptures. It's about the triumphant return of our King, a return that the whole world will witness. And when He comes, we will see Him."

She paused, her hands now still, resting once again on the Bible in her lap. "It's always been there, right in front of us. We just have to read it as it is. Christ is coming back, once, for all to see, and we'll be there, clothed in white, standing before the throne. That's the story. That's the truth."

Rebecca sat back, the weight of her words hanging in the air, not as a burden, but as a quiet, resolute hope, a hope that had been there all along.

Her voice broke slightly, the sorrow creeping in as she spoke of what had been lost. "James, my husband, and I... we changed what we believed. We trusted what we were taught, that we'd be spared, that we wouldn't face the worst of it. So when the tribulation came, we were completely unprepared. We weren't watching for the signs because we didn't think we'd be there to see them."

Rebecca swallowed hard, the pain of memory weighing down her words.

"We should have known we were in the Tribulation, but we didn't. And James... he didn't see it either. He didn't understand. He took the mark, thinking it could not be the mark of the beast, because we were told we would not be here. Thinking it was just another thing, just another part of life."

"All I am saying is don't just accept everything you hear. Read and study the Bible for yourself, and when you do, pray for understanding." She paused. "You still have time."

Rebecca's words hung in the air, carrying a weight that was impossible to ignore. She took a deep breath, her gaze locking with yours for a moment, and you could see the depth of her conviction in her eyes.

The air seemed thick with the tension of her words she was about to speak. "The Rapture is not just a moment of mercy, of gathering. It's a declaration that the time has come for justice. No more will the evil of this world go unpunished. No more will darkness reign unchecked. The wrath of God, long prophesied, will follow the return of Jesus. As the seventh and final seal is opened, the earth will shake, and God will pour out His righteous judgment on those who have rejected Him, who have turned their backs on His Son, and harmed His children."

Rebecca's gaze intensified, her eyes locking with yours as if she could see beyond the present moment and into the future that was soon to unfold. "This is why the Rapture won't be quiet, why the world will witness it. It's not just a gathering, it's the vindication of God's people. It's the moment when the church is revealed to have been under God's care all along, when all who held fast through trials and tribulations are lifted up for the world to see. It's a moment that will leave no room for doubt."

"God's wrath," she continues, her voice thick with grief. "It's not like the tribulation we endured before. This... this is His righteous anger. The world mocked Him, persecuted His people, and now they will face His wrath. And the worst part... the worst part is, they'll know. They'll know they had a chance, but they hardened their hearts."

Tears began to fill her eyes. "I can't stop thinking about it, those left behind..."

Rebecca sat for a long moment, as her tears gradually stopped, but the weight of everything she had just shared lingered in the air like a thick cloud. You could see it in her eyes, the pain, the love, the desperate hope. And now, as her tear-streaked face lifted to meet yours, there was something new, a fierce urgency, a determination that seemed to rise from the very depths of her soul.

She spoke to you, and she spoke past you, as if addressing the universe "If you're reading this," she began, her voice raw but steady, "I'm pleading with you." The words hanging heavy, and though her voice was trembling, the emotion behind it was unmistakable. "Please, please don't put this off. Don't walk away from this moment thinking you have more time, thinking you can come back to this later. I've seen what happens when people wait too long, when they push God aside, believing that tomorrow is guaranteed. But it's not. Tomorrow isn't promised. You don't know what's coming."

Rebecca became very serious, "But you..." she says, "you're still here. You still have a chance."

She wiped her face, her eyes wide and red, her voice hoarse from the flood of emotion. "I'm begging you, please, don't wait. Don't be one of those who will be left behind, or the people you love. You still have time right now, but tomorrow... tomorrow might be too late. Don't wait for tomorrow. Turn to God now. Ask Him for forgiveness now, because He's waiting for you. And after everything I've seen, everything I've lived through, I can promise you... you don't want to wait until it's too late."

Rebecca's voice cracking under the weight of what she was trying to communicate. "I'm pleading with you because I love you, because God loves you. If you walk away from this moment, if you turn back to the world and leave this behind, you may never get another chance. Please... turn to God while you still can, and tell the people you love, tell them the truth, because they need to know too. Don't let them be left behind. Don't let them suffer what James is going to suffer."

You could see the love and concern in her eyes for you. "God loves you," she whispers, her voice trembling. "He loves you so much. And He's waiting for you." Her voice dropped to a hoarse whisper, the final plea thick with emotion. "Please... turn to Him. Turn to Him now... just do it."

You sit there, staring down at the final words of Caught Up in the Tribulation, the weight of the story pulling at your heart. The book feels heavy in your hands, as if the pages themselves carry the gravity of everything Rebecca had just shared with you. Your mind races with the decision you're about to make, your thoughts swirling with the warnings and hope she so desperately tried to communicate.

You glance up, ready to speak, to tell Rebecca what you've decided... but she's gone.

Your eyes search the room, confusion tightening in your chest. The chair where she had sat is empty, as if she was never there at all. You blink, scanning the coffee shop, but there's no sign of her.

Was she really sitting there? You try to remember, but the memory feels distant, foggy—like a dream slipping away as you wake. A chill runs down your spine. You glance back at the book in your hands, feeling the weight of it once more, and the reality of her words sinks deeper into your soul.

Was she ever really here? Or is it a voice that has always been calling out to you from somewhere deep in your soul?

A PRAYER FROM THE AUTHOR

Heavenly Father,

I come before You today, not just as the author, but as someone who desires to lead each reader closer to You. Lord, You know the heart of this person praying with me right now. You know their struggles, doubts, and desires. I ask that You draw near to them as they reach out to You.

Father, I pray that this reader feels Your presence, that they recognize Your love and the redemption You offer through Jesus Christ. As they call upon You, may they truly experience the power of Your grace and forgiveness. Let this moment be the start of a new chapter—a step closer to You and a deeper understanding of Your truth.

Holy Spirit, work within them. Open their eyes to see Your plan, soften their hearts to accept Your mercy, and break down any barriers of fear or doubt that may be keeping them from fully surrendering to You. Help them to see that redemption is not earned, but freely given by Your love.

Lord Jesus, I ask that You cover this reader with Your peace. Let them know that no matter what they have faced or will face, Your grace is enough. Lead them into a relationship with You that transforms their life and brings them hope beyond the pages of this book.

I thank You, Lord, for every reader who has come this far. May Your will be done in their lives, and may they know without a doubt that Your love never fails.

In Jesus' name, I pray. Amen.

J.B. McKISSACK

ABOUT THE AUTHOR

J.B. McKISSACK is a devoted pastor and author committed to biblical truth and eschatology. Born in the American South, John's life was transformed at age 31 when he found life-changing faith in Jesus Christ. This profound shift led him to Bible College and missionary work in the Dominican Republic, where he and his family had a children's Bible school and faithfully shared the love and message of Christ.

John now pastors a small rural church in Southeast Texas. His love for end-time prophecy fueled this novel, where he offers a fresh perspective on the return of Jesus, vividly depicting a world where all witness His coming and believers are revealed in epic style.

John first envisioned this powerful return of Christ 29 years ago on the mission field, which became the foundation for this novel. After years of trying to write it, a recent moment of intense prayer reignited his passion, confirming that now is the time to share this story. Through this novel, John invites readers to explore the most spectacular event in human history: the moment when God reveals His true believers to the world. **All eyes shall see!**

Dear Reader,

Thank you for joining me on this journey through Caught Up in the Tribulation. As we navigate these complex themes and interpretations, I wanted to share a perspective that may offer further clarity. It is important to emphasize that I do not hold the belief that the mark of the beast will necessarily be invisible to the human eye. While interpretations can vary, I find it essential to recognize that Scripture, when taken as written, only states that John saw the mark in a vision. This detail leaves room for thoughtful consideration and personal reflection.

I encourage you to explore the Scriptures deeply and prayerfully. Let your study be a source of insight and spiritual growth, and remember that understanding prophecy requires humility and openness.

For those who wish to delve deeper into the material and themes discussed in this book, I invite you to visit my website at www.jbmckissack.com. There, you can download a free "Caught Up in the Tribulation Study Guide", designed to guide you through further reflection and discussion.

Thank you again for reading. Your journey, your faith, and your understanding are uniquely yours, and I am grateful to have been a part of it.

With blessings and gratitude,
J.B. McKissack

www.jbmckissack.com/studyguide.html